MOONRISE OVER
NEW JESSUP

MOONRISE OVER NEW JESSUP

a novel by

Jamila Minnicks

ALGONQUIN BOOKS OF CHAPEL HILL   2023

Published by
Algonquin Books of Chapel Hill
an imprint of Workman Publishing Co., Inc.
a subsidiary of Hachette Book Group, Inc.
1290 Avenue of the Americas
New York, New York 10104

LIBRARY OF CONGRESS CATALOGING-IN-PUBLICATION DATA
Names: Minnicks, Jamila, [date]– author.
Title: Moonrise over New Jessup : a novel / Jamila Minnicks.
Description: First edition. | Chapel Hill : Algonquin Books of Chapel Hill, 2023.
| Summary: "It's 1957, and after leaving the only home she has ever known, Alice Young steps off the bus into the all-Black town of New Jessup, Alabama, where residents have largely rejected integration as the means for Black social advancement. She falls in love with Raymond Campbell, whose clandestine organizing activities challenge New Jessup's status quo and could lead to the young couple's expulsion—or worse—from the home they hold dear."
—Provided by publisher.
Identifiers: LCCN 2022038753 | ISBN 9781643752464 (hardcover) |
ISBN 9781643753744 (ebook)
Subjects: LCSH: African Americans—Alabama—Fiction. | Civil rights movements—Alabama—History—20th century—Fiction. | Alabama—Race relations—History—20th century—Fiction. | LCGFT: Historical fiction. | Novels.
Classification: LCC PS3613.I6525 M66 2023 | DDC 813/.6—dc23/eng/20220928
LC record available at https://lccn.loc.gov/2022038753

10 9 8 7 6 5 4 3 2 1
First Edition

For my mama, in her place among the stars.

In this here place, we flesh; flesh that weeps, laughs; flesh that dances on bare feet in grass. Love it. Love it hard.

—TONI MORRISON, *Beloved*

MOONRISE OVER
NEW JESSUP

PART ONE

ONE

The moon rises and sets, stitching eternity together, night by night. Love-spun thread binds family when even years, or blue skies, stand between one and another's touch. Generations travel the same footprints, reach hands to the same climbing branches, and warm the same brown skin under the Alabama sun. Maybe "family" brings to mind only blood, marital relations, and it's easy to understand that way of thinking. But love by my hand tethers generations to generations, as well as kin by skin, in this place where all in me, and of me, can thrive.

Yet even the strongest thread will snap with constant tension and no slack. The heavens overflow with memories lost. So as life requires I hold taut and I give. In most ways, my people know, if, in some, they never will. But in all ways, my moon rises and sets for family.

So in eternity, the time had come for me to leave the home where I was born. The sun was setting and the half-bald red sweetgum around the fields announced November just a few days coming. But 1957 was still October-old when our landlord ended up face down on the ground for trying to drag me behind him to the toolshed. I was the last to leave the home house in Rensler: Daddy had passed a couple weeks before, and I had settled him next to Mama, though his burial left me scrambling for the rent. My sister Rosie was rooming with a nice family in Chicago, doing hair, and my need to keep a roof over my head had mellowed my worry to wonder about when her next letter would arrive. There was plenty of gleaning left to make November's payment, and then I'd scratch around for whatever came available to buy myself some time. I had never planned, or wanted, to leave Alabama. But with old man Todd shouting curses at my back, his face split open and gushing sweetgum-red, my plans to stay began to fade.

After sleeping a night at the neighbors, and an hours-long walk with the dawn, I arrived at the bus station with just my thrown-together knapsack. The man behind the counter assured me that my little money would carry me to Birmingham. Not Nashville, or Louisville, or Cleveland, let alone Chicago. Birmingham, he said. And no further. In those hours I waited on the bus to depart, the world came undone piece by piece. Unable to get to a place I never wanted to go, with ticket in hand to a place I knew not a single soul, first, the landscape flattened. Direction was next—north, south, east, west, all headed towards the unfamiliar. Then finally color, until everything faded to black and white. I rode the bus into this flat, directionless, colorless world, until it shushed to a stop in my new home.

Not that I knew it at the time, no. My ticket read Birmingham, and all I knew was that we had stopped somewhere between nowhere in particular and the big city. We had traveled a hundred country miles, or maybe ten. Stopped once, twice, four times—I don't know. I was huddled against my window, watching the world blur by as the man seated next to me kept up one-sided conversation about returning north after visiting with his wife and children down country. Somewhere along the way, he started worrying me about the brown paper bag on my lap, and the chicken grease soaking through to my dress, but that oily stain hardly ruined anything. The grayed threads had known color when I first sewed it. Red plaid. But that stain just turned light gray to ash, and ash gray to black, so somewhere near Needham, I offered him the chicken. He took it and finally left me alone.

We shushed to a stop and the bus emptied—some, getting off, hugging loved ones "hello"; some taking luggage from the belly of the bus; and most everybody stretching, smiling, and laughing underneath the blue-sky day. But the stops were all the same to me, so I stayed inside with my head against the glass, feeling the sun's warmth on the window. That's when a red-heeled shoe clicked its way up the sidewalk. Two of them, if I'm honest, though it wasn't so much the shoes that caught my eye, but the bronze stockinged legs inside them. They continued up the way towards a sidewalk café before disappearing through the *front* door.

My eyes traveled from the café to the paved sidewalk to the row of brick-front shops lining the wide avenue. The sun gleamed from the white tile at the bus depot, and a polished chrome dog leapt over the door. But a couple folks—one, like me, and the other, nothing like me—looked around, unsure of what we were seeing. When the man seated next to me returned smelling of cigarettes and shoe polish, he urged me off the bus with a dime from his own pocket.

"Miss, our next stop ain't for quite a while, and this here is a good place to stretch your legs. Why don't you go on inside and get yourself a Coca-Cola before we pull off again?"

Before stepping foot to pavement, I hovered in the doorway of the bus. To the left and right, the avenue, the sidewalk, the storefronts, extended to the horizon in either direction. But reaching the front door of the depot, the Colored entrance was nowhere in sight. To my right, a shoeshine man chewed a toothpick while studying the shoe, and the polish, in his hands from every angle. Behind me, from the bus window, the man urged me through the door; only, the last thing

I needed was to be arrested for going through the front just to buy a Coke.

"Help you, miss?" asked the shoeshine man. Until the words eased from his mouth, he'd done his level best to ignore me. With the weather-beaten hand-me-downs on my feet, it was no wonder why.

"I'm looking for the Colored entrance, please," I said to the pavement, not wanting to be pegged ignorant of city ways and where they hid the Negro doorways.

"You won't find one of them here," he said. "Just walk in."

"I'd prefer the Colored entrance. Please," I insisted. He seemed an unusual man, perhaps a prankster of some sort, with the long limbs, triangular head, and bulging eyes of a chameleon. Just the sort to make trouble for folks and dart away.

"We ain't got one of them because ain't nothing but Negroes in this town, is what I'm telling you. Look around and see if you see any whitefolks other than these sorry few from the buses." He smirked and returned his attention to the shoe in his hand, satisfied he knew the lay of the land.

A dark brown man sold bus tickets and answered questions inside while two soldiers in Army-issue khaki rushed past me: one, with the deep mulberry skin of the ready harvest, and the other, my same sun-gold cinnamon with dark freckles on his cheeks who placed a hand to his peaked cap. A light-skinned woman with a wild mane of bottle-red hair rushed into a yellow cab driven by a portly man of pecan complexion. He sped past an ebony police officer in white gloves holding palms up, meaning "stop." A deep bronze man across the street wore paint-covered bib overalls, smoking a cigarette next to another bib-overalled man—cocoa-brown. And the family by the drink machine? The mama, she was high yellow, but her husband was a rich, deep brown to match some good, peaty soil. One child favored him, one her, and one fell to a brown somewhere in the middle. And that was just within those few feet of me at the depot. Up and down the avenue, Negroes of every shade came together like the dusk in a fall forest.

I should've been glad, relieved, to find such a sight on my journey. But my knees gave out and I sank onto the bench next to the shoe-shine man. I buried my face in my hands and sobbed.

"Ain't *our* folks' usual reaction when they first arrive in New Jessup," he said, patting my shoulder with the light taps of a man unaccustomed to comforting people. I stopped crying in time to wave the bus off, too exhausted to shed another drop.

"Is there a church house nearby?" I asked.

"Pastor and Mrs. Brown'll take right good care of you up at Morning Star Baptist," he said, and with walking directions, he sent me on my way. But after I took a couple steps up the sidewalk, he called out. When I turned, he spoke to the stain on my dress and the marks on my arm that weariness had me forgetting to hide. "But miss, if you looking for whitefolks, and I don't imagine that you would be, but say you are? Well, you'd have to get all the way to the other side of the woods to find a single one."

I SLEPT IN a room with flowered wallpaper and mauve carpet and a bookshelf next to a desk, although, maybe *slept* isn't the right word. I fell into a bed, behind my eyelids, and disappeared from the world in that room—too weary to dream about where I came from, or where I was going. In that bed, one hour turned into two turned into blank-ness until I woke with the dawn when the door latched.

With hardly a footfall, Mrs. Brown had left a tray of warm butter-milk biscuits, strawberry preserves, and thick slabs of good country ham on a tray next to the bed, though instead of eating, I turned over and watched the sunrise signaling the end of my overnight stay. Out the window, the neighborhood street climbed a hill, with gold crown-ing the peak like salvation. Promising that if I reached the horizon, Chicago was just on the other side—just beyond the place where day met night, just beyond the place where trees met sky, just beyond the place where gold touched pavement, my sister Rosie waited. The food cooled while I watched the sun come up from underneath thick quilts. Even wrapped in warmth, I could not shake the chill of two dresses, some underclothes, my weather-beaten hand-me-down shoes, all of Rosie's letters tied with string, a half-used ticket to Birmingham, and the unused dime for that Coca-Cola being everything I had in the world to complete a journey I never wanted to take. But without any better options, sunrise hinted that the horizon was waiting.

After a gentle knock, the door creaked again. A hand came to rest on my shoulder with the permanently curved fingers of a mama's caring touch. Mrs. Brown was a wisp of a woman, with acorn skin and sweet, smiling eyes. I thanked her for the food and the kindness of a place to lay my head and promised to get out their hair as soon as I visited the privy and washed up. Smiling kindly, tolerably, she said,

"You're welcome to use the *restroom*, child, and nobody is rushing you out the door."

The Browns were wonderful, patient, and over some days, the warmth of the parsonage steeped into me slowly. The house smelled of lavender and peppermint and had real wallpaper on the walls. Little cakes of soap were always nestled atop soft, thick towels in the restroom. Knobs for hot and cold called water from pipes underground to fill the tub, and Mrs. Brown used machines to wash and dry her clothes, beat her rugs. The house was comfortable and modern, and, I figured, everything Rosie must have in Chicago. Only, I was still in Alabama, maybe four stops into a journey I had not figured out how to complete.

Pastor preached the Gospel of New Jessup, chapter and verse. One day, he laid a photo album in my lap out on the porch. It was open to a round-faced man who was wiping a handkerchief across his sweaty brow with one hand and pointing a finger to the sky with the other. He favored Pastor, save for the gray hair all over his head that had just started creeping into Pastor's temples. Pastor Brown smiled silently at the pages, his gaze lingering on the photograph, enjoying a memory. Leaning closer, I read the faded newspaper clipping on the opposite page from the 1904 *Tunnel Springs Star*:

> All community-minded Colored People willing to sow, and build upon, the soil of this state will find a welcoming respite in New Jessup, Gilliam County, Alabama. All trades taught, and professional class welcome, as we seek to leave nothing wanting in construction of our community, wholly adherent to the virtue of self-reliance. Work is plentiful, and land is available for purchase (outright or by work agreement) to those endeavoring to assist in the settlement of all-Colored New Jessup.
>
> This is unimproved land waiting for strong men and hearty women to join in our efforts. Your ideas about town building will be valuable, as we seek to grow to more than ten-thousand Colored settlers seeking to call Alabama home. If you make suggestions that the community adopts, you will be given the opportunity to receive your share of the benefit.
>
> Upon arrival, enquire after Ralph Greene, Duke Royal, Clifford Campbell, Jenson Franklin, Isaiah Bell, Luke Morris, or Dayton Laramie.

My sleeve crept up while I read, revealing the sausage-thick bruises on my right forearm again. Other than offering aspirin and ice, neither Pastor nor Mrs. Brown had asked about the marks—or the way I was favoring my right shoulder. Now, Pastor's eyes locked on my attempt to pull my sleeve and hide the skin. He picked up midthought, as if continuing aloud a conversation begun in his mind.

"Because this town, you see . . . it was born of the swamp, from days of tribulation. But from tribulation comes perseverance, and perseverance, character, and character, hope. You hear what I'm saying, Sister?"

"Yessir, Pastor."

"That's my father on the page during his first sermon in the sanctuary across the street." He pointed to the man, then the clipping. "And this was the advertisement that brought my family here when I was a little boy. It was a long road to build that church. A lot of labor, a lot of nickels and dimes. When we pulled up in our wagon in 1904, there wasn't much to New Jessup but swampland and opportunity. Including the opportunity to thrive amongst our own community," he said, with a final glance at my wrist, now covered. "Amen?"

"Yessir, amen, Pastor," I said, and we never opened the door on my leaving Rensler again.

The address on Rosie's last letter had no telephone, so I wrote her with the same information, over and over, for weeks—news about our daddy and my whereabouts. Meantime, one day, walking back from the post box, Mrs. Brown showed me a large room off the church fellowship hall, where an explosion of clothing donations overflowed from the collection bins. No need to ask whether I sewed, she said, since all we country girls were born with needle and thread in hand. Some of the pieces were worn, needing repair, but there were plenty of store-bought, never-worn clothes among the piles. After a day or so, we finished separating everything and I asked for that needle and thread.

She sat me at a Singer instead. The stitches flew on that sewing machine, straight and even, through all sorts of clothes. Design ideas filled my mind with something other than the sunset-silhouette behind me, or the horizon ahead. I busied myself from morning until night, inspecting, patching, French seaming, reinforcing. I attached taffeta, ruffles on little girl dresses; gave little boy coats corduroy and flannel on the collars; hand-embroidered delicate patterns on the wrists and plackets of women's blouses; and reinforced men's dungarees to work plenty more shifts.

While sitting at the sewing machine one day, Mrs. Brown approached me with a wool skirt-suit sheening purplish-navy with a

VTL tag stitched in the collar. The fabric was pristine, unworn, and it needed nothing but the right-sized woman to snap it up. Refusing my "no thank you, ma'am" and "I couldn't possibly, ma'am," she insisted I cut it down to fit me. So, over some days, I refitted it for my frame.

After around a month with the Browns and still no word back from Rosie, Mrs. Brown suggested I wear that navy-blue skirt suit for an outing, just the two of us. As the setting sun reflected red clay across the horizon and the clouds, we pulled into traffic on Venerable Ave.

"I'm sure you know by now there are worse places than New Jessup," she said as we sat in her Buick. "You still haven't heard from your sister, have you?"

"No, ma'am. Not yet."

"Do you have anywhere to stay once you reach Chicago? Or any money for a rooming house? Pastor and I can give you a little something to put in your pocket, but where will you go?" I shrugged. It was not the first time she had asked, laying the horizon ahead of me again that early December day—winter being the time of year that Rosie had described Chicago as "knock-you-down hateful" in her letters. "Well, till you find Rosie, or at least save up a little, what's say you stick around a spell? I have somebody I think you should meet."

We parked and hustled up Venerable Ave. towards a tan-skinned woman locking the door to the Taylor Made Dress Shop. Mrs. Brown started in right away, bragging on all my sewing. The woman looked me over from head to foot in silence; then she lowered her glasses and looked over top of them, inspecting me with a look practiced in finding flaws.

No, ma'am, I had not worked as a seamstress assistant. Yes, ma'am, I had just learned how to use a sewing machine. No, ma'am, I had no formal training. Yes, ma'am, I graduated high school. No, ma'am, I never worked with satin, lace, silk, or sequins. And yes, ma'am, I was new in town. She invited us inside, where she inspected my work closer. She needed not look at the tag inside the collar to know I had cut down a Vivian Taylor Laramie original. But she looked anyway, maybe to confirm that somebody had nerve enough to alter work created by her hand.

"What is your name again?" she asked my reflection in the mirror.

"Alice. Alice Young."

"And you only recently learned to use a Singer sewing machine, Alice Young?"

"Yes, ma'am. Just a couple weeks ago."

Her lips pursed in a little smile and she nodded at Mrs. Brown.

"Well, you'll stand up straight, hold your head high, and enunciate in my shop," she instructed. "You'll be on time and dress the part. You'll carry yourself with distinction, both here, and throughout New Jessup when you work at Taylor Made. Are we clear?"

I have no idea whether or not I knew I was home. What I knew, and wanted Rosie to know, and come see, was that this, too, was Alabama.

TWO

Didn't matter that I was five, and Rosie six, when she promised never to leave me. Her words were full of the kind of truth only children can tell—bursting with the belief and imagination of an uncorrupted heart. And in devout adoration of my older sister, I believed her. Even years later, well after she thieved away in the night, I was grasping at the air she left behind.

She promised on the day when we made acquaintance with a sugar maple so ancient it invented sugar. Maybe it was two trees joined at the bottom—I never really knew why the two massive trunks came together in that V the way they did, but it called to us on a clear day as sheep clouds grazed across the sky. Me and Rosie were born eighteen months apart, some years into the landowners and bosses now blaming "The Depression" as their reason for their shorting my family's wages. By the summer of 1940, me and my sister were old enough to know a weed from a shoot and fetch water from the pump, so we helped our folks doing field work—planting, tending, and harvesting whatever the landowners wanted in the ground. Mama also sold pies at O'Dell's Grocery—the Negro store in Rensler—and sometimes Daddy delivered guano for a fertilizer dealer or cut timber. But mostly, we were in the cotton.

That day, me and Rosie raced through our noontime dinner because we were convinced the clouds were just low enough to glance the branch tips and turn to spun sugar. We meant to climb that sugar maple and get a taste. A middling climber by then, I knew better than to look down. Rosie scrambled up the right trunk, and me, the left, because I was smaller and those branches were closer together. As branches do, they thinned as we climbed higher until I reached one that creaked. I looked down. We were sky high and I froze, hugging the trunk tight and pouring water from my eyes. The sound of my own wailing filled my ears until Rosie's soft, but firm, words eased in between my sniffles.

"Stairsteps going up, stairsteps going down, Alice. We got to come down from here."

I refused and screamed when the branch groaned. My arms were more splayed than hugging the tree, and with Rosie safely on the other trunk, it would have been my fall alone. I looked down, wondering how the next branch had been so close coming up and was now a mile away.

"Stairsteps going up, stairsteps going down, Alice. We got to come down from here." Over some seconds, her soft confidence warmed and soaked through me. Slowly, like the way a pat of butter melts over cornbread fresh out the oven. My eyes cleared, and the next branch down was, all the sudden, right there. Big and beefy and ready to hold me safely. Then the next one, and the next one was easier still, until bit by bit we worked our way to the ground.

About halfway down, our parents appeared at the base, shielding their eyes. Daddy had an arm behind his back. The forest around us was so quiet their whispering voices carried into the leaves.

"Great Jesus," said Daddy. "You see this? You see your girls up there?"

"I see them, Marion. Be calm—they coming down."

"See what I mean, Safi? Now tell me I'm wrong."

"Nobody said anything about you being wrong. Mrs. O'Dell will take Rosie, but Alice just turned five a couple days ago."

"She'll take Rosie *and* Alice, is what I know. My daughters is going to school. They ain't finna be mining nobody's coal."

"Mrs. O'Dell reminded me she's nobody's babysitter, and there's only one of her. Teaching is serious business, she told me."

"Like you don't know that. She just got her back up because you wanna start your own school."

"Well, whatever the reason, she said next year for Alice."

"Alice won't be no bother. She got just as much learning as kids Rosie's age—knows her letters and numbers already. What difference do it make to Laverne O'Dell how old she is?"

"Well, maybe you should ask her then, 'Brother Young,'" she said, in that near-breathless way Mrs. O'Dell addressed my daddy. For Mama, she always called "Sister" from the back of her throat and through near clenched teeth. "Because she certainly said 'no' to me."

"Safiyah." He drew Mama's name out longwise to tickle her good humor. She gave him the closed-mouth, deep chuckle he was looking for. They finished their playfulness and stopped talking when me and Rosie got close enough that they thought we could hear.

The second my toenail kissed the earth, Daddy was on me. He snatched my upper arm, and before I could open my mouth to cry out, two lashes seared the back of my legs. Fresh dirt peppered the leaves on the ground, and it was only when he turned his attention to Rosie, who was trying to sneak away, that I saw he had yanked a baby sweetgum sapling clean out the ground, with soil still clinging to the roots. It was an indignity to survive death from a tree only to be whupped by a tree.

He quit after those few licks. We did not dare sniffle or cry or raise a word of objection—instead, me and Rosie spoke to each other in pitying glances as we walked behind our parents back to the rows. Mama did all the actual talking.

"You two should've known better. High as you were, me and your daddy would have been able to do nothing but watch you fall. All the ways this world'll try to kill you in a tree, for y'all to be out here giving your lives away?" she said. "You won't be out here doing the world's work for it. Not as long as me and your daddy draw breath, you won't. I bet you won't do that again."

Later that night, Mama had me and Rosie at the table for our lesson, when she told us that Rosie would start first grade the week following, and I would start school of some sort. Both of us would be in the same one-room outbuilding behind O'Dell's Grocery, where Rensler's Negro children from little to big shared one teacher and one classroom during the week, and Rensler's Negro Baptists worshipped on Sundays. We were to work hard and mind our manners because we were going to college. My sister took the news without a thought, chanting absentmindedly as she worked through her spelling.

"*Firrrrrst* grade, second grade, third grade, college!
Firrrrrst grade, second grade, third grade, college!"

But right away, *BIRD* stumped me. Side-by-side, Rosie continued working while I held my pencil straight up, the end pressed, unmoving, unable to arrange the letters in my mind or draw them on my slate. Because soon, my sister would be on the other side of a classroom, next to new playmates who knew all her same spelling words and math problems, leaving me to fend for myself under the black-marble glare of Thousand-Year-Frown O'Dell. A woman, me and Rosie had decided, whose cheeks drooped down the sides of her mouth like slid-down egg yolks. My inside laughter about her frown had allowed me to ignore Mrs. O'Dell anytime she teased me about blanking on my Easter speech Easter past. To ignore her in silence as she fed on my still obedience like candy.

Now, I would actually have to listen to what she said to me, when Mama was the best teacher in town. *A, B, C, 1, 2, 3, CAT, DOG* was scratched all over my slate, and I could even do some of Rosie's figuring and spelling. But that night, my word was *BIRD* and the letters were like steam escaping my mind. After a couple of distracted attempts, Mama excused me and I went out to the porch.

Daddy was outside mending the cotton sacks. I sat on our old porch steps and stared at the night and the kindly members of my family who I imagined taking pity on me from the stars: my four Big Papa and Big Mama stars; countless aunties, uncles, and cousins. Family I had never met looking down at me, listening for my prayers. Silently, I asked them to undo the news of school.

Daddy let me stew for a minute before he asked if I'd been struck mute.

"No, sir."

"Then what's got you aggravating your mama in there, and out here like you can't speak."

"Nothing."

"Nothing's so big as nothing, Lil Bit," he snorted. "So what's the matter with you."

"It's just . . . Mrs. O'Dell."

"What about her?"

Laying the sacks on his knee, he leaned forward, nodding his head and wrinkling his forehead in all the right places as I told him about a couple instances of her picking with me. But when I finished, there was no consolation or promise that we could skip her school and keep getting our lessons at home. Mama would start her schoolhouse one day, he said. Meantime, Mrs. O'Dell was the only teacher for Colored children in Rensler.

"Ain't no child of mine ever gonna bust rocks for being truant, hear?" he said, ignoring the confusion on my face as I nodded my head. As a child, no more explanation was due, and I knew better than to ask. His gruffness was a warning and a promise that there was something even too old for Daddy in his words. He was a tall man, but "it" was taller, and just beyond the reach of his long, strong arms. Its brow was set just a touch more than Daddy's and its jaw just a little more square. But though it was gnawing and clawing to get to his girls, Daddy contained it, held it back from us, in the things he didn't say. "That O'Dell woman'll be the least of your life's worries. You go, show her just how empty-headed you ain't, then come home." He turned his attention back to the sacks and let me get back to my stars.

Rosie finished her lesson and joined me on the steps some minutes later. As she sat, I stretched my arm to match my thumbnail to the bright yellow crescent inside the moon.

"What you doing?" she asked.

"Trying to put some magic in my thumb."

"Oh, I wanna do that, too." She sat next to me and outstretched her thumb. "I feel it coming down my arm. It's warm like pee."

"Yeah, warm. That's right," I said, maybe convinced, maybe not wanting to be left out.

"What you gonna do with yours?" she asked me.

"Make it so you stick by me at school. So you can't never leave me."

"*Aww*, girl, don't waste it on something silly as that. You know I ain't never leaving you."

"Yeah? You promise?"

"Promise." Her arms must have been little-girl short, but they wrapped tight around me and eased some sweetness back into my world again. I felt so good, I even let her boss me. "Now, we got to think real hard and come up with a good use for this magic before we lose the moon."

THREE

Miss Vivian Taylor Laramie was a serious woman who with-ered assistants with a simple glance over top of her glasses. She didn't laugh much, but come springtime in 1958, she was keep-ing me busy at that Singer from *can't see* to *can't see* and rented me the apartment over the shop she owned with Mr. Earnest Laramie (who everybody called Cap, for "Captain," since he was head of our local law). With its pullout sofa, small kitchen, indoor plumbing, and shelves full of books, it was comfortable and spacious and the lone-liest place in New Jessup to send, but not receive, letters after work.

After a wrong bus to get to the picture show one night, I ended up in front of a HELP WANTED—NIGHTS sign in the window at Marvin's Diner. I took a few shifts there to fill my evening hours with the noise of being alive—which turned out mainly to be Mr. Marvin Johnson in the order window hollering my name if he thought I answered the bell too slow. He kept me running between the checkers-playing old men with grabby hands; to quiet, polite young men with watch-ful eyes; to booths filled with rowdy high-schoolers; to young fam-ilies with crying babies; to folks rushing in at the end of their shifts across the woods; to fathers and sons out for their regular meal. Mr. Marvin's nightly smile came after we locked up and he sent me off with a loud, tired huff and a tight crack across his lips that said, *Well, I guess that's it*. But laugh? Mr. Marvin? Never.

Now, Mr. Dale Campbell had a laugh to be remembered. It was one of the first things I'd noticed about him when I started a few weeks before Miss Catherine passed. First, it exploded as a great bark, followed by slow chuckles, each one lower in register than the last. He would wind down until the funny stopped, his shoulders still bouncing up and down as it smoldered; all, usually, the result of some tale he'd told himself. So it was normally him filling the air with his laughter and lies. But one night, his laugh burst through the air of the empty diner so unexpectedly I nearly dropped the glass in my hand.

"You'd better hop to it, then!" he boomed over Jackie Wilson from the jukebox and the rain keeping time with the beat.

Behind me, pots and pans crashed in the kitchen as Mr. Marvin trashed uneaten food and fussed about the night's receipts. It was raining hard; the sky so dark since the beginning of my shift that the sun set on the day before it rose. After a third thunderclap shook the building, flashing the lights, Mr. Marvin stormed out the kitchen and turned the sign from OPEN to CLOSED. There I stood, watching the raindrops explode onto the plate glass as lightning cracked across the sky. Caught, the fool on foot and with nobody's umbrella, I was in no hurry to step out in that storm. So I was drying the glass in my hand, and drying it again, when all that commotion started in the Campbell booth.

Mr. Dale handkerchiefed tears running down his cheeks, laughing so hard, I thought he'd been affected or something. He hardly seemed able to breathe, let alone notice me watching from behind the counter. But his son Raymond, across the table from him, just smirked a lopsided smile and sipped his coffee. They both had that same dark amber skin, its color reminding me of long-steeped sun tea. The same tall, lean body, full lips, and gray eyes belonging to generations of the Campbells. Except for his velvet coils cut a little closer to his scalp, Raymond was the spitting image of Mr. Dale probably thirty years prior, suggesting that he would also be handsome well into his salt-and-pepper years. Though not much of a talker.

"Calm down, Pop. You're getting yourself excited," he said, just as cool as he pleased, his grin propping up one cheek. But Mr. Dale threw palms at his son, pushed the story right back at him and told him to keep on lying. In the weeks since Miss Catherine's passing, they had never laughed like this, so I figured, after spying their clean plates, that they must be feeling better about things—this stormy night, the first that Mr. Dale had finished his pie. Their carrying on peopled that empty diner with voices as I made my way over with the coffee pot.

But Raymond laid working man's fingers atop the rim of his cup to refuse another coffee, offering me a ride home instead. And after thunder rattled the building again, raising fresh curses from Mr. Marvin that caused even two mechanics to flinch, I took the ride.

Raymond sprinted through sheets of rain to pull his rattletrap under the awning—an old Frankenstein car with a Studebaker nameplate. Me and Mr. Dale climbed in, and then he eased us into a storm battering us from all sides. Almost right away, Mr. Dale started wishing, aloud, that they had driven his Cadillac, teasing Raymond about his budget ride:

"Metal on this thing's only good for writing paper."

"Even the Almighty's desperate to put this thing outta its misery."

"If F-O-R-D stands for 'fixed or repaired daily,' or 'found on the road dead,' S-T-U-D-E . . . well, Studebakers must have a hell of a fate."

But suddenly, and seemingly without cause, a group of men minding their business under an awning on Pinckney Ave. caught Mr. Dale's attention. He stopped chuckling and started fussing, thundering about the shame no-count scoundrels brought the community. Men who had done no worse than a little woofing now and again—calling me "pretty round brown," wondering whether heaven was letting all the angels out, promising me the stars and moon, stuff like that—on my normal walks between the diner and my apartment. Men who were certainly not the menace he was making them out to be.

But he kept on about how New Jessup Negroes should have more pride than this, and when he was young and who would have snatched him up and what harm would befall Raymond if he ever, *ever* found his son in one of Pinkney Ave.'s juke joints or pool halls. He wished he *would* find Raymond out there—"wished" like you do for somebody to spit in your eye or stomp your foot. Without knowing then how deep, and personal, the offense to him, Mr. Dale's reaction seemed outsized. I had heard the stories of how New Jessup came about, but this night, in the rain, was before I realized how much of our town was truly *in* him, *of* Campbell blood. Even still, by this night when Raymond first drove me home, I had stopped looking for COLORED ONLY signs; the surprise of seeing Negroes exclusively, and everywhere, had almost smoothed into expectation. I considered Mr. Dale just being cranky about some young folks.

Especially after Raymond rolled his eyes, smiling at me like a man who knew that lecture from cover to cover. I shrank into my seat, trying not to let the father catch me smiling at the son while wondering why the son was trying to make me smile in the first place. In the weeks since returning home to bury his mama, he had been pleasant at the diner, if hardly talkative. Just as Mr. Dale started repeating himself, Raymond pulled to my curb. He had an umbrella in the trunk, and as he hopped out to get it and walk over to my door, all that bitter turned sweet in Mr. Dale's voice.

"See, Alice?" he bragged. "I didn't raise a man for Pinckney Ave., now."

The car door opened to rain crashing down on Raymond in waves as he held the umbrella just for me. He winced as the rain pelted him, bouncing from his skin and soaking his clothes. The downpour blasted the nylon over my head in tiny pops as we scrambled up the steps to my apartment. I had been on a couple dates since arriving in town, and always had keys in hand by the time we reached my door so they had no cause to linger. But butterflies fluttered from my stomach to my fingers as I fumbled through my pocketbook. I needed no double-take glance to tell me he was nobody's sunset silhouette. It was not the chill in the air, or discomfort, making my teeth chatter. Instead, under the light, he was just the handsomest, most pitiful-looking man in all of Alabama.

"Alice," he shouted over the drumming *tat-tat-tat-tat* on the roof. "I'd like to take you out sometime."

The words left his lips as condensation, and I said "yes" before the cloud dissolved into air.

"Tomorrow, then? Dinner?" he said, with that smile teasing the end of a frost, the beginning of spring, as I nodded. "I'll pick you up at seven?"

"Seven o'clock, then. Goodnight, Raymond," I said, breathing the scent of the rain, of him, of the good feeling, and allowing myself a smile after too many nights of not remembering one.

FOUR

"**A**gain, you say?"

The question hovered over the table like the waiter crumbing the stray bit of lettuce from the white linen tablecloth. Raymond's gray eyes sparkled in mild, if spirited challenge, causing fresh air to rush back into our date after he stopped dead from explaining the difference between the Jessups. And just in time for Billie Holiday to sprinkle a little of her moonglow over us from the speakers. Around us, other diners clinked silverware on plates with heads huddled together in intimate conversation. Practiced in the art of turning a blind eye, our white-gloved waiter was doing a fine job of ignoring me and Raymond's own foreheads practically touching—even if his expert discretion also meant that he took his sweet time exchanging salad forks for soup spoons. He finally served the soup, and mine looked delicious—described on the menu as "potatoes † leeks † cream." Of course, in a place with crystal chandeliers and oak paneling on the walls, the name had to be French. Alone again, I dipped my spoon into the bowl in a smug, playful victory, but with the first taste, it was my turn to be surprised. I didn't complain, although I did lower my spoon and my expectations.

"Again, you say?" he repeated, the smile warming on his face as he scored his own point. But he switched our soups instead of telling me that vichyssoise was *supposed* to be cold, forgoing his crab bisque for my mistake.

"I stayed with Pastor and Mrs. Brown for weeks when I first came to New Jessup. Not to mention that I work for Mr. Marvin and Miss Vivian, remember. They stay reminding me about how special it is here, about building the community and their families' roles in it. But yes, I do enjoy hearing you tell me the story of New Jessup. Again."

"Again," he snorted, blew on a spoonful of chilled soup, snorted again, and slid it into his mouth. The heaviness that had descended upon our first date finally drifted away. If being at ease was discovering another person on earth completely fluent in the same alphabet of letters, head tilts, sighs, and flirtatious eyes, then we had found ease from the moment he picked me up. Between the time I slid into the car and when the waiter poured our water, there had been no empty space in conversation. Even the songs playing overhead, our laughter, our silences, meant something between us. And the words he did say! This man who had barely addressed me with more than pleasantries for months had called me a little proper, a little country, Alabama coy with a little spice. He even called himself admiring my voice (my "soft voice") so closely he had to pull his chair around and sit next to me.

I was enjoying him, too: the way his lips curled up at the corners as he talked, or how they pressed together when he started to get bashful. The soft spot for his mama was still an open wound, and there was a tenderness in his eyes when he learned about my parents being gone. And the couple times Mama and Miss Vivian hovered over my shoulder, correcting my "ain't" for "isn't," he said, "You ain't gotta do that. Please don't correct yourself with me."

Our conversation was a creek flowing into the river finding its
way to the sea, streaming into the history of New Jessup without
hesitation. Raymond was one of the town's proudest descendants
with his own story to share. When he started talking about his
granddaddy—"Big Poppa" Clifford Campbell—his face lit up like
Christmas. But slowly, in noticing his mouth, I saw the parts of the
story that turned his lips down. Particularly when he began talking
about the swamp.

His eyes turned serious but kind—the sort of look asking my permission to bring this talk to our table. We were in the middle of a
nice time getting to know each other, and none of our talk about
siblings or favorite foods had had anything to do with whitefolks.
In fact, since stepping off the bus eight months before, the only ones
I had seen were in the news doing nothing new under the sun when
it came to Negroes, so I wanted to usher them away from our table.
But like it or not, even New Jessup's Negroes' fates had been tied to
whitefolks since tobacco was prince before cotton became king in
Alabama.

I already knew that, back when Jessup was born and thrived
as a place without an acre of farmland, the town still fattened off
the blood of Negro people in every other creative way. I had never
been across the woods, or had occasion to go see, the old holding
pens where traders held our folks for auction in Jessup, or the town
squares where husbands screamed for wives, and mamas begged for
children to be taken off the block. It was a city accommodating slav-
ery's every need, from blacksmiths forging shackles, chains, brands,
and all the tools of bondage, and its wickedness; to saloon owners forcing Negro women to serve food and drink downstairs, and
cater to men's other appetites upstairs; to cotton gins separating seed
from fiber, and mangling Negro hands in the process. I knew that
the docks had been built, and railroad tracks laid, to allow for train
cars and boats to be loaded down with the tobacco, then cotton, that

brokers sold to the four corners of the earth, from Jessup. That banks showered plantation owners with money in Jessup and that hotels, theaters, and restaurants popped up and filled with whitefolks. There was a slaughterhouse, a fertilizer plant, and later on, textile and lumber mills. Lawyers, dentists, undertakers, dressmakers, butchers, and more, all hung their shingles in Jessup. Carpenters, road builders, stone masons, built and expanded the town, creating places where society women, preachers, newspapermen, and so on all lived, and worked. And these folks were no more averse to enslaving and tormenting Negroes than their brethren and sistren on the plantations.

Jessup grew until emancipation created "the Negro problem"— that whitefolks needed us but had no desire to live by us. A "problem" hardly acknowledging that our proximity to whitefolks had never done us any favors. Raymond's smile returned when he started talking about how new freedmen gladly separated into a community called Negro Jessup, far on the other side of the train tracks, where those who had worked from field to house and everywhere inside Jessup reconstructed their lives on useless farmland, given by the very people who had held them in bondage. There, men and women who had made meals of pig's feet, chicken backs, corn pone, and chitlins built two-story houses when most whitefolks were still living in one; men and women scarred by the whip and the branding iron sent children to professional schools, who then returned as doctors and businessmen, architects and engineers, tradesmen and teachers. Negroes opened a hospital and a savings and loan and rode their horses, drove their carriages, over pavement. Miss Vivian's grandmere opened the original Taylor Made Dress Shoppe, where she designed dresses for the town's most fashionable ladies, and Raymond's great-great-granddaddy turned his training as a blacksmith into the town fix-it shop. Negro Jessup was modern and thriving and building ever closer to the whitefolks' side of town and making whitefolks wonder who was living on the other side of the tracks from who.

I knew this story and enjoyed watching him be proud of it. At first.

But Raymond started drawing figure eights on his salad plate as he began talking about the 1903 riot that left six dead and drove the rest of our folks into the swamp. With shotguns, deeds, and the threat of torches in hand, a white mob evicted our people and absorbed Negro Jessup as their own. As Raymond began describing this evil, his face clouded and the light in his eye dimmed a touch. Since coming to town, Mr. Marvin and Miss Vivian had recounted this horror to me a number of times, and I had my own share of Rensler nightmares to add atop the heap. But this was our first time out together, the first time he'd said this many words to me. Our first real opportunity to learn about each other in this place where we were free from sitting around rehashing the misdeeds of whitefolks. As he settled into the telling, he knocked some lettuce off his plate. Too embarrassed to be sure about what to do next, the pity on my face only made him lay his fork down.

So when the waiter made his way towards us, just before he served the soup, I teased Raymond into ushering talk of whitefolks back across the woods.

"I really enjoy hearing you tell the story of New Jessup. Again," I said.

The shock was immediate and lasting since the waiter took his time clearing the crumbs and sliding our bowls on the table.

"You must've been bored to death listening to me talk. That makes sense about Mr. Marvin, but Miss Vivian, too, huh? I can't believe you just let me go on like that," he said as I took a spoonful of my bisque. It was delicious, and I felt slightly bad for enjoying it as much as I did. But with talk of whitefolks excused from the table, he seemed alright. Better than alright when he smiled and asked,

"Did they tell you how we paid for it? The land?" The greens and yellows reflecting in his eyes suggested he relished this part and wanted to answer his own question.

"No. You tell me." Crossing the last couple of inches between us, he leaned in close enough for my perfume and his aftershave to mingle and told Mr. Dale's version of the truth: that Big Poppa Clifford was one of several pouring money atop money in the swamp. Coins and bills they managed to smuggle out in the overnight hours of the riot. Whitefolks had taken everything for their own, including every Negro dime in the savings and loan. But after some days, folks in the swamp started pouring money from socks, coin purses.

"And twenty-dollar gold pieces, too. The Ladies Economic Improvement Society had agreed to sew them in the backsides of doll babies."

"Stop lying." His grin said he was satisfied about my surprise. "Now I know you telling a tale, Raymond Campbell."

"Dale Campbell tells it for true," he said. "Socks, mason jars, flour sacks, silk purses, doll babies, you name it. He says nickels, dimes, dollars, and even twenty-dollar gold pieces piled up like a king's ransom out there. And remember, this was a time when you could buy an acre of land for fifty, sixty cents in Gilliam County." He lowered his voice and whispered right in my ear. I flashed hot. "And I'll tell you why I believe it, too. Plenty of old-timers around here still do that—keep money hidden around the house. Including my father. He says that if a Negro's got thousands in the bank, he'd better have millions under his mattress." I clutched my stomach trying to keep the laugh inside, but it escaped as he described the bankers' faces watching all that money pile up in the swamp instead of nestling inside their bank vault.

As the pile grew, so did the ideas about what to do with the money. Some of the doctors and lawyers and businessmen styled themselves the Talented Tenth because a man named DuBois wrote somewhere that the educated few should lead the masses. Quarrels erupted between the families about which 10 percent among them was talented enough to lead the many, and which 90 percent was

destined to follow the few. Who among the blacksmiths and tai-
lors and haberdashers and road builders and carpenters and brick
masons and cooks and nursemaids and housekeepers and shopkeep-
ers were the contaminants, the worst of our people, unworthy of
having an opinion? Because the swamp was equal ground for everybody to catch fever or get snake-bit, argued men like O'Connor
Greene, Sr., Clifford Campbell, Dayton Laramie, and Duke Royal,
among others. Tempers cooled after it was decided that money collected by all would be agreed upon by all, and not just a Talented
Tenth of them. In the winter of 1903, with Negro Jessup gone and
everybody's children cold and starving, there was no appetite for
such talk.

Some left, but many stayed and poured that money towards
swampland considered by the government and land speculators to
be too damned to develop. Happy to part Negroes from their money,
whitefolks handed over the deeds. In return, the old-timers left miles
of treacherous swampland between the Jessups—calling them the
Trust Lands because the deeds were held in trust. With the rest of the
land, folks got to work and rebuilt what was lost to the other side of
the woods.

The elders invited Booker T. Washington to come for a visit in
1913. Whitefolks north to south and shore to shore loved Booker T.—
born enslaved and telling Negroes not to be troublesome to our white
neighbors? Whitefolks ate it up when he said the races could live
social lives as separate as the fingers, but that Negroes should stay
close enough to continue working across the woods. And while they
celebrated him telling us to stay in our place, he was calling Negroes
to Tuskegee Institute to learn better ways to farm and build, to take
what we learned in physics and mathematics and chemistry courses
back to better our own farms and communities. Sure, whitefolks still
needed us, and many Negroes obliged, working in homes and businesses over in Jessup. But when it came to living, whites and Negroes

alike stayed to their sides of the woods, and New Jessup thrived. Thanks to delivering a speech that whitefolks wanted him to say, Booker T. delivered a message Negroes wanted them to hear.

"Stay out," Raymond said, chuckling.

"I ain't never heard you talk this much," I told Raymond. "Usually, it's 'good evening, Alice,' 'no thank you, Alice,' 'thank you, Alice,' and 'goodnight, Alice.'"

"My voice is that deep, huh?"

"Down there with the low keys on the piano." He blushed purple when he smiled.

We continued comparing our own notes—the differences and similarities piling up in the spoken, and unspoken, language between us like the gold and silver pieces piled up in the swamp. As Eartha Kitt sang in French through the speakers like it was her native tongue, me and Raymond discovered each other. Our path forward seemed as chipped into stone as the Ten Commandments—older than the world, definite, and alive. So much so that when I told him about Rosie and the moon's magic in my thumb, he pressed it gently to his lips, saying maybe he felt something, too.

"I don't even remember what we wished for," I said. "These days, it would be for her to come back to Alabama where she belongs." A woman walked past our table, maybe on her way to the ladies' room. I only caught her back, but a blue dress skimmed her shapely frame, and her bob hairstyle barely reached the bottom of her ear. Nothing like Rosie as I remembered her. But in that moment, I placed every wish in the universe to see my sister's face when the woman passed by again.

"You think she'd like it here? Your sister?"

"I do. She would marvel at this place."

"Yeah, as far as places to live in the Jim Crow south, it's far from the worst. Still," he added, "I never thought I'd be living back home."

"But you are living back here? You ain't got a job or anybody special waiting on you in Montgomery?" He shook his head and half-
smiled to melt a whole frost.

"I quit my job in Montgomery after being here a few days," he
said. "And that was all I had to quit."

ON THE FIRST GOOD SUNDAY after the April rains, Raymond picked
me up, he said, for a piece of fish at Waverly's Fish Shack—where they
caught what they caught, and you got what you got. The Waverly
family fished the Tombigbee at dawn, sold filets during the day, and
served it fried until all gone. But instead of pointing the car towards
the river, we headed outside the city proper: past the last tall building, past the welcome sign, past where the pavement turned to red
clay. Another few minutes later, around a bend in the road, an ocean
of cars and their parts came into view. Rusted-out frames, car doors
of assorted colors, motors and other metal pieces, stacks of tires—
everything having to do with any automobile ever built—extended
from the edge of the road to the end of the earth. Or at least, to a
forest thick with cypress mingling with bent and twisting live oaks,
leaf-crowned sugar maple, and magnolias starting to bud.

He slowed and turned into the yard of a long, white house with
green shutters. Mr. Dale was on the porch resting Sunday away
behind his eyelids, while his oil-black Cadillac slumbered next to the
porch stairs. Another driveway on the right led to their auto shop,
flanked by two wreckers with CAMPBELL AUTO painted on the doors.
The land extended so far in that direction that birds flying above the
property appeared and disappeared into the white sun of the day.

To the left of the house—to the opposite end of the earth, or, at
least, extending to the same line of tall and hunched trees—was soil
worked by somebody who clearly knew what they were doing.

"Y'all farm this land?" I asked as he pulled the keys from the
ignition. He shook his head.

"I told you Mama had a garden," he said, like every flower and vegetable garden was measured in acres and not square feet.

Mesmerized, I was already through an expanse of grass yard before I even asked to see a blade. Ahead, there was a row of tall and short logs between the carpet of green and the golden, spent stalks of a dead cornfield. I spied the edge of a vegetable garden in the back, where weeds littered neglected, if neat, hundred-foot rows of soil. Trees dotted with pink and white flowers teased of peaches and cherries growing beneath the blossoms. But beyond the cornfield—for further acres than the eye could see—was an array of hydrangeas and azaleas and roses and peonies and camellias and crape myrtles and jacaranda and forsythia and hibiscus and bushes and trees and vines of flowers I didn't recognize, exploding on the land until God just ran out of color.

I had made one off comment, wondering aloud where I would ever find good fruit again. Living inside the city proper, the avenues had begun growing lush with dogwoods, and flower bushes were starting to show their buds—the time of year when my little strawberry patch back in Rensler would be bursting with sweet, juicy berries. Not that I was nostalgic for breaking my back on somebody else's land, but I did miss tending things, having my hands in the dirt, pulling my food from our little kitchen garden at the home house. Overstuffing myself with peaches and figs until I was sticky with the juice. So after one lament about store-bought fruit, on one of the first blue-sky days after the April rains, Raymond brought me out to Miss Catherine's garden and asked what I thought about getting comfortable inside.

We made a plan: Raymond tuned up Miss Catherine's old cobbled-together tractor and we decided to skip the cornfield that year, plant the vegetable patch, free the flowers from weeds and ivy, and trim the sucker branches from the fruit orchard. From that first Sunday, and on every Sunday thereafter, we jumped out of church clothes and into gardening clothes, busying ourselves on the day that He told us to "Let there be rest."

One such Sunday, we were on our way out to the fig trees and found devastation in the turnips. The culprits—rabbits—shot off together towards the cornfield, suggesting that the dead crop was harboring a warren. We rushed back to the house, where Raymond picked a gun from the case, closed the door, and turned the lock.

"Two's better than one, you think?" I told him.

"I can't teach you to shoot while hunting rabbit. Another time," he said, kissing my forehead that way a man does when "another time" means "never."

"Who said I need teaching? I could pop a bottle off your head at a thousand paces." By then, in addition to my soft voice and Alabama spice that he liked so much, he had added "tale teller" to my list of attributes, on account of stories I would tell him about my day, or bits here and there about my coming up. He read me up and down, then bellowed a laugh bigger than I had ever heard from him.

"And who taught you to do that?" he said, his chuckle barely contained.

"My mama." He exploded anew.

"Your *who*?"

"Why'd you say it like that? Everybody's gotta be able to shoot critters on the farm. And she was the better shot, anyway, so she taught me and my sister."

"*Hunh.*" His mouth was cracked open in a smile as he considered my face with eyes full of skepticism. I played a little huffy.

"What would Miss Catherine do if she found rabbits like this?"

"*She'd* shoot them. But she knew how to handle a rifle. Most women around here? Don't."

"Well, you forgetting that I ain't from around here, baby. So why don't you go on ahead and open up that case for me?"

He obliged and watched as I selected a right-sized .22 from among the host of shotguns and rifles they had for everything from pheasant to deer. We headed out the front door into the clear day. Through the grassy side yard, the dead cornstalks we had decided to chop down in the fall coming provided a haven for critters. The dropped leaves shushed and crunched underfoot, and when we kicked at them, looking for holes in the ground, too-fat corn snakes hissed before slithering off. Crows pecked at crumbs before they cawed and took flight, and plenty of fleeting footsteps dashed away as we stalked. For all our effort, though, we found nothing more than honeybees drunk on nectar from the flowers nearby. Without any dogs to flush the rabbits out, we had to wait.

Meantime, we set up Coke bottles on the stumps just to shoot something. He had a good eye, too, but ate a word every time I squeezed the trigger and shattered some glass. Finished wasting bullets, we sat at one of the tables in the grass. Entranced by the sun's kiss and the restful shushing of stalks, we relaxed back into our chairs exchanging slight, flirtatious smiles.

"Your mama taught you to do all that?"

"I told you she did."

"Did she learn from her mama?"

"I really don't know. I never asked her. Just knew, of my parents, she was the better shot."

"What about between you and your sister?"

"She hits where she aims. Used to, anyway. She never mentioned shooting nothing in Chicago."

"Why'd she go north?"

"Milk and honey and all that. You know that tale."

"Yeah, I've heard it," he said with a soft, relaxed laugh. "I'm glad you stopped in New Jessup, though. Caught ahold of your senses before you got too far." The reason I had left Rensler had never been spoken. Not to Miss Vivian, the Browns, nobody. And I had no intention of telling Raymond, especially when the best I could hope for was pity or rage or, God forbid, indifference. None of which would have changed anything. So perhaps it was the sleepy bees or the endless blue sky, or the stir of misty memories about Rosie, but I spoke before I thought.

"Wasn't that hard," I said. "I barely had enough lint in my pocket to get the bus to Birmingham, let alone another one to Chicago." He tilted his head and raised an eyebrow, his gaze still burning a hole in my temple when I turned away from him to face the vegetable garden. But reviving my last moments in Rensler at the sight of Miss Catherine's garden brought a crushing to my chest. That talk didn't belong in this place.

"Alice?" Concern shaded the way he said my name and I turned back to him. "I thought your bus ticket was *through* Birmingham *to* Chicago."

"No. Just Birmingham."

"You have people in Birmingham?"

"You awfully inquisitive today, Raymond Campbell," I said, ready to move on. He was not, as told by the way he lowered his chin and waited, watching me. "No. No people in Birmingham that I know of."

"Then why did you leave Rensler so suddenly?"

"My landlord got impatient about November's rent. Originally told me don't worry about it, get my daddy's marker squared away, and we'd work it out. Changed his mind, I guess, got pushy about it, so a couple days before it was due, I left."

"*Before* it was due? And what do you mean 'pushy'?"

"Just . . . insistent is all. He wanted his money. He didn't think I'd have it by the first of the month." Knew I wouldn't, actually, as I was gleaning for him and he was the one paying my wages. And he promised that I couldn't pick enough cotton to satisfy what he wanted. But watching clouds take over Raymond's face on that perfect, blue-sky day was no time to tell him all that. *Never* was the time I planned to tell him what old man Todd actually said, or did, when he menaced me, silhouetted by my last Rensler sunset. Still, Raymond pressed the issue, combing the fingertips of his right hand on his left cheek like he was getting agitated.

"Pushy how?"

"Ain't important, Raymond. I'm here now. That's what's important."

"Alice. Pushy how?"

"Raymond. Listen to me. It ain't important. What matters—"

"—did he—"

"No. No. But he did threaten to bring the sheriff to put me out." Even without knowing the whole of it, he pressed his hand against his mouth, and his chest swelled as he sighed.

"He was gonna bring the sheriff to put you out and your rent wasn't even due yet?"

"Raymond, it was time for me to move on. Everybody I ever loved was gone from that house, so ain't no use getting upset about it now. I ain't thinking about all that anymore."

"But why did he . . . ?" He trailed off then, knowing neither of us could see inside the mind of old man Todd, nor did we care to. Instead, he snorted a small, unsmiling laugh—more in disgust than amusement. The quiet that followed overflowed with unasked questions and untold answers dancing together.

After a few minutes, a rabbit slid into the corner of my eye about fifty paces off, emerging from the corn followed by two of its friends. They headed straight back to the turnips. I jerked my head to the side and he turned to look. They were moving, and he kicked up a tired, one-sided smile.

"Pop a bottle off the top of my head, huh? I—"

"Shhh."

His grin kicked a little higher.

"You really think you can hit one of them?" Raymond said.

"I would get all of them if you weren't sitting here running your mouth," I whispered, already up and ready to finish this critter, and this conversation, for good. "But we only gonna get one shot and I intend to get one with that shot. So hush and let me deal with this varmint." He laughed just as I pulled the trigger. With Rosie, and Birmingham, and sunset silhouettes still on my mind, I shot and came close—but I blamed his laughter, that came after, when I missed.

FIVE

My daddy was nice-looking, not even forty years old, with a strong back, and a good head on his shoulders, when my mama passed away. Naturally, women visited to console him, bringing food and patting me and Rosie on the head. But with two teenaged daughters, a quiet way about him, and deep-well grief, they trickled off after a while. All except Mrs. O'Dell, a "Mrs."—I came to learn—only the way women of a certain age marry the Lord. After Mama passed, Mrs. O'Dell started sending treats home with us from the store at the end of the school day, talking like her and Mama had been the best of friends.

"I just saw Safi the other day, bless her heart. We were talking about your daddy's love for our sour pickles. You know, I make those myself for the store."

As her cold shoulder warmed to me and Rosie, she even started riding out to the house to offer Daddy rides in her car. But after he declined one too many times and sent her away again, that mean marble glint returned to her eye.

After she left the last time, Daddy took to working a long stick of white oak to make strips for a new laundry basket. The piece was a couple inches shorter than him—so around six feet long—and the width of his two thumbs. He shaved splinters with his pocket-knife from end to end before notching the top, splitting off a strip, and starting to shave again. As he split, shaved, split, and shaved, stooping, rising, over and again, I asked about his intentions with Mrs. O'Dell. The *shoo shoo* sound of his work slowed briefly, but he continued, not looking up when he said that was a big question for a little girl. I was thirteen.

"Well, she is our schoolteacher, Daddy," Rosie said, "so if you put her off, she gonna take it out on us."

"Y'all two need to worry about y'all's schoolwork and y'all's duties at home. That's it. Not about that O'Dell woman coming around."

But me and Rosie stood to lose whether he made her our step-mama or he didn't. She had been our misery for years, and married to the Lord or not, she would either become a permanent fixture or a woman scorned. Newly thirteen and almost fifteen was no license to question Daddy about his affairs or defy my daddy. Still, me and Rosie announced that we were boycotting school until he not only put Mrs. O'Dell off, but he told her not to punish us for it. My daddy was good-natured until he wasn't. But instead of whupping us, he stayed steadily working that white oak, talking without raising his voice.

"Y'all ain't going to school because you worried about your teacher picking with you? I hear you right?" We both nodded, shifting side to side on our feet. "*Hunh.* Well, don't that just beat all? While we at it, my darling daughters, let me tell you what else y'all ain't finna do."

The *shoo shoo* continued, though one sideways glance from him uncrossed Rosie's arms and sent them shooting pin straight to her sides.

"Y'all think you grown enough to tell me how to handle my business? You think you need to tell me not to go around with Laverne O'Dell?"

"Daddy, we—" I started.

"What you ain't finna do is think just because your mama's gone that I need one woman, let alone two young girls, to boss me. You going to school. Know why?" The question was obviously a trick because he meant to answer it himself.

Rosie muttered, "To learn."

And I said, "To put something in our heads"—our dejected words tumbling over each other like struck bowling pins. My daddy didn't even look up from his work.

"Because what you ain't finna do is get hauled off for truancy, only to be sold to some snaggle-toothed, yellow-eyed cracker to die in a mine. Not my daughters. Ain't no redneck jailer finna put my daughters on the block for being absent from school."

Like all Negro parents we knew, Mama and Daddy never explained themselves to their children. Daddy working coal in his youth was old news, but judging by the slack-mouthed astonishment on Rosie's face, this was also her first time hearing that Daddy had been sold into the mines. For truancy.

"Your schoolhouse is open from August till May, ain't that right?" he said.

"Yessir." We were nearly breathless.

"And the classmates you started with? Bosey Jackson and the rest of his little brothers, Darby Thomas, Mo Marie Saint, they all in the fields now, working to help they families, ain't they? How many kids around here you know whose main job it is to go to school? Bring practically nothing home but good marks from August till May? Not many. So what you ain't finna do is say another peep about boy-cotting nothing, hard as me and your mama worked. Say what you want about Laverne O'Dell, her and her father keep that schoolhouse open, come hell or high water, without a dime of support from the county. So if school's in session three hundred and sixty-five days of the year, that's where you'll be. Believe it."

Rosie found her voice and started to speak. "Daddy, we just meant—"

"I know what you meant. Now let me tell you what I mean. Y'all two think Mrs. O'Dell picking with you is the end of days? Well, you ain't never gonna know what it is to have the truant officer haul you away from this house. Not as long as I have breath in my body. You didn't know they still sold Negroes, did you? Easy as pie, too." He snapped his fingers. "Catch us up for truancy, vagrancy, loitering, false pretenses, fill the jailhouse, and sell everybody off.

"You ain't gonna know nothing about gas sneaking its way from the bowels of the earth to steal your breath without sound, sight, or smell. Blackdamp. No, not my girls. My girls gonna trust the air they breathe and not spend the rest of they days wondering if that crushing in they chest is a trick of the mind or not. No. What y'all two are gonna know is college. That's what me and your mama promised each other long before we promised you. So if Mrs. O'Dell wanna give y'all good marks and pick with you, you'll fill your heads and forget the rest. You finna quit all this talk about boycotting school, hear?"

"Daddy, we just tired of Mrs. O'Dell being sometimey," I said. "She never had a kind word for Mama, hardly put up with us, to be coming around now, bringing treats."

He looked up briefly from his work and said, "This is the last word I'm gonna speak on this, so listen good: her coming around here ain't no treat to me, neither."

IT WAS A few weeks after the rabbits when I told Raymond about the parade of women knocking on our door back in Rensler after Mama passed. A brewing confrontation had forced me and him from the Campbell yard. Not between us, no—we were in full-bloom love, and he had surprised me one Sunday with a little snub-nosed, powder-blue Henry J, built by his hand the same way he had done with his Studebaker in Montgomery. He called both cars "boneyard specials," though mine had little in common with his: mine was all gleaming chrome with marshmallow whitewalls and not a single dent. But I had never driven a car or dreamed of owning one.

While me and Raymond sat in the car going over the knobs and dials, a red Packard carrying Widow Hughes from church eased into the yard and parked next to the Cadillac. She rose from the car with foil-topped Corningware in hand. Though I had witnessed similar unannounced visits and was familiar with the casseroles piling up in the Campbell Frigidaire, this time a gray Oldsmobile was practically on the Packard's bumper. With Campbell Auto closed on Sundays, this was usually some of the quietest stretch of road in New Jessup. But the day Raymond taught me to drive what we came to call "Blue Lightning," the yard filled with so many cars we had to take my lesson to the road.

Raymond's excitement about surprising me had cooled when we pulled onto Route 40. It was no wonder why, with Miss Catherine gone barely four months and Mr. Dale's gentlemanly dismissals being routinely dismissed. The car bucked as I stalled constantly. Whenever I did get going, my whisper of toe on the gas sent the Henry J flying forward, causing us to spew red dust when I mashed the brake. After one such time, my heart leapt into my throat when we lurched and almost ended up in the ditch. We switched sides so he could get behind the wheel and turn the car around, then switched back on the road facing the house in the distance. When his eyes migrated towards the yard full of cars, I nudged him, and his smile asked for some reassurance.

"It stops, you know," I told him. "Over time. All the women, they go away."

"Yeah?"

"Yeah."

"It was like this with your pop?"

"My teacher, baby," I said. "Even my schoolteacher."

Talking, I crept along slowly telling Raymond about Mrs. O'Dell, the failed boycott, and Daddy's lecture. The car jerked and stalled again. In the middle of Route 40 on a blue-sky day, as I caught my breath, he was also quiet, and I thought, stunned speechless by the jolt.

Until he said, "The jailers . . . sold your father?" I had started to reach to turn the key, but pulled my hand back. I realized it was my daddy's story that had stunned him. "What year was that?" he asked.

"1917, 1918, thereabouts. His older brothers were all off at war."

"Why didn't he serve?"

"He was nine years old."

"*Christ.* You pulling my leg?"

"I would never joke about something like that."

It's hard to imagine who I would have told my daddy's story before Raymond. When I showed up at the Browns with bruises on my wrist and injuries to my soul, their kindness allowed for recovery without too much prying. The diner was for taking and serving orders, not long conversations about my life, my people, and at Taylor Made, well-dressed, well-meaning women talked about the recipients of their generosity from fundraisers and donations and benefit galas with a benevolent *tsk*. My folks deserved better than to be summed up by a pitying glance, yet merely talking about Mama and Daddy as "passed," as I had done to protect them, was its own type of dishonor. My memory was the thread tethering their time on earth to a legacy; speaking of them as only "passed" deprived them of living an entire life.

Still, Raymond's reaction struck a note somewhere between pity and judgment and made me want to close my mouth. I turned the key and started the car. Tried the hand shifter. Remembered the clutch. Pressed the clutch. Slid the shifter to first gear. Feathered the brake too light to release the clutch. And stalled. All of it, too slowly, like I was doing everything underwater. I moved to turn the key again and he laid a hand over top of mine.

"So what happened?"

"They let him go."

"But . . . how?"

"I don't know. After six years, they opened the door and he walked out."

"That's not what I mean."

"I don't get your meaning, then."

"I ain't trying to pry, and I know it's upsetting to think about what happened to your pop. You don't have to tell me if you don't want. But he got from there, somehow, to us being here. And . . . I wanna know *how*." The admiration in his eyes was too bright to look at, except from the corner of my eye. "I mean, you know the story of the swamp."

"Yeah, I know it."

"As many times as I've heard it, and as much time as I've spent in the swamp myself . . . I still can't hardly imagine how they created New Jessup from these woods. I hear about your pop, and I wanna know *how*. And . . . I wanna thank him for whatever he did to get you here."

"Well, it was my mama, too."

"I know, I know, I know," he chuckled softly. "Please? I just . . . tell me?" I started the car again but let it, and Raymond, idle for a minute.

"Well, he served six years on that thirty-day sentence," I said, and slid the car into first gear, slowly easing my foot from the clutch as I warmed into the rest of it. "I don't know why they held him or released him when they did. The jailers had told his folks he died in that mine accident, with the gas? So by the time he worked his way back to Stillings County, a neighbor told him his folks picked up and moved on to keep the rest of his brothers and sisters away from the truant officer, police officer, whatever. My daddy worked the Black Belt from end to end trying to find them, he said, picking up every skill there was to pick up. He cut timber here, worked docks there, slaughtered pigs here, delivered guano there, and worked cotton everywhere."

Still going slowly, slowly, the speedometer crept up. "Second gear," he said.

"After five, six years like that, my mama's daddy hired him to work on their share down in Macon County. My mama? She had this way about her. Folks always remarked she was a beauty, and she was—she had this coffee skin that shined dark copper in the sun, and these full, pillow-like lips and cat eyes. But even as a little girl, I knew 'beautiful' wasn't the right word."

"What was the right word, then?"

"'Beguiling.' You know that word 'beguiling'? It's like mysterious, spellbinding. Somebody who draws you in."

"I know 'beguiling,'" he said, the smile in his voice hinting at a compliment. "Third gear."

"Anyway, she had these eyes that could read you without her ever saying a word."

"*Hmmm.*"

"So the year my daddy came to help them out on their share, there she was—getting ready to graduate high school and planning on Stillman College in the fall. Wanted to be a teacher. He got on well with my mama and her folks. They liked his traveling stories, and that he could do whatever was needed around the farm. But my parents started dreaming together under *can't see*-wide skies: he wanted land big enough, with soil rich enough, for them to parcel among all their people. She wanted to open a schoolhouse on their own little patch of Alabama.

"By and by, they fell in love, but my granddaddy put them out when Mama's dresses got tight with Rosie. No Stillman after that. They scratched around a couple months till they found a house to rent and settled in Rensler. The landowner was thinking about selling some of the property, and there was enough day work around so they wouldn't have to sign any share agreement. Mama used to call our house a 'shotgun blast' of a house on account of all the holes. But it was on the land we thought would be ours one day, so they fixed it up, and me and Rosie were born there. We never bought it, no, but it was the only home I ever knew till I came here."

We had driven straight past the house and around the bend in the road. When the clay turned to pavement, and the city loomed large ahead, the WELCOME TO NEW JESSUP sign came into view. I pulled over to the side of the road, not ready to tackle traffic in town just yet.

"And I guess you could say, here I am."

SIX

In those early days, other than Wednesday nights and Sunday afternoons, me and Raymond mostly dated at the diner when him and Mr. Dale settled into the Campbell booth. One early summer night, there was hardly a moment to chat them up with a diner full of hungry folks and Mr. Marvin ringing that bell every five seconds. In the booth behind Raymond, an Alabama red-clay boy named Curtis led a group of teenagers over hamburgers and milkshakes, loud-talking and guffawing in that rat-a-tat stupid way unique to high school boys.

There was an air-breathing ease with which Negroes went about their day in New Jessup; particularly the young folks in town who had never known any other way. But it had taken me some getting used to, not seeing WHITES ONLY signs and backdoor Negro entrances. To really believe that every single thing in a city, with its double-digit-storied buildings and avenues to the horizons, was owned, and run, by men and women who looked like me—the world outside New Jessup existing mostly in the news.

These kids came to the diner on dates, or to laugh in their stupid, rat-a-tat way with friends. If Mr. Marvin heard them getting too rambunctious, his high wrinkled forehead would pop into the order window, calling them back for a stack of dishes. Many a youngster found themselves elbow-deep in the suds, and every so often, parents would march a misbehaving child to the swinging door to enjoy a quiet moment while their kid cried in the back.

But like Miss Vivian and the Browns, Mr. Marvin was a generation ahead of me—old enough to remember Negro Jessup, old enough to want to forget the swamp, old enough to be there when Booker T. came—and he had not an ounce of humor for a word against our town. After what I thought to be too many questions about my people and my background for a job slinging diner food, he'd taken me on with a clear warning that my first instance of equal-rights troublemaking would be my last, and to keep an eye for any such talk in his place. I could hardly imagine anybody speaking "New Jessup" and "agitating" in the same breath. For what? But when these boys, usually boisterous, shot curiously quiet words over the table at each other, it caught my eye. Nothing but kids, some of them had barely finished squeaking when they talked.

When I walked up with their food, the table's mood was thick as honey. Curtis leaned towards me, crooked a finger for my attention, and whispered—asking about my philosophy.

"What philosophy?" I asked, sliding that boy his cheeseburger.

"It's alright, it's alright. We're all gonna be freedom fighters," he said, not fighting for the freedom to speak loud enough for Mr. Marvin to hear. "Soon as my brother says we can come to their NNAS meetings, too, we're all gonna join up. Right fellas?" I scanned the table. None of the other boys even twitched an eyelash.

"You joining *what* meetings?"

He sighed and spoke slow like I was slow.

"The National Negro Advancement Society. You're in, right?"

"I certainly *am not* in that mess." He furrowed his brow. "Why on earth would you even ask me that? Y'all know you have no business talking like that in here."

"But . . . I thought . . . *Ow*, man! Don't kick me!" he hollered at the boy across the table.

"Y'all better hush that talk before Mr. Marvin kicks you out and bans you from here," I told the table. Raymond—back-to-back with Curtis from the Campbell booth—turned his ear into the conversation. I thought nothing of it—he had started making it known he was listening for fresh comments. He did that with men who came in one, two at a time, usually smiling as he watched me chat them up and put them off.

Curtis snorted at my threat—his voice, greasy with confidence.

"C'mon Alice, you and I both know he would never ban us from here."

I swiveled my neck from one side to the other in that full diner, making sure he followed what I saw.

"We busy tonight, though. It's gonna be a mess of dishes back there."

"*Aww*, you know I'm just kidding, Alice. Just kidding," he said as the rest of them rat-a-tat laughed and they got back to the business of being high school boys. Curtis had always been a ringleader. Mouthy, fresh, with something perpetually in his winking eye. But never had he mentioned the NNAS to me until that night.

The crowd thinned until it was just Raymond and Mr. Dale waiting around, Raymond making eyes at me, and Mr. Dale chuckling about it. The boys had left their table in a sorry state, with bits of meat and buns strewn about and snowballs of food-filled napkins among the stacks of empty plates. The mess was normal for teenagers, if not preferred, especially after sifting through it and finding no tip. I pushed it all into the garbage pail and wiped the table down with the rag and bucket. After Mr. Marvin turned the OPEN sign to CLOSED, and slid into the Campbell booth, Mr. Dale read him for allowing the kids to badmouth Booker T. in the diner.

Finished cleaning the kitchen at the end of the night, Mr. Marvin sat down in the Campbell booth to tally the receipts while I finished cleaning the boys' table. Though the money was good, Mr. Marvin's fragile good mood evaporated when Mr. Dale reported what he'd overheard.

"You talking about Curtis Greene, Dale?" Mr. Marvin asked. He was ordering denominations of bills on the table, and had just begun tapping their edges together, preparing to count, and stopped mid-tap. "O'Connor's boy with the big ears? Hugo's kid brother?" he said. His voice was strangled by the heat simmering underneath his collar. Mr. Dale was all slow-pouring molasses in his needling. He treated getting a rise from Mr. Marvin like that second slice of pie Raymond had put a stop to.

"That's the one," Mr. Dale said. "Never knew you allowed such loose talk in here."

"You better hold your tongue, man. You know better than to say that to me."

"I know what I heard, Marvin."

"And you ain't said nothing to him or any of them?" Mr. Dale frowned slightly and shook his head.

"Thought you had a handle on your place. Is that not the case, Marvin?" Mr. Dale asked. From his tone, and the look on Mr. Marvin's face, whatever threat was implied was received. "I mean, I'm glad to do it if you think you need the help, although I'd probably bring Cap along for that discussion."

Mr. Marvin reared his neck back but smiled. A harmless enough thing, by itself. Like a rattle—until it's attached to a viper.

"You wait a minute, Dale. My old man built this town, same as yours. Broke his back in that swamp, same as yours. So don't dare sit here now acting all holier-than-thou. What'd you hear?"

As I wiped the table, Raymond tried to defuse the situation. But when Mr. Dale told everybody to ask me if they didn't believe him, Mr. Marvin glared at me like I had sprouted a second head.

"What's he mean, 'ask, Alice'? You heard something?"

The rag bobbed around the frothy, greasy soap bubbles atop the bucket water.

"Yessir, but they were just being kids. Stupid talk, you know. I would tell you if there was something to tell. I reminded them of the suds and they straightened right up."

"Yeah—just kids, Mr. Marvin," Raymond insisted. "Don't pay Pop any mind."

Mr. Marvin grunted softly, his eyes traveling back and forth between me and Raymond as if considering the budding thing between us. He sighed, cooling, and things seemed like they would have died had Mr. Dale not stoked the fire.

"Maybe you *should* have Cap, or some of his deputies at least, sit in here during the evenings."

"That's the second time you said that to me, Dale Campbell. The first time, I let it slide. The second, let me promise you there won't be a third."

"He's the law in New Jessup. It's what we would do any other time."

"I don't need help! You know, it sounds to me like you dangerously close to saying 'Cap . . . or else we tell all to the whitefolks,' and I assure you I don't take kindly to such threats. My house is in order. I know you ain't going across the woods to spout off about Marvin's Diner and some instigators."

"Nobody said anything about whitefolks, Marvin. You know me better than that. I'm talking to you and not the Business Council. But I am saying to get a handle on it before somebody gets it in their head to make trouble."

"Mr. Marvin," I said, "you know those boys. They just being stupid kids. Ain't nothing to get upset over."

He said some words meant to be the end of a lot of things if not heeded.

"Listen here, young lady. Me and Dale was little boys when they rode over to Negro Jessup and robbed us blind of our inheritance.

Our inheritance. I'm talking generations, not just a few months." He paused to let the point sink in. "So let me tell you something, Alice. I ever hear that you let these kids slide in my place again? It'll be the last night you ever welcome in Marvin's Diner, hear?"

"Yessir."

"Let me find out you sympathizing with them—"

"—No, sir, not me. Not ever—"

"—Mr. Marvin, you think that's fair?" Raymond said.

"Wait a minute, Marvin," Mr. Dale put in. "It ain't this poor girl's fault."

"Raymond, ain't nobody asked you to stick your bill in, son. And you, Dale Campbell? You gonna stop acting like your shit don't stink because your family hosted Booker T. My daddy was there, too, cooking up all the food. My family has just as much stake in New Jessup as yours, so you can wipe that smile off your face. Since you decided to sit on your ass and say *nothing* to these kids, you can sit on your ass and say nothing now." He sneered back at me. "So Alice, I promise that you and that pretty face of yours will be out on the street if I ever hear you're in here sympathizing—"

"No sir, not me. I assure you," I said. "I would never sympathize." His threat only made my words flow faster and more urgent as the idea of being blamed and ostracized—of maybe being outcast, or even being called for a talk with Cap—frightened me to pieces. "I promise you, Mr. Marvin, that New Jessup, doing for ourselves, this place, all of us together. It's the most beautiful place I ever saw. I promise I'd never bring harm here."

THE CADILLAC EASED its way to my curb on nights Raymond meant to impress. After our first date, we'd rattled around in his car, my car, for a while, but just as the climbing roses blanketed every trellis with red, he called me up after a diner shift insisting I take off Saturday night. It was as close to pleading as I had heard cross his lips, but after letting him cool his heels for a day, I said "yes." He slid up to the shop in Mr. Dale's oil-black ride that night, and we had a fine dinner as June yawned into July in 1958. Afterwards, he said he had a surprise.

I was surprised all right when he parked the Cadillac on Pinkney Ave.: home of every no-count rascal, hoodlum, and scoundrel in Gilliam County, let Mr. Dale tell it. But I had walked to and from the diner past the jukes for months without much hassle, watching hip-hugging dresses swish and sway up the sidewalk. Men wore jackets and hats, and sprinklings of music filled the air. I usually dropped a quarter from my tips for the doo-wop boys while waiting to cross the avenue and watched cars with fresh polish cruise by on weekend nights.

Outside the Cadillac, one line from the jukes ended where the next began, with folks two, three, deep across the pavement. A couple walked arm-in-arm up the street, whispering to each other the way couples do. Folks stood around talking, laughing, women twirling necklaces around their fingers, while a woman's lowdown blues meandered from one place, meeting up with a jazz piano from another, and mixing with a saxophone from a third, creating a street melody all its own. Raymond ran around and opened my door.

"What are we doing over here?" I asked.

He cocked his head to the side slightly and smiled. "I brought you here to meet some of my oldest friends. We're gonna catch up with them inside while we watch Big Mama Thorton sing about a hound dog," he said with a sly grin.

"And does Mr. Dale know you parking his car in front of a juke joint on Pinckney Ave.?"

Without an answer more than that smile, Raymond offered a hand and pulled me up to the sidewalk. We hustled down the alley to the back door, where a light, bright, baby-faced man flicked cigarette ashes to the ground. He was so light that, from a distance, I thought we were sprinting towards the first white man I ever saw in New

Jessup. Raymond's tug turned insistent as my steps stuttered, and my heart fluttered, but as we neared, the man's thick lips and coily hair eased my mind.

"What's up, doc?" Raymond greeted him with a back-slapping hug.

"How you living, young boy?" he said with the shining eyes and sly smile of false modesty. "Not a doc yet." He turned that sly smile on me, and by the time we shook hands and he said "Matthew Washington" in his melodic voice, those bright eyes had traveled up and down my front with seeming approval. Mr. Not-A-Doc-Yet, indeed, with his thorough examination.

Matthew crushed his cigarette under his shoe and hurried us inside, through wall-to-wall people, towards the bar. There, Patience Armstrong—with her velvet midnight skin—was at the bar demanding every eye. Men clamored around listening to her deep-purr voice, but when Matthew knocked on the wood and called out to his sunshine, the smile she beamed at him drew men's protests for miles. She wished her admirers a "good evening" and we four headed to the edge of the dance floor.

Perfume, cologne, sweat, and lust mingled there. Women, dancing, hiked knee skirts to the thigh, drawing appreciative grins from men with jackets hooked by fingers over shoulders. Bodies swayed in time to the music and each other, while folks filled round tables at the edges, telling lies, toasting gin, and playing cards. I looked around my feet.

"They don't pitch peanut shells here?" I shouted to Raymond over the music.

"What!" Raymond said.

"On the floor. No peanut shells."

"Thought you'd never been to a juke."

"You ain't never asked me that. You asked if I ever been to Pinckney Ave." His smile said he was surprised. His eyes said he enjoyed it.

So, pressed together with our hearts beating to the same rhythm, we danced—trading eyes and kisses—until I lost my last breath. When my legs gave out, we found Matthew and Patience at some pulled-together tables in the corner with other friends from high school. Looked like I knew them from somewhere, though I had trouble placing them. After introductions, me and Patience escaped to the ladies' room to powder our noses, and on the way back, she pointed Matthew and Raymond out, huddled among the group of men. She shouted over the music as we wound our way around all the swaying bodies.

"Will you look at these guys? Can't even wait for us to get back before they dive into shop talk."

"What shop talk?" She shook her head slow, that puzzled way to question if I was being serious or naive. Then she leaned close to my ear and said, "You know, the NNAS."

I stopped. The low, blues growl had couples' limbs weaved into each other as they swayed together on the dance floor. At the tables, the men were laughing. What she was saying made no sense. In the heard, and unheard, conversations between me and Raymond, he had never mentioned the NNAS. Not once. Even that night Mr. Marvin half-accused me of sympathizing, Raymond was mum. I caught Raymond's eye just long enough to watch his surprised smile drop to a worried frown as I stepped backwards, away from him, and into a couple on the dance floor. The woman shouted at me, refusing to pardon my clumsiness. In the midst of her yelling, I found my bearings among the forest of people and took off out the door.

The mass of folks still crowding the sidewalk slowed my progress, and he caught me easily, wrapping his hand around my arm with that working man's grip—strong enough to insist, but gentle enough to ask, that I stop.

"What's wrong? I thought we were having a nice time!" With nothing better to do than wait to get inside the jukes, a million eyes watched for me to explode into hysterics, or to see him grovel, or whatever. Not knowing the whole story, what any outburst could really mean, disappointment pierced my beating heart and flooded my veins. The face of the man I loved and barely knew paralyzed me there on that concrete. After some seconds, I mustered a calm breath and told him to take me home.

There were no words in the car—not even the radio for those few blocks. Just the hum of tires on the pavement. The fuzzy headlamps of oncoming traffic etched the shadows into his face, and our hands, intertwined, trembled together until we reached my curb.

"Please tell me what's wrong," he said. "Tell me, and I promise it won't happen again."

"You lied to me."

"When did I—"

"The NNAS, Raymond? You?" He sighed and muttered "Patience" like a curse word.

"I didn't lie, Alice. I'm sorry, but I didn't lie. I just . . . I couldn't tell you before tonight."

RAYMOND SET MY kitchenette chair on the other side of the coffee table and sat down. He had only been inside my apartment a handful of times, and then, only to wait on the sofa if I was late getting ready. Not because of Miss Vivian's warning to be mindful of overnight visitors, or the swaying window sheer in Miss Hattie's window across the street whenever he pulled the Studebaker to the curb, no. And my place was clean and tidy—a second-floor walkup with a sink, corner shower, and commode in the bathroom; a sofa bed, hot plate, and kitchen table that folded down from the wall. With only one chair. Raymond was outsized; had all that Campbell land inside of him, that New Jessup inside of him in the things he didn't say. Not that that stopped us from falling deep, into love outsized on its own. But enough to lose my head and all too much to stay long inside my tiny apartment.

A wash of soft light streamed through the window, nestling the carpet beside our feet. I had to keep my eyes on it, to fill my view with its brightness, so that, maybe, Raymond's hand-wringing would disappear from my tear-clouded vision, and the sound of his heavy breathing would stop splitting me in two. Yes, we had the said and the unsaid between us, but this? Flattened me. How on earth was this man—this man!—the wrecking ball New Jessup faced? How could he be the one ready to destroy it all, bring agitating and the whitefolks' chaos? Not Raymond. Not a grandson of New Jessup. The man asking me *how* the old heads, my daddy, brought us here, to this place, together. Not Raymond.

But the chair looked too small for his tall frame. Standing, he could easily touch palms to the ceiling, or, seemed like, hands from wall to opposite wall. The vast feeling of him included the lie, which, like the water he had placed before me a few minutes earlier, was done quietly. Intentionally.

"I had it all planned out how to tell you myself. She shouldn't have said anything."

"Wasn't like you lacked for time, though. We been going together since the end of March. You were right there that night at Mr. Marvin's—"

"—I couldn't until tonight—"

"—and you sat there listening to him fuss me out—"

"—but it ain't what folks think—"

"—that I was some kinda sympathizer—"

"—I took you tonight to tell you and show you it ain't what you think."

"How do you know *what* I think, Raymond? You ain't never asked me." I waited, and when his only response was a grimace, I swallowed an ache threatening to rip me apart. "That boy Curtis asked me, Mr. Marvin asked me, but not you. And now that I think on it, that feels purposeful. Was it?" He nodded, regarding me carefully as I breathed deep. "Why? Because Mr. Marvin hollered at me?"

"No. I just couldn't yet." I kept my mouth shut. "My friends you met tonight . . . any of them look familiar?"

"I don't know. Why?" I snapped.

"It's just that, those are the few of us running this chapter of the NNAS for now. You know the governor, the state, has been hassling the NAACP about their membership lists, so NNAS leadership had stopped allowing new chapters in Alabama. We never had one in New Jessup, or Gilliam County, so after me and the guys convinced leadership we could operate under the radar, we decided that, in order for us to tell anybody, we have to bring it to the fellas, let them check you out first."

"Check me out! Y'all been gossiping about me!"

He sighed, as if trying to get his bearings.

"Men don't gossip, but—"

"I could strangle you right now for correcting my words."

"Not to gossip. Will you listen? I had everything planned that I wanted to say, but you—"

"I *what*?"

He sighed our conversation into another long pause, collecting himself. When he finally spoke, it was more measured. Sounded rehearsed.

"They were there to chat you up, ask you questions about yourself. Your background, how you're liking New Jessup. Get a feel for you, see if you're the kind of person who would support our efforts, likely be discreet. They were in the diner some nights watching you, yes. Watching me and you. I'm glad, too. I was ready to pour my heart out to you like a fool."

"Then you should have, as soon as you started getting to know me."

"It was all so new then. You and me; me and the fellas, Patience, and our work. We didn't know what we were doing at first. Me and Matthew and my brother Percy, we were . . . the only ones who had ever done any equal-rights organizing. In Montgomery."

I leaned back against my couch and cocked my head to the side.

Two clouds—each its own storm—swirled and merged inside me.
One, rage that he had turned me into a sympathizer whether I knew
or not, agreed or not; and the other, his absolute conviction that
he had done the right thing. I breathed deep, swallowed hard, and
clenched my teeth to keep the tempest from flooding out in tears.

"You never mentioned any organizing in Montgomery, neither."

"I had it all figured out what to say. Give me a chance."

"That's rich—a chance? You had since March for chances, baby,
especially since y'all were involved in this business before you and
me ever started up. Even after you suspected, and then you *knew*, I
disagreed, you kept it from me, and that's a lie—don't care what you
call it."

"I told you I built the Studebaker, and you know I built your car.
We built, serviced, and drove cars to get folks where they needed to
go during the bus boycotts. But for those cars on the road, things
could've collapsed. Early."

"Get outta my apartment."

His grieving face contorted into somebody I hardly recognized. I
had laid my feelings bare to this man—about him, my family, New
Jessup. Never made a secret of how much I not only loved him but
loved the town. A place that Rosie could love, come back to. A place
to be ourselves among ourselves.

"You are not the man I thought you were, Raymond Campbell.
Integration? Here?"

"Alice, will you listen? Please?"

"I am listening, which is why I asked you to leave."

"Integration ain't our fight here. It's the opposite, really. Me, the
fellas, and Patience, we all started talking after Mama's homegoing.
About equality—real equality for New Jessup. Just a bunch of local
boys, you know. And Patience."

"I said get outta my apartment."

But he kept going, his eyes full of pleading and worry.

"We were talking about *our* home. Hugo and Major are married, both living here and starting families. I'd met you, saw how happy you seemed here and really, really started thinking about home, what I was doing. I loved my neighborhood in Montgomery, loved growing up here. I—"

I stood up, walked to the bathroom, and turned the lock behind me. He talked through the door, and I listened—breathing deep and trembling angry—as his voice vibrated the wood between his mouth and my ear.

"Open up please, Alice. Alice?" I refused to speak or open the door. "I intended to tell you everything tonight, show you that good people are involved in this."

I said nothing.

"Alice, we live on the Negro *side of town*. Every time we pay taxes, the city's still taking our money, skimming from the top to keep it across the woods. If whitefolks are owed a dollar for their roads, their schools, they get two. We're owed a dollar, we get a dime. It's time to control our own money, first off. This work means keeping folks from across the woods outta our hair and our pockets for good! Outta everyday conversation."

"They ain't been in my everyday conversation since I stepped off that bus eight months ago."

"C'mon, Alice! I'm sorry!"

"Not nearly sorry enough! Why, Raymond? And some secret, by the way. Curtis Greene knew?"

"They overheard us early on. When I was talking about you. And this. He knows to keep quiet, but he knew you and I were going together, and he assumed . . .

"Anyway, this is us trying to move towards the vote *without* integration. The time is right for us to show the world that things are separate already here, so let them be equal! Negro communities, settlements, even municipalities, have been around since before emancipation. Hobson City is right here in Alabama. Major served in Korea with a guy from Mound Bayou, Mississippi. Like those places, we become our own city, make it plain that integration ain't what we want, telling everybody the world over that if there is a fight, it's about resources, not fellowship. Let whitefolks run on tickets in their own elections and let us do the same."

"You gonna to get yourself, and me, kicked right outta this town because of the NNAS."

"Alice, please listen to me. The momentum behind integration and voting, together, will run us over if we don't think about our community. Even the NNAS is pushing in that direction—you know that. But we convinced them that we don't need mixing to vote. Integration won't do anything but spread us out with one man voting over here, another one or two folks over there, all casting ballots for the same whitefolks everywhere. Separation is concentration of our folks, our votes and our power. We can get our folks on the ballot, have our own city council."

I snorted so hard I hit my forehead on the door.

"A Negro city council? Then what? County council? How about a Negro president while you at it?"

"Alice, c'mon. We're a well-resourced *side* of town, darling, and we already run things on our own. But we pay taxes here that come back for the Jessup City Council to dole out, you hear me? Not the *New* Jessup City Council to spend as it sees fit. So we make it work for us, is the thinking. The neighborhood where I stayed in Montgomery—"

"Don't mention another mumbling word to me about Montgomery."

"Fine, but imagine if, around the country, where Negroes are already living, we're resourced and building communities of concentrated political power. Whitefolks want separation too, so if we can all agree on that then why not? Pop was only invited to join the Business Council because they are terrified of race mixing in the schools, wanted our folks to tell if any instigating is going on over here. You hear me? Terrified and not believing that we don't want it, neither. Municipality takes all that off the table. It's us saying we want nothing whatsoever to do with integration. Nothing. There are still plenty of fights but mixing ain't one of them.

"NNAS thinks this could lead to big changes. Negroes running on tickets in Negro cities, to start. Then yes, county, statewide offices, and up the chain, we could start to see some of our own candidates on the ballot. And in our own cities, we take care of our own, like we do here. My folks raised us to be good examples. New Jessup can be an example, a model, for what we can achieve around this country. We want, and have, our own everything—it's about us, taking care of us."

Through the door, he told me their reasons for keeping this secret from everybody—not just me: other longtime friends, brothers and sisters. Even Mr. Dale and Miss Catherine had never known—not about Montgomery, because of her heart problems, then not about this scheme because it was only supposed to be a dream, cooked up at her homegoing by a bunch of boys she helped raise to become men. And Patience. A dream pushed by an organization that could get me fired from every job I had and put out of New Jessup. A dream that Mr. Dale was supposed to report to the Jessup Business Council whenever he rode across the woods, whether it was his son doing the dreaming or not. A dream that had turned into this nightmare of a night.

I listened to him, unable to face this dreamer. And this liar. The same man who picked me up in that Cadillac, who scooched next to me at Le Chat. Who built me that boneyard special and who had told me he loved me over and over and over . . .

"You lied to me," I said softly enough that he would only hear it with an ear pressed to the door. "Let me stand there with Mr. Marvin hollering at me."

"I'm sorry about that. I tried. But I didn't lie. I just couldn't tell you about the NNAS without telling you everything. I had to put my feelings aside and wait till the fellas could see you. Agree. It's how we stay quiet. Safe."

"You can't possibly believe this'll work."

"It's what I've got to hang a hat on. We're still figuring it all out, but this is our home too, Alice. We love it here, same as you, and ain't nobody trying to bring harm. You believe me, don't you?"

I opened the door and looked at his face. What I believed mattered not; Raymond believed himself. The storms of his conviction, my hurt, grew and grew as he talked—outgrew my living room. New Jessup. Alabama. Even if he hadn't outgrown me and him yet, talking the way he was talking, he would one day, so I had to focus on the pool of moonlight on my floor to avoid his grays. *Not his eyes*, I told myself, or that storm would overcome me. It crumbled me to hear him struggle with his words; but when he said my name, I refused to look and be turned to dust by his anguish when mine alone was too much to bear. Even the feel of his heartbeat racing underneath my palm as he opened his arms, inviting me into his embrace, almost broke my resolve. I promised I would never tell. But I pushed him with my gentlest hand against his heart.

"I asked you to leave, Raymond, and I meant it. Please go."

SEVEN

That started the long, miserable weeks before I began telling stories. The Henry J sat on the curb at my apartment collecting dust, and when the Campbell men came into the diner, I let the other girl handle their table. Each time, when I realized that they must have noticed Blue Lightning missing from the lot, and they were waiting to run me home, I snuck out the back door.

I kept my word and held his secret to myself. What would I say, anyway, to folks who had trusted me, taken a shine to me before I knew anything about Raymond Campbell? And why tell them? I was done with him, which is what I told Miss Vivian when she caught me glooming over some designs I'd dog-eared in a magazine. But the colors were all drab; the fabric looked thin and scratchy, and I couldn't remember what even caught my eye. Nothing tasted right during days that managed to fit twenty-four hours between the shop opening and lunch. I had finished steaming a delivery of bridesmaid dresses again, and settled into the magazine, when she walked up.

"Some folks just ain't who you think," I told her. She could hardly hide her offense. "Aren't. *Aren't* who you think. It's fine, Miss Vivian, really."

So when he came around a couple days later, he had to pull teeth to get her to tell him that I took my lunch in the park up the street, on one of the benches next to the playground.

"You're a hard woman to find when you wanna be," the voice said over my shoulder as his shadow stole my sunlight. He came around the bench and I laid my book in the spot where his eyes asked to sit next to me, so he sat on the other side. I refused to look at him and didn't speak. Instead, I bit my sandwich and watched a pretty little brown-skinned girl squeal all the way down the slide, with a freedom and glee I remembered at that age. But different, too—full of New Jessup confidence that this would always be her world. When she got to the bottom, she ran around and got back in line behind the others, fidgeting, waiting. Every time another kid went, and she got closer to the front, her eyes brightened and her finger pointed to the top of the slide, telling the others of her adventure. She looked about my same age when me and Rosie discovered the magic in our thumbs.

"I've been thinking, and since it looks like you ain't planning to speak to me, I'll say my piece and go. But this work I'm doing? It's gonna make New Jessup a better place for all of us. Including you."

"Now I'm included. But if you woulda asked me, you'd know I have no quarrel with the way New Jessup is right now."

"We don't aim to change anything except to incorporate it. Our only goal is municipality. Independence. So even if you and me ain't together, and you never spoke to me again, this work is because of you. For you. Has been since the beginning."

I peeked at him out the corner of my eye.

"*Hmph.*"

"I . . . look . . . I . . . " He paused, rubbing his hands hard enough over top of his thighs to wear out the denim on his coveralls. "I can't . . . I can't do this if you won't look at me. Please? I'm sorry for not telling you, but will you just look at me?" A glimmer of hopeful smile crossed his lips when I turned my head. Perhaps he saw my nose reddening or my tears welling, but that smile disappeared right quick. "We're working on one thing at a time. Because if folks hear the NNAS's name called right now, they hear agitating, integration, and nothing else. First, we show New Jessup that independence, and not mixing, is our intention. Then, we start working on a safe way to vote.

"But like I said: even if you and me ain't together, if you never spoke to me again in life, you're included whether you like it or not."

"Because I live here and I'm gonna be affected by you no matter what?" My remark was granite though my resolve turned to dust with the frustration, near resignation, in his sigh.

"No. Well, yes and no. Either way, it's because when we were all talking about home and family in the very first days, I had you swirling around in my head. I couldn't think about home without thinking about you. You've been part of this since the beginning."

His two hands swallowed my one and, after some coaxing, he brought my thumb to his lips and closed his eyes. It wasn't freedom I felt when I knew I would forgive him. Or glee, not like that little girl and her friends who were watching, pointing, giggling at our hard-won sweetness. It was looking at him and realizing that me and Raymond had as much choice to stay apart as the moon had to decide whether to rise and set. It was knowing that, with our eternity stitching together, night by night, my life would require times of holding tight, and times of letting go.

SO BEGAN OUR DAYS of deeper love and passing time, with shared glances and smiles—sometimes secrets, mostly flirtation. Like that late-summer Sunday, with my legs stretched out and ankles crossed, when we lazed away the afternoon at Waverly's. On our blanket, Raymond turned on his side and propped his head in one hand, tapping his finger against my anklebone to bring my skin to life. Watching, waiting, urging my little turtle birthmark to waddle to the water and swim away.

"C'mon, Little Turtle." He touched it, tickled me, and I laughed to inhale the whole, blue sky. And I wanted to laugh, after a car ride during which he asked me to really get to know his friends. My heart was full for Raymond; my arms, ready to wrap around and protect him. And if I was to embrace him, his work, then I was to hold Hugo Greene, Major Royal, Abel Gaston, Patience Armstrong, Thomas and Lisle Morris, and Matthew Washington close. Wives knew, but girlfriends didn't, except for me and Patience.

When I looked at the side of his head and told him this hardly meant I was joining their meetings, he snorted softly and said, "The way you sprinted from the juke, and left me cooling my heels those few weeks? Trust me—no one is expecting you to join the NNAS."

And he was right. They were a good group, never pressing my feelings about their doings, never challenging the freedom I felt in New Jessup. They had grown through the ages together—thick as thieves and twice as loyal since they were small, including those whose grandfathers, like Raymond's, had built from the swamp. Everybody worked, had families, so on the rare occasion I saw any of them, it was usually to shoot something or go to the jukes. With Raymond's friends, I could be the country girl who shot the pheasant I put on Raymond's plate, and he could still be quietly confident, if now brimming with new love.

Once or twice, a topic they were chewing on among them snuck into conversation. I never stopped them, but I never engaged, either. Ultimately, and without a word from me, the mood would shift. Somebody would blink. Clear their throat. Change the subject. I understood their work, their goals. But every waking hour of my life before New Jessup had been navigating a world of invisible lines and unwritten rules just to stay alive; breathing all the blackdamp of hatefulness just because of the color of my skin. New Jessup was freedom to shed all that. Possibility for a future without it, too. I trusted that they knew how to keep the NNAS on a leash, to redirect the group's focus from mixing with whitefolks to respecting and organizing Negro towns across the country. I had to trust it. But I had no desire to sit around with anybody regurgitating the evils of whitefolks. To keep inviting them into the room, only to have them steal all the air.

One day, I was running errands for Miss Vivian when I saw Patience dash out a yellow cab, across the sidewalk, and into a building up the way. When I walked by the plate glass, she was standing in the middle of a bunch of little girls in dance costumes. They hung on her every word as she talked, glowing as they clamored around her. She glanced at the window and lifted a casual hand to wave, so I waved back, but since neither of us were going to do more than that, I left her to her business and went about my own.

Later that evening, on my way to the diner, I spied Patience looking through the window at Taylor Made as I came down the stairs from my apartment. I called out to her and she started, her bright-white eyes widening and her full lips parting in a slight gasp. She regained composure quickly and pressed her lips into the kind of smile for both calculating and hiding. Her voice was dusky enough to be alluring, and she had this clipped, proper manner of speaking that caused me to call upon my Taylor Made English more than I didn't.

"I didn't mean to startle you," I said. "I thought you heard me on the stairs. We're closed for the evening, and open ten to six, Monday through Saturday."

"That's alright. I came to see you. Are you heading to the diner? I'll walk with you."

Her life of studying dance, and her work as a dancer, explained the way she floated rather than walked. She had danced professionally in New York City, but after doing it since childhood, she had tired of the strain on her body and the travel. I was thankful, briefly, that Rosie's city life in Chicago sounded better than the way Patience described living with four other girls in a small apartment and work-ing two, three jobs for the privilege. A city girl at heart—grown up in the middle of New Jessup—Patience had never hunted, fished, or even been in the woods. But New York City was too much city for her, she told me.

"I was surprised to see you with the kids. I thought you worked on Pinckney Ave.," I said. She laughed a little. "I guess you never really do know about people."

"I suppose not. But yes, I teach dance, tend bar on occasion, and . . ."—she hesitated—"do a little writing."

"What kind of writing? Like books?"

"No. Just whatever comes to mind. More scribbling than any-thing else."

We crossed Pinckney Ave. and she lifted a surprised eyebrow when I threw a quarter into the doo-wop boys' bucket. As the side-walk thickened with folks, her voice lowered in volume. She thought a minute while a group of people passed going the opposite direction, then said, "I'm glad you stopped in the window and waved today."

"Of course."

"It's hard to just get the two of us alone without all the guys around."

"Yeah. It can be hard, with everybody working, trying to live their lives. But it's a good group." She nodded.

"Look . . . Alice? I really came by to tell you that I didn't mean to cause problems that night when you first came to the juke."

"I never thought you intended to cause problems. Just . . . bad timing, I guess," I said, wanting to keep what happened with me and Raymond between me and him.

"Good. So . . . you think you'd be interested in joining us, then? For meetings? Now that you know everyone?"

Her face fell when I said, "Oh, no."

"But why not?"

I shrugged, glad that Raymond and the fellas had never put this question to me. Had avoided it, if I'm honest, by blinking, clearing throats, and changing the subject. "I understand what y'all are doing, but it's not for me." My answer seemed not good enough, the way her eyes narrowed briefly.

"But what about Raymond? The rest of us?"

"My lips are sealed, if that's what you're asking."

"Sort of. What if he gets caught?" I stumbled over a crack in the sidewalk.

"I'd deny any knowledge of it, that he had any knowledge of the NNAS, their presence here. Just like y'all agreed to do." She sighed.

"It'd be that easy for you? To lie?" Her tone was soft, disappointed.

"If it meant helping, I suppose it would have to be."

"You can do that, but you can't join us? Raise your own voice?"

"It's not for me, Patience. It's just . . . not for me. That's all."

"This work would be so much faster if we didn't have to sneak around." I shrugged, wishing she would respect my wishes to end this conversation. "I mean, Cap can't expel all of us, especially if our numbers grow. And you obviously have strong feelings about it, upset as you were that night at the juke. But look! You came around."

"Patience, I'm happy here. In my wildest dreams, I never imagined such freedom in such a place. Write my sister about it all the time, wanting her to come home and see it for herself. I'll keep y'all's secret and do everything in my power to keep y'all safe, but . . . the NNAS just ain't for me. I just ain't trying to be a part of it."

She stopped walking and took hold of my elbow gently. Her lips parted and she paused, as if to say something other than the *thanks for the talk* and the *good evening* she finally uttered, before turning around and going back the other way. We saw each other a couple more times with our beaus before autumn, and things were as cordial, friendly, as they had always been. But when Matthew eventually returned to school for the semester, he carried any reason I had to spend time with her back to Howard.

OTHER THAN WORK, the harvesting and canning needed to be done when summer whispered into fall, and that was more than enough to fill my time, anyway. The peaches were first, and with so many, I set some to ferment like my family used to do back in Rensler. Mr. Dale was in a teasing mood after a supper of stewed rabbit as we three sat on the porch on a night chilled by autumn air.

"My son got himself a country girl," he said, while swirling the wine around in the glass. "I bet you never had peach wine and rabbit back in Montgomery."

"No, sir. Can't say I did," Raymond said with a castoff look like there was something on his heart.

"Well, I'm glad you're home, son. Settled. I just hope you're winning more than you lose at those card games with the fellas."

"Yup, I could get used to this," Raymond said, turning those grays on me to ease my unease again.

EIGHT

Winter had crisped the air and turned everything red and green the night we snuck away from the Christmas dance. Mrs. Brandy Wicks and her army of pedigreed volunteers had prepared the U.S. Jones High School gymnasium to the envy of the North Pole. Shimmering gold fabric swagged gracefully overhead, and floor-to-ceiling ivory curtains with gold embroidered doves hung every few feet along the walls. A whole cypress was dressed in gold ribbons and ornaments, and the dance floor was crowded with young to old—all in finery—moving joyfully to the band. A child shrieked, inviting others to the windows overlooking the river below, where the Waverly flotilla—each motorboat decked out as reindeer—towed Mr. Marvin's Santa boat and his sack full of gifts to the dock. In the commotion, Raymond tugged my hand, and we eased into the corridor behind Matthew and Patience—me, in my first Taylor Made original.

Raymond had asked me to the dance within seconds of forgiveness. I told Miss Vivian when I returned to the shop, after color had returned to my world, as I hovered over dog-eared pages again. She slid her glasses over her nose, studying my new mood, then studying the photo that was to become my dress. After half a look, she frowned.

"That piece will require some intricate work on the hem. And if you don't cut it right on top, it'll sag and you'll look like a clothes hanger all night with fingers dug into your underarms. Look here, too." She tapped the magazine photo. "It doesn't fit her right at the waist. Makes a nice dress look cheap. Even if it is a nice dress," she admitted with a smile that said I was onto something. "In that emerald-green satin, I think, for you." A look up and down my body and she agreed with herself about the color. "It's just my suggestion, of course," she said. "You do as you please, though," said Miss Vivian, said my mama, when neither of them ever meant it. Two sides of the same mirror without the resemblance, offering words that were more challenge than choice. "You do as you please," said Mama with a glance over her shoulder and Miss Vivian over top of her glasses. "It's your choice, of course," said Mama when I whipstitched my doll baby, or Miss Vivian when I finished a hem with the Singer. Each time, these words, from Mama, from Miss Vivian, came with a look that said to think twice if I was thinking.

Over some days, Miss Vivian watched from afar as I fiddled with the muslin, but she closed that distance quickly to fix any thread out of place. Her pins precisioned that sample to my curves before she sent me to fetch the emerald green satin from the back (*Not the forest, that's too brown and have mercy, how could I not see that?*) She left the cutting and the hand stitching to me, although she watched with all four eyes. After it was finished, and she tugged the zipper during my final fitting, she fetched the dog-eared magazine. Against my dress, the model looked as creased and frayed as the paper. The strapless satin hugged my curves, flaring out at the hip in a bubble skirt. I had never owned anything looking like somebody poured liquid emeralds all over me.

"See?" she said as she compared my dress and its improvements against the picture. In that dressing room, mamas, sisters, grandmamas, cousins, and friends observed, teased, and pouted over women on this very pedestal from their chairs in the corner. My chest ached, and tears threatened as Miss Vivian fussed and fixed because, with her, my corner somehow didn't seem so empty.

"You see the improvements?" she asked.

"Yes, ma'am, Miss. Vivian. Thank you. I appreciate everything you've done for me."

WITH RAYMOND, THERE were always more secrets—especially when Matthew and Patience were involved. We four strode through the corridors of U.S. Jones High School—away from the gymnasium, where Christmas music filled the air; away from the chaperones tugging teenagers from dark classrooms—Raymond, with the gentle metallic swish of the liquid in the flask over his heart. For a tour, Matthew assured the skeptical eye of a squat woman with his megawatt smile as he reminded her that he was on winter break from the Howard University School of Medicine. She walked away with a final warning to behave, and when she was out of earshot, Matthew tapped his own breast pocket.

"Well, ain't y'all's tuxes full of surprises tonight?" I said. They both snorted softly.

We walked a corridor ten miles long, with lockers extending from sunrise to sunset. One classroom after another staggered along the way, each one top to bottom with schoolbooks, a midnight-clean blackboard, and a massive teacher's desk made of the whole pine. After passing through the geology and chemistry labs, the classrooms where they took algebra and calculus, and after happening upon some kids practicing anatomy in the biology room, we wandered around the corner and slinked into their moonlit history classroom.

I ran my finger over the spines of books filling the shelves: fat ones, skinny ones, hardcover, and paperback. Rows of thick American history textbooks were shelved neatly along with books about the Kingdom of Kush, Carthage, and the Songhai Empire. We found four desks in the corner, away from the glass in the door, and Raymond shared his flask.

"What's this?" Patience asked.

"Peach wine," Raymond said.

"Where'd you get it?" she asked.

"The peaches," I told her. A blank look crossed her face as she waited for the second half of the answer, and when the meaning became plain, she smiled.

"*Oooh*," she sang, "our little Miss Alice is a moonshiner? It's good."

We sipped in the low light of the classroom as they all talked about the good days, the old days, ruling the hallways like New Jessup kids tended to do. The moon was generous with its light on our skin, streaming through the window as a creamy night sun. It lent a soft glow to the men's white dinner jackets, Matthew's buttery complexion, the perfect, dark amber of Raymond's face, and enviable glow of Patience's night skin, especially against the eggplant purple of her dress.

But looking to the front, middle desk, my eyes softened, searching for skin like my own. Not that they had benches, no—students at U.S. Jones High School sat in real desks. Still, I looked for skin like mine, with one arm bent over top of her head, resting on a middle part between two plaits, its hand clutching inside the elbow of the other, tired arm with its hand high in the air. Her white cotton sleeve, puffed, pulled taut against her arm as it quivered, waiting, with fingers wiggling. Waiting, with cheeks puffed while Mrs. Thousand-Year-Frown O'Dell asked the class if anybody else— anybody except Rosie Young—had the answer. I could almost reach into memory and see, hear my sister be the smartest among her schoolmates sitting in that classroom, until my fingers grazed my leg for the fabric of our scratchy, matching wool jumpers and came up with only satin.

After a chaperone's flashlight floated by, I stood to look around. The globe next to the teacher's desk was yellowed, aged, with little veins crisscrossing the earth without regard to the borders between land and sea. The books caught my attention and I went to the shelf.

"This school, these books. Y'all must've paid a fortune in book fees," I said.

"Some," Patience said, "but the county bought most of this stuff. Books, desks. It all comes second-hand, though. From across the woods."

"This looks like nobody's second-hand to me. Must be a book in that shelf for every student."

"Probably two," she said, and the three of them shared a sad, remembering chuckle, each losing themselves inside the same speck of terrazzo on the ground.

I picked up an American history book and opened it to a lesson from present-day—sent from the other side of the woods. *Filthy nigger* had been scrawled inside the front cover in thick, black marker before someone rubbed it out as best they could. Frayed paper edges clung to the binding where the first seventy pages of the book were once attached, with enough paper remaining to show pen marks. N-I-G here, G-E-R there, M-O-N here, K-E-Y there. D-A-R here, K-E-Y there. Insults hurled at New Jessup's children in puzzle pieces. But other than the inside of the cover, the missing pages, the book had the normal margin notes and fingerprint smudges of a well-used text.

I stood and flipped slowly through a few pages. Not really wanting to see anything else, but not wanting the kids to see it either. Not the high schoolers learning in these desks. Not, one day, the little ones right up the hallway who were now clamoring to tell Mr. Marvin Claus their secret Christmas wishes. Not that little girl from the slides at the playground. Not her. Never her, or any of them. Any of us.

Not that we had this sort of ugliness in our textbooks in Rensler, no. The county never even sent books to our school. But Christian names were for whitefolks and their hunting dogs. To step off the sidewalk, lower our eyes, go around back, come here, get away from there, do this, don't even *think about* that, be quiet, and never complain was still no guarantee against a "filthy nigger" sneered in passing or a "you know how niggers are" dripping from nice-lady talk between companions wandering by. Folks inhaling confidence by exhaling these cutdown words. Slash after slash, year after year, generation after generation, leaving wounds that either lay open, weeping forever, or that keloided into a callous into an armor. An armor I had allowed to soften on our side of the woods. By Christmastime in that moonlit classroom full of books, among hallways built for Negro children, in a town where we thrived among our own, my guard was down and this hatefulness seeped right in. Invisible, yet sinister as blackdamp.

"What've you got there?" Raymond asked in the quiet voice of somebody already knowing. He had walked over, and he took the book from my hands before slidding it atop Matthew's desk. Matthew looked inside the cover and slammed the book shut. Patience shrugged.

"Like I said, probably two," she said.

"*Gah.*" Matthew made known his disgust. "They're still doing this shit?"

"Why would they stop, honey?" Patience responded with cool sweetness that did nothing to quell Matthew's agitation.

"You know what? You're exactly right, sunshine. Just another reason we need our own money for our own town."

Raymond nodded and sighed with a breath to discharge the static as me and him slid back into our seats. "Yeah, you know I'm with you, doc."

Patience looked at Matthew, then Raymond. She snorted softly and said, "Though in a perfect world, fellas, Negro and white kids alike would be learning from the same books." After a beat to think about her comment, each of Raymond's words in response were as considered and cautious as one in search of stepping-stones to cross the river.

"Well, I suppose you're right. But you see the teachers still tear out the bad and keep what's useful. Looks like they're working through the books for next term."

"Of course," she sang with the soft chill of sarcasm that I had come to learn was her signature armor. "They have to make sure that our kids can read between the lines."

Raymond was somebody who accepted the cold outside, drew the drapes, and stoked the home fires. Over some months, his dreams for the future of New Jessup had warmed into me, too. So much so that I enjoyed making him bite his smiling lip when I called him Mr. Mayor. With her armor, it was hard to tell about Patience yet, but Matthew was one who lamented the cold and reacted to the chill. Normally good-natured, the book riled him.

"Well, we need independence for New Jessup," he declared. "Let them keep their raggedy-ass textbooks." A quiet moment followed, and then, without warning, Matthew shoved the book with both hands. It sailed over top of the desks in front of him, crashed into the back of another chair, and slapped to the ground. Summoned, a chaperone's footfalls quickened up the corridor.

"What'd you do that for?" It was Raymond's turn to be agitated. Matthew's slick grin returned, spreading across his face. "Now somebody's coming! Stupid!"

"Raymond, you're looking at a grown-ass man," Matthew said. "Ain't nobody putting me in detention." He winked at Raymond, then stood, offering a hand to Patience. She rose from her seat, glancing at the book on the ground, the ones on the shelf, with the elegant dignity of somebody, herself, calloused to insult and this need to disturb our peace. Seconds later, her eyes were smoldering again for Matthew. He smiled wider. "What's say you and me finish our trip down memory lane, sunshine." They walked out and left me and

Raymond huddling in the shadows, meeting the chaperone seconds before she made it to the door.

"Oh, no ma'am, we just got a little turned around, is all." Matthew was all bluster just outside the classroom. "It's been a while since we've been in the building . . . Must've left my brain back at the Howard University School of Medicine . . . Oh, yes, ma'am. Studying to be a doctor, you know." He sweet-talked as his words, their steps, faded up the hallway.

"I know butter never melted in his mouth," I told Raymond.

"Never." When all was quiet, I rose, fluffing and inspecting for wrinkles on my left side while, to my right, Raymond descended to a knee, pulling another surprise from his tuxedo. This one, a star captured inside a red leather box.

"Well, ain't your pockets just full of surprises tonight." I chuckled nervously, and he laughed. Nervously. Then, he began.

"All that talk a few minutes ago? About the book? All that? Coming to the classroom wasn't supposed to be about—"

"Raymond Campbell," I interrupted, too loudly and lightheaded with excitement. "I know you'd better tell me what this *is* about and not what it *ain't* about."

"Marry me," he said. He never asked a question because it wasn't a question. He slid the ring on my finger, and I tasted his sweet lips until that chaperone returned and yanked the door open.

"Raymond Campbell! I know you know better!" she mewed. "I expect this from your brothers, but not you! And let me find out that Matthew Washington had something to do with this, too. All that bragging about 'the Howard University School of Medicine.' I'll fix him."

Raymond grabbed my hand and we showed our heels, hustling up the hallway to the gymnasium. We reached the doorway out-of-breath laughing, but just before we walked in, he stopped.

"You think you can be surprised one more time? Pop's been so down in the mouth missing Mama that I promised I'd propose in the dance. Only reason he came out tonight was to see us get engaged, and I'd hate for him to miss it." He pulled the ring from my finger before I had time to poke a lip out. While he put it back in the box and tucked it inside his pocket, I looked through the door.

"In front of all these people?"

"Heaven help me, but yeah. It was the only way to get him out the house. So," he leaned in, kissed my cheek, and rumbled into my ear, "you'd better say 'yes.'"

He inhaled his courage and we walked back in, finding Matthew and Patience by the punch bowls. Him, wearing an old Cheshire Cat grin behind a cup to his lips. Raymond asked him to take a walk up to the bandstand, leaving me and Patience together. She offered me a cup, but when I declined, she nodded her head left, and we moved for a better view of our beaus moving through the crowd. Separated from others around us, on our own island in conversation.

"So, you two are getting married," she said, her dusky words floating only to my ear. "Been going together a good, long time."

"About eight months, *mmm-hmm*."

"Matthew and I have been together going on eight years. Always told me that he and Raymond weren't the marrying type. I suppose he was wrong." She sipped and I shrugged, trying to find Matthew and Raymond after they absorbed into the crowd. "But I guess eight months is a good, long time to get to know somebody."

"I think so."

"His favorite color, favorite meal."

I didn't know the color. Knowing all the colors in the world except his favorite pricked me a little.

"He loves catfish, salmon croquettes, liver and onions, and baked chicken thighs with peaches. And anything with stewed carrots," I said.

Pretending not to notice her small, uncaring smile, I turned away from her, spying them again as they jostled each other approaching the bandstand. They pulled the saxophone player's ear, who nodded and held up an index finger before bringing the horn back to his lips. Matthew hugged around Raymond's shoulders as his neck swiveled, taking in the room around him, where New Jessup dripped gold and draped itself in finery, clapped backs, bragged about dresses, filled the dance floor, lined up for Mr. Marvin Claus, and drank punch.

With Raymond seconds away from bringing everything to a halt, Patience said, "And, of course, you know about the bus in Montgomery."

"He told me about the boycotts, yes," I said under my breath, waiting, vibrating, and now, pricked again.

"No, not the boycotts. Getting off the bus, first day, him and Matthew."

I shook my head and she sighed from behind the cup at my squinted confusion.

"A bus? You know what he's up there doing and you in my ear about a bus?"

She paused, considering my face.

"Look Alice, I was hoping that, maybe, you and I could talk. Really get to know—"

"Ladies and gentlemen, boys and girls, please welcome Alice Young to the bandstand. Let's give her a round of applause and encourage her on up here!"

In the commotion, I looked at Patience, maybe waiting on her to finish her thought or apologize for being messy, I don't know. All I knew was that, in a moment I was supposed to be surprised, I was surprised. But she lowered that cup and jerked her head towards the bandstand instead. When I was slow to move my feet, she said, for everybody watching, "You'd better get a move on, girl! There are about fifteen young ladies itching to be Alice Young right now."

When it was all said and done—again—Mr. Dale took me for a spin around the dance floor. With his chest stuck out, he insisted I call him Pop from now on. Raymond, Matthew, and Patience talked and watched from the punch bowl. Even from the distance, I knew his eyes; I wasn't worried about him. From the distance, I looked at her, and saw her mouth behind that cup again.

"POP'S WAITING IN THE CAR," Raymond said, dropping me off after the dance. He was bathed in the glow of my doorway light during our first free moment together in hours. His surprise looked like confusion at first when I asked him about the bus. But his face melted when I told him that Patience mentioned it while he was at the bandstand. "Besides . . . after our disagreement . . ." he said, hesitating, "I thought you didn't wanna hear any more about Montgomery." Though not an accusation, it cut deep to know he could have kept something from me that he wanted to say. No, I had no interest in regurgitating the world's evils. But he had entrusted me with his beating heart, so if there was something inside him needing to get out, I meant to be the one protecting him, comforting him.

"Raymond—when it comes to things like this, if you wanna tell me, I wanna know. And I certainly do not wanna hear about something on your heart from somebody else's mouth."

"Yeah, well, I've known Patience a long time. She's a good friend. Funny, sharp as a blade, and I never question where we stand, even if her name is like a practical joke sometimes. There's more to her than meets the eye."

"That's what worries me. She's working with y'all on this underground project, to be jumping the gun on your news to me. Twice now."

"She has her own ideas, but she would never speak outside the group. She's too loyal for that. If anything, she just wants you more in the fold. She'd *never*," he said again, rushing to interrupt my question. "But Pop's waiting on me in the car. I do wanna tell you. I just need more than these few minutes, though. Come by early, whatever time you like, and we'll go out in the garden. I'll tell you everything. I promise. Tomorrow."

NINE

Pockets for secrets were plentiful in the house where Raymond grew up. Not just for people, but for things, memories. Like on Christmas Eve, when Miss Catherine's paring knife stayed hiding from me. Although I knew she must have one in her kitchen, I had given up on finding it and brought my own to the house months before. But after peeling the first potato, the handle separated from the blade—it just broke in half. So I pulled the drawer next to the stove, next to the sink, emptying both. I climbed on a chair and opened every overhead cabinet, shining a flashlight and running my hand over the dark corners in the shelves, convinced that, if light could reach it, I could find anything. I was so convinced that it was just beyond my fingertips, so preoccupied with where to look next, that I only noticed the car horn after the glossy, blue-black wings of crows taking flight outside the window caught my attention. I abandoned my search, grabbed Pop's brown wool cardigan from the coat rack, and headed out to welcome Percy and Dot home for Christmas.

Christmas in the Campbell house had, for years, been a dwindling affair, with older siblings trading holidays with in-laws. Thanksgiving here, Easter there, and so forth. Raymond's older sister Regina always traveled from Montgomery to Bessemer to spend

Christmas with her husband Edward's family, and his older brother, Trevor—married to Sallie—stayed in New York City with their children and her people. Raymond and his youngest brother Percy came home every year from Montgomery, and since Percy's wife Dot was also his high school sweetheart, they ferried back and forth during their visit between her parents and his. But since Miss Catherine had passed in February 1958, only Raymond had set foot in their home house. Finally, at Christmastime, a Studebaker—identical to Raymond's nearly to the dents—pulled up in the yard. By the time I got to the porch, the front doors were open—Percy, bent inside the driver's side, with Dot just a voice and some feet from behind the passenger side.

"Hi," she called out, high and excited. But when the screen door yawned and snapped, and yawned and shut behind me, with Pop and Raymond off in the shop, she stepped from behind the car door and said, "Where's everybody else?" Before I could answer, she shrugged off her disappointment and slammed the car door shut, heading straight at me. She was just as itty-bitty as I remembered from Mr. Marvin's when I'd served the Campbell tables at Miss Catherine's repast. A whir of golden-brown skin, white gloves, and a crimson-red skirt suit with matching pillbox hat, she marched across the yard and up the porch, where her brown eyes looked up into my brown eyes. She stuck her hand out, and her face lit up with dimples deep enough to hide plenty of secrets.

"You remember me? My name is Dorothy, but everybody calls me Dot."

"Sure I remember you. Good to have you home. They been talking about y'all's visit all week. Just excited."

"Hardly excited enough to greet us, I see. Percy's *been* blowing his horn."

"Yeah, well, they at the shop," I told her. "Been there all morning." She shook her head but smiled and rolled her eyes.

"Just like a Campbell man to leave you in the house cooking while they're off tinkering on something."

"Maybe, but what else they supposed to do but get in my way?"

She laughed and it reminded me of an Ella Fitzgerald scat—knowledgeable and musical as a tease.

"Don't let these men fool you, honey. If they can rebuild a transmission, they can fry an egg."

Before she even wrapped arms around to hug me, Dot was the warmest embrace of any potential girlfriend I had met in New Jessup. With jobs keeping me busy from *can't see* to *can't see*, I had very little free time. And something about my interactions with Patience had me always considering how my words sounded. Like maybe, if she could understand me better, she could *understand me better*. But Dot opened the door to her heart and invited me to get comfortable inside.

"Anyway, thank goodness I'm here. You getting on alright?" Dot asked, looking past me at the front door. Over her shoulder, out in the yard, Percy's car door was still open. He had stretched tall with his arms crossed over top, and he was watching the conversation without a word or any expression on his face. Certainly no holiday cheer. Some gloominess was to be expected, this being his first Christmas home without Miss Catherine. Mamas aren't supposed to die and leave their families staring at holidays ahead. Leave their families staring at a slaughtered, butchered turkey without any idea how to cook it.

As a child from down country, I understood death as a part of life. The undertaker prepared Mama beautifully, we prayed over her, and buried her in September 1948. Only, whenever the stalks rustled, or a hat hid a woman's face in town, there was Mama, just beyond my grasp. Like maybe she would change her mind and come home before supper. But passed on? Gone to glory? Gone forever? *Forever* only became real at Thanksgiving that first year, when she wasn't there to show me and my sister how to prepare the turkey, so I read

Percy's stone face as missing Miss Catherine at the holidays. I was partially right.

His voice was as deep as Pop and Raymond's but as buzzy with "welcome" as a swarm of wasps.

"Are you wearing . . . my mama's apron?" he asked with such calm hostility it took me a second to register his words as complaint. Dread melted over me then at the magnitude of my mistake. Not only was Miss Catherine not coming through the door, but I was wearing her clothes. I fumbled quick, shrugging out of Pop's sweater and laying it in his rocker. My trembling fingers refused to unloose the knot on the first apron I reached for whenever I entered her kitchen.

"Yeah, I—"

"Don't take it off now. You're already wearing it."

"Ain't a problem. I could—"

"I said you don't have to take it off."

"No, really, I—"

"Well, look what the cat drug up!" shouted Pop from up the driveway, Raymond hot on his heels. With one final scowl at me, and Miss Catherine's apron still hanging from my neck, he turned his back and spread his arms wide to receive them. They stopped short of a hug, though—covered in grease and not wanting to muss his traveling clothes. While they were all bellowing their togetherness, Dot nudged me with her elbow.

"If Raymond didn't warn you about my husband's *Percy*-nality, he should've. He can be a hard man to like when you first meet him. Plus, he's grumpy from the drive and missing Mama Cat, is all. We'll get settled, get some food in him, and he'll be alright." But when they told him why they were in the shop on Christmas Eve, the teasing eyes Percy turned my way were full of menace, even if my car being on the lift was none of my fault.

What had started as a funny scraping noise when I turned the key in the ignition ended with me bucking into the Campbell's driveway when the sun was still barely a yolk on the horizon. By the time I rolled to a stop in the yard, Raymond and Pop were on the porch hollering and waving hands, so I killed the engine to hear what they were saying. Both of them sank their foreheads into their palms.

"We were telling you not to cut the engine!" Raymond said through clenched teeth as he strained to turn the ignition. When he failed to muscle Blue Lightning back to life, Pop fetched the wrecker so they could haul the car to the garage, where they had been since just after dawn. Only a few hours after Raymond had promised to tell me about Montgomery and that bus. But with my car on the lift since first light, then Percy and Dot pulling up earlier than expected, there was no time to have that conversation.

"Thought those Henry Js were indestructible." Percy was talking to them but eyeballing me. Some seconds passed in silence, and then, comfortable with his upper hand, he moved on to his own opinion about the car. They fussed about head gaskets and radiators and water pumps, each daring the others to be wrong. Thick clouds of confidence blew between them as they ridiculed each other's ideas.

"Since I'm here, I may as well go on and take a look," Percy finally said. Pop snorted and shrugged, regarding the state of the two Studebakers flanking his Cadillac, both looking more at home in the boneyard than the front yard.

"You still have some coveralls hanging in the shop," said Pop. "But I'm telling y'all right now, it's the head gasket."

Me and Dot headed inside, where she surveyed the torn-up kitchen and the handle and blade laying next to the potatoes on the table. After a big laugh, she lifted a false bottom from the drawer next to the stove and pulled out Miss Catherine's paring knife. Hidden there because, she said, things had a habit of getting nicked for the shop and returning broken, if at all. Which explained everything I needed to know about what happened to my knife. Properly knived and aproned and always talking, she settled at the kitchen table with the rest of the potatoes and turned them under the blade until they were bald.

With the potato salad chilling and the 7-Up cake in the oven, I was sticking cloves in the ham when our small talk turned to a friendly interrogation about me and Raymond. She talked like Raymond danced—skillfully and nonstop. Requiring careful attention to stay on track with two people more than capable of leading wherever they wanted to go. Even if it was all in fun.

"Anyway, like I was saying—I've known that man since he yanked Percy off my pigtails in the schoolyard; hardly said anything then, either—just popped him upside the head and dragged him away. Yeah, Percy liked to think of himself as a ladies' man, even as that bad little boy, he was always a talker . . . you know the type, can't help but to have their mouth running." She paused, and when I said nothing, she went on. "My husband always had a little girlfriend over here, and another little girl hanging around over there. Different ones every week, seemed like. Till me, anyway.

"Not my brother-in-law, though. With the talking, I mean, though he always had girls buzzing around. But he's a tough nut to crack, so that's probably why. Never saw him hold a hand or have much conversation, and like I said, I've been knowing him since the schoolyard."

"*Hmm*" is what I said with a little grin. She smiled, revealing a perfect line of pearly teeth, telling me she knew I knew she was getting at something.

"Always a tough nut," she said again. "That's why, when you slid his food in front of him and he turned that purple at the repast, we all knew he was gone as gone gets."

"Raymond turned purple?" Cunning cracked across her lips and sparkled in her eyes as she drew those couple words from me.

"You listen to what I'm telling you—gone as gone gets. Let me find out you put something in his food."

"Something in his food," I parroted, sucking my teeth at that tiny girl and her enormous accusation. "You saying I put a root on Raymond?"

"Not exactly. All I'm saying is that he's a hard man to get close to; so quiet, you know. Not a hand holder, not a talker, never smiled as wide as he does every time he comes in here sneaking food and spying on what I'm telling you. And if you would've told me a year ago that my brother-in-law—Raymond Campbell—would one day propose marriage in front of all New Jessup? I would've called the nuthouse on you. He's a hard man to . . . get close to," she repeated, and the meaning changed. I set the cloves down and turned fully around to face her, leaning myself into the corner where counter met counter.

"You sound like you got something on your heart, Dorothy."

"Nothing on my heart, honey; just making conversation. And why do I have to be Dorothy? I told you, everybody calls me Dot."

Dot's chattering was both welcome and bittersweet. With the scents of Christmas Eve supper mingling, and me in Dot's interrogating embrace—the way we danced around each other, with and without words—the Campbell kitchen, always comfortable, glowed with such warmth that it raised Rosie to my mind. Not that Rosie was such a talker, no. And she was even taller than me, lighter brown, and had started doing hair because, like me, beauticians cringed to see our miles of coils coming through the door for a press. But that year when Mama was really gone, leaving us to prepare the meal, we closed the door, together, on holidays past. I had Rosie for two more years after that before she was gone, too, and now I wondered who my sister was celebrating with, and whether she also had somebody like Dot chattering in her ear, making her feel warm and think of me.

We all trimmed the tree as the sun lowered, singing carols and flinging tinsel at each other. When Percy asked where I got my pipes,

I told him, "All the women in my family have nice singing voices, I guess."

"I suppose I'll have to take your word for it." He smiled with that same slick-mouthed, mean-spirited teasing he had been calling Christmas cheer for me all day. Mindful that I had walked out the house in Miss Catherine's apron, I gave him some leeway. But when Pop started talking about the Studebakers, and everybody was having a good laugh, I said I had never realized Dr. Frankenstein made twin monsters. Percy's jaw tightened up right quick before he left the room, muttering about some ornaments in the attic.

The air was thick with everybody's longing at supper, though Dot did her best to fill the empty spaces with cheer. But sometimes, the quiet needs its respect. After a long pause, with plates wiped clean and the remnants of our feast on the table, Pop looked towards the remains of the potato salad. Talking more to Miss Catherine's crystal bowl than to any of us, he said, "She would've been so pleased to see her boys, their wives and wives-to-be, here with their old man at Christmas. So pleased."

His hand rested on the table, its fingers curled up, with nothing to hold on to. With Pop on one side of me, and Raymond on the other, I took each of their hands, trying to bridge something we were all missing. Percy looked right in my face, with Dot's hand circling between his shoulder blades, and said, "Yup. Seems like she should still be in *that* seat."

"DON'T THINK I'VE MISSED A THING, little brother," Raymond warned after they started talking again. The rockers' wicker stretched and groaned underneath the weight of two grown brothers in conversation on the porch. They chose to ignore the sound of the board creaking through the crack in the door—the board flexing underneath my foot. Grabbing the doorframe with one hand, I leaned my ear to the sliver of opening and stilled everything except my breathing. Coming to bear news I knew Raymond would want to hear, Percy's voice buzzed angry and assured me I should listen rather than announce myself.

Just minutes before, they had left the family room together— Percy's arm wrapped around Raymond's neck in a playful jostle—to go outside for a private nip. They left me, Dot, and Pop talking until Pop's mid-thought snoring took hold and threatened to turn contagious. Me and her smiled as his gentle exhales filled the room with the Sandman's dust. I yawned and yawned, wanting little more than to close my own eyes and drift off to sleep. So when Dot said, "You should just stay. There are plenty of places to sleep in this house that are not up under your man," I gave in to an idea he had been pushing for months.

She left the room to get me a scarf, some bobby pins, and some Pond's, but before I took my face off and pinned my hair, I went to find Raymond and tell him. The front door was cracked open, and the rocking chairs rocked and rolled over the porch slats.

"Then what are you *doing*?" Percy said sharply. "First, you were coming back to Montgomery right behind me. Then, you were staying just long enough to get Pop squared away. Now, you're staying forever and buying into all this bullshit again?"

"You, of all people, know that ain't what's happening," Raymond said.

"What I know is you're fooling yourself to stay here and do what y'all are cooking up. You need to come back to Montgomery, where change is actually happening."

"You never thought about coming home? Because look around you, man. This is our land. We have space here. Room to grow. And we don't have to move off the sidewalk for anybody. You yourself were talking with Hugo and Major about how y'all are starting families, so what is your problem?"

"You weren't singing this tune before Mama passed. That's my problem," Percy said. "Wonder what changed." Raymond spoke quiet like a second language and it was agitating his brother. After a silence that seemed intentional, Percy got louder. "And Dr. King! What you're cooking up is squarely in contradiction to him."

"Ain't he preaching economic equality for Negroes? And voting?"

"And integration!" Another silence. "Raymond, you better talk to me, man. You're the one got me joining the big folks' church, up there on the political action committee and everything at Dexter Avenue Baptist, in the bus boycott, all of it, to turn your back now. What are you *doing*?"

"I ain't turning my back. I'm getting married and staying put. Period. There's plenty of work to do right here."

"You ain't staying because of the work. You're staying because of *her.*"

"Say 'her' like that one more time and find out what happens, little brother."

"This woman dumped you, let's not forget, because of this work!"

"'Alice,' Percy," he said, hissing the end of my name at his brother. "Not 'this woman,' either. *Alice.* And yes, I do remember."

"Fine. Now, you got *Alissss* up in Mama's house, in her kitchen, in her apron, in her chair! Calling Pop 'Pop!' She was ready to cut you loose over equal rights, and for that, you put a ring on her finger?" Percy's voice rose as he managed to say my name without an ounce of respect on it.

"How many times did Dot turn you loose for much better reasons?"

"We ain't talking about me! We ain't talking about me! And let me tell you something—*Alissss* got a smart mouth to be talking about the Studebakers the way she does. Frankenstein's monsters? After what we built and used them for?"

"Damn, Percy, quiet yourself already. This is how you want Pop to find out what all we were up to in Montgomery? With you out here crying on the porch while he's missing Mama the way he is?"

"You and Matthew shoulda been told him what we were up to. Don't put that on me."

"Well, now ain't the time. Lower your voice."

"I ain't no little kid anymore, Raymond. *You* are gonna *stop* telling me what to do."

The chairs rocked and rolled over the floorboards in silence, while the sound of Pop's soft snoring drifted through the house. But Percy's voice was rich with aggravation and deeply vexed out there with Raymond, who had always smiled with good humor at my jokes about his Studebaker.

"Alright, so Pop doesn't know," said Percy. "But what's *Alissss* think of it now?"

"Keep on pushing, Percy. Just keep on."

"Well?"

"She's on board. Wants to keep New Jessup the way it is," Raymond said.

"What do you even know about this girl?"

"Everything I need to know."

"She ain't even from around here."

"No."

"Then where are her people, Raymond? Where are they?"

"Ain't around here, neither."

"Well ain't that a bitch? My brother, comes back home—"

"—Lay off, man—"

"—got his nose wide open behind some cute gal—"

"—I said lay off, Percy—"

"—Look, I ain't the one to tell you to turn down a good time. Hell, have all the fun you want with her—"

"—Percy, you say—"

"—But don't have her coming out *my* mama's door on Christmas Eve in *my* mama's apron—"

"—another word against Alice—"

"—like she owns the whole goddamn place—"

"—and you and me are gonna have a misunderstanding—"

"I just wanna know who this mystery woman is trying to take my mama's place—"

"Her folks are dead, and probably her sister, too. Happy? So lay off, man, and don't you dare say a word to her about her people."

Raymond's voice rumbled through the doorframe and turned the pit of my stomach to jelly. Every time we spoke about Rosie—in the garden, in the house, in New Jessup—we spoke of her as alive. She *will* love it here. There *are* jobs here for her. He'd be happy to build her a car, teach her to drive it. All things I had written to her and more. Even though letters to the home house in Rensler, asking for word, yielded nothing but the disappointment of silence, I still knew we were just missing a connection. Now here he was telling Percy and not me—never me—that he actually believed my worst imagined fear. The words made everything in my world tremble.

"I'm sorry about her folks. But she could be anybody. Don't you wanna know?"

"I know all I need to know, and I know this: you start a word with Alice about her sister, and I'll bust every last tooth out your head. Even if she brings it up, you change the subject." The chair's wicker creaked as the rockers quickened across the floorboards when one of them stood up.

"Well, then bring her back to Montgomery, then, because this ain't you."

"It is me, Percy. It's us. Campbells founded New Jessup."

"Shit, it ain't me, man," Percy said. "Because you mark my words, Raymond: ain't no pussy in the world good enough to pull me back to this place."

Something crashed, a glass shattered, and a loud thump banged the other side of the wall.

"You lost your goddamn mind?" Percy shouted, his voice strained.

Raymond said nothing; just more thumping against the wall. The commotion finally gave me a reason to push through the door and stand there speechless, stunned. Raymond was gripping a fistful of Percy's coat and had his forearm pressed against Percy's chest like an iron bar, pinning him against the house. Paint-colored flecks floated to the porch slats underneath Percy's feet.

"Let go of me, man! I promise you don't want me hollering out here!"

I shouted Raymond's name. They turned identical faces to me with the same grays speaking different languages, both men panting small clouds from their mouths.

Pop and Dot's footsteps hurried up the hallway, and Raymond let up on Percy when they came through the door. The scarf was in Dot's hand and the bobby pins ticked to the floor when she saw the aftermath of the fight. In the silence, Dot demanded answers.

"What in the world happened out here? Fighting? On Christmas Eve? Y'all should be ashamed of yourselves; too old for this mess! Broke a glass—somebody's gonna clean that up, and it won't be me or Alice. You hear me? Are you listening to me? Y'all are brothers! Brothers! There is nothing in the world that should come between you, make you get to this; shoot, just all of it. Trifling. Stupid . . ." She kept talking, not knowing she had plunged the knife deeper into my heart, talking about nothing coming between siblings. Their words seemed heavier than the argument between me and Rosie, for which her only course of action had been north. But Dot kept on chastising everybody. Pop was wide-eyed at the paint flecks still sprinkling from the Percy-sized dent in the siding. For their part, Raymond and Percy said nothing; just glared at each other until Dot ran out of steam and they apologized for the disturbance and the damage. With the commotion petered out, Raymond opened the door and Dot offered the scarf to me. I refused, holding my palm out.

"I just came to ask if I could hold the keys to the Studebaker," I said. "It's getting late, and I should go."

HE DROVE ME INSTEAD. Past the boneyard, and around the bend in the road, the city was lit up, but in sleepy silence awaiting Santa's arrival as the darkness hung heavy with stars. He sighed hard enough to blow wisps of gauze across the night sky. With his sun tea glowing under the streetlamps as we entered the city proper, he waved good evening to the WELCOME TO NEW JESSUP sign.

"How much of that did you hear?" he asked, breaking the quiet.

"Nothing. What happened?"

He nodded slowly, in disbelief. Uncertain enough to confirm my lie but suspicious enough to raise an eyebrow at the pavement ahead.

"He wants me to come back to Montgomery," he said, after thinking about my tale a beat. "He's disappointed, is all. *Hmph.* Montgomery, Montgomery," he sang-talked, then blew the heavy air from his chest.

"Sounds like you miss it."

"I think about it every now and again. I don't miss getting hassled, arrested, that's for sure."

"But you do miss something."

"Sure. The guys, of course."

"Of course," I said, though I had never wrapped my head around why he worked for integration.

"The conversations I had in this very car with folks I drove around during the boycotts."

"I didn't mean any harm by that Frankenstein monsters comment—" Before I could utter a full apology, he raised his hand from the steering wheel to stop my thought.

"Don't mention it. Percy either needs to learn some manners, or to get as good as he gives," he said, with an edge of annoyance still in his voice. "If anything, you surprised him, is all, and I'm glad for it."

"Yeah?"

"Yeah. I like the fight in you. And he can act like he doesn't, but Dot's the same way." He snorted. "So's Regina. So was Mama."

"Well, I wasn't raised to be nobody's punching bag. Still, I did walk out the house in Miss Catherine's apron, so I can't say I don't understand."

"It's no excuse. And anyway, he thinks the sun rises just to hear him crow. Always been like that, but especially because of the work he's still doing in Montgomery. But go ahead and ask him whether he wants to move to a mixed neighborhood. Watch how quickly he tells you *no*."

"That makes no sense to me. I'm sorry, but it don't."

He drew a deep breath and let it out.

"You sure you wanna hear all this?"

"Look. I said what I said that night because I was angry. But if you have something on your heart and you wanna let it off, I don't want you stuffing things inside, neither." After some quiet seconds, his words started. Short, tight sentences at first. The kind still wrestling with truth to be told.

"Percy and Dot? They still live in Montgomery. In a neighborhood called Peacock Tract. Where Regina lives, too." He paused and jumped a little in topic. I wanted to give him space to open up. "You never really got to know my sister Regina, my older brother Trevor."

"Just talked to them at the repast a little."

"She's seven years ahead of me. Trevor's five. She moved to Montgomery to attend State, married Edward. Stayed put. So . . . when the time came . . . me and Matthew were going to State . . . we moved in with her. Percy came a year later. Anyway, there we were. Five adults, my little nephews, all in this house smaller than Mama's. Together. We got on each other's nerves, sure, but . . . I loved it. The house. The neighborhood. Peacock Tract was my first experience outside New Jessup where I really started to see how special, and unique, our way of life is. When we're separate.

"We all lived with Regina and Edward through college. Her neighbors up and down Lapine Street were families and folks there a long time. Kids playing ball, skipping rope. Folks visiting on the porch. Old folks outside telling everybody to get in before the streetlights came on. Calling to us about the track squad and our grades. Spent a lotta time underneath the hoods of cars up and down the street, like here, with my old man. Growing up on the outskirts of New Jessup, me and Percy didn't have that as much. I miss my sister's house. Her neighborhood. My friends there. And sometimes, yes, my work there. Dr. King had vision and gave voice, a path forward, to address so much of our frustration, with hope and dignity."

His eyes narrowed, and his sentences shortened, punctuated streetlamp by streetlamp.

"The bus depot. Regina came to get me and Matthew. Our first day. First moments off the bus. There's a little hill. She was late, running up the street after parking the car. Sidewalk was crowded but she's tall, like us. I saw her, lifted my hand to wave. Get her attention. I hardly even grazed that white man but didn't matter. He yelled assault, and in no time, I don't know how many others were holding me, Matthew, calling us both every ugly name under the sun.

"I wasn't some dumb kid, you know. Knew that whitefolks took Negro Jessup, drove us into the swamp. I knew that they ain't evolved in any way but their methods of oppression. But you know the worst part of it? Not riding in the back of the bus to Montgomery. Not the Colored entrance at the bus depot. Awful as it was, not even the struggle."

"Were you hurt?" He shook his head and continued.

"I could read the newspaper. Think for myself. I had parents who prepared me for the world. Wasn't even totally taken off guard. Disgusted, angry, yes, but not entirely surprised until the worst part. You know what happened?" He paused as we pulled behind other cars waiting to make the left onto Venerable Ave. His face pinched as though pained by the next part. Always the last, worst, unexpected seconds between getting dragged off somewhere and escaping with your life. Either way, everything in the world turns slightly off kilter as long as there are days to be lived. He looked at me, drew his eyebrows together, considering my face. "My sister," he said. "She lost her shoes running up that little hill. Running to beg those men to let me and Matthew go. *Beg* them, Alice. My sister lost her shoes. She groveled for our lives, and in the commotion. Somebody. Took. Her. Shoes. Why?" he asked with such desperation that I jumped in my seat.

"I can't answer that, baby. I don't know."

"Anyway, we got to the car, drove to her house after all that at the bus station. There was nobody but Negroes up and down Lapine Street, far as the eye could see. It was something to come home to that kinda community in a city that's supposed to hate you."

He pulled the Studebaker to my curb, and I raised my hand to stroke knuckles along his cheek. He turned his head and kissed them instead, hiding his pained smile behind my fingers. I wanted to wrap myself around this man and his dreams and never let go.

"You wanna come up, have some tea?"

"It's late. I should get back before I fall asleep at the wheel."

"I don't want you to go back. I want you to come up and stay with me tonight."

TEN

Socked feet, heavy feet, men's feet trained to remove work boots inside Miss Catherine's house made their way to the kitchen just after Dot left for the chicken coop.

Me and Raymond had awakened together on my pullout sofa, fully clothed like each other's presents yet to open. It was my first time seeing his clothes rumpled, his smile, unshaven; my first time atop his chest riding his first deep breaths of the day. We unwrapped arms and legs slowly, drank coffee together slowly, did everything slowly until it was time to get back to the house.

While me and Dot fixed breakfast, Percy came to the kitchen scratching at the stubble on his face. He kissed his wife's cheek, then mine, with the same lips he'd used to muddy my name the night before. His arm, squeezed around my waist, felt intended to be an admission, an apology, and a fresh start. I told myself to smile as I poured his coffee from the percolator.

But showers and shaves did little to wash away ill feelings between the brothers during breakfast. Raymond ate quietly with the newspaper open between them, and Percy filled his usually talkative mouth with one forkful after another. It was only when the aroma of turkey hit the air, and Pop complimented the smell, that any kindness spread between them.

"Does smell delicious. Mama's recipe?" Percy asked Dot. She shrugged and shook her head as she swiped jam on his toast.

"Ask Alice. She put it in."

"*Hunh*," he said. Raymond folded the corner of the paper down and regarded his brother with wishing eyes. Percy winked at him, though. "Pretty and can cook, huh? Good on you, man." Raymond nodded with a wary smile, and that was how, on Christmas day, they declared a sort of peace on earth between them.

After we opened presents, the men headed to the yard to study under the hoods of those Studebakers, finally leaving me and Dot to finish supper. She was being obstinate, telling me we needed to leave some eggs in the henhouse to turn to chicks. I told her to fetch as many as had been laid instead of just what we needed for the chocolate cream pie. With a pout, she picked up the peck basket and left, and a few minutes later, heavy footsteps let me know one of the men was watching me baste the turkey from the doorway without me even having to turn around.

"Raymond tells me you grew up in Rensler?" Percy said. When I looked over my shoulder, he was already lowering himself into his chair at the kitchen table. He pulled Dot's chair and patted the seat as an invitation. Outside, Pop laughed and loud-talked Raymond about the cars, and Dot's journey to the coop would take at least twenty minutes there and back. He poured two glasses of tea and slid one for me.

By early afternoon, the bird was warming gently, slowly, as I thought me and Percy had agreed to do since breakfast. I joined him at the table warily, mindful about my language, just like with Patience. Wanting to be understood.

"That's right. It's a tiny place between the Escatawpa River and the Mississippi border. You won't even find it on some maps, but it was my home."

"How'd you find your way to our tiny place from your tiny place?"

"I wouldn't consider New Jessup tiny at all," I said. The temperature on his smile was much lower than mine, so I dialed mine back. "I've never encountered an all-Negro city before in my life." He lifted an eyebrow.

"Well, what did you *encounter* where you came up?"

"It was a farming community and a small town."

"Segregated?"

"Naturally." The corner of his mouth kicked up like he was amused about something, though I said nothing funny.

"Naturally? You always talk this proper with Raymond?" When I didn't answer, he said, "Because you can relax around me. I don't bite. I'm just trying to get to know the woman who stole my brother's heart."

Only, the coolness in his tone suggested he thought he already knew me. Knew enough, anyway, to sneak into the kitchen under the cover of family distractions that had opened this window of opportunity. Pop barked laughing again, Raymond's laugh beat the air, and Percy smiled with cool eyes—a splash, a wave, a ripple.

"And you were on your way to Birmingham?" he asked.

"Chicago. My sister is there." He opened his mouth to say something but, I assume, having been warned off of asking about Rosie, he moved on.

"My brother told you about his work in Montgomery?"

"He did."

"That he roped me into Dexter Avenue Baptist, equal rights, all that?"

"Not that he roped you into it, no. But he told me y'all were both part of it."

"And what he told you about our work in Montgomery, you can't get behind?" I shook my head. "Why not?"

"Because what for?"

"Because Negro blood is being spilled all over this country for demanding our rights. Life ain't New Jessup everywhere."

My body turned rigid with anger; my deep breaths, hot enough to singe his lecture right from the air. Not just because I was tired of Percy being nasty to me, treating me like I wasn't missing my own people at Christmas, too, but because he wanted me to defend myself for daring to be happy, free among my own people.

"You really think you need to tell me that, Percy?"

"I think it's worth the reminding."

"You say that to me like you know me."

"This is me trying to get to know you, like I said."

"It ain't enough that I love your brother, your daddy, New Jessup just like it is?"

"Segregation, separation, whatever, doesn't work like this in most places," he said, letting out the big sigh of a crusader failing to convert. Smugness pulled his lips to the side.

"The bus boycotts." I said. "You ride the bus now, with you and Dot sharing a car?"

"Sometimes, yeah."

"And you're allowed to sit in those shelters waiting on the bus?"

"Sure am."

"When the bus comes, do you sit up front next to the whitefolks?"

"Sure do," he said proudly, like he was telling me something. Maybe getting through. "Sometimes."

"And did I read that folks got shot at those bus shelters after the boycott ended?"

"There were a couple of shootings, yeah."

"One of them, a woman. Expecting too, wasn't she?"

"Yeah."

"So you sit in those shelters, and up front with whitefolks on the bus. You do that because you *can*? Or because you *want to*?" He shrugged, not seeing any difference. "Because when I rode the bus in New Jessup, before I started driving Blue Lightning, I sat where I *wanted* to."

Catching my meaning, he huffed at me with those steely eyes. We sat in silence a moment until Pop called him back outside. Percy looked down at his full glass of tea, pushed it away, and walked out.

ROSIE CHECKED IN ON ME THAT NIGHT, coming in as quietly as she had left before she left again. Another time in our lives, me and her would have talked about this Percy business:

> *You believe that Negro? Some nerve talking to you like that. Want me to say something?*
> I handled it, Rosie.
> *You shoulda told them you heard them out there on the porch the other night.*
> I said I handled it, Rosie.
> *Alright, alright. Well you let me know if you want somebody to handle it for real, Lil Bit. I'm just right here.*

That's something like how I imagine it would have gone if she had spoken. Always ready to sweeten the world ahead for me.

That night, I settled into sleep in Regina's room with the curtain open. After celebrating a Campbell family Christmas until the moon was well across the sky, we were all too tired to drive anywhere. A misty moonlight poured into the window as I lay in bed, softening everything it touched. The mist tickled my feet, my legs, and stuck the cotton nightgown to my skin as though the moon's magic was touching me, warm and slightly damp like Rosie had claimed when we were small. I got up and looked through the window for the old man pines in the distance, but instead of trees, I found Rosie looking back at me, looking in on me—leaned forward just slightly, with her hands resting on the sill, her eyes scanning around behind me.

And of all nights to show up . . . why this one?

What took so long? I asked. Where was she when old man Todd turned up in the field, silhouetted by sunset? Did she see that bulge in his pants, or know he would demand November's rent behind the toolshed? Did she hear him tell me he would hate to put a tight young filly like me out in the cold with winter just around the corner? Where was her voice in the reminding that he had known me since I was born? She was the one who warned me about Tena and Ellie and Mo Marie and other girls who were once our schoolmates, so how could she have left me to that same fate? Did she see him snatch me, try to drag me, or how I planted my feet and twisted my wrist away so he fell face-forward into the dirt? Who cared about Percy, when she left me with that man spitting curses at my back, promising to come for my ass that night? Where was she in the five minutes I had to shove things in that knapsack rather than wait on him to show up and make good on all his threats? Percy was grieving, being a pest, sure, but it was my sister who had not written for almost two years before showing up in that window.

Those were just some of the things I wanted to say, behind my eyelids, in my dream. She said nothing, just sighed through a regret-filled smile before she disappeared, without a word, into the mist.

ELEVEN

Raymond propositioned me in the camellias—on a Sunday when we had just gotten back from church. In January, shortly after our engagement, we walked into plants tall and thick enough to be their own forest; their luxurious perfume almost intoxicating enough to distract me from the ulterior motive behind his smile. It was the same chilly, gray day when Mrs. Brown settled into Pastor's office chair and opened his schedule book. We were taking our vows in Morning Star Baptist, and I planned to wear the white dress, so they wanted to talk to us, she said, about the meaning of marriage beyond just shivering at the sound of each other's name. Point made, she returned to humming the joyous recessional still lingering in the air and flipped to Monday night, readying her pen.

"The diner." I shrugged our excuse without mentioning Raymond's own Monday night activities. Tuesday, I worked. Pastor's schedule was full on Wednesdays. Thursday, I worked. Friday, Saturday, I worked, I worked, and Sunday, Pastor took his rest. She stopped humming and frowned, flipping pages slowly as if turning to God's secret eighth day. I offered to switch a couple shifts and asked to get back with her. Then me, Raymond, and Pop drove back to the

house—Raymond's thinking-quiet taking over the entire car ride—
and an hour or so after she flipped those pages, we were in the flowers.

LONG BEFORE ME AND RAYMOND sat across from Mrs. Brown that
day with Pastor's schedule book, I had followed the shoeshine man's
directions and found Morning Star Baptist right where he said—
*around the corner, few blocks, can't miss the white, white staircase
up to the massive doors with the cross engraved between them.* By
the time I arrived, the stairway offering salvation to anybody reaching the top was tinged soft gold by near-November's setting sun. I had
hardly stopped moving since leaving Rensler the prior evening, and
still had the entire world laying ahead. Atop the stairs and through
the door, the vestibule itself was larger than my whole home church.
Inside, the sanctuary was so drenched in gold that even the tapestries
shined with metallic thread.

I sat in the pew closest to the door, both exhausted by the journey
and wearied by the unknown. The glossy wood, stained glass, and
blood-red velvet carpet were opulent enough that, after a few moments
to take it all in, I stood up to leave. Quickly. Convinced that this was
no Negro church. Not that I saw any whitefolks on my walk, though I
was hardly looking. But knowing that whites calling themselves good
Christians burned crosses meant to be a message for Negroes they
considered guilty of any trespass, I pushed through the door between
the sanctuary and the vestibule, nearly crashing into a brown-skinned
man in a gray three-piece suit and wingtip shoes. He had a round
face and a round belly that heaved when I startled him. But he smiled
quickly and gave a little laugh of nervous shock.

"Excuse me, miss. Thought it was empty."

"I was just leaving," I said, and moved my feet. Feeling fortunate
enough to run into a Negro, but not wanting to meet his boss.

"No rush—it's open for a reason," he called out with a confidence suggesting he had the right to welcome whoever he pleased

into this church. With my hand on the brass doorknob to the street, I stopped and turned around. His smile grew wide, lifting clusters of tiny black moles under his eyes to crest the hilltops of his cheeks. He placed a hand on his heart in introduction. "My name is Justin Brown, and I'm the pastor of this church. New in town? I've never seen you around here before." I took a breath. Half a breath. Not knowing who I expected to run into, I thought there would at least be somebody between me and the pastor. Perhaps a secretary or cleaning lady. Somebody to point me in the right direction. Maybe tell me what he was like. What to say, or whether to just make tracks.

"Yessir. I mean, no, Pastor. I mean, I'm just visiting. I was just leaving. I just . . . got off the bus."

"Visiting? Somebody I can call for you?" He cocked his head and furrowed his brow, the kindness in his voice only thinly veiling the faint suspicion creeping into his questions.

"No, Pastor. I just got off the bus for a spell. Going to see my sister in Chicago."

"So nobody's expecting you, meeting you here?"

"No, Pastor. I just got off the bus." Still smiling, he lifted an eyebrow about the fumbling way I answered his question.

"Nobody called for you here or sent you here?" he insisted, but gently.

"No, Pastor."

"Asked you to come here or directed you here? For anything?"

"No, sir. I just . . . at the bus station . . . I just don't quite know how to find my sister."

"Thought you said she was expecting you." Through the tears gathering in my eyes, his gloss black shoes called to memory that shoeshine man, and made me wonder why on earth he sent me to somebody who would tap at the crack in my spirit. He had patted my shoulder like a man unaccustomed to comforting people, but could he really not see that those kinds of tears fell because I was less than a day after fighting off old man Todd, just a couple weeks since Daddy passed, and in the middle of a journey I never wanted to make? Sending me here, then, seemed an especially cruel prank. Every moving thing felt like it stopped and bore its weight right on my head.

"I can't say for sure, Pastor. I ain't heard from her since April."

After a deep breath, his suspicion eased and we called the address from her last letter. Tried to, anyway. The operator said there was no phone. With the light almost gone on the day, Mrs. Brown appeared in the doorway to his office to call him for supper. My invitation for a meal turned into a night turned into a few weeks, and with still no word from Rosie, turned into worry that I was overstaying my welcome. Particularly when Mrs. Brown asked, again, whether I had received any correspondence without even glancing my way from her knitting. We had all settled into the family room after supper, and I was embroidering a design on the placket of a blouse. The question surprised me so much I laid my needlepoint in my lap and started packing my knapsack in my head.

"People surprise you. Sometimes, they come back," she said. I looked at her, saying nothing, though I cleared the half-packed knapsack from my mind to listen. "Many of the Negro Jessup families that left? They came back. Many times, carrying advertisements similar to those that brought Justin's family here in 1904."

She looked up—her thick glasses enlarging her sweet eyes—and rested her knitting on her lap. Her hair was wrapped in the same tight pin curls as I had recently learned to do with my press, only different shades of gray crowned her head.

"Some Colored towns boasted of riches in their advertisements, offering want upon arrival. Not here, though. Folks coming here knew what they were getting into. Those wanting to work found a community willing to share down to their last. Willing to teach trades, offer a comfortable bed, keep bellies full. I come from a farming family, and we often had folks turning up just like you, your kin. They worked, saved up to buy their own land if they wanted, or moved on, but our work was crucial. I like to think my family fed New Jessup so it could grow and grow.

"When the ones who left came back," she continued, "they were floored by what we had done with the money. They came back, and they're still coming back two, three generations later. New folks are still coming to *stay* here, too," she said with a suggestion in her tone and the slight curve of her smile, though, until then, staying in New Jessup, particularly without Rosie, had never been a thought. My sister had been in Chicago for six years. She wrote of friends, and said she liked her job and that she missed me and wished me and Daddy would come. Those weeks, all I thought about was finding her doorstep. Finding, seeing Rosie was the journey, so I knew she would never just pick up and move back to Alabama, to a place where we were both starting over. So stay? Without Rosie? I changed the subject.

But sleep escaped me overnight and I lay awake staring at the ceiling. Back in Rensler, I used to sit on our old wood porch steps—their splinters long smoothed away by age and wear—when I couldn't sleep. The night skies were like all the quiet inside me surrounding me in the world. Even with eyes open, the endless heavens out in the country were onyx black; as completely dark as the back of my closed eyelids. The crickets' never-ending song was the memory of sound left in my ears after the heavy brass schoolhouse bell stopped sounding. And each of the diamond-bright stars overhead was somebody who had once walked this earth with my same coils, my same skin, my same laugh or turtle birthmark. Their blood coursing through my veins, star-bright inside of me. I could sit there for hours and be with the sky. Be the sky. See all of myself as Alabama.

Still unfamiliar with the creaks and groans of the parsonage floors, I stayed in my bedroom so as not to rouse Pastor and Mrs. Brown. Instead of the porch, I pulled the desk chair to my window.

Though the city lights stole all but the brightest of starlight in the sky and made the moon just a quiet outline, the crickets, the stars, the dark, were my chimes, my blood, my quiet blackness, as inseparable as out there on my Rensler porch steps. But the street outside the window climbed the hill towards the horizon, where Rosie was just on the other side. In Chicago. She had left with all the desire in the world to leave Rensler. And me. Gone for six years by the time I found myself in the parsonage, we had reconciled on paper long ago. *Just come*, her letters had urged.

When the night began to lift and the horizon called again, I turned on the light and prepared a paper and a pen to ask my sister a question that was really two questions. One, for the method of it. And one, for the pain of it:

How *did* you leave Alabama?

Before two weeks were out, with no word back from Rosie, I took the job at Taylor Made.

"WHAT IS THAT LOOK ON YOUR FACE, RAYMOND?" I asked in the camellias. "You look like you up to something."

"Now that we're engaged, I don't want you serving other folks, sewing other ladies' dresses. I want others serving you, dressing you. You're about to be Mrs. Raymond Campbell," he said proudly. "I would never have asked for your hand if I planned to worry you about nickels, dimes, or anything else."

I laughed, telling him that I knew a weed before my letters and numbers. That I liked working for Mr. Marvin, loved working with Miss Vivian. When I asked what I was to do with myself all the live-long day, he raised an eyebrow and swept his upturned palm in front of us, suggesting I start with the camellias and reckon with the whole rest of it over the course of my life.

"All this is about to be yours, darling. It's a lot to manage. And when you ain't running your own household, you'll get your hair fixed or whatever the ladies do around town."

"I can still take care of Miss Catherine's garden, y'all's house. Your mama had everything pretty well set up already."

With a patient sigh that revealed some minor, if ongoing grievance, he said, "You call it 'Miss Catherine's garden,' and 'y'all's house.' Not like you're at home here, but like you work here. You're right that this is Mama's legacy, but it's also our inheritance. It's your turn to be the lady around here."

The glossy forest of camellias, just like the rest of their acres, was once dense swamp where men like my daddy had downed beginning-times cypress, diverted and drained water that had stood a thousand years, and killed snakes the size of their thighs. My daddy, who said he knew every inch of the Black Belt, had never mentioned a place with a Negro hospital, schools, a theater, jobs—all with white-folks across the woods. While I appreciated that Raymond wanted to share his inheritance, *What if my family had . . . ?* formed in my chest and stuck there.

But even without such a head start, New Jessup dreams had privately eased into me at Miss Vivian's Singer. My imagination was widening, freeing itself to the possibility that my days of sewing and talking could lead to my own inheritance. Her daughter Earnestine was the only one of her girls still living in town to help out, grudgingly, from time to time. Other assistants with plenty of training came and went after a few weeks of Miss Vivian's withering eye, leaving me and her long days and dog-eared pages and talk of dressing new generations. And Mama had worked, so I really knew no other way. Not that I dreamed aloud to anybody, or even asked Miss Vivian how she had been a career woman, wife, and mama. She kept close guard on her personal affairs and would have rightly considered questions on the subject an intrusion. So, I dreamed of inheriting Taylor Made in letters to Rosie, and only in letters to Rosie. Dreams never spoken to Miss Vivian. Or Raymond.

He waited expectantly for me to say something, the pride beaming across his face about the idea of holding the umbrella over my head for the rest of our days, protecting me from the storms of life as he had done the night he asked me on our first date. I had been right that night that he was the handsomest man in all of Alabama, and he had been willing to be my refuge from the world's abuse. Asked to be, in fact, and was proud of his ability to provide my every wish and need. I had long ago welcomed him into me, too. Maybe even the night of that storm. My blood, hot with starlight, coursed faster as the condensation from our breath mingled under the light of the doorway. His voice rang in my ears long after he left. And maybe I dreamed of him behind my eyelids, maybe not. Either way, he was there.

So out there, in the camellias, standing on tiptoe, I placed a soft kiss on the apple of his cheek, and his smile grew wider. Holding the key to Raymond's smile meant being able to unlock his happiness, something more spectacular than all the colors of the garden. But it also meant I could reach straight into the depths and take his deepest sorrow in the palm of my hand. So I meant to take precious care of Raymond, and to love him the best way I knew how.

Meaning something had to give. I stayed on with Miss Vivian, but slowly, I cut my shifts at Mr. Marvin's until I ate there more than I worked there, until I didn't work there at all. That gave me nights free near the middle of March in 1959, when I invited Patience to my apartment to look through wedding books. Matthew was in town for March recess, and we four had supper and went dancing one night, giving me and her little reason to do much talking. At the end of the evening, she held my car door open and leaned in, asking whether me and Raymond had our wedding planning under control.

Raymond coughed nervously and fired up the car. Matthew snickered.

I had tried luring Raymond to look through Miss Vivian's fabric-covered wedding binders one time. A slight, proud grin traveled up his cheeks as he chewed his sandwich and flipped through some laminated pages like he was doing something: A Vivian Taylor Laramie original gown for his bride; my pick between the civic center, the church fellowship hall, and a Collier House ballroom for the reception; a list of Chitlin Circuit bands at our disposal; pictures of four-tiered wedding cakes; and invitations from the stationery shop written in calligraphy penmanship. When I noted all the high prices, he looked over it, nodded, and said, "That's why I work as hard as I do, darling." But when I started asking his opinion, he rose to his feet with sandwich in hand, kissed me on the head, and said again, "That's why I work as hard as I do, darling," and vanished into thin air.

"No, it's just me," I told her as the silence of his nervous, guilty inhale weighed the air inside the car. "Miss Vivian's helping, but she told me to go through and pick some ideas for attendant dresses. You welcome to come by and take a look."

The next night, with legs folded underneath my coffee table, Patience turned the pages of those binders in a way I thought a woman who only wore pants could never do. Her younger sister's wedding the summer past broke the ice on our conversation, and pleasant memories of the day jumped across her face: A smile as she recalled their baby sister (only ten) twirling around the dance floor, or her twin brothers taking the groom out for a talk after he fainted at the altar. Her glances reached all the way to Detroit, where her family had moved while she was in college. As she talked, I recognized her kind of loneliness well—that choice between the place, and the family, we loved. But she laughed with her sly smile at the way folks assumed she was glad to leave the south for a "better life" up north.

"You know what I tell them?" she said.

"What's that?" I asked.

Making her voice duskier, and exaggerating a drawl she had long ago begun to hide, she said, "It's different." We laughed. That kind of air-clearing laugh suggesting a mutual love of Alabama, an appreciation that the soil was not responsible for the dirt of man. Our common ground, finally, for nurturing a budding friendship.

Talk turned to things between her and Matthew. Flipping through the dark dress swatches, she said, "I won't wear white if Matthew and I ever get married. Not cream, not bone, not ivory."

"What color, then?"

"Black." She turned the page and I watched from the corner of my eye as she slid into the red section. "Or maybe red."

"Red *is* a choice," I told her.

"Like this one." She pointed to something the color of kidney beans that was plain as a house dress—the sort of color meant to hide spills and spit-up. She held the book to me in honest, eager expectation, but all I could manage was a slight head shake. She huffed and kept flipping. "Well, I wouldn't wear a dress, anyway," she said.

"Cream would be so pretty against your skin, though."

"No white—not cream, not bone, not ivory is what I'm telling you. None of it. If we ever get married, it's going to be black all the way. Pants."

"Miss Vivian would fall out to hear you talking like this. She only makes white, you know, and if a bride even asks for ivory, she casts a glance, gets suspicious."

"Well, ask her about black, then. I'd be curious."

"You ain't serious. You gonna wear black up the aisle to marry Dr. Matthew Washington? That I'd have to see to believe."

"I sure would, and he'd be thrilled to see the day. I told him way back that he's not getting this milk free."

"Getting milk free? But . . . ain't y'all been together eight years?" She nodded. "And y'all ain't . . . in eight years?"

"Keep on. I'm still deciding whether I like you."

"I'm just saying."

"Nobody said anything about me and Matthew being saints. Just about me and Matthew being unmarried. I know he wants a boy and a girl and a white picket fence, and if he wants that with me, he'll do it the right way. I wouldn't say 'no,' though," she murmured. "Eight years *is* a good long time."

As the night deepened from lavender to lilac to plum to midnight, she turned to a mulberry swatch that reminded me of the silk she wore at the Christmas dance. A silk that stunned as much for its color against her skin as the fact that she wore a dress at all. When I reminded her of my astonishment seeing her in something other than pants, and suggested she wear dresses more often, she answered with the gentle thump of a knife on my coffee table.

"You sound like Matthew," she said. "But there's nowhere to put my switchblade."

Her grin suggested this knife was more prop than weapon to her. As it lay on the table, she sat back with arms folded across her chest, awaiting my reaction. My surprise came not because she wanted to defend herself. In a scrape, me and Rosie were taught to duck and jab; kick and elbow; knee and wrestle—whatever we needed to do to get away. I searched my mind for an occasion when I used a weapon to fight back, and thought about that time I cracked a white boy in the jaw for rushing through a dust cloud to spray a shook-up soda on me. The car had skidded to a stop just feet in front of me and Rosie on our way home from school, kicking up a thick cloud of red clay dust. Him and his friends busted through the cloud, spraying the soda and shouting "nigger bath." Half-blinded—by the gritty mist of red clay and Big Red stinging my eyes; soaking my hair, my dress; getting in my mouth, my ears—I swung my writing slate with two hands and hit him square upside his head. But the day old man Todd tried to drag me behind the toolshed, I had no weapon other than the hard-pack dirt he hit, face first, when he fell. Still, here she was, trying to make me think she was ready to gouge somebody.

"Where'd you get that?" I asked her.

"New York."

"What about all that nonviolent resistance stuff I thought y'all agreed to?"

"I didn't make those rules, and the rules for Colored women aren't always so neat."

"Right, but . . . you ever used a knife, Patience? To fight somebody?"

"No. But I wouldn't hesitate if I had to."

"Show me what you would do with it." She took the switchblade in her palm, stuck it out straight to the side, and clicked the button. Chopping the inside of her elbow came immediately to my imagination. After she dropped it, the scramble would be on against somebody with boiling blood because she had just pulled a knife on them. Self-defense or not. "I suppose that's one way to do it," I told her.

She lowered her arm and raised a surprised eyebrow.

"I didn't figure you for the fighting type, always talking about folks getting their heads bashed for wanting equal rights."

"I ain't extending invitations for anybody to beat my head in. Where I came up, whitefolks chomp at the bit for that sorta opportunity. But there is violence that comes to our doorstep, whether we conjure it or not. So you pull a blade when that violence comes knocking? You better know what to do with it."

STANDING AND STRETCHING the kinks out after a long night hunched over my coffee table, Patience asked about Rosie. And not just a passing mention, either; no casual question of what she was like as a sister, as a child, but the exact date she had left our house in Rensler. The sudden mention of Rosie's leaving surprised me more and cut deeper than that switchblade ever could. As Patience stood waiting on my answer, Rosie's scent and the feel of her hands plaiting my hair came to recollection. But the memories were dull, like the ripples of an old splash. Fading. And I realized I had forgotten her voice completely. What was sharp—always sharp—was the stricken look on her face after I spoke the words that had driven her away, and then, the feel of her cold, empty side of the bed in the middle of the night.

Folks in Alabama called Bronzeville, Wentworth Avenue, and Cottage Grove like we knew Chicago. The correspondence from loved ones promised those streets were paved of gold. I shared the same parts of Rosie's letters over and over in conversation: she did hair, it was cold, the "L" stood for "elevated" train tracks, and she lived in a house with a nice family. Only, as time passed, the black and white outlines of the lives other folks' relations were living filled in with the color of marriage and new jobs, children, travels to new cities from the new cities. But Rosie's story stayed the same black and white.

"She left in October of 1951," I said. "I don't remember the exact date."

"Why'd she leave?"

"You know how it is. Milk, honey, all that. She had finished school the year before, and without college on the horizon, I think she just wanted . . . well . . . maybe . . . well . . . she just had a lotta reasons."

Patience got quiet as she slipped on her jacket, regarding me as the sadness of my sister gone north started to close on me like a curtain. The night ahead promised to be one long wish for a picture of Rosie as I read through her letters again until I fell asleep.

"I could send somebody to the building. See what's what," she offered.

"What do you mean?"

"I have people in Chicago. I'm sure they'd be happy to go check up on her."

"You'd do that for me?"

"Of course. May take a while to hear back, but with luck, maybe we'll hear something before your big day. Don't look so shocked! I didn't mean to upset you."

"It's been almost eight years since I've seen my sister. Nearly two since I've heard from her. You'd really do that for me? I know we don't always see eye to eye but—"

She held up her palm to interrupt me. A hand she could use to finally close the whole sky between me and Rosie.

"Let me see what I can find out. Okay?" she said. After I nodded, she left.

WE HAD A FEW LUNCHES TOGETHER on my bench before the day she was so late we almost missed each other. I had waited with the cake book and my sack lunch as usual. It was early April by then, with a nonthreatening gray sky muting the sun. But by 12:15, I had finished my tuna salad and half the pages in the binder. It had been a few weeks since Patience's offer, but not wanting to appear overly anxious, I'd decided to let her tell me when there was something to tell. As I waited, I put the book aside and lost myself inside the sounds of children's singsong games and peals of laughter that teased my dulling memories. The ball rolling to my feet at 12:23 broke the trance, and I gathered my things.

Just as I was leaving, Patience hustled into the park with her macramé shoulder bag bouncing from her hip. Her scribblings, she apologized, had run away with the time. I shrugged. After a moment's hesitation, she asked to show me something, and she reached into her bag. The composition book she pulled out as we walked back to Taylor Made was filled with pages of her handwriting, and titles were scrawled across the top every few. She leafed through and settled on one, handing it to me as we walked. The heading screamed JIM CROW RIGHT AT HOME IN THE WINDY CITY.

I stopped in my tracks.

"What is this? And who is Johanna Riley?"

"Johanna is my pen name. It's an article I've been working on with those contacts in Chicago I was telling you about. The *Chicago*

Defender is going to publish it. My scribblings," she said with such soft pride that my surprise was slow to come. I stood there wondering for a minute whether I should be happy for the thing making her face glow. Of course folks had opinions about equal rights. Newspapers were full of stories of the same atrocities being done against Negroes everywhere. New Jessup had, in fact, been built because of such an atrocity. Paid the price for years in that swamp and found its way. For many more than me, the town's arms were still open. But embracing our town while challenging the rock of its foundation was a hug with a knife in our back, and ears pricked for talk that sounded like a push to bring integration, or any hint of it, to our door.

But she was writing about . . . Chicago.

"Would you like to read it?" she asked, holding the book open in my face as we walked. I pushed it back at her.

"I thought your contacts were family."

"Some family, yeah. Some reporters. Some folks I've been interviewing, too," she said. "Alice, I—"

"Why are you writing about Chicago? You scribbling about Rosie?"

"Sort of. Maybe. I hope not."

"You ain't making any sense." She sighed.

"North isn't so different, you know, about segregation. Here, it's the law. There, they just draw these sneaky red lines on maps. Banks use the maps to issue loans that prey on folks and city services are a joke, if they exist at all. The result is segregation no matter how you slice it." Quickening my pace, I wanted to get as far away from Patience and these words as possible. Like my sister, she kept stride easily with longer legs. But unlike my sister, she was hinting that Rosie was unsafe up north, and calling the whole world's attention to herself as a woman named Johanna Riley.

"I didn't come here to talk to you about red lines. We was supposed to meet and look through cakes. And maybe . . . if you had news about Rosie."

"I haven't heard word yet; that'll take a while, like I told you. You'll be the first to know when I know anything. But this *is* about people *like* your sister who have been going north forever for opportunity, only to be excluded from good houses, schools, everything, because of some red lines on a map."

"But that ain't Rosie. My sister lives with a nice family and does hair."

"Okay. But other folks live in rat-infested firetraps with filthy drinking water and no heat in the wintertime. People freeze to death, it gets so cold." She wasn't hearing me, understanding me.

"I ain't interested in a lecture, Patience. My sister wouldn't live like that is what I'm telling you," I said as we reached the Taylor Made doorway. I opened the cake book, and we both bowed heads over it, pointing, whispering nothing sweet until the end.

"I'm sure she lives with nice people," she said. "It's just—"

"Raymond, Matthew, or any of the others know about this?" I asked. Her neck stiffened and her face tightened. Pausing to answer, she turned one page, then another, and pointed at a cake. Her voice deepened and cooled.

"Why would that matter? This is under my pen name, not on behalf of the NNAS, and being published all the way in Chicago, so there's no reason for them to know."

"You know people around here listen. Talk. You think about what drawing attention to yourself really means if folks read these articles and find out *you're* Johanna Riley?"

"How would something like that happen?"

"I don't know, but what if it did? Y'all are quiet here . . . working underground."

"I can tell you're upset about your sister—"

"Stop putting this on Rosie. *My* sister—"

"Lives with a nice family and does hair, I know—"

"Don't live inside no red lines! Stop talking about her like that!"

I thought I had finally understood Patience—both of us longing for long-gone family. But this article made her loneliness seem more deliberate; an intentional choice, like sometimes, she wanted an ocean between herself and others, and sometimes, she meant to drown the very people she presumed to love. Or work with. "This ain't about Rosie! This is about you drawing attention to yourself and everybody around you. Why?"

She turned a page in silence, then another one.

"Because what's municipality going to do for Negroes around this state, in Chicago, all over this country, who don't have the luxury of waiting for their own city when everything else is falling down around them? We should be leading the push for equal rights, including the vote, right in Gilliam County."

"New Jessup ain't falling down," I continued under my breath. "It's thriving. Look around you. You said yourself the north, with integration, ain't 'better.' Just 'different.' Why not give this a chance to work here and everyplace?"

"Do you want to talk about this or not?"

"You playing with my life, too, Patience, especially standing here talking about Rosie. And even if I ain't coming to the meetings with you and the fellas, I worry about them, too. What would they say about all this?"

"I used to think I could get this municipality nonsense out of Matthew's head. But this is the only way I get heard anymore, Alice. I thought I could tell *you* my excitement, at least. If nothing else, that you'd keep this quiet for me?" I stopped flipping pages and looked up at her. Her hopeful head tilt and little smile suggested some friendly bargain had already been struck. Some agreement in her mind for which I was already sweetly, if concretely, indebted to her. Her same hand doing these scribblings was the one capable of finding my sister.

"This is you calling yourself my friend?"

"I am your friend. This article is being printed all the way in

Chicago, and it's about Chicago. I'm just asking this one favor. My scribblings are the only way I get heard. Otherwise, the deep voices always overrule you."

"Those deep voices are your friends, Patience. And besides, you got one of the deepest woman voices I ever heard."

She sighed and said, "*Woman* voices." The words were full and round as they pinballed around the entryway. Miss Vivian, inside at the counter, looked up. We bent heads back over the pages, flipping through to the end of the book. She pointed to the very last cake and said, "I actually do like this one," before she left.

TWELVE

Such was the up and down nature of things between us over the next few months. Attempting a friendship required me and Patience to put talk of the article away. Time passed without news of Rosie, but her endless interest in my sister, and about my life growing up down country, allowed me to recapture memories that had begun to drift away. The sugar maple. Mama's long braid and practiced, swooping penmanship. Daddy's traveling stories and the *swish swish* of the white oak. My porch steps and diamond skies back home. And she pretended to ignore the catch in my throat whenever I asked for news about Rosie, and "soon" or "not yet" were the answers.

I had to teach her something about defending herself. She asked once how I would use her switchblade.

"I wouldn't," I told her. "I have my hands, feet, elbows, and knees, and if I need it, a rifle."

Her decades as a dancer meant she was agile and learned quick. She was good at escaping wrist holds, ducking, blocking, and the like, and in return, she even taught me some dances that had Raymond doing a double take whenever we all headed to the juke.

But a skim of ice could develop between us in the flick of an eye. Knowing full well Miss Vivian's pride in dressing traditional brides,

Patience repeatedly thanked goodness that Miss Vivian would be for-ward-thinking enough to design black wedding pants for her when the time came. Miss Vivian would quick-flick her eyes at me as she stooped, pinned, and considered the pearl-colored silk she was sculpt-ing around my body. When she asked why I stayed in Rensler, and I told her that I had neither the money for school, nor the desire to leave Daddy by himself, she turned the conversation into one about a pet bird that she had once released out the window to its death because its wings were clipped. That was irritating, but hardly as tiresome as the amount of time she spent talking about the similari-ties and differences between whitefolks north and south. Persistently conjuring them to the park or my apartment, or bringing them into conversations when we were with our beaus. Sometimes, she asked what they were like in Rensler, wanting to hear me speak for, or against, whitefolks when life was bursting with better things to talk about.

"They whitefolks, Patience," was all I said, and we both under-stood that was the end of it from me.

But she liked to have a word about everything and enjoyed toe-to-toe banter with the fellas. She could hold her own with them in most ways—more than I could, or cared to; after all she'd known them since the schoolyard, and in their NNAS work.

One summer night, Emma Jean Greene held a birthday barbeque for Hugo. The evening had wound down to just the two of them, Matthew, Patience, Abel Gaston, Major and Meenie Royal, and me and Raymond, sitting in the yard, talking in a circle of chairs. Standing and stretching as the lightning bugs started their show, Matthew yawned that him and Patience were leaving. Long days working at Blakely Memorial as part of his summer break had him aching for a good night's sleep. After teasing Matthew for leaving so early, Hugo welcomed him back any time to "help finish off this eighteen-point buck."

The lightning bugs even blinked, wondering how the buck had grown so large. Eyes that had watched Hugo take an *eight*-point buck found each other. I was on that hunt. As were Major and Raymond. Hugo's one drooped eyelid squinted almost closed, and he flashed his gap-toothed smile. Emma Jean shook her head slowly, a renegade blonde-tinted curl falling in her face and teasing her quick rabbit nose. Laughter waited to be ignited like gunpowder.

Raymond started.

"Eight . . . *teen*?" he said.

"You heard me say it."

"I heard you say it, but you sure you meant it?"

"Couldn't possibly," I said. "Unless we talking all told on the day. I'll spot you those two rabbits you got, but even two points apiece, you still way short."

"God sent me an eighteen-pointer himself, now! Said 'C'mon up to heaven, Mr. Deer. It's time for you to meet your maker.'"

I looked right in Hugo's good eye and said, "You need to either leave God outta this or sit over there and tell this lie." I pointed all the way to the other side of the yard. "So we ain't all riding your lightning bolt straight to West Hell for this exaggeration."

"Now Alice, I know *you* ain't talking mess, miss lady huntress."

"Not about no eighteen-point buck, I ain't. You are correct." But Hugo refused to let up, the play fueled by raspy chuckles and tittering giggles around the circle. Finally Major sat back in his chair, his long legs spread wide, arms across his chest, his U.S. Army eagle straining against the muscle of his forearm. He was plainspoken and liked to exaggerate the roundness of his words.

"*Awww*, Hugo, stop all this, man. Just the other day, he was twelve, and when you got him, he was practically fresh out his mama's lady business there."

"Major!" shrieked Meenie. But it was too late. The laughter rocked and rolled and bent us over. Meenie turned from a creamy moonshade to bright red, and black tear tracks trailed from her eyes, through her rouge, dripping from her face to the grass. The laughter roared like a fire only capable of snuffing itself. Yet in the middle of it all, Patience smiled, her shoulders just bouncing slightly—familiar enough with Hugo's exaggerations, but unfamiliar enough with hunting to understand the scale of this whopper. That whole time, her small grin read more embarrassment than amusement.

When only the soft snorts and headshakes of the funny memory remained, Patience said, "Alice? Your mama taught you to shoot, didn't she?"

"*Mmm-hmm*. She sure did."

"You think you could teach me? It's just, well, Matthew never took me hunting, and none of y'all have ever offered," she said, scanning her wounded indictment among the men. Fresh, nervous laughter murmured around like an irregular heartbeat.

"But . . . when did you become interested in shooting, sunshine? Let alone hunting?" Matthew asked, confusion narrowing his already sleepy eyes. "You can't even stand blood."

"Maybe if somebody would've offered to *take me*, I could've learned to appreciate hunting," she said with a sweet smile to coat the sharpness of her accusation. "So . . . what do you say, Alice? You'll show me?" I agreed.

But before we had a chance to get out and pop some cans and bottles, Raymond came to pick me up one night to see a show. The slow, heavy breaths of his thinking-quiet filled the car as we drove along.

"What's got your jaw all locked up tonight?" I asked.

"Nothing you wanna hear about."

"If you about to strangle somebody, I certainly do wanna hear about it." The DJ started a new song on the radio. Raymond glanced at it, annoyed, in no mood to hum along with Ray Charles talkin' 'bout that river. He kept fingers wrapped tight around the steering wheel instead, so I cut the music off.

"Raymond, I don't care what it's about, you tell me."

He clenched words inside his jaw at first, but he opened up, slowly, about the *Defender* article—then, others in the *Washington Afro-American*, the *Atlanta Daily World*, the *Birmingham World*, and the *Alabama Tribune*—all calling equal-rights organizations to Gilliam County, and New Jessup, Alabama. Patience's ideas flowed from his mouth, so it was no surprise when he called Johanna Riley as the writer. The artery in his neck throbbed when he said that the articles called for us anesthetized New Jessup Negroes to wake up and join the fight for integration in Colored newspapers around the country.

I listened, hoping my heart was only beating loud in my ears. That was hardly the night to come clean about what I knew. It had been months by then since she had told me about the *Defender*; long enough for a secret to turn to a lie to turn to an outright betrayal. Patience needed no switchblade to stab anybody; turned out, she used words, pens, promises—her pleading for me to keep quiet, too closely tied to her offer to find my sister in Chicago.

"She don't live around here, though?" I asked, patting his leg. The muscles were rock hard with tension. Too hard, I imagined, to feel the slight tremble of my nervous fingers. "This Johanna woman?"

"I've never heard her name called if she does."

"Well, sounds like she don't know New Jessup to be saying all she's saying. Must not, because if she was from around here, she'd understand why everybody wants to live in the town that Campbells built." My own nerves eased seeing the corner of his mouth kick up slightly. "I know she wouldn't dare speak against it, anyway, and get run out like some agitator. And if these integrationists are half honest themselves, they all wanna live here, too, huh baby?" His jaw, and the artery in his neck, his leg muscles, all relaxed. "Yeah, they wanna live in the town that Campbells built, Raymond, and this Johanna Riley woman ain't gonna change that. For Negroes? New Jessup is *it*." The air in the car lightened when he gave me his full smile, even with the rest of the truth hiding, burrowing deeper into the darkness whenever we drove underneath the streetlamps.

PERHAPS IT WAS CRUEL to take Patience into the woods because, for all her talk about switchblades and growing up in New Jessup, she was a city girl who had never even stepped foot into Miss Catherine's garden, let alone into the thickets of longleaf pine and ancient cypress on the property. We passed the stumps between the grass and the corn, headed through where God ran out of color, and into the trees with a bag of bottles and cans, to the same trail that me and my men walked to hunt deer. We often found them in a grassy clearing, but the journey to that grass was through stinking, sucking muck that had her cursing and scaring off anything interesting for miles.

"Thought you wanted to learn to hunt, to be carrying on like this."

"I do. But I've never been out here before. I grew up in town, remember."

Already knowing that, I told her to step light, be quiet, and keep an eye out for diamond-headed snakes.

After we reached the clearing, I showed her how to load the gun and balance it on her shoulder, how to set the sights, disengage the safety, lock the bolt, and then, how to breathe and slow the world: to inhale the smells of the moss, the ferns, the scat, and the swamp sulphur—all the smells of death giving life. Exhale every other care on her mind. Inhale to quiet everything except the sunrays singing though the canopies. Exhale to release the inside noise. Inhale, exhale the land like Mama had taught me the second I was old enough to aim. Until the only things that existed in the world were my eye, the barrel, and its target. With the *swish* and *click* of the bolt, and the feather of my trigger finger inside that trance, those bottles and cans jumped and popped.

I loaded the gun and handed it to her, watching her waste ammunition on the trees. She bored of it even quicker than I thought she would and sat in the grass watching me nick cans and bottles. She whistled when a bottle exploded into a mist of glass, all while she lazed underneath the three o'clock sun. As I reloaded, I said, "Raymond told me that Johanna's been writing all summer."

"Does that surprise you?"

"What surprises me is that he's still surprised, since the articles are calling the NNAS, of all things, to come here."

"You say anything?"

"No. I should've but—"

"Why didn't you?" she cut in as I slid the bolt. I flicked the safety instead and turned eyes towards her. Her words had the easy flow of a challenge won as she played with a long blade of grass in her hands, bending and straightening it, careful not to snap it in half. Just bending and flexing it. Playing with it, like she had with my tenderest hope of finding my sister. As she sat there with that smug look on her face, there was no doubt in my mind that she had used my longing against me. Just like with my search for Rosie, that blade of grass could snap as soon as she decided. Her attitude churned something murky inside me.

Above, that three o'clock sun crossed the sky towards three thirty, and all around us, every tree looked like the longleaf pine marking our entrance to the clearing. After I finished scanning our surroundings, the look I directed at her promised I was not in a trifling mood. Her curses and complaints were the only path she left for herself in and out of that clearing, so I knew she'd never find her own way home. She lowered her hands and turned her eyes away from my gaze.

"My sister is the only family I have left in this world. Where is she?"

"I don't know yet. Soon. Probably soon," she said. "But not yet."

"Did Raymond tell you not to talk to me about Rosie? Does he know that you're doing this for me?" Her answer to both questions was silence. "What's taking so long?"

"I'll reach out. Folks are busy, but I'll reach out. Find out. I'll tell you what I find out by week's end."

I returned her safely from the swamp, and at week's end, she left me waiting, listening to the kids' singsong games in the park. Patience—a woman for all the people—never bothered to show her face.

WE CROSSED PATHS a few days later—the Saturday a week before our wedding. With time off from Taylor Made and a weeks' worth of preparations to finish, Raymond had nonetheless convinced me to waste the day splashing around upcreek from Waverly's with Patience and Matthew in the heat and light of summer's longest days. As we drove, he hummed along with the radio, tapping the wheel to the beat with those knobby fingers. His low, satisfied hum vibrated from his chest to fill the entire Studebaker.

At the river, Matthew and Patience were waiting with a basket full of fried fish, oysters, hushpuppies, and greens from Waverly's. Children played with their mamas and daddies, and chased frogs in the water, while young lovers played their own games either on hidden rocks or deeper into the woods upcreek. Splashing in the water, flirting, and kissing gave us little reason to talk until we all settled on our blanket. As we enjoyed the late afternoon sunshine, two of Cap's deputies weaved their way through the crowd, tipping caps at the ladies, greeting the men. They meandered over to us, asking for Patience Armstrong by name and making no mistake of looking in my eye. When she refused to acknowledge them, as though they were joking, the shorter one squatted on his haunches and said, with a quietly boyish smile, "Please don't make us handcuff you in front of all these folks."

"Handcuff me! For what?"

"Ma'am, please—"

"—You dare 'ma'am' me and threaten me in the same breath! I deserve to know what this is about!"

"Cap just wants to talk, ma'am. Just a talk."

"Well, call him and tell him he can find me by the Tombigbee. Or better yet, you two go get him and you can all take a dip."

Around us, the mamas and daddies wrapped arms around children's backs and led them away, with glances lingering over shoulders. Young lovers emerged tentatively from hiding places and watched like curious deer. But the more the deputies tried to calm her and encourage her to go, the more she argued. When she stood up to storm away, the one on his haunches sprang up and took her by one arm, the other grabbing her on the other side. Just to talk, they said. Cap only wanted to talk. Matthew and Raymond both shot up, but before Raymond was fully on his feet, and while Matthew was already talking, I grabbed Raymond's hand and yanked back with all my weight. He jerked, and when she saw why, her glare burned through me as my hand slipped and I fell to the ground. Just a talk, the deputies assured, and sure, Matthew, alone, was welcome to go with them. He packed up their things, and they walked off with every eye watching them weave back through the crowd.

"Let's go," said Raymond as he started packing our things. "I've gotta get down to the station and talk to Cap." I sat still as every eye at the river migrated from the back of Matthew, Patience, and the deputies to the scene unfolding on our blanket. "Alice, you hear me? I said let's go," he said low.

"I don't want you involved in this mess. She's in a heap of trouble, Raymond," I told him.

"How you know about what kinda trouble she's in?"

"I saw, same as you and everybody else, those deputies come and pick her up. I don't need to know the kinda trouble to know what a heap looks like."

"Which is exactly why I need to find Cap. This must be some sort of misunderstanding."

"Then let her tell him that. I don't want you involved in any misunderstanding belonging to Patience."

WE PACKED UP and left as a couple needing privacy for a brewing argument. But the words we started having in the car ceased when Raymond pulled around the corner and behind Cap's patrol car parked at my curb. It sat empty, but the license plate read NJessup1, and it had "*Cap*" painted in small cursive on the topside of the hood. We eyed a truce to each other and climbed the stairs to find Cap leaned against my doorframe with his landlord's key to my apartment in hand.

Cap was a heavy-muscled Harry Belafonte in a tailored police uniform. He tried to hide his square-cut jaw and deep, chiseled dimples underneath a neatly trimmed beard and mustache, but women still whispered "arresting" about his no-nonsense eyes anytime he walked by. His only flaw, if he had to have one, was that slightly flattened boxer's nose he'd gotten before Miss Vivian got ahold of him, so the window sheers fluttering up and down Venerable Ave.'s still evening had likely all taken in his presence before we arrived. Waiting to get a glimpse of his business over here. Well after the hours for a landlord visit. And in his patrol car.

"There's our bride-to-be," he said, smiling as he slid his key into my lock. Nodding us all inside, he directed me and Raymond to the sofa while he brought the kitchenette chair to the coffee table. I breathed in and out, in and out, summoning the quiet. The cars passing by under the window; the gentle hum of the Frigidaire; the pipes gurgling; the squeak of the wood underneath his feet as Cap uncrossed his left ankle over his right knee, then crossed his right ankle over his left knee—all faded to nothing but the words coming from his mouth and my heartbeat.

Patience loved her people, she said. Was forever talking about how much she loved her own people. Negroes. But wasn't I a Negro? And Raymond and Matthew and all our friends—weren't they all Negroes? Wasn't New Jessup built by, and filled with, Negroes who educated her, cared for her? She was forever talking about loving her people but seemed ready to drown the actual people who had raised her up and held her up. The people who had pride in everything they built for her to pass to her generations. She was forever talking about loving her people, but somebody had to actually love them.

Love them the way I knew I was loved when I returned to Taylor Made after the day she stood me up in the park. Miss Vivian was hunched over the same pile of buttons she had been when I left—pearl buttons, every single one a slightly different shade of pearl—for my wedding dress. The dress she had made by her hand for my body. She looked up at me and smiled. Nodding towards the small pile of progress she had made in my absence, she invited me over to stand next to her and continue, fingertip by tip, sliding each button next to another, considering whether their pearls matched enough to keep or set aside like I used to do with Mama and Rosie sorting field peas. She smiled at me and I knew I was loved, that she was in my corner, and that nobody could question my love for my people, for New Jessup. It was that love that brought Cap's name to my lips when I asked what his "talks" with instigators looked like. She stood stalk-straight and slid the glasses off her face.

"He would never tell me, exactly," she said. There could've been a slight tremble in her voice, though maybe it was my imagination. "But I suppose it depends on why he feels *he* needs to be the one speaking with them. What I do know is that whatever conduct sparks the conversation will not be repeated. Why?"

After months of Patience's slick comments during my dress fittings, Miss Vivian was only half surprised by news of the articles and the search for my sister that was meant to keep me quiet about all her scribblings. Still, with head cocked slightly, and narrowed eyes, she said sharply, "You and Raymond aren't involved in any of this, of course."

"No, ma'am. Never. You'd be hard pressed to find folks who love this town more than us." With one last inspection of my face, she slid her glasses back on, returning attention to the buttons.

"I knew there was something about that girl. I wanted you to have friends, but I never understood why you insisted on bringing her around."

"But what *will* Cap do to her?" I asked.

"You needn't ask that question, Alice," she said as she moved a button into the castaway pile. "Patience should be asking what *she's* doing to Patience. What she's doing to all of us."

"I'VE KNOWN YOU since before you were born, Raymond. Matthew, too," Cap said, playing with his watch. "Knew your fathers, Matthew's mama, since we were all knee high in that swamp, and your mama since Dale brought her back here after Tuskegee. Thought I knew folks pretty well in this town, but you know who maybe I don't know very well, apparently? Patience. You know Patience well, Raymond?"

"You know Patience. She's a friend and Matthew's girl," he said, his eyebrows pulled together in confusion. "What's this all about?"

Cap turned to me, squinting, reading my face. "Vivian tells me y'all are friends. That she's come to know Patience since you started bringing her to the shop. Anything *you* have to tell me? Anything I should know about?"

"We're friends, yessir, but—" Before I could finish my thought, Raymond called on that organizer training that he learned in Montgomery.

"Is this an interrogation, Cap? If so, why are we being questioned?"

Cap scanned his eyes between us, back and forth, thinking quietly before he spoke to me.

"Alice, Vivian's been mentioning a bad feeling about Patience. Said she's mouthy, disrespectful when she comes around. Makes me wonder why either you or Raymond spend any time with her."

"But what is she charged with, Cap?" Raymond asked. I squeezed his hand.

"She was helping me with the wedding, picking cakes, talking music, stuff like that," I told him. "And plenty of girl talk. She's pretty much the first girlfriend I've had since I've lived here."

"She say anything to you to make you think she's up to anything? Maybe into something illegal?"

"No, sir. She was just helping, like I said. Why do you ask?"

"I don't know yet, but Vivian was adamant I talk to her, and *before* your wedding. Said she didn't want to mention anything to you because she wanted to encourage you to make friends. But she was insistent I check her out, make sure there wasn't something . . . else."

"Cap, your deputies came to the river and picked her up in front of half of New Jessup because *your wife* doesn't like Alice's friend?" Raymond said.

"Raymond, watch your tone, son. You know that my job is to handle any foolishness around here. Has been since way before you were a thought of a boy. And let me remind you that you prefer it that way."

"What's that supposed to mean? You about to actually start reporting our doings to the sheriff, or at those Business Council meetings?"

"You ever known me, your father, or Marvin to do that before?"

Raymond waited a beat before he said, "No."

"If anybody—and yes, that includes Vivian—is this persistent that something isn't right, it's worth following up. So I'm going to ask you both—you sure you don't know anything Patience may be up to?"

We both shook our heads. Raymond could rightly deny knowing the identity of Johanna Riley. And the rest of it? Denial of the NNAS, any instigating, among those of us who knew, was the expectation. Still, the blade of grass came to mind as Cap talked. The way it bent and flexed according to her will. When all the mercy had been in her hands. "Well, if you do hear something, be sure to tell me first. Especially about any instigating. That's the one of very few things white police care about in Gilliam County. You let me take care of it first, hear?" Raymond blinked and nodded a convincing enough denial for Cap to stand and get ready to go.

"What's happening with her?" I asked.

"She's waiting on me down at the station. Radio chatter said Matthew went with her?" When Raymond nodded, Cap shook his head. "That's regrettable. But if she's clean, she'll be home by sunrise. If not, we have to see what we're dealing with." He cleared his throat as a reminder for Raymond to join him in leaving my apartment. After watching Raymond peck my cheek, they walked down the stairs together and pulled off in opposite directions of Venerable Ave. with window sheers flapping in the still night.

IN THE HOURS when phone calls caused only worry, I twice picked up, then cradled the receiver, thinking to call Raymond at home. I grabbed my pocketbook and went down to Blue Lightning, sitting in the car for a minute before abandoning my plan to head either to Campbell's or Cap's jail—a small, gray brick building standing alone on the opposite side of New Jessup. So I sat up all night instead, dragging the kitchenette chair to the window, listening and watching for the Studebaker to come back. The dark was still that night, Venerable Ave. strangely quiet, and I waited so long I fell asleep sitting in that chair. Waking with still no word from Raymond, and trusting his silence meant trouble after ringing the house to no answer, I drove out their place, steadying myself. For what, I had no idea.

But the Studebaker and the Cadillac were parked side by side in the yard. Nobody answered when I knocked at the house, but a tool zipped faintly from the direction of the shop. When I walked through the door, Raymond was alone, waist-deep under the hood of a car. His muted greeting suggested it was no accident I had not seen or heard from him. He was in coveralls, wrestling a bolt or something underneath the hood, and went back to it.

"Where's Pop?" I asked.

"Towing job. Across the woods."

"I was waiting to hear from you after you left."

"Picked up the Morris boys. Got Matthew from the police station. Came home."

"You coulda called me and told me. I was worried sick."

"*Mmm-hmm.*" After failing to work that bolt loose, he grabbed a louder tool from the shelf and undid the jam with the same ease as his silence undid my nerves. Overnight, the fear I felt for Raymond out there in the unknown had me ready to dial a phone and take off in the dark before I sat myself down, locked up in a chair by the window. Calling Pop would have only roused suspicion if he had not arrived home—and showing up to the jail? Even if he wasn't there, Patience was, encountering the consequences of my love for New Jessup. So I was frozen, locked up like that bolt all night in that chair. Now, I found him alive, whole, and in arctic silence. "What are you doing here?" he finally asked.

"Looking for you, I told you. I just said I was worried sick."

"Well, you found me," he said, standing to face me. He wiped his hands with a rag, his grays implying, *So, now what?* It was no worse than the limited, terse way he dealt with other people, but no better, either.

"Raymond Campbell, I know you ain't acting short with me! Not about Patience Armstrong you ain't!" Expressionless, he watched me go on for a minute about how little I appreciated the closed-off way he was dealing with me. Then, in the middle of my words, he bent back underneath the hood of that car. I turned to leave, but he called out, stopped me cold with accusation in his tone when he told me that somebody had named her as Johanna Riley.

"She had the notebook in her bag full of articles," he said. The air thinned.

"Who told?" He looked at me but said nothing. "Who Raymond?"

"No idea, I guess."

"What do you mean, 'you guess'?"

"She told Matthew you knew. Said you're the only person that did know, as a matter of fact."

"And you believe her?" He raised an eyebrow but said nothing. "That's exactly why I didn't want you involved in this mess—because look what she was doing behind your back. And now she's trying to make her problem our problem."

"But you did know?"

"About one article. The first one, in Chicago! None of these others over the summer." He inhaled and exhaled deep.

"And you didn't think to tell me? Not only didn't you tell me, you had nerve to keep it from me that night we were in the car?" I looked down. My toe was tapping in my shoe.

"Because you woulda told her to stop looking for Rosie."

"Rosie? Now you've really gotta catch me up. What's your sister got to do with any of this?"

It took a few deep breaths to steady myself again. He was as comfortable in silence as a warm bath, and said nothing, waiting on me to respond.

"Patience said she had connections in Chicago who would go by Rosie's address. Reporter folks who could find her. I thought if you knew, you'd tell her to stop."

"Why would I tell her to stop?"

"Because of what you said to Percy on the porch Christmas eve."

I brought all that truth to my lips knowing I would never tell the truth of what he was really asking—whether I was the one who told. The one question bubbling in this argument and waiting to boil over. He froze while the conversation with his brother played back in his mind, and he grimaced when I figured he remembered the nastiest parts. Or maybe the part when he admitted thinking she was dead.

"Alice, I just meant I didn't want him bothering you."

"Whatever the case, Raymond. I'm just saying why I didn't tell you. She promised, but told me to keep quiet to you and Matthew and the fellas."

"She swears she didn't tell anyone but you."

"And you believe that? From her? Over me?"

"You didn't say anything to Cap?" Raymond asked me.

"No, I didn't."

"Miss Vivian?"

"No. I wouldn't! Do you honestly think I'd want Miss Vivian, or anybody, to accuse me of sympathizing with Patience Armstrong or Johanna Riley or whatever she's calling herself? I'm nervous enough with your municipality work just because you're doing it with the NNAS." The expectation had been to deny—to sever from the group anybody caught so that the rest of the body could continue to live. But my loyalties began, and ended, with Raymond. We were joined together, so anything that hurt him, threatened to expose us, I meant to take care of it. Sometimes that meant balancing scales, and keeping him safe, keeping his work concealed, would always outweigh the guilt I felt for lying to him about my talk with Miss Vivian. When he sighed, I had no idea whether he believed me wholeheartedly. But I knew that I had sowed enough doubt in her for the love between us to be the reason that his scale would balance in favor of giving me the benefit of the doubt.

"Well, somebody said something, which means Cap and his deputies are gonna be on the lookout. We were trying to do this, just the fellas, but . . ." he stopped short, letting the thought hang there with no intention of sharing it with me.

After an eternity, I asked, "What's happening with her?"

"She's probably halfway to Detroit by now. Cap's deputies drove her to Birmingham themselves before first light, where she would get the train. She'll never stop writing now unless Matthew can set her straight."

"She say anything about y'all's work with the NNAS?"

"Sounds like not," he said. "And after all this? I sure hope it stays that way."

THIRTEEN

I bumped the car to the curb of Washingtons' Confectionary and Cream and looked right through the plate glass. There was no crowd inside: no tired mamas with misbehaving children, crowded together with proud mamas and good children, crowded together with teenagers thinking love is sweet, crowded together with folks near the end of their workday bringing candies to loved ones at home. No one to block my view from the driver's side straight to the trouble on Mr. and Mrs. Washington's faces in the window; their vacant eyes joining the Chocolate T. Bear sculpture's blank stare at the sidewalk. As I stepped in, Mr. Washington nodded in acknowledgment of my "good evening" and disappeared into the back; the clap of his wingtips and soft chug of the Lionel train along the wall the only sounds other than my *hello*. Thinking that he was heading back to get Raymond's groom's cake, I stood with Mrs. Washington in silence for a minute. She wore Matthew's troubles on her face like a death mask. Normally a woman with a kind word and a warm smile for everybody coming through the door, she turned chilly eyes to me.

Months before, those same eyes had sparkled on the night of our Christmas dance engagement. She had insisted on making a champagne chocolate groom's cake for the first of "her" sons to marry. Made with the same silky chocolate they used on the raisins Raymond loved. I asked if she would package some of those up, too, while I waited. Hoping to make her smile, I bragged that they were his most loved candies.

"I know they're his favorites," she said. "I gave him the first ones he ever had. Twenty years ago." When she pushed up with a lot of effort never before required by her stoutness, I met, for the first time, the woman who Patience had scoffed about when I once called her a guppy.

"Barracuda's more like it," Patience said. "Take my advice and watch your tongue around her."

Behind the counter, her eyes narrowed as her gaze skated across the top. No need to wonder if Mr. Washington was listening. The couple times the bell chimed, me and her stood and waited for him to reappear, scoop an ice cream or bag some candies, then slide out of sight again. Each time, she regarded my attempts to keep light banter going with stony silence. Without any shouting over my shoulder, without her stories flowing freely, every *swish* of the sliding candy, every *chug* of the lonely train, every gentle slap of his wingtips, crashed into my ears from the walls of the lifeless shop, until finally she spoke.

"Did Raymond tell you that he and Matthew were friends since the first day of first grade?"

"Yes, ma'am."

"Those boys, and Percy? They were inseparable through college. The two-and-a-half musketeers, we called them," she said. "I knew every scraped knee and broken heart they ever suffered. Mr. Washington and I were the ones who bought Raymond a microscope for his birthday one year because he was always wondering about the insides of things. It was because of that microscope we all thought he, and Matthew, would attend medical school. They were *that* inseparable. You understand?" She taped the paper package closed, waving my money away when I tried to pay for the cake and the candies. "I don't know what changed," she said. "Perhaps it started when Matthew actually decided to study medicine, while Raymond just came home to fix cars." Her sons, indeed, as that barracuda bared her teeth. With a practiced toss, she slid the candies across the counter so they came to rest directly in my face.

"Raymond and Matthew are still thick as thieves, Mrs. Washington," I said as I took the bag. The paper crumpled in my grip.

"You think so?"

"Yes, ma'am. I know so." I cleared my throat to tamp the rage down, not wanting to give her expectant eyes the smart remark she was trying to draw. "Raymond loves working with cars, and he's great at it. He never mentioned anything about being a doctor to me."

"Well, I guess it'll just remain a mystery, then. Why y'all told Cap you didn't know anything about Patience's doings? Why would you say something like that, Alice?"

"Because we didn't know, Mrs. Washington."

"How could you not? There's never been a secret between those boys since the first grade and you can't get me to believe that Matthew isn't covering for that girl. Not to mention that the two of you are girlfriends. You're one of the only women I've ever known to befriend her."

"Yes, ma'am, but she said nothing to me. And it doesn't surprise me that Matthew didn't know. Patience has her own mind."

"*Hmph*. Well, will you kindly let the rest of New Jessup know that? That she has her own mind?"

"Ma'am?"

"Look around you, Alice. Folks watched *my* son get hauled off to jail right along with her at the river! There isn't a soul in town that doesn't know they've been dating since high school. Our business is suffering because of *that* girl—her behavior, and her mouth. Meanwhile, she got a one-way ticket away from here, and the Campbells are over there living high, with no son or soon-to-be daughter-in-law getting arrested and besmirching their good reputation. But Washington is a name in this town, too. We've been here too long to be treated like lepers."

"Mrs. Washington, I don't mean to contradict you, but neither me nor Raymond knew about those articles, and I wouldn't be surprised if she kept Matthew in the dark. And anyway, it sounds like she's gone for good, or at least a long while."

"I don't suppose you expect me to shed a tear?"

"No, ma'am, I don't expect you will."

"Not a single one. He should've left her wherever he found her all those years ago. Matthew is going to be the first doctor in our family, only now, he's talking like he might not even come home. All because of *her*." She glared her private appraisal of me, and then said, "Maybe Raymond was better off just fixing cars after all."

At that, I slid that crumpled bag back over the countertop at her. She stepped out from behind the glass display, threw the candy in the trash, and walked towards the back of the store. If Mr. or Mrs. Washington ever returned with his groom's cake, I was gone before they got back.

FOURTEEN

Pushing up my veil, I crossed the vestibule and pressed through the front door into an ocean of blue sky vast enough to touch me and my sister at the same time. While New Jessup's stewards, and many of its oldest heads, perspired shoulder to shoulder inside the sanctuary with sons working secretly for the NNAS, and while cars full of folks took a first look at me in my wedding dress from the street below, I closed my eyes and felt marigold warmth on my face. Wishing, or maybe praying, I asked the sky to fold itself together and bring Rosie to my side. It was my wedding day, and she was only there in my mind.

She broke her little-girl promise to me in October of 1951. That spring, she had graduated high school with top marks and flew over the moon when she got the acceptance letter to Stillman in the mail. After supper, Daddy sent me out to the porch while he talked to my sister alone. Though unable to hear their words, Daddy's voice buzzed with the frustration of a final word being challenged, and she burst through the door in tears a few minutes later. There was no money—scholarship or otherwise—to send her, and he wouldn't let her move to Tuscaloosa by herself at seventeen. She had to work for a year to save up.

We worked the rows together that summer, but come fall, after I started my senior year in high school, she was offered a job with a white family by a woman who had worked for them for generations as a maid.

"We looking for somebody to assist me," a woman named Mrs. Trueblood told Rosie one day when we ran into her at the grocery. She had always taken a shine to my sister, and was pleased when Rosie accepted her offer. It was October, and she was glad to get out of the fields, but at the end of the first week, she was waiting for me on the porch at the grocery when school let out. $1.45 of $10 was all she'd earned after they docked her wages for her uniform and meals.

We left from the front of the store and walked home quietly. The shoes she carefully shined and carried in a bag every day were on her feet, getting coated by the red clay dust climbing up her white tights, turning them the color of sunrise. Suddenly, she grabbed my hand.

"You and me. We gotta tell Daddy we need to leave here. Ain't no way there's gonna be money next year for college for me, let alone for both of us."

"But this job, with Mrs. Trueblood, it's—"

"Peanuts. Listen to me, Lil Bit. Even if I go to school next year, you won't be able to. You gonna be in my same spot. There are jobs up north that pay good money. And there are good schools."

"I don't wanna go north, Rosie. I don't wanna leave Alabama, and Daddy ain't gonna wanna leave, neither." We started walking again, but the quiet was combustible. She sighed and began talking to the breeze.

"We gotta get outta here. We don't wanna go from cooking and cleaning for whitefolks to cooking and cleaning for Daddy to cooking and cleaning for a man just like Daddy."

"What's that supposed to mean? Daddy worked so you could finish school. How many of your classmates dropped out to stay in the fields? He asks for hot food and a clean house and that seems fair to me."

"Only, I ain't in school anymore. Am I, Alice? I should be a freshman at Stillman."

"Just one year, he said. We'll save some money, and you go next year, and I'll go the year after."

"Oh, Alice," she said. The heartbreak deflated her. "Ain't no money for college here. This is it for us, you understand? All this *nothing* is all there is for us!"

I pleaded with her to stop talking like that. One more year, and she could go. But she wanted college so she could get a job where she could wear pantyhose and ride the subway and work in an office and be a career woman with an educated man. Not a man like our father.

"What's so bad about a man like Daddy?" I asked.

"I just want somebody with some ambition. I don't wanna be with somebody in dirty overalls, both our backs bent, me, knocked up every year for the rest of my life. Then dead."

"Now you talking about Mama, too? It ain't her fault. It ain't their fault!"

"This ain't about fault. It doesn't have to be our fault for this to be what it is. I'm just saying it doesn't have to be that same way for us if you and me tell Daddy we wanna go—"

"I don't wanna go north. This is our home. I'll save the money, and you can have whatever I make, too. You'll go next year. You'll see."

"Alice, please listen to me—"

"If he made us work during the school year, we could've saved, but he never made us."

"Will you wake up, Alice, and listen to me, girl! I'm trying to get you to see!"

"Rosie, will you just please shut up with this? I'm sorry about your school, but I ain't talking to Daddy about this. So stop asking."

Her frustration turned mocking, as hurtful as I'd ever seen, as she taunted me.

"It's gonna be you knocked up with your back bent over," she said like a curse. "And I—"

"Will you shut up with all this, Rosie? Just shut up with it! Because you crazy if you think you'll ever do better than a patch of land in Alabama or find a man on this earth better than Daddy."

The words stunned her into silence, which is how we finished the walk and supper. After we ate, she told Daddy she was having woman trouble, so he kissed her head and she turned in early. In place of the rent she took when she crept out that night, she left a note promising to send the money back, with interest, when she settled up north. When the crisp bills arrived in an envelope some months later, Daddy refused to touch them, or anything else from her, ever again.

Now, on my wedding day, I wanted to bend that blue ocean sky, meet her on those church steps, and tell her that we had both had it wrong. I wanted to tell her that she could save for college, be a career woman, wear pantyhose, marry an educated man if she wanted. To say, look at me in my Vivian Taylor Laramie original, about to stand up in front of a hundred folks in finery. To shout about men and women in dirty overalls who built this town. I wanted her to meet my man—grandson of a town father, son of a town steward, and father of a new movement, aiming to make New Jessups every place the blue sky touched. But the cars driving by kept driving; the folks walking by kept walking; and only Miss Vivian met me on the steps, blotting the perspiration from my face as she pulled me inside.

After a blur of a ceremony, I had a wedding ring on my finger, a new last name, and a set of lips on mine. During the reception, Dot loudly, and not soberly, announced my conundrum: a delicate lace jacket designed as part of my gown that buttoned, and unbuttoned, in the back. Even that little slip of fabric, something neither me nor Rosie had ever dreamed possible for us. When I scanned my other in-laws for the *lady* Miss Vivian had assured would help me out the jacket, Dot promised that the big bow on my tail meant I was Raymond's present to unwrap. They fell out laughing when Raymond, with his own tipsy smile, pulled the pocket knife out his tuxedo trousers as his proposed solution.

"I know you said you didn't need a honeymoon, but I'm gonna take you somewhere special for the weekend, at least," he said as he turned Blue Lightning away from the home house and deeper into town. We ended up at the Collier House hotel—ten snow-white stories rising to the heavens in the middle of New Jessup. The honeymoon suite had plush cream carpet that swallowed my toes and a floor-to-ceiling view of New Jessup's skyline lit up in the night. A cork popped, and then there was the expensive sound of champagne fizzing into glasses. Raymond wrapped around me from behind, kissed my shoulder, and handed me a coupe. We sipped silently, tangled together and watching headlights below drive to their destinations: the hospital, the jukes, the theaters, the high school on the hill, a drugstore, or just home to lay their heads.

The sweet champagne on his breath wafted to my nose from behind me.

"I don't think I've ever known you to partake of anything other than brown liquor, whiskey and tea, or shine," I said. His soft chuckle vibrated through his chest, against my back, and I hummed my relaxed approval.

"It's true I do enjoy a good nip every now and again. Even champagne, although that ain't for every day or everybody." He pressed soft lips to my shoulder again. "But sometimes, a man likes something sweeter than shine, a little lighter than brown liquor. Something to make his head spin and heart race. Something to let everybody know he has a *hallelujah* on his heart, and maybe, something a little more worldly on his mind. Something on his lips to make him hear color and see sound. Like right now. I could cover my ears and *see* you purring; close my eyes and *hear* that pretty pink on your mouth ready to say my name. Yeah, sometimes a man needs something sweeter than shine, darling. Something to make his head spin and his heart race."

PART TWO

FIFTEEN

Pop limped into the pool of light at the bottom of the porch steps. My feet were in Raymond's lap on the swing, which quieted even its mechanical groaning when Pop's condition came into view: the caked, dried swamp muck to his elbows and knees, and a long slice up the inside of his left pants leg. The ripped fabric flapped, revealing a rag wrapped around where the high top of his boot would have been had it not been missing. We scrambled up and got him inside, coming home like that from a job that wasn't even ours in the first place.

"Ours" since the day Raymond propositioned me in those camellias. "Ours" as in this house, this land, and this business belonged as much to me as them. And if this was to be my land, with every leaf and crumb of soil my responsibility, then so, too, were these to be *my* men to love and care for—both of them. Every eyelash in the eye, every splinter, fever, sore muscle, and hunger pang. So when they came in dragging from the other side of the woods, this whitefolks' towing lit me up inside.

He grimaced in pain with each step, even with an arm draped around Raymond's neck. Knowing what little I knew about towing at the time, how he completed that job was beyond me. We sat him in the kitchen, and I sent Raymond for rags, washcloths, anything absorbent enough to stop the dark puddle forming on the floor underneath Pop's foot. Even unwrapping it was a mess. He flinched at the approach of my touch, but I had to remove the rag still darkening with his blood.

Raymond set the washcloths down by my knee and then started pacing behind me. His steps stuttered when Pop roared after I unloosed the knot and pulled away the makeshift bandage, caked to him with swamp muck mixed with blood like another skin. All because the son of a man with whom Pop had been trading since toy trucks was inheriting the business and decided, one day, that we worked for them.

Negroes had been working across the woods, for folks who paid their wages, since the first Jessup. Buses and cars went and came, carrying hands and hearts experienced in toil and calloused by the resilience they relied on day to day. Like the men who worked at the lumber mill, who caught their cross-woods bus from Mr. Marvin's parking lot. Through the plate glass at the diner, I would watch them close their eyes and take a deep, grateful breath as they returned to New Jessup soil. Some took their lunch pails and walked away, others waited on a New Jessup bus for the final leg of their journey, and still others came into the diner for a meal with friends that sometimes involved conversation about their foreman, Bossman Tate, who was forever calling "y'all niggers" too slow getting across the conveyor while the saw was ripping timber. New Jessup men knew better, and every last one of them agreed that they would stick to how they knew to stay alive. When one day Bossman Tate's tirade ended in a frustrated offer to show "y'all niggers" how to jump the saw, most of the men had sense enough to snap their eyes shut and slap palms over their ears. So they only saw the two halves of Bossman Tate being carried off by the conveyor belt.

But Dale and Raymond Campbell worked for Dale and Raymond Campbell. The paychecks I deposited in the savings and loan were signed by the owners and proprietors of our shop. They were men, mechanics, shop owners; not tools to be picked up, handled, summoned, by anybody. None of that had changed.

Yet calls had started trickling in from Fitzhugh Auto across the woods for favors that only favored them. Even before we married, the phone would ring as I fixed supper or as I was cleaning the dishes. Then, after I moved in, it rang as we settled in for Steve Allen, or on a Sunday after church. Rang after I said "goodnight" to my two men and curled my hair; rang in the middle of our dreams. All because of one time Pop had agreed to help Wade Fitzhugh out a jam, back when there was not a carburetor to be found at the Fitzhugh Auto boneyard.

Thirty years before and across the woods, Fitzhugh had also been a young man with newly inherited businesses when Pop traded him a carburetor for a headlamp he needed. They turned that phone call into a yearslong trading relationship, but Pop had always traveled over there. Not as an employee, or necessarily as a friend, but because neither of them wanted Fitzhugh pointing his car towards New Jessup. And a couple times when Fitzhugh's only wrecker gave him fits all those years ago, Pop jumped in our truck and helped him out once or twice. In thirty years, Campbell Auto had received that call less than enough times to make a handful, and never once had we sent an SOS of our own.

But they were friendly enough as things go. Both men had sons and agreed that separation was best for everybody. So when the Jessup Business Council—a group of white businessmen, state politicians, the sheriff, and other similar local white men—thought to invite a few New Jessup men to participate, Fitzhugh insisted on Pop because he knew every car and driver on our side of the woods. Cap attended as head of our local law, and Mr. Marvin was the third because he

fed every stomach on our side of town. Asked to bring news of instigating after the Supreme Court desegregated the schools in '54, they
assured the council once a month, sometimes twice, that nothing of
the sort was happening. Even if Pop, Cap, and Mr. Marvin heard,
knew about, and quietly handled activities never, never reported in
those meetings.

Earlier in the day when Pop tore up his ankle, I had smelled the
rain. The air was cooling, earthy—the kind that sent the squirrels
scrambling, frantic about the coming change in weather. My men
were sniffly and irritable in the morning, so I invited them home by
their noses with my pot roast for supper. When Raymond came in
alone, I'd blamed the scent of rain. By then, "the favor," as we came
to call it, meant Chase Fitzhugh could be counted on to call over in
nasty or too-pretty weather, claiming that all four of their wreckers
had broken down at the same time. Act of God? Missing screws?
Didn't say.

"Hi Alice! Who's on deck?" was it for explanation.

He had been placed in charge of the towing because, Fitzhugh
told Pop, it was getting time for both of them to pass the torch, and
the father appreciated the "neighborly way" we were "helping the
boy along, giving an old man the freedom to allow his son to find
his own way? Just long enough for the boy to get his feet underneath
him?" "Neighborly" the way Booker T. encouraged Negroes to stick
close and do the work folks across the woods either could not, or
would not, do themselves. But Chase's calls quickly became "neighborly" in the same way as blackdamp—ever present and insidious.

The calls crept up in frequency from a couple times a month to
at least once a week, each time, Chase's tone honing from request
to demand. His voice, fortified by the boundless expectation that
we would hop to, no matter the time, day, or weather, no different
than the downcountry whitefolks I grew up knowing too well—a
hard glare at a Negro suggestion that planting in wet ground would

lead to root rot and a paltry harvest, or a huff about our decision to stay home from work when our bodies were so wracked by coughing spells we couldn't get out the bed. Like when my daddy was coughing, then coughing blood those months before he passed, or when I assured Chase at 1 a.m. that everybody in the Campbell house was down with the flu. Raymond took that call just a few hours later, bundled and slathered in Vicks and still sweating out a fever as he pulled away. Not that Chase had the right to expect anything because "just to help the boy along" was only supposed to be every blue moon, and never supposed to be permanent. Because the Fitzhughs, for better or worse, were our "neighbors."

The night Pop was hurt, a car had run off into the woods deep on the other side of Jessup and crashed into the muck that stole his boot. By the time Raymond came home from the shop, the crisp fall chill had cleared away both the smell of rain, and the dark lambswool clouds from earlier in the day. After supper, in the porch swing, me and Raymond directed our attention and lovers' talk past the grass yard, the cornfield; past the fruit trees and the vegetable patch; past where God just ran out of color, where our own house would be getting underway soon. Until Pop hobbled up the driveway.

Raymond paced behind me, unable to watch or help, except to be slow changing the bowl of water reddening every time I wrang out another rag. The cloths piled up on the floor, bloodied with memories so soaked into the threads they would never wash away.

"I asked what happened to you," Raymond demanded a third time, when his first two times went unanswered.

"That call that came in this afternoon. The car was tore up and stuck pretty good, and then, I had a problem with the winch." Pop winced. The bleeding slowed but had not yet stopped. "I was being careless—tired, you know—smelling the rain coming and rushing. I was trying to get my balance and my foot slipped on the same tree root that snagged the car. That thin, jagged metal sliced me good."

"Why didn't you radio for somebody to come help you?"

Pop turned his head slowly at Raymond, as if repeating himself was almost equal to the pain in his leg.

"Because I was in the muck, son. Having a problem with the winch. And I was rushing, I told you, trying to get back before the storm came in."

Only, there ended up being no storm; just the leaves changing with autumn and my father-in-law bleeding on the kitchen floor, missing a boot, after a tow he never should have been doing in the first place.

WITH TWO MEN IN MY CARE, I rarely gave a second thought to what I had to do, what I had done, to keep them safe. Like with Patience. I had bundled up my talk with Miss Vivian and eased it through the sliver inside me next to the other secrets on my heart, the other words I would never reveal: next to Raymond's work for the NNAS; next to his building cars for the bus boycotts and driving folks around in Montgomery; next to the sunset silhouette that drove me out of Rensler.

The only one who I'd spoken everything on my heart to was Rosie, and even then, I had not heard back. In the space of my distracted thoughts, seeds of wonder sprouted into a question—why had Rosie become frozen in that last letter? Nobody had told me she was gone, and I knew—I just knew—I would feel something if she had passed. So I continued writing my letters—at least once a week, on Thursdays—repeating news of Daddy, leaving Rensler, finding New Jessup, my inheritance at Taylor Made, Patience, the NNAS, municipality, my marriage. My life, piling up, page after page of these new events and secrets—everything nobody else could know.

That Thursday, with Pop's ankle on the mend, and the two of them stuffed full of hoppin' John and collards and engaged in a drowsy disagreement in front of the television, I slipped back to me and Raymond's bedroom and closed the door. With a pen and some stationery, I confessed everything to my sister again, laying out every detail and justification for my part in having Patience sent away. I read the words over again after my tears dried on the paper. They were the only apology I ever meant to utter, especially when, that night, I considered for the first time that maybe my sister would disagree with me about New Jessup, what I had done to protect our way of life. The ink grooved deep into the paper, my words defensive, challenging: "you would have, too . . . " and "this is our way of life . . ." and "you can't judge me without being here." I thought, even hoped in some strange way, that she was refusing to write because of the woman I had become. The woman, I reminded her, she had no hand in raising after she abandoned me in the middle of the night. So at the end, I asked only that she send word that she was safe and I promised to stop bothering her. Just send word. I dug through the desk for a stamp and laid it in the pile for the post box the next day.

With the sunrise, I slipped the letter into my apron pocket. The men were asleep and I stepped through cool morning air thick with a low autumn fog to make my way to the hen house. After a detour twenty steps off my path, I was at the trash barrel, where the paper with my dried tears and defenses and plea for word went up in smoke with a single struck match. "With all my love, your sister Rosie," was how she had ended every letter, including the last one I had from her, dated April 1957. So with all my love, I burned the wounded words I came so close to sending to my sister. In the hazy air over the fire, I tried to envision her face—her eyes, her smile, her nose. But she was drifting from memory's reach.

I stood there and watched the fire, and then, just stood until Raymond came outside and waited silently next to me. His soft, confused eyes questioned why I was burning anything so early in the morning.

"Do you really believe Rosie is dead?" I asked. He exhaled with such pained surprise at the question that I knew he could still hold secrets from me. And while knowing he could keep secrets from me didn't absolve me of having my own, the little pocket inside where I stored all the other confidences opened again and prepared to swallow his lie, told, like mine, for no better reason than love.

"Of course not. I told you . . . I just said that to Percy so he'd leave you alone." After kissing the weak smile hiding his words, and taking one last glance at the ash in the barrel, we went back inside. Where our life—with its joys and heartaches and all—belonged to us and not some man across the woods who refused to stand on his own two feet.

AFTER POP'S ANKLE, the calls slowed but didn't stop. I started seeing them off and waiting up. Although I had come up wearing a scarf over my plaits in the fields for anybody to see, Miss Vivian had assured me that no lady in New Jessup would be caught dead out her house with her hair in curlers and a rag on her head. So if I was up before they left, either for Raymond's Monday night meetings, or if a call came from across the woods, I only pincurled my hair and prepared for bed once my whole house was home.

Most times, it was a couple hours on the living room sofa, or sometimes at the kitchen table next to the phone, which is where I was waiting on Raymond one early morning when the logging truck rumbled by the window. It was late October, and the sweetgum was blazing crimson in the height of fall. I shot up from slumbering on my elbow, thinking it was the wrecker coming back, but when I looked outside, a pickup loaded down with men zipped by on the road as the sun spread across the horizon. Behind it, a logging truck hungry for logs lumbered to the shoulder next to the camellias. The pickup turned off way at the opposite end of the garden, turned left, and disappeared into the pines. I fixed the coffee, looking and listening for any signs of work while I started breakfast, but the distance between us swallowed the roar of any chainsaws and turned swaying treetops into a trick of the wind.

We'd married August 8, 1959, and left the honeymoon suite at the Collier House for Raymond and Percy's old bedroom. It had moss green carpet, car wallpaper, and their two beds pushed together in the middle of the room, short-sheeted by my new in-laws before they left town. He dropped my suitcase and we walked right back out the house, past the high corn, past blood-red roses, through the bursts of hydrangeas, inventing names of colors since God ran out, until we finally stopped at a wall of woods so thick and dark with trees it looked like somebody cut the lights out inside. Behind there was another mess of land belonging to the family, where we'd dreamed about building our own house.

We walked Pop out to the land a few days later, and he craned his neck all the way back, scratching his chin, looking up at the canopy of ancient cypress and live oak extending to the sun. Then he turned his eyes to a line of giant carpenter ants marching across the never-disturbed ferns and moss covering the forest floor as we explained our plans.

"You wanna build . . . way out here?" he asked with amused skepticism.

"It's just on the other side of the garden. This way, we ain't gotta clear any of the fruit trees to make way for the house," Raymond said.

Pop's laugh burst from him so loud and spontaneous it sent the birds fleeing from branches overhead.

"Your husband has finally lost his mind," he said, his shoulders heaving with soundless chuckles. "Y'all don't wanna take down some itty-bitty cherry trees, some little old peach trees, but you wanna down these thousand-year-old cypress?" He laughed so hard he looked to be choking on the sound. It was teasing fun, if just around the bend from ridicule. "I'm old enough to remember what it took to clear these trees, all these men out here. Why do you think so much of it's still standing at the edges of town?"

He cared nothing about me and Raymond's conversation with Harold Jenkins about the project. That builder didn't have equipment fancy enough, Pop told us, to finish our house before Easter. But the Jenkins had driven nails in the first Jessup, and every Jessup since, Harold boasted as he inspected the site, gave one or two of the trees a fleshy slap, and declared that we needed five bedrooms, not four. Four bathrooms, not just three. Two stories, and not just one with all this good wood.

Pop straightened up and looked over to his place. The way his face fell, the other side of the garden may as well have been the end of the earth. It was close enough to see his house as a speck off in the distance, but far enough that a holler would disappear in the air between us. A two-minute drive, I measured, from door to door.

"See? Two minutes," Raymond said when I objected that it was too much house for Pop alone and worried about his laundry, his meals, his nighttime company. Who needs all that space to be alone? I argued. With nothing bouncing around, no life to fill it or soak into the walls. To sit with the quiet company of nothing. Thinking of that, watching him crane his neck, squint his eyes, and look off towards his place, I promised him a room in our house big as me and Raymond's bedroom (bigger, even!). They raised those identical eyebrows at me. Pop snorted his appreciation.

"Thank you for your charity, Alice," he said, "but I have a home, right off yonder. Y'all are welcome to visit any time."

CYPRESS LOGS TWICE AS THICK as a man is tall lined the truck bed when I got home that first day, and it seemed things would go smoothly. It crawled by the kitchen window on four near-flat tires to offload at the lumber mill. All that, but in the distance, it hardly looked like a single leaf had fallen. After carrying on like that for another day or two, inside the wall of trees was a forest of stumps.

Raymond drove we three into a dining room fit for giants one crisp night after supper. The Studebaker crawled through such dense pine and magnolia that the thick, gnarled branches groaned and snapped against the metal. The trees swallowed the tire-track driveway behind us and hugged us tight inside, where the golden hearts of stumps big as eight-tops glowed softly in the moonlight. We three climbed atop one and soaked in a midnight sky priceless with diamonds, out there in me and Raymond's Alabama. Raymond inhaled the enchantment deep into his lungs, and with his arm wrapped around me, my head against his chest, I heard his heartbeat quicken just before he continued words started between them earlier in the day at the shop.

"See, Pop? I told you these trees would come down quick."

Pop snorted and laid his head back, resting on the tree's golden heart.

"*Heh heh*, yeah. But what about these stumps?"

"Harold said the excavator'll make quick work of the stumps."

When Pop stopped cackling, he said, "Alright. But back in the day, the old-timers used dynamite."

"Say old man, speaking of the old-timers?" Raymond started before he paused. "You . . . know that thing we were talking about earlier?"

"This again?"

"Will you just hear me out?"

"Go on ahead with your fairy tale," Pop sang dismissively. I squeezed around Raymond's waist to give him a little courage.

"You're sitting in my living room right now, old man. You know that? So you gonna hear me out or what?"

"I'm sitting on a cypress stump right now, Raymond," he said. "A cypress stump that Harold'll need dynamite to get rid of, you watch what I'm telling you. *Boom*." But Pop was at home atop that tree, eyes closed underneath our saints watching from above. "Same as they used when I was in short pants, living in these woods with New Jessup coming up around me. So before you say anything, remember that Big Poppa built all this up with his mind bent on Negroes owning the land, whether we were our own city or not. So why now?"

I had not imagined how, when, or if he would broach the subject of municipality with his Pop. We had not discussed it, and I figured news of seeking city status and any revelation about his work with the NNAS would go hand in glove. Which meant I thought it was Raymond's news to share. So as I listened to his heart pounding, and his words, to reveal the whole truth of his doings, my heart started beating a little fast, too, since I had also kept this secret about the NNAS from Pop.

As Raymond explained about dollars and dimes, wanting to preserve what the town fathers built, a star's mischievous wink brought to mind Mama and Daddy and white Jesus. Rensler was the kind of segregated where whitefolks went anywhere they pleased. Including Mount Glory Baptist—a church house full of Negroes—where a giant picture of white Jesus hung behind the altar on Sundays though we had not a single white worshipper among us. Yet there He was, arms outstretched with ruddy, pink skin, and long, wavy brown hair offering salvation.

But when I was little, Mama would drag feet on Sundays. When we were just ready to go, she'd say, "C'mon, let's all go pray to white Jesus." Me and my sister would laugh, because of course Jesus was white. He was right up there over the pulpit, and all around Rensler, whitefolks seemed to be doing just fine. Without cracking a smile, Daddy would tell me and my sister to pray for Mama and ourselves. That we were raised in a church of godliness, and we were to repent and ask for His grace.

But one Sunday, under that portrait, Pastor preached 1 John 1:8–9.

"If we say we have no sin, we deceive ourselves, and the truth is not in us. If we confess our sins, He is faithful and just to forgive our sins and cleanse us from all unrighteousness."

Forgiveness from *all* unrighteousness? For the sale of my daddy and the nigger baths and the sunset silhouette trying to drag me behind the toolshed? For 1903 and the swamp? All manner of hatefulness forgiven, and a place in heaven assured, because of words confessed with a last, miserable breath? Under that beautiful night, as the star winked at me and our kin watched us from above, the same question formed in my mind that I'd had when I was a little girl: who was seated next to my folks? My people? Was the rich reward we had been promised for our earthly suffering only an eternal blackdamp? Because it seemed no kind of heaven for Negroes if our tormentors could just apologize and follow us right into the stars.

"It ain't about desegregation, Pop." Raymond continued a thought I'd missed. "I can assure you me and Alice's children will go to New Jessup schools with students and teachers who look like them. But since the beginning of time, whitefolks hear 'integration' and they automatically call it 'infiltration,' when Negroes around here ain't even interested in fellowship. We want our resources. The nickels and dimes we're already owed without them telling us how to spend it. Nothing more."

"You think they won't fight you over nickels and dimes, son? That was greed and envy in the hearts of men driving us into the swamp, just *because* we had some coin to our names."

"I know it, but at least we take mixing off the table. Look, you got a better solution, Pop, I'm all ears. But I don't want my kids in a desegregated school, and this movement has new life on both sides. For whitefolks, that's young blood reviving old ideas about violence and intimidation. For us, it's fresh ways of thinking, including this. We can't stop this momentum, but we can take this energy and make something for ourselves. We already have separation here, and it works."

With his head still rested in his hands, his back still on the stump, Pop trained his gaze on me.

"Did you know about this municipality scheme, too? First I ever heard anybody in this house mention this was today." He seemed unsurprised about my sheepish shrug. "So you want this too, then? You're on board with it?" he asked me.

"I don't want New Jessup to change, if that's what you asking. I want our people to stay separate, to have our own heaven here on earth, and I can only hope it's like this for our kin up there, too."

He sat up then, looking steadily at Raymond, and I braced myself to hear him admit his doings with the NNAS.

"Tell me the truth?" Pop said.

"Truth," promised Raymond.

"Your Monday nights playing cards with the fellas? This is what y'all been cooking up all along?"

"Yessir, for a while there. Till all that business with Patience, anyway. Been laying low since then. But we have a short window for a big change, so," he paused, and I just knew the whole truth was in his lungs, waiting to pass his lips, "it would sure mean a lot to have your blessing. Maybe you could help smooth the way with some of the old heads for us? You always said Campbell meant something in this town. That it was our duty to put our community first. This is me, the rest of the fellas, trying to do that."

The opportunity for truth came and went on the breath leaving his mouth. Floated off and vanished. Pop looked at Raymond with a mixture of pride and fear in his eyes. Then me. He stared at us for a long time before he leaned back on top of the stump in our living room, looking up at our saints as they winked, spied, and protected us from their place inside the sky. Then, he said, with equal parts apology and permission,

"You do what's best for your family, son. That's all a man can ever do."

SIXTEEN

Even the sprinkling of carols from the supermarket speakers seemed unable to soothe Percy into conversation at first. He followed me around the store like a man who never set foot inside a grocery: hovering at my shoulder, watching me check prices and pick the brands I thought best, peering at the labels like he was newly discovering the idea of selection. When we reached the end of the aisles, he placed a hand on the front of the buggy, telling me to wait while he looked left and right, like we were crossing an intersection in the car. We only started talking in earnest about halfway into the trip, just when we reached the baking aisle.

He was only with me because Dot twisted both our arms after he showed up to the house full of Christmas cheer for everybody, and a slight winter's chill just for me. Me and Dot spent mornings together while the men walked, and worked, the job site before breakfast—her, rubbing a seven-months round belly and eyeballing my flat one. Squirming and shifting, she breathed hard, trying to get comfortable as the baby twisted around inside her.

"Mama Cat always told me these Campbell babies are hard to birth, but easy to love," she said, rubbing her stomach and trying to put a brave face on the baby giving her fits. But she seemed pale and tired, like being big hurt her, though she insisted I lay a hand on her belly to feel the baby kicking. That child kicked three times—*whack, whack, whack*—not once, and I joked that she was too small to be expecting such a mean-seeming baby.

"My baby isn't mean," she scolded as she winced and grabbed her back like he was mean. "Just active, and that's a good thing. Besides, you know any child of Percy Charles Campbell has to start life fussing about something." She winced again and put her cup down, changing the subject.

"You wouldn't even know there's a house being built out there," she said, looking out the window towards the pines.

"It's just a big patch of mud right now, but it's supposed to be done before Easter," I said. "Harold says after the holidays, it'll go quick. But Harold *always* says it'll go quick."

She nodded absentmindedly as she sat back in her chair, looking out the window. Her eyes didn't even register my joke; instead, she just looked outside at our land, deep in thought, with the common sigh, and the drifting eyes, of a Negro woman somehow exhausted by the world. Her eyes squeezed at some memory she kept to herself, and I dared not ask what ached her other than the baby, because she would tell if she wanted to tell. I needed not know the particulars of slight to know the look and language of hurt, to know the world well enough to know how hard she was working to keep this wound from stilling her heart. But her voice—breathy, soft, and slower than I had ever heard—surprised me with something other than the sadness behind her smile.

"We're coming home, you know. Me, Percy, and the baby. He wants to be in New Jessup, to work with Raymond, to raise our family here," she said.

"I never heard a bigger lie," I told her. She smiled and shook her head that quick way that said she was satisfied with my reaction to her surprise. "Dorothy, you talking about *your* husband? My brother-in-law? Percy *Charles* Campbell?"

"Unless you know another one."

"Well, he must've been body snatched, then, to be talking about coming home to New Jessup, Alabama."

"You'd better hush talking about my husband like that."

"I'm just saying . . . now, I have *really* heard it all."

"Yeah, honey. He's planning to tell Pop and Raymond at breakfast. By the time we laid head to pillow last night, he'd already plotted our house right next to yours, down to the paint on the walls."

"What color paint then?"

She smiled and looked at me with the sparkles returned in her eyes.

"You hardly have to ask. Whatever Raymond picked, you know."

"And he's . . . gonna join Raymond for those meetings, too?"

She nodded.

"Percy has his own mind, make no mistake about that. But Raymond does know how to move his brother. Sometimes, it's talking. Sometimes, they used to tussle—you saw that at Christmas last year, and lord, I hope that season of their lives is over. But mostly, when the talking doesn't work, Raymond just . . . does his own thing. No words; just deeds. Percy can't help but notice, think on it, and then poke out his chest like it was his idea all along. Just like he is about this move, bless his little heart; he's pretending to forget that I've been wanting to come home since college. But my husband is a smart man, Alice, and he can be reasonable, given some time, you know?" There was a soft edge of pleading and demand in her voice. "Like when I told him last night he'd better not plan on feuding with my sister-in-law forever, and you and him need to have a conversation. He grumbled about it before going to sleep but woke up saying he thought y'all should talk. Whatever. Just have a conversation with him? For me?"

So with Percy behind Blue Lightning's wheel, the two of us drove to the supermarket for ginger ale, canned pineapple, and some other things we needed on Christmas Eve. Along the way, he ground the gears and complained that "they" had yet to fix my car properly although an entire year had passed. But other than wishing they had listened to him about the water pump, the ride was jerky and quiet. When we arrived at the ginger ale, he picked up the Schweppes and I grabbed the store brand.

"That's high today," I said. "And I have a coupon for this other one."

"But this is the one she keeps at the house." I put mine back and he placed his in the buggy. Then, he watched me put 7-Up in the cart with a slight, questioning frown. "She likes this one," he said about the Schweppes again.

"Ginger Ale's for her. 7-Up's for the cake." He nodded and we moved on in silence that felt like somebody needed to fill it as we next wound our way down the baking aisle.

"I'm glad to hear we'll be neighbors," I told him. He nodded and scanned some prices for instant pudding. "Your brother, Pop, they over the moon. Your father told me him and Miss Catherine always thought their closest grandbabies would be in Montgomery."

"Yeah, they used to say that all the time. Trying to guilt Regina and Edward or Trevor and Emma Jean to move back, or at least come home more often." He picked up a can of evaporated milk, bounced it in his hand, and placed it back, label front, on the shelf.

"I'm glad, too."

"Yeah? I know you and Dot are close. She's happy, I'm happy." Safely around another corner, he walked next to me with eyes now averting the Kotex.

"And I know you and your brother are close. I'm glad you'll be working with him again—I know he misses that. And I'm thinking that, since y'all are close, and me and Dot are close, and him and her are close, and me and Raymond are close, and me and Pop are close and you and Pop are close—"

"*Mmm-hmm*—" He raised an eyebrow.

"That maybe you and me can try being real friends."

"I know Dot wanted us to talk, and Raymond told me you heard what I said last year on the porch."

"Both those things can be true, Percy, and I can still mean what I say. I ain't got no quarrel with you. Never did, if I'm honest, because I know what it is to miss your mama, your kin, at Christmastime. But there's enough people in the world telling us we ain't worth nothing for family to be breaking apart over some stupid words."

"You think so?"

"I know so. I come from people, too, remember. Everybody says things we wish we could take back, but there comes a time to let it go," I said, talking to him, praying to Rosie.

While he thought on my words in the aisles—checking products, asking about this and that with mild enthusiasm—I could tell he was using the silences to work something out in his head, like Dot said. So no real thawing occurred until we finished our shopping, he put the packages in the trunk, and he got back behind the wheel.

"New Jessup has grown up so much since I was a little boy. Being away, and then coming back home, I can see that now. You know, when you're growing right alongside a city, you don't always see it. But I remember when there was nothing super about this market. It was too small to serve the community back then. And now, look. We have a Custer's General Store on one end of town, and Brooks Supermarket on the other, all owned and run by Negroes.

"As a boy, I couldn't understand what a big deal Negro ownership was because I didn't know any different. I knew Fitzhugh owned his place, and that we owned our shop and didn't see any difference between Pop and him. Don't get me wrong; I knew they were white-folks, and that they lived 'on the other side of the woods,' not to be trifled with. But they weren't here, either. We were. This was ours."

"I still wake up sometimes thinking that shoeshine man at the Greyhound station is playing tricks," I told him.

"Shoeshine man?" He smiled his confusion.

"Story for another day."

"Well, Dot's wanted to come home since we finished at State. I refused outright, told her that New Jessup was full of backward thinking Booker T. Negroes who couldn't see the swamp for the trees. *Ha*. And you should've heard the conversations I had with Raymond about coming back."

"I heard *one*, remember."

He winced and blushed at my little joke.

"I am sorry. I never meant for you to hear that."

"Go ahead, Percy. You were saying? About coming home?"

"Well, when you asked me where I sit on the bus, and why? *Hoo*, did you ever yank my chain! I was so mad I had to get up and walk away from you, girl. Talked Dot's ear off about it that night till she threatened to put me on the couch in my own mama's house. But you? Challenging *me* about integration? Some woman popping out my mama's house wearing her apron? How dare you." He threw a wry smile at me that hinted almost as handsome as Raymond's. "But you were right: I was killing my spirit to make a point. This is a fight about resources, so let it be about resources alone and let's quit fussing about the things we *don't* want, which for me, was that seat on the bus.

"I stopped all that worrying, all that wondering with those kill-you-quick thoughts—the kind that fester and eat you up inside. Does this woman next to me despise me or will she tolerate me? Does this man maybe even respect me? And if he does respect me, what happens when somebody who doesn't respect me gets on this bus and sees us sitting together, maybe talking? What if the one who can't stand the sight of me has a friend who decides they don't mind me, but the friend also wouldn't mind seeing me get my head bashed against the window? And if it is a white woman sitting next to me . . . what if I bump her purse, or worse, her arm, or worse, her leg? It ain't always the consequences that'll kill you quick, but the imaginings of the consequences eating you up inside."

"Yeah, all that blackdamp. All that wondering just worrying the life, the spirit right outta you."

"What do you know about blackdamp?"

"My daddy was in a mine accident as a boy. He just died a couple years back. It's why I came here." He nodded his condolences with his eyes on the road. "And when he got sick, near the end there, he swore the blackdamp finally caught up with him. Couldn't stop coughing, could hardly ever catch his breath. It was awful to watch him suffer like that." The view outside the window was blurred by his speed, and by the tears filling my eyes. "But he said the coughing? He'd been expecting something like that. To lose his breath one day. That he'd felt that blackdamp in his head his entire life. He wasn't scared of dying, he told me. He said he wished he hadn't spent every day of his life *thinking* about dying, scared to trust the air."

"Damn. I am *so* sorry, Alice," he said with enough force behind his words to release the last of the dam blocking his heart for me. He patted my knee and I let the tears clouding my eyes finally fall down my cheeks.

CLIFFORD EUGENE CAMPBELL II was born in early February 1960. Raymond had picked up the phone expecting to hear Chase on the line at that hour, but soon called from the kitchen with the excitement. Dot had a rough delivery, but both her and baby were doing fine, and when Raymond said the name aloud, me and Pop had to take a seat. Pop was teary-eyed that Percy—*Percy*—named his son after a New Jessup founding father. Especially after months of bragging that a boy would be Percy, Jr.

"Hot damn, a boy!" said Pop like a broken record with red-rimmed eyes. Then, he'd say, "A boy, hot damn! Clifford Eugene Campbell the second. And they're coming home. They are coming home!"

The call started us three talking about family. What it meant, and what it meant to be taken away. Even though the towing was still occasional, it was coming regularly enough that Raymond had dragged feet getting to the phone. Fitzhugh and Pop were still the old heads in charge, so my father-in-law insisted they be the ones to have the conversation. In every neighborly way, Pop meant to end that towing for good.

"We've been trading since toy trucks," he said. "Serving together on the council for years. This all started because he said Chase needed some help coming along, but he should be 'along' well enough by now. We're family men. Fitzhugh should get that." I don't know if he believed he could change it or not. But overjoyed by the baby news, he said it.

Those days, Campbell Auto was fixing cars from *can't see* to *can't see*, and they needed help. Lisle Morris had long since wanted to quit the timber mill, and Thomas Morris was looking for something other than his work as a bouncer around Pinckney Ave., so Raymond convinced Pop to bring them on at the shop. Percy and Dot had their Clifford and their house underway, me and Raymond were nearly finished planting the vegetable garden for the year and our house was almost complete, me and Miss Vivian were birthing pastel Easter dresses, and the whole of it was wearing us out, even as the towing slowed. Then one day, I woke up with my head swimming and feeling bleary-eyed in the spring of 1960. I made breakfast and prepared lunches and got us all out the door as usual, hoping it would be a quiet, early night. But as I pushed up from the stool to turn the sign at Taylor Made, Miss Vivian—standing next to me—separated into three of herself.

"Alice?" all three Miss Vivians said, with their twelve eyes regarding me. "Are you alright? Because you look quite grim." The Miss Vivians started chasing each other around, faster and faster like they were going down a drain, dragging the rest of the color and light of the world with them. I closed my eyes, but the night behind my eyelids was spinning, too. A heavenly drain of light that refused to empty.

"Alice!" she called out as I crashed into a rack of Easter dresses due for delivery in a few hours. She called my name, over and over, as she dug me from a mountain of silk and chiffon. I laid there with the world spinning, unable to move.

Miss Vivian put me on the sofa in her office with a cold compress over my eyes and called Raymond. She told him to bring me home and put me to bed right away. But as the world blurred by in Blue Lightning, and as the car stopped and started at the lights, my eyes could find no focus. Horns honking, car doors shutting, people shouting, flowers blooming, everything tapped from the tin can of my inner ear. With my head in my hands, we rode along until the car jolted to a stop. I erupted sick all over the seats, and Raymond's three stricken faces followed suit right away.

We crawled into the house and he cleaned us up and put me to bed, sitting with me until we both fell asleep. As the light faded with the day, I woke to Pop in the doorway with a medicine bottle and a soup spoon.

"Mrs. Laramie called the shop, said you fainted and asked if Raymond got you home okay," he said, screwing his lips into a frown at his son, wrapped around me from behind. Pop shook his head. "You still dizzy?" he asked me.

"*Mmm-hmm*," I said, too afraid to even nod. "We both got sick, so don't get too close. Might be something going around."

Pop snorted and rolled eyes. "Raymond's got a weak constitution. Never could be around sick without joining in. But what I suppose you got is what Catherine had with Trevor. Don't look at me like that. She had no problems with Regina—at least, not that I knew about. An easy baby even through delivery. But then came my boys. With Trevor, she had these fainting spells, like what you're having. All the doctors wanted to run tests like they do on the women across the woods, but my mama said, 'she ain't sick; she big.'"

Pop smiled, letting his eyes float towards Raymond, lying behind me with his hand draped over my stomach. "With Raymond? She had terrible indigestion, and, um, wind coming from all over her body. Said she was on fire inside. Percy? He was all of it, plus a sick stomach, and he was active. Punching, kicking, I bet screaming if I listened. I should've known about that boy," he laughed to himself. "So seems like you have a Trevor going on."

Even sucking teeth at my father-in-law made me mildly woozy, so I settled into the pillow and locked my lips tight in protest of the hundred-year-old ginger tonic he poured in the spoon and put to my face. A Trevor, he called my dizziness. Even if, as he talked, my stomach felt full. Like I had eaten an entire meal, although I had been sick all day. After I told him to get his crusty bottle away from my face, he left to get some fresh tonic from the drug store. Raymond glowed like a new star. In the middle of my husband grilling me excitedly about how I was feeling, what I was feeling, whether I knew I was expecting for sure, and didn't I know Campbells make boys, the phone rang.

He got up and took the call. Still dizzy, I held the wall all the way down the corridor, reaching the kitchen door just in time to hear him hang up. I wore complaint on my face.

"I'm having a baby," he said with excitement in his voice. "You better believe we're gonna end this towing for good, darling. Soon," he promised. "Meantime, just stay in the bed for me? I'll be back before you know it. Alright?"

Although he walked me back to the bedroom, tucked me in, pulled coveralls over his clothes, and kissed me goodbye, by the time the wrecker was pulling past the house on the way to the road, I was watching him leave from the picture window.

SEVENTEEN

Me and Raymond agreed that the NNAS work was all his. I was nothing like Patience and felt fine sending him to meet with the fellas in Hugo Greene's old father's cottage—a one-room house, no bigger than where I grew up—built, as the town fathers had built as young fathers, to be a refuge for their families. Just in case. Hidden, and secure enough to be safe, many of the cottages had been allowed to disintegrate from lack of use over time—a testament to the optimism that our city would be ours forever. Clifford Campbell's cottage was the most optimistic of all, with its caved-in roof, broken windows, and walls sagging towards each other as if deflated. But Hugo had fixed up his family's cottage to be a usable hunting cabin and offered it for their meetings. Raymond described it as a pile of sticks coming from the earth that looked like the earth was coming back for it. The only eyes on them out there, he said, had four legs, glowed in headlamps, and responded slowly to warning shots. So they were safe in the middle of a swamp and its slow-to-react eyes, inside a shack so full of holes Raymond came home perfumed of cypress and open-hearted moonflowers. At home, me and him dreamed together. About municipality and what it meant, sometimes, with him falling asleep to my whispers of "Mr. Mayor" in his ear.

It took about two weeks to confirm that I was expecting. Raymond glowed like new money, boasting to Percy on the phone as I finished fixing supper the night we got the news. But his good humor evaporated almost as soon as he hung up. Over my shoulder, he flipped pages back on the wall calendar. They slid backwards from April—March, with a look in my direction, February, January, and the *thump, thump, thump* with his forefinger for all the Xs and Os I had ignored in 1959, breaking promise after promise to quit Taylor Made. O, the circle around the day I would give my notice. X, the countdown. Over and again, I had circled a new date, fixed fried catfish or baked chicken thighs or other such favorites, and kept working. We went on like that for months after we married, but the day Doc Patterson confirmed I was expecting, Raymond thumped his demand on the calendar.

"I remember us saying it was finally time to sit you down, darling," he said to me. "Months ago."

Pop came into the kitchen, saw Raymond punching his finger, scooped mashed potatoes, string beans, and the big piece of chicken, and took his supper to the family room, where he cut the TV on to a Western blaring gunfire.

"Raymond, I quit Mr. Marvin's before we married," I reminded him. "I'm hardly on my feet at Miss Vivian's, mostly sitting at the sewing machine."

He looked at me, his eyes softened by my lie. With lips pursed in the tiniest sliver of an apologetic smile, he shook his head so slightly it was almost impossible to see.

"Thought Doc Patterson said these dizzy spells were from your pressure."

I nodded, started to say something, though I didn't know what at first. Certainly not my dream of one day owning Taylor Made, which had never been spoken. When tongues have the power of life and death, it had always seemed safer somehow to write my dreams to Rosie. Raymond was born into his inheritance—the shop, the land, everything flowed to him as a birthright. To me by marriage, yes. But I hoped that, somehow, Taylor Made could flow to me without having to speak for it, beg for it. That maybe I could have his same dignity of expectation.

So first, I made some joke about idle hands that just clouded his face in confusion. Then, he just held the pen to the calendar to circle the date himself.

"Raymond!" I called with an urgency that caused him to look at me over his shoulder. The pen stayed poised and ready to strike. "I thought maybe, one day, one day, baby, with her girls not wanting it, Miss Vivian's shop might . . . become . . . mine." He turned fully around then and lowered the pen. "She took a chance on me when she didn't have to. Taught me all sorts of things about sewing, New Jessup. Always treated me like her own, so I thought . . . maybe. You can understand that, can't you? You have the shop, something for you." He paused and let out the sigh of a man already decided. A man trying to soften the blow of taking away my every day, and my future, at Taylor Made. Or maybe he knew enough about how things really worked to know I was only dreaming.

"You know, Mama had heart problems for a lotta years," he told me.

"I know." My hope deflated as he stepped towards me, covering me in his shadow.

"So your pressure is nothing to trifle with as far as I'm concerned. Not to mention that we already agreed you'd quit."

"I know."

"I know you're close with her," he said. "So you go see her as much as you like. Every day if you want. But with you having my baby. Especially with your pressure, Alice . . . it's just time." He put the pen in my hand and closed my fingers around it. "Now, put your circle on the calendar and we're gonna hold to it this time."

TWO MORE WEEKS OF XS AND OS went by without a word to Miss Vivian about quitting. When circle day arrived, I planned catfish. Distractedly tapping her pen against the countertop, she wondered, aloud, yet to nobody in particular, whether it planned to rain outside. Suddenly, she snapped to attention, looked at me, and, with a slight frown, disappeared into the stockroom.

She returned with an armload of our store boxes, from large to tiny, made of deep garnet cardboard and with VTL stamped in gold foil on top. The mark of her true originals, except for the one at the very top, which was robin's egg blue. She slid it all across the glass to me.

"What's this?" I asked her.

"You won't know until you open it," she said, smiling.

Soft knit, gingham, voile, lace, and plaid knit maternity dresses piled high in the larger boxes. They were so soft—too soft to wear, and too expertly made to believe they were just for me to get big. There were two new hats and a black leather pocketbook closer to the top of the cake of boxes, with the robin's egg blue the last box she wanted me to open. It was about the size of my hand, had a top and bottom, and a fancy white ribbon holding it together.

"There's no reason to be slovenly just because you're expecting," she said, watching me marvel over the gifts. I tugged the satin bow on the blue box. Inside, wrapped in soft cream silk, rested a silver rattle with *Tiffany* stamped on the bottom. The metal felt smooth and cool to the touch, and the inside swished as I waved it next to my ear.

"Oh, thank you, Miss Vivian. This is all very generous." I smiled, if sort of confused, because no names had been discussed this early on.

"Tiffany's is the brand," she laughed softly, catching sight of my confusion. "This is a special time for you, and I wanted you to have all of this. Today. Because I'm afraid I'm going to have to let you go."

With reassuring grace, she told me that she never employed expecting mamas in the shop, just as Earnestine walked from the office to the dressing room with a swag of lace draped over her forearms and just-showing bump. I did not dare accuse her of going along with whatever scheme Raymond put to her, though it was unsurprising that she would—married folks' business was not her business, and she would never interfere in decisions between husband and wife. So there was no begging or pleading to change her mind. Decision made, my quarrel wasn't with Miss Vivian.

I gathered my things and left, gaining steam during the ride home. Planning to tear past the house and towards the shop, I slammed brakes when I saw Raymond in the yard. His neck was bent over a clipboard with the Jensen's Furniture truck driver, and they disappeared into the dust cloud when my car skidded to a stop. He emerged with a half-amused, half-confused grin propping up one of his cheeks.

I raised slowly from the car. Knowing what he did, and why I was racing into the driveway before the 10 a.m. sun, he must have banked on me not showing out in front of company. But he was mistaken; I didn't know that man with the clipboard, or the other ones waiting in the truck, all averting my gaze like men caught somewhere they'd rather not be. I glared at Raymond from behind the car door, wishing he would say one mumbling word to my face. He said six.

"Just in time, darling. Furniture's here."

I slammed that car door.

"You smiling in my face? Something funny to you, Raymond? Let's see if you still smiling when I get rid of some things you love most."

Storming up the porch, through the house, and to the bedroom, I had designs on a dresser drawer full of things he refused to pitch but would never miss—his high school varsity track letter; a tin of jacks with half the pieces missing; a plaster mold of a leaf; a small piece of fool's gold; a broken watch—all piled atop some old T-shirts and socks with stretched, brown elastic. He was right on my heels, talking fast about how we had agreed this would be my last day and that I needed to calm down because of my pressure. That hardly helped. I yanked the drawer out the dresser and turned it over on the bed. Everything spilled out. He kept talking as a navy-blue folder from the Himes Insurance Agency, thick with papers, fell from the bottom of the drawer to the top of the heap.

It slid to the floor and splayed open. Three sheafs of paper, each held together by a staple, fluttered to the ground throughout the room. The one with "burial policy" landed face up next to my foot. The others fell further away from me, and while I bent down, transfixed by the clump of papers next to my toes, he picked the others up from the ground. And then, while I read, he started talking again. But I heard nothing for those minutes as I read his final wishes for a closed casket wake and cremation.

"I put that at the bottom of that drawer to forget about it," he said. "And I guess I did forget about it."

"What is this, Raymond?" He came no closer when I held the paper in the air next to my face. With a deep sigh, he pulled his lips over his teeth like even that heavy breath was an admission.

"It came from a Monday night."

"And? Don't get closed-mouthed on me now. I am not in the mood."

"We agreed you'd stay outta NNAS business. Remember?"

"What else you got in your hand, there?" After a moment's hesitation, he handed me a life insurance policy and the last will and testament of Raymond Louis Campbell, signed, witnessed, and notarized. "This is NNAS business? Not mine, is what you telling me?"

"If you needed it, the fellas knew about it."

"I ain't talking about the fellas, baby. I'm talking about you and me and you doing things behind my back. What's this all about?"

"I wanna keep Monday nights outta here."

"Only, this is in the bottom of your drawer." I shook the cremation paper at him. "You ain't asking the fellas to do this. You asking me." He considered me, running his fingers over his lips the way he did when he was thinking through his words. I didn't know how immediate my concern should be—whether something had happened, or was getting ready to happen to him—but the quiet provided fertile ground for fear to blossom with possibility inside my head. And that scared me to tears.

But he would not, could not, be rushed, and spoke in his own time. So fighting back those tears, fighting fear, I waited until he spoke.

"During a meeting a while back—before Patience was put out—me and Matthew started talking about the bus in Montgomery. Then Hugo jumped in about getting stopped by some redneck police on a back road while him and Emma Jean were driving to their honeymoon. Major was shot in Korea and almost died because the medic only gave him a transfusion of white blood under threat of court-martial. The jeers and threats Patience endured onstage, city by city, as a *professional* dancer. Thomas visiting their grandmama down country. Abel buying cigarettes. And *Jesus Christ*, Lisle at the lumber mill? By the end of the night, we were drowning in each other's miseries. All of us." He sighed. "The flood of untold stories between us that night, Alice. You just never know. You just never know."

My rage about Taylor Made wouldn't hold after my newlywed husband—a twenty-seven-year-old man with cars for wallpaper and our first baby on the way—revealed that he was planning to be burned up in anticipation of the imaginative cruelty of whitefolks. His final wish, to hide the remains of his last horrifying moments so he could rest in peace. Disappointment and anger still flooded my body, yes. But rage grows and gloms onto other fury, and the wrath of whitefolks anticipated in these papers was nothing I cared to join against my husband, who stood there, alive, with toes wiggling in his socks. My eyes traveled to his grease-blackened knees, then, to his hands, the red-stitched nametag over his heart, all leading up to a face with deep worry lines squinted between his grays, which were floating above dark circles.

My rage wouldn't hold, although this was Raymond—again— insisting, when he got me fired. Insisting on being the man turning the world. Fixing cars the way he insisted, keeping the books the way he insisted, nitpicking two construction sites at his insistence, going to his meetings at his insistence, pursuing municipality, then the vote, at his insistence! When I looked at him, at the dark circles under his eyes, seeing the toll of all that insisting, world-turning, he stood there, a man exhausted. With those papers in my hand saying "cremation," anger, frustration—resentment, even—would all have their day. But not rage when the world outside New Jessup harbored every sort of fatal rage for a Negro with cars on his wallpaper.

"I didn't tell you because I wanna keep Monday night talk outta here," he said again. "I come home to you to dream, darling. To live. Sometimes, as much love as I have for the fellas, and for the work, sometimes, it's suffocating to talk about whitefolks' dirt *all the time*. Like we're just reacting instead of growing our community in ways the old heads never dreamed! Into the future. The focus should be on us, living fully independent of some old rednecks that ain't never gonna change." His fists were clenched and trembling, so I dropped the papers on the bed and wrapped my hands around his, letting the tears fall down my face. A touch I needed to give, and, as his hands relaxed and unclenched, a feeling I needed to feel.

"And I'm sorry about Miss Vivian," he went on. "But you're up all night, waiting on us with this towing, keeping the house, working the garden, working a full-time job, and now you're expecting? This sickness? I didn't ask for your hand to worry you to death."

"You ain't gotta worry about all that, baby. Home is fine, and Doc Patterson said I just need a little rest, is all."

"Home ain't fine unless I'm providing for my family. If I'm not, none of this other work is worth the aggravation. Now, I'm sorry about Miss Vivian—"

"You don't know how sorry you about to be, Raymond Campbell," I grumbled without any teeth to it. "You always trying to fix things, but I—"

"I am truly sorry, Alice. But I just wanna care for you like you deserve." I met his lowered neck and pleading eyes with lips pressed tight, refusing the smile he was looking for. He wiped at the salty trails on my cheeks with his working man's thumbs.

"Had nerve asking for cabbage with supper tonight, knowing I was getting fired today. Did she . . . ?" I started to ask whether Miss Vivian objected, talked to him sternly, asked him to reconsider when he called her. But it hardly mattered, so I thought better than to feed more disappointment to the lump in my throat. He waited for my question. "Some nerve, indeed," I told him.

"Well, tell me about myself after we get this furniture settled? She was supposed to talk to you at the end of the day, give me time to get the house together. But it's finished."

We got into the Studebaker and made our way behind the pines. Our house appeared in the hazy forest sunshine as though it had always been there hiding in the trees, just waiting on us to come home. Those old cypress, now our new house, whispering their return to the woods.

Harold and his crew were hard at work nearby, installing the septic at Percy and Dot's. He looked up from some blueprints and waved us in with machines whirring behind him.

"It's finished?" I asked. Raymond shrugged, smiling as the soft light cast a spell over me. I looked at the front door, knowing, but still dreaming about, what lay inside. "And it's ours?" He nodded.

Ours. The roundness of the word was almost too big to form my mouth around it.

We walked every inch of that empty house while the movers waited outside. I ran a hand over the creamy yellow of the walls, the glossy white windowsills. We glided stocking feet over heart pine in the family room, and in the parlor, with its giant window looking out front, past the gravel yard, through the slivers in the pines, towards the garden. We slid down the hallway, onto linoleum in the kitchen, where my fingers grazed Formica countertops and the cool metal of the oven and Frigidaire. We shuffled to the bedrooms in the back of the house, where, although soft morning light filtered through the window, I imagined my own family's sleeping heads safe on their pillows.

I marveled at one of the hallway bathrooms—everything new and not a smudge in sight—gleaming and shining and belonging to us, built by *us*. Through the window, Harold smiled and waved a palm at my wonderment.

The moving crew put everything where I asked to the inch, their muscles straining, their breath short, as they carried the mahogany dining table and china cabinet in without a scratch. They unrolled all the rugs, assembled the beds, slid the dressers and nightstands into place. They unloaded the crib and placed it underneath the mobile in the nursery and put the rocking chair engraved with "Campbells" next to the bassinette by the window. They arranged, then rearranged, then rearranged the television cabinet, couch, and armchairs in the family room. They even placed vases and decorative plates where I asked. Before long, everything was in its proper place, Raymond signed the paper, they were gone, and it was me and him. Us. And ours.

EIGHTEEN

June was flawless in 1960. Summer's mildest warm breezes welcomed the mornings. The garden was thriving, bursting with color; the light was rising earlier every day; and all my in-laws packed into me and Raymond's home behind the pines. Dot, Percy, and baby Clifford had arrived and were staying at ours while they waited on their furniture from Montgomery. And despite his teasing and phony protests during the build, Pop had long since claimed our guestroom as his own room.

In the hours before Dot and Percy's first good sunrise home, I started the percolator and settled in at the kitchen table clipping coupons. The light was just slivering through the trees from the edge of the world, stretching cypress shadows towards my kitchen window. Over some months, the dizzy spells had phased out, and were replaced by nerves about my stomach expanding and my clothes tightening and what that meant inside me. So when Dot's bedroom slippers shushed up the hallway and into my kitchen our first morning together, and she leaned down to hand me a half-asleep Clifford, I stiffened. Nobody had taught me what to do with a baby, so whenever I held him, tickled his belly, made gibberish talk or funny faces, I checked her eyes to see if she read my discomfort. She had caught on, but instead of scolding or teasing, she laid him in my arms anyway and started chattering about the fixings for the coffee.

"Don't drink that milk! You shouldn't reach high, either, keeping the coffee all the way up there on the shelf where only giants can reach it. Let me get the stepladder and I'll climb up and get it."

That morning, and the days that followed, starting at this grits o'clock hour, it was the same with Clifford.

"Dribble a little formula on your wrist, honey. Like this. Hold him like this . . . raise his head up. Like that. Nestle him against you like this. Hold the bottle like that. Don't bounce him! Lay him on your knee like this. Pat his back. *Oop!* See? There's his little belch. If he squirms a little, just hold him tight. Not quite that tight, honey! Put this cap on his thing or he'll urinate right in your face. Don't be afraid to get in there and wipe him clean, too. Now the powder, just like that. Wrap the diaper around his middle like this. Slide the pin through right there. Quick, now, so he doesn't get too cold. He's fine if he cries a little—he's just being fussy. Not hungry or wet. See? Look at my little man's eyes drooping already."

"How do you know what to do all the time?" I asked.

She huffed.

"I don't."

"It seems so natural to you, though. Being a mama."

"We'll learn together as we go, honey. You'll be alright."

We eased from friendship to sisterhood with as much thought as the flowers opening their buds. I had somebody to hang the wash with, and out there with me digging in the garden or fetching eggs from the chicken coop. And not just anybody, or even a friend. A sister. I knew what a sister was supposed to feel like, and here she came. Not that she could take Rosie's place. Nobody could do that. But Dot was her own kind of sister to me, and Rosie was her own kind of sister. I just had two dear hearts: one with me every day, and one silent. Somewhere.

One night, Raymond came home from doing payroll and asked to speak to me in the bedroom. He closed the door behind us quietly enough to destroy peace. So carefully the click of the catch revealed a secret.

"What's going on, baby? What's this about?" I had to call his name a couple times before he spoke.

"I just got off the line with a guy named Maceo in Chicago—"

"This is about Rosie?"

"Yeah, but let me explain."

"You about to tell me she's gone?"

"No. Just give me a chance to explain."

"What, then? Don't keep me waiting, Raymond. Where is she?" He sighed the way he did when he had already arranged the words in his mind and I was pushing him faster than he could get them out.

"Maceo is a community organizer in Bronzeville. The neighborhood where she lived. He's trying to get a municipality together there; says it's all Alabama in the area. He didn't know her—"

"You say 'didn't' and 'lived.' Where is she?"

"The house where you send your letters? She's not there anymore. Sounds like she ain't been there for quite some time."

"How does he know that? And if she ain't there, where is she?"

"The other day, me and him were talking about folks we knew in common and I happened to ask. He doesn't know your sister, but tonight, he told me he thinks he knows the house. The street, anyway. There was a shady mortgage dealer that owned a lot of houses over there, selling bad loans to people, changing the terms, whatever they needed to do to make sure folks would lose their house. Then, the lender would reclaim it and resell it. Do it all over again."

"But Rosie rented a room. She never bought a whole house."

"No, but if she was paying rent in one of the places he thinks she was staying, she would've been put out, too."

"To go where?" His shrug was just another dead end street, and I didn't have the heart for it. "That's all he told you? There must be more."

"That's it for now. I just talked to him a few minutes ago and then came straight to tell you. He seems plugged into the Alabama community up there, so if she's there, I think he can find her. But I wanted to talk to you, see if that's what you really want."

"Whatever he has to do, tell him to do it! That's my sister. Why are you hesitating?"

"You once asked me whether I thought something had happened to her. Did she ever tell you where she worked? About her friends? Anything?"

"Her letters were always about general stuff: asking about school, work, Daddy. She mentioned a couple friends—first name, anyway— but not the name of the beauty parlor where she worked."

"Can I see the letters?" he asked. I hesitated a beat at his request, and I don't know why. But I retrieved them, and his eyes scanned quickly, turning pages. With every passing second, I wondered if he saw something I'd missed. I savored her penmanship, tried to remember her scent, but he read fast, for words, meaning. The way one reads for clues and not the beauty in memory. But he folded them up and handed them back to me.

"You really wanna know what he finds out? No matter what?" he asked.

"This man? He's actually gonna look for her? And find her? Because I don't wanna get my hopes up, just to be let down, like with Patience."

"I believe that if he looks for her, he'll find something. My question is whether you wanna know."

"You keep asking like you think she's dead."

"I don't know what to think, darling, because I don't know," he admitted for the first time in all our years together.

"Well, I think my sister is alive, Raymond. She was born because Marion and Safiyah Young loved one another, and she's still loved. Love don't just disappear; don't matter how long it's been. So till somebody tells me different, Rosie Beatrice Young is alive, and always has been to me. Yes, I wanna know. You tell me as soon as there is something to tell."

I SAW ROSIE in mid-October, and I do have Raymond to thank for that. My baby came several weeks early—October 22, 1960, when Doc Patterson had assured me of mid-November. But already tired, breathing heavy, as the baby kneaded my insides like dough, he assured me during my checkup that I was laboring and admitted me to the hospital after I, again, refused his offer to be put into twilight sleep.

Blakely Memorial had just begun allowing men into the labor rooms those days ("Not 'delivery,' 'labor,'" he made sure to tell me to pass along to Raymond. "For delivery, there is still the stork club.") When Raymond showed up, the way he froze, open-mouthed in the doorway, suggested he may have preferred waiting in the stork club for everything. But he stayed as I twisted, struggling to find a comfortable position against the cramping and squeezing, pulling and tearing, hour after hour after hour. He grimaced, watching, puzzling through how to fix something he couldn't fix for me, especially after Doc Patterson checked on me time and again, frowned, and said, "not yet." When it felt like the baby wrapped its fist around the base of my spine and squeezed, the pain shocked the jelly of my insides and a wet, crying scream escaped my mouth. Doc Patterson whispered to Raymond with a hand on his shoulder. My husband nodded, then knelt next to my bed, his face now begging forgiveness as the nurse plunged a needle into my arm.

"Alice, they're gonna make you more comfortable . . ." were the last words I heard before soft sunlight warmed my veins and

Alabama's humid, honeysuckle air filled my nose. Summer's daytime buzz filled my ears as around me, long goldenrod fingers tickled my ankles, my knees, up to my hips. While diving fingers in and out of yellow waves, I laid full, open eyes on my sister's beautiful face again.

The warm breeze grazed my cheek as we stood there, face to face, in those clumps of goldenrod. The field was unfamiliar, but her smile dazzled pearl-white in the sun. My screams pierced blue skies above. Doc Patterson's voice told Raymond he had to go. *Now.* Rosie wore a mint-green cotton dress.

"Where are you, Rosie?" I asked.

Nothing.

"Are you in Chicago? Do you have a place to live? Are you cold? Where are you, Rosie? Say something!"

Nothing.

"Why won't you speak to me?" Without answering, she squeezed her arm around my shoulders just like she did the night she was six and promised never to leave. My groans and pleas echoed between my mouth and the heavens: Where did she live? With our parents? Did she know Daddy was gone? Had she received my letters? Was she married and did she hurt and was she scared and would she come live in New Jessup? But she never spoke, just squeezed me close—a little tighter when it hurt worst—letting up after each contraction until the sky, the grass, my sister, dissolved on that warm wind.

Then, the baby cried.

"She's beautiful," said Doc Patterson as she wailed while the nurses cleaned her. Overwhelmed, I cried, too. My sister was gone that quick. Raymond had been put out for the delivery. Now, it was me and a baby that I was supposed to mother.

"She?" My voice came out gravelly from all the screaming and being worn out from my journey. With what he said, and far away as my voice sounded, I thought the medication made me a little deaf.

"You said 'she'? But my stomach was low and Campbells make boys, and—" Doc Patterson's laugh dismissed every notion of a boy.

"Well, *she* is a girl," he said with amused certainty. "And it's probably too early to say this, but she looks just like your husband, I mean, *just* like him."

After the nurse cleaned her up and wrapped her in a blanket, they held her to my face, and he was right. She was a girl, and with a patch behind her ear that made her all Campbell.

"What's her name?" he asked.

Stunned, scared, and still without my sister, I squinted at this too-bright sun as my heart filled in places I didn't know existed and said the first name that came to mind.

"Hi, Rosie Beatrice," I whispered to her as I reached up and touched the soft baby fur on her cheek.

"That's pretty," he said. "Do I remember correctly? That's your sister's name, right?" He was still doing something below my waist behind the curtain, so I hoped he couldn't see my tears or hear them in my voice.

"Yessir, my sister in Chicago. She lives up there now, doing hair."

EVERYTHING BLURRED AND HALOED against the white-white antiseptic walls screaming with sunlight. Somebody was beating a drum inside my head. On my side, facing the doorway to my hospital room, my eyes were too sticky to open all the way, and as I shifted, the ache of my daughter being born, then being away from me, formed two halves of a pain that stole my breath. I stirred a little more and groaned as the everywhere throbbing on my body, the sick feeling in my head from that needle, brought vomit rushing to my throat. I swallowed it back down and pushed myself up in the bed.

"Whoa, whoa! What are you doing, darling?" came the deep voice I loved from the chair behind me. Although haloed in angry sunlight, working man's hands gently urged me by my shoulders back down onto the pillow.

"You were out cold. Thought I'd have to come into your dreams to get you," he said.

"You already there."

"*Ha*. Your mind never stops working."

"It did for a while after that needle. My head still ain't right."

"I know, and I know you said you didn't want it. But you were suffering so bad, and they had to turn the baby and—"

"It's alright. I'm alright."

Only now, I was suffering. With sticky eyelids and the light giving everything a halo, I tried to remember Rosie's face. October 22 of 1960 was nine years to the month since I last saw my sister's face. She had dissolved away so completely from my dream that all I remembered was her mint-green dress, the warm breeze, the field of goldenrod, and the endless blue sky. But whether that woman was my sister at seventeen or twenty-six, I had no idea. Nine years of hardly knowing her had passed. Nine years, when even simple seconds were gone forever. Raymond leaned close and laid ginger kisses on my hand and forehead.

"I must look a fright," I told him.

"You're the most beautiful woman that ever lived."

"Listen to you tell a story. You see the baby yet?" He nodded and smiled like a man in new love all over again.

"Six pounds and twelve ounces, ten fingers and toes on the most beautiful baby girl God ever put on this earth. I can't believe she's a girl! Pop almost fainted." He kissed my forehead again, and just then, the pain of her leaving me rippled through my stomach and chest. He bolted upright.

"You alright? You need the nurse?"

"I'm fine, baby. Just a little tender is all." He exhaled and kept up his excited talk.

"A girl! Rosie Beatrice Campbell," he said, and with his pride came the pain of being unable to see my sister's face, hear her voice, or feel her touch. I lay back in the bed, exhausted, and let the tears flow from my eyes to the pillow.

"Yeah, baby, Rosie Beatrice Campbell," I said. "But maybe, going forward, let's just call her 'Bea.'"

NINETEEN

Me and Dot had become Tuesday Morning ladies. With my head in the shampoo bowl, Miss Charlene herself massaged my cares away with such tender, loving kindness I thought I would cry. I was half-sleep, though, tuning out her lecture on the virtues of the bottle versus the breast while still awake enough to roll Bea back and forth in the beauty parlor bassinette. Under every hair dryer was a woman waiting on her turn in her beautician's chair, and in every chair was a woman warned to hold her ears as red-hot straightening combs or marcelling irons threatened to sizzle scalp and skin. Wafts of bergamot hair grease and Dixie Peach Pomade floated by on the finished ladies saying their goodbyes, and throughout the shop, gossip, laughter, secrets, and conversation worked their way around us like licks of tobacco, clinging to us like the smoke.

Suddenly, everything quieted to just the radio, the gentle hum of hair dryers, and the rolling of the bassinette wheels on the floor. But in the middle of my first good scalp massage since having Bea, my eyes refused to open and examine the curious stillness of women's tongues. Their voices eventually started back, first as a trickle, then into a stream of conversation and laughter much more animated than before. After some moments, two women, each confident in her opinions, approached the shampoo bowls to my left. The chairs squeaked, and then they began a polite, competitive conversation.

"He's a lawyer, you know."

"So you've spoken to him, then?"

"No, but you just saw him walk by here with Abel Gaston, didn't you? I've seen them together a couple of times by now."

"That doesn't mean he's a lawyer, Claire. It means he's the friend of a boy *barely* a lawyer."

"Why do you have to say it like that? Abel's a nice young man. Has lawyering in his blood."

"He may very well have lawyering in his blood, but nice? Don't you think that's a stretch?"

"I certainly don't."

"Well, my Jessica and plenty of other New Jessup daughters wasting time by the telephone may have a different story to tell."

"He's always been very nice to my Eloise, Margaret."

"I'm sure." Her words were so certain they were accusatory.

"I know what you're getting at, I know what you're getting at! And you should know that Abel Gaston always tips his cap to my daughter and makes way for her to pass on the sidewalk." Silence only intensified whatever indictment was hanging in the air about Eloise or Abel, who was known to be selective and to harbor short-lived affections. But who was, as with the rest of Raymond's friends, unknown as NNAS. So hearing his name scratched my solace. Rolling the bassinette, entranced by the scalp massage, I listened for any hint of awareness about Abel's more secret activities.

But Miss Charlene called the round before the women said anything more about him. This was her place. She owned the building, the business, and every day that happened inside.

"That's enough, ladies. First of all, Margaret, Attorney Jones *is* a lawyer. Finished with Abel at Howard Law and decided to practice here."

"How do you know?"

"You act like I ain't been doing DeBorah Gaston's hair for thirty years. Which brings me to my second point: I've known Abel since he was rolling in this bassinette. Him, Eloise, Jessica, and Raymond, too, rest Catherine Campbell's soul. Our children ain't perfect, but what you ain't finna do is dirtmouth anybody's child in here."

With eyes still closed, I probably sighed too loud hearing her ready to defend Abel. But she gave me those few seconds to relax my constant watch. Her fingertips traveled every inch of my scalp, working not just the knots from my hair, but the knots of tension that crept in at the mention of anybody's name I knew to be associated with the NNAS. I had stockpiled half-truths, nontruths, and some-truths ready to quell any suspicion whenever somebody called the men by name around New Jessup. And, of course, I would've denied outright the presence of a single member of the NNAS in the city. Their becoming public would not be this day and would not be my doing. So sometimes, to protect us all, I told some-truths, half-truths, and nontruths to almost everybody I knew. Sometimes, even to Pop, and yes, sometimes, even to Raymond.

Properly chastised, Miss Margaret mellowed from accusatory to piqued interest in her tone.

"Alright, so he's *Attorney* Jones," she said. "What *else* is there to know about this mystery man?"

"His name is Simon, Sidney, Steve—something with an 'S.' He's a Georgia boy, and DeBorah assured me he's got impeccable home training. Was staying with the Gastons until he found a place to lay his head, last I heard," said Miss Charlene.

"And . . . what about the rest of him. Was he looking for somewhere to lay that, too?" asked a voice I didn't recognize.

"Theresa!" said Miss Charlene. "You sit back under that hood and dry up! At least another twenty minutes!"

"But—"

"Go."

"It's just that he's a sizable man, Miss Charlene! That's all I was saying! Eclipsed the sun walking by just now!"

"*Mmm-hmm*. Go."

Theresa huffed and walked away, banished to the dryers to think about what she said.

"But he *is* single?" confirmed Miss Margaret. Miss Charlene snickered. Then, in a voice thick and gravelly with the gossip, she said,

"Last I heard? Single as a one-dollar bill."

So by the time Raymond returned from his Monday meeting a week or so later, it was hardly the first time I'd heard about Simeon Jones. I was still up, waiting on my house to be home and finishing Bea's 2 a.m. feeding when I heard the car doors shut outside. Entering, smiling, Raymond took the baby from my arms first thing, and dipped his nose close to her milk-and-powder scent. I frowned my yawn and he chuckled lightly.

"Bea must be wearing you out. You're usually wide-eyed and watching me park the car through the picture window."

"It's two-thirty in the morning, Raymond Campbell, for all your fooling. You usually home Monday nights by eleven. Midnight at the outside."

He had nerve to be in a joking mood, coming in the house hours late. And energized. After we said goodnight to Bea, we finally made it to the bedroom, where I could put my hair up and lay my head down. He slid next to me on the bed, smelling of sun-dried cotton pajamas, pine, and the open-hearted moon flowers that overran the Greenes' old father's cottage. All excited and playful, he propped on his elbow, fingering my locks as I pin-curled my hair. He was still wide awake, wanting to talk to *me* about something that happened on a Monday night.

"We have a new guy. A schoolmate of Abel's from Howard, but he knows Matthew, too. He started a job over with Gaston, Miles, and Peters after they graduated."

"You met him before tonight?" I asked.

"A couple times. He's only been in town a short while."

"*Hmmm*. And does old man Gaston know that his son and newest lawyer are both NNAS?"

"No. And folks move to New Jessup all the time, so a new lawyer won't raise any suspicion."

"Maybe not suspicion. But a new lawyer, single, our age, sizeable, apparently, and hanging out with Abel Gaston?"

"How'd you know he's single? And sizeable, you said? I didn't mention any of that."

"Because he may not have raised suspicion, but he has raised eyebrows, baby. Every woman in this city from eighteen to eighty already knows he's in town." His wrinkled brow demanded an explanation, but with the clock reading 2:45 a.m., and my alarm set for just under two hours, it was not the time to explain to Raymond woman talk at the beauty parlor. "I hope y'all are being careful."

"We are. And it's good to have a couple lawyers for this next part. We gotta file our paperwork soon, and him and Abel are gonna be a big help with that."

"What's Simeon like?" I asked.

"Smart and eager to make New Jessup our own city. Already has good ideas about writing our own laws, stuff like that."

"Not too eager, I hope. Like he's talking about the NNAS all over the place."

"No. He knows the rules. Me and the guys made sure of that. Made sure of that," Raymond repeated to himself with a little smirk and said no more about it. By the time I finished the last curl, with his energy draining away, he told me drowsily that he had invited Simeon for Thanksgiving. Ready to slip into dreamland together, I took my place atop his chest and fell asleep to his heart beating and soft breathing and the faint cologne of cypress and open-hearted moonflowers.

WITH THE SUN ROSE my hope that this would be the last I ever saw, or heard mention of, Chase Fitzhugh. In my phone, yes, but also, in the newspaper. No more pictures of his grinning face in campaign ads for city council. I had tired of happening upon photos of him "working" whenever I opened the Jessup *Call and Ledger* to clip coupons, wondering whether the cutout of his mouth on the back of the clipping was worth the five-cent savings on Swan's Down. His campaign slogan, "A working man's working man," shamed a lie, with his soft-looking hands waving at the camera and his coveralls nearly pristine. I knew working men's hands when I saw them; knew from scrubbing working men's coveralls just *how* they dirtied and where the fabric wore thin. Knew that my men wore the grease of his labor and that I laundered his supposed-to-be toils from their clothes. Knew that Pop's ankle was forever marked by the lie of Chase's work ethic.

The ads went on for months, making promises and good bedding for the chicken coop if I didn't cut his face apart for coupons. Other than that, they changed nothing about life for any of us in New Jessup. And he was hardly alone in refusing to court our votes. There was one ad promising to "keep Jessup safe with every gun at the Sheriff's disposal," and another promising to close Jessup schools before our children darkened their doorsteps. They all ran some version promising that no water from their fountains, or food from their lunch counters, would pass our lips, without a peep about releasing New Jessup tax dollars back to us. A safe and fair vote was our aspiration, for folks who had our best interests at heart. But wearing out my shoe leather begging these whitefolks to do right, only to vote for folks stealing our money? No, I never tried to cast a ballot for men intent on keeping us out of Jessup—never once having bothered to ask whether we wanted "in" to begin with.

And "in" where? Miss Vivian dressed me, Miss Charlene pressed my curls; my family always, always had food from our land on our plate, with help here and there from Brooks Supermarket when their prices were right, Custer's when theirs were better. My daughter was born in the south wing of a four-story Negro hospital, where the only white was the walls and the floors. But nobody bothered asking us anything. Instead, during election season, whitefolks convinced themselves with stories of Negro invasion that they spread among each other like infection.

Ultimately, Chase Fitzhugh owed his loss more to some woman named Julie than to any Negro in three counties, thanks to ads showing him doing everything but working—mostly walking into, or stumbling out of, bars on the other side of the woods. About three weeks before the election, just before I went into labor, a full-page spread showed two pictures side-by-side: one, of Chase underneath the hood of a car, then another of two men holding him up by the underarms leaving a place with *Julie's* blazed in neon cursive across the front. "Would you trust *this man* with your brakes? What about your city council?" the caption read with such ominous warning that if I were registered, and knew no better, I would have been thoroughly discouraged from voting for him.

All the while, the buses and cars continued riding between the Jessups, carrying the men and women who worked the laundries; cleaned everywhere from homes to slaughterhouses; watched babies; worked the docks and factories; cooked in their restaurants. People like Miss Evie, who attended our church, could always be counted on for another installment of "The Adventures of Edie—A day in the life of a housekeeper whose employer thought so little of her they never bothered to call her by her right name." Every word they uttered in her presence she carried back to us across the woods to entertain those called shortened names, nicknames, and out their names. Those letting the sting of this shared indignity be the antiseptic, and the shared laugh, the balm—in the comfort of New Jessup, where she was Miss Evie with a "v." Back and forth, back and forth, across the woods, our folks were hearts and eyes and brothers and sisters. Some, even NNAS. Some, even my men. And during election season, they carried stories back to my men at Campbell Auto of folks talking about, laughing about, Chase Fitzhugh.

That Friday after the election, after Chase's worst—true, false, or otherwise—had been splashed for months all over the papers for his fellow whitefolks to look down on him, fear him, disregard him, discard him, our phone rang and kept ringing.

TWENTY

A couple days before Thanksgiving in 1960, me and Bea were bundled against the chill out on the porch swing while she finally settled her crying. She may have been the spitting image of her daddy, but Alabama quieted her just like it did me. Even with the salty tear tracks crusting her baby-fat cheeks, and water still collected at the corners of her sleeping eyes, my daughter was perfect in ways this world never deserved. I could watch her little stomach rise and fall with baby breaths for hours, and her tiny fists opening and closing captured my imagination for all the things I wanted for her in life.

The woods were dark as the bright fingernail moon nestled in the shadowy tree canopy above, and the swishing leaves almost totally overtook the season's waning crickets. But the night was heavy with melancholy. As Bea drifted off to sleep, I promised to show her how to catch the moon's magic one day. Thinking of the moon and its magic, of family, on that melancholy night, Rosie slipped easily into mind. The sugar maple, school, her little girl arms that sweetened my whole world, yes, but also whether my sister would be a mama now. What it would be like behind the pines with Dot and Rosie and a mess of cousins being together. So I was already feeling a little sad when Pop pushed through the door.

"There's Big Poppa," I said in that drowsy, singsong way one talks to babies. He jumped, startled. "On his way across the woods. Again."

He came over and stood in front of the porch swing. My father-in-law was still strong as an oak in his coveralls and heavy coat, even with his salt-and-pepper head exposed to the elements for any cold to jump right in. Before he tied boots to his feet, I sent him grumbling back inside for his hat. When he returned, he bowed close to tickle Bea's chin with the strings dangling from the ear flaps. She stirred a little, poked her tongue a couple times, but didn't open her eyes. Pop yawned.

"This can wait till daytime at this point," I said. "It must be three o'clock in the morning."

He shook his head.

"Got a full shop, so even if it could wait, we ain't got time to have towing backed up. Especially from the other side of the woods."

"Ain't ours in the first place, to be backing us up."

"Yeah, well, me and Fitzhugh agreed that it all ends with the new year. You know that. Just a few more weeks now."

"I know that, but does Chase know that?"

"He's got no choice but to know it. It's done."

"But Fitzhugh's retiring at some point," I reminded him.

"It's done," he said in that way to be a father's last word on it, whether he believed it or not.

We quieted, looking into the forest. The trees swished in a lazy breeze, and the crickets' waning yet never-ending song threaded the beginning of time to the end. The groan of the porch swing was deep, resonant, and rich as a song I used to sing with my family as we sowed, planted, and picked. It was my daddy's song, learned as a little boy, passed to us, never to be lived by us. But my sister sang it from the depths of her soul like a premonition. I held my daughter tight and, maybe as a prayer or a hope, as the crickets pulled all time together, I called it to the forest. For Rosie. For Bea. For Mama. Pop watched me in silence.

> Sometimes, I feel, like a motherless child,
> Sometimes, I feel, like a motherless child,
> Sometimes, I feel, like a motherless child,
> A long way from home,
> A long way from home.

The air was so thick with fading hope that the song just needed a voice to sing it. With the *sometimes* hinting at maybe better times ahead. Like sometimes, often times, folks figured out how to build. Sometimes, often times, folks figured out how to survive. Sometimes, often times, sisters returned to Alabama after being gone without a trace for many years.

"I don't miss those years in the swamp," he said. "They were hard. But doggone, girl, it does something to my heart to hear those words again. Everybody I know is proud of what we built here, but nobody I know sings those songs anymore."

"We did where I came up. My sister sang it like nobody's business." Nothing could hide the disappointment on my face over the years-long wait to hear from Rosie, so I just let the tears collect if they wanted to collect, and fall if they wanted to fall.

"You should've seen 1913, after Booker T. came," he said. "Folks long gone from here streamed back into town and couldn't believe what we had accomplished in ten years. We were nowhere near where we are now, but it was a sight. I remember when folks came back. I remember," he said, sitting on the swing and putting his arm around my shoulder, rocking us back and forth with his foot into his memories.

"When Booker T. came, he stayed in the Collier House. It was brand-new at the time, and the tallest building in either of the Jessups.

My father was one of the first on our side of the woods to have an automobile. A brand-new Tin Lizzie, girl!" He chuckled. "Was still fixing buggies, forging iron, you name it, but he also taught himself, me and my brothers, everything there was to know about that Model T.

"We picked Booker T. up from the hotel and drove him to the Gilliam County fairgrounds for his speech. Passed the house where I was born, and my father pointed proudly at the house Daddy Campbell, my grandfather, built. But a little white girl glared out the window at us like we were invading. I was only three when the whitefolks came and didn't remember the night, but the feeling of it was still in her eyes.

"We New Jessup Negroes got to the fairgrounds with no idea what to expect. We had to stand in the back, but Booker T.—I'm talking a man born into bondage . . . bondage, you hear me? The same man who became an advisor to the president of the United States! That's the man who rode in my father's car. That's the man who took the stage.

"The crowd was silent as a cemetery for a long while, and I started to sweat even though it was still cold outside. But then, he spoke, calling our arrangement 'his greatest ambition realized.' Somebody shouted and we all looked around. Then they started clapping and hollering agreement. All us Negroes were glancing at each other, wondering did Booker T. just tell these whitefolks to stay outta New Jessup, too? Did he tell them he was sad for any man relying on his skin color as proof of his measure? In his own way, he did. Booker T.—from bondage to an advisor for McKinley—praised *us* New Jessup Negroes for our work ethic, skills. That's why we needed to stick close to whitefolks, he said. Because we have know-how, bounce back. And they ate it up because all they heard was 'Negroes stay around, but on your side of the woods.'"

"You think the Fitzhughs were at the fairgrounds that day?" I asked.

"Probably. At least some of their kin."

"I wonder if *they* heard the message to stay out."

"I'd like to think so."

"Because you know what else I wonder?" I asked as the question formed on my chest and squeezed.

"What's that?"

"Whether the Fitzhughs were also part of that mob with deeds and shotguns acting a fool back in 1903." He sighed.

"Probably."

This night was no better and no worse when it came to the towing. Every time the phone rang was that blackdamp coming again. But when Pop stood, pulled Bea's blanket tighter to her neck and jostled my housecoat at the collar as though getting ready to leave, getting ready to step off my porch because Chase reached to our side of the woods again, that night, no different than any other in so many ways, still made it harder for me to breathe.

"This has to *stop!*" I said quietly, sharply. He froze. "We supposed to be free of all this! It ain't their right to decide when it stops! This is our lives, but they act like we supposed to be at they beck and call. If I tell him we sick or sitting down to supper, he blows air into my phone like our lives ain't our own—like somebody needs to get up. Now. He does it in that way that tells me he's more interested in what whitefolks were up to in 1903 than the fairgrounds. And we gotta rely on his daddy's word to stop it when he's the one telling us to just help bring the boy along? Ain't that *his* job? Ain't Chase *his* child?"

Pop stood there quietly watching my frustration.

"And for what? To prove he can? To prove to the world he ain't nobody's Negro? Well, you hear that, trees?" I said to the dark. "Chase Fitzhugh ain't nobody's Negro! He ain't nobody's Negro!" Pop sat back down and wrapped a tight arm around me, shushing until my breathing slowed. Hardly different than I had just finished doing with Bea.

"I know it's frustrating, but it's only a couple more weeks. You're tired; you should be in the bed." I took a deep breath and blew it out, trusting Wade Fitzhugh's promise even less than I had trusted old man Todd's.

"You know the rules, Pop: my baby is up, I'm up. My men are up, I'm up."

With one last jostle, a kiss to me and Bea's foreheads, and a sigh, he was gone.

TWENTY-ONE

There was one more call before Thanksgiving, and then, it was quiet until the men started shouting.

"Show them how we do it down south! Yassuh! Stomp him! Stomp him, good! That's right! New Yorkers sure cry a lot after a little bitty hit!"

Raymond and Percy were holding our babies with the same expertise as the men running up and down the field on television. Pop jumped up and crashed back down to his feet, causing an empty thud to boom from crawlspace to attic. And with a pie box in each hand, each large enough to be their own serving platter, Simeon Jones bellowed, "That's what I'm talking about!" as me and Dot exchanged quiet, disbelieving glances in the archway.

Me and her could have walked into the room and barely been heard above the fray. But the Tuesday ladies' shock when we traded Thanksgiving guest lists under hair dryers had emboldened me and her to feel a little sneaky. So when we were in the kitchen, and heard that new voice join the chorus, Dot put a finger to her lips. We crept out, to the right, and up the hallway, peeking around the doorjamb of the wide archway leading to the family room. There they were, facing away from us, towards the television in the corner. So the first thing we saw was his broad back, with shoulders wider than Percy

by probably three inches on either side. And Raymond—at six foot
three—stood a good head shorter than Simeon. As they stood in rapt
attention watching a play on the television, my first thought was that
we should've picked more greens.

I started to turn on my heel, but Dot slapped my arm before sliding herself into the archway. It swallowed her whole. After the play
ended, they turned to congratulate each other about Texas beating
up New York and caught sight of her in their side vision.

"Hey Alice," she said, "you suppose that, in Georgia, they don't
speak to introduce themselves when they come into somebody's home
for the first time?"

Simeon spoke then, smiling an embarrassed smile. And he kept
speaking as he carried the pie boxes back to the kitchen with something to say about everything and everybody. Well, the babies obviously got their good looks from their mamas; our pecan and sweet
potato pies on the sideboard put his offerings from the bakery to
shame. And were those collards he smelled? From our garden out
there? Where we taught God himself how to grow things? He filled
the air with that deep-well voice. Nothing bad about it, in and of
itself, but the syllables, the words, the phrases all seemed ready-made,
waiting to be plucked from a shelf. He was smooth, fluent in the language others most wanted to hear. Like a river rock; although I was
left to wonder whether he was the kind to throw that rock and hide his
hand.

But I smiled and spread hospitality with our feast, which was
more than could be said about my brother-in-law. Percy was usually
the one trading big talk with Pop over the table, so at first, it seemed
he was allowing our guest the space to open up and tell us about himself. But the more thanks and cheer Simeon spread, the closer Percy
hovered over his plate. That same icy undercurrent once reserved for
me had Percy only speaking when spoken to, and offering a snort
instead of a laugh every so often.

On the porch for shine and brandy after supper, me and Dot sat in the swing with the babies, while the men took the rocking chairs. Percy trudged next door to take one of the chairs from their porch for Simeon and returned to find our guest in his regular spot between Pop and Raymond. So Percy carried the chair all the way to the other side of the porch and placed it between me and Dot on the porch swing and Pop. Point made, he rocked slowly, so close to Dot she had to sit cross-legged on the swing.

Simeon turned to Pop, gearing up to throw that rock at all of us.

"I don't think I've ever seen a prettier place than New Jessup, Mr. Campbell, and I'm from Atlanta," he said. "How much further back do these trees go on the property?"

"All told, other than the garden, my house over there, the shop and boneyard, another couple hundred acres or so," said Pop as he sipped on his brandy.

"Indeed, indeed. Y'all going to build on it? Or would you consider selling some of it?"

"Oh *nooo*. It's good for hunting. Where do you think that turkey came from?" Pop said with the pride of the one who shot that year's bird.

"Impressive! It sure was a beauty, Mr. Campbell. My father's a lawyer, too, so I never handled a gun myself."

Percy grinned, inserting himself into the conversation.

"Seems like, if anybody needs to know how to shoot straight, it's an attorney," he said.

"*Ha*, Percy!" Simeon said. "Always quick with the lawyer jokes."

"You took that as a joke?"

Raymond's eyes, behind Simeon's head, said *be easy* to Percy. I didn't know Simeon except some beauty parlor talk, and these few hours he spent with us on Thanksgiving, when he spoke the language of what he thought I wanted to hear. And with the way me and Percy got on at first, I knew my brother-in-law's first impressions could be both dead wrong and firmly held. But if my own intuition wasn't enough of an alarm, that look from Raymond assured me that even a broke clock is right twice a day. Percy leaned back in his chair, the clouds formed by his breath getting bigger and bigger.

"I've never seen this much land owned by one family. Is a lot of New Jessup like this? Undeveloped, I mean?" Simeon asked.

"Well, you know downtown's built up pretty well," Pop said. "City planning was always important. You can tell that from the way the architects worked their way out from the old town, built up the business districts and neighborhoods using that grid system. It all centers on the original high point, where the high school school sits now," Pop said. "City will hopefully keep growing, spreading out according to that plan, but outside the city proper, like here, I guess you could say there's still a fair bit."

"What about all that land between here and Jessup. Who owns that?"

"You ask a lotta questions," said Pop, his eye and smile turning wary.

"My apologies, sir. I'm an attorney. Mama always said I have an inquisitive nature."

"We told you about that already," Percy growled low.

"Why?" Pop asked, setting his brandy down.

"Well, it's just, I'm thinking, sir," said Simeon, "that New Jessup is an attractive place to settle down. Folks'll start moving here if y'all's secret gets out."

"Secret's been getting out for nearly sixty years, Simeon, and folks have been making it their own ever since. But that land is in trust, never to be developed."

"But with things heating up all over, sir, New Jessup could be an attractive place for all sorts of folks to settle their families, I bet. They'd be safe here."

Percy leaned forward in his chair and looked across Pop to Simeon.

"Didn't you just hear my father tell you that folks have been moving here for sixty years? And besides, we *told* you about this already," he said. Simeon smiled his same disarming smile as he had all night. But like water in search of a crack, the direction of every word uttered in my house seemed intent on drawing Pop into some discussion about agitating. Only, I had been telling some-truths, half-truths, and nontruths to anybody needing to hear them: Miss Vivian; Miss Charlene and the Tuesday ladies; every time I set foot at Waverly's, Mr. Marvin's, the grocers, Morning Star Baptist, or even at my own supper table with my own family. Even to Pop, who not only would have blown a gasket to know the municipality work he was talking up to the old heads was in concert with the NNAS, but who was one of the men in New Jessup responsible for doing something about it. But now Simeon showed those dimples with rock in hand.

I rocked the porch swing and bumped Percy's chair. He turned irritated eyebrows at me, but he was too close and not the only one out there agitated, so I read him right back. Behind him, all the way at the end of the rockers row, Raymond tilted his head to tell me and his brother to stop bickering. Simeon took a sip of his brandy, leaned forward, drawing breath to say something else to Percy. Before he uttered a word, Raymond cut him off.

"Hey, man," beat the air, his voice echoing through the trees. Then, he stood and walked towards me, with eyes trained *on* me. "We told you Thanksgiving was something special out here, didn't we?" He was bragging.

"Sure did, and indeed it was."

"Yeah, our stomachs are full, we're all happy and healthy, and me and Percy have the love of the two most beautiful women in the world. Right here in New Jessup, Alabama."

Leaning in to slip Bea from my arms, he came close enough for our three heartbeats to touch. And placed a hand on my knee to tell my toe to stop tapping.

AS WE PREPARED to close our eyes on Thanksgiving night, Raymond propped on an elbow and asked what I thought about the evening. He'd been so excited to have Simeon in our home that, of course, his question was about our dinner guest. I was glad Simeon's big talk was gone and also not glad his big talk had gone elsewhere. Because here was another one: another man whose name was to be listened for, whose background I had to cover for, whose whereabouts I had to vouch for. Raymond had never asked me this question about the fellas, Patience—a group whose loyalties to each other were fully formed before I ever started coming around. Friends we saw at the jukes on Saturdays and church on Sundays; who went to the swamp together on Mondays and shadowboxed Cap any day. They and their families had charmed their way around weddings, Christmas dances, school benefits, and barbecues with the generations who founded, and provided stewardship, for New Jessup. I kept the confidences they kept themselves, but all I knew about Simeon was that he was new, Atlanta by way of DC, and pulling ready-made lines from the shelf. They picked him, though, which was why I didn't answer his question right away.

"Turkey came out well," I said. "But you think the pecan or the sweet potato was better?" Though I made the sweet potato, he cocked his head and pulled lips to the side, unimpressed by my dodge. "What are you really asking me, then, Raymond?"

"Your opinion about our guest."

"Why?"

"Because I wanna know. Humor me."

"Honest?"

"Honestly."

"I think he likes the sound of his own voice too much." He chuckled as if unsurprised by my answer. "You laugh, but his 'yes, ma'am' and 'yessir' are way too big."

"How's that?"

"The way he says 'yes, ma'am' with his full chest. He sounds like he's calling it to the bottom of a well and it's bouncing back. It's too big. Big enough to seem insincere, especially with the way he says 'indeed' a whole lot."

"I can see that. He certainly ain't Alabama."

"No, he ain't. Ain't no mumble to him. He's all boast, without any humility. Is everybody like that in Georgia?"

"Dr. King's from Georgia, and you've heard him on the television plenty."

"Yeah, well, I ain't telling stories for Dr. King. But I do tell a lotta half-truths around here for men you came up with because y'all are thick as thieves and twice as loyal. Simeon? None of y'all know him well and he ain't Alabama, which makes me nervous."

He nodded as if that was the response he was looking for. "You know about the Rule of Three—three guys need to give approval to tell anybody about us all being NNAS. But did I ever tell you who gave me the okay to tell you?"

"No. And what's that have to do—"

"Hugo, Major, Abel, the Morris boys, and Matthew. Everybody who was here at the time."

"Except Patience."

"Except Patience," he admitted. "But you know what they said about you?"

"Thought y'all weren't gossiping about me." He smiled that caught-in-a-half-truth smile—his front teeth bit gently into his lower lip. "You can put your eyeballs back in your head, Raymond. A half-truth is still a whole lie."

"Well, we weren't *gossiping*. But they did say that you were charming, but not overly chatty. Sweet, but suffered no foolishness. Matthew said that asking too many questions was the quickest way to end the conversation, and Abel told him don't find out what happens if you try any sweet talk."

"I don't remember any of that."

"They remembered you from the repast, too. We said only wives, no girlfriends, and they told me I was crazy for even asking them, as little as I knew about you. But they came back, one by one, giving you the thumbs up. Good thing, too, because I would still be pushing.

"They knew that I would keep pressing for Simeon when he came, too. It's different because he's from HQ, so the question wasn't whether to tell him, but whether to try and send him back. Me, Matthew, and Abel had to push hard with the rest of the fellas, because they wanted him gone from New Jessup."

"I vote with them," I said, as if I had a vote.

"Matthew knew him from DC, and Abel went to school with him," Raymond said. "I watched him in action at the Gilliam County courthouse, and let me tell you, he's the real deal in the courtroom. Defended a Negro arrested for trespassing over in Mathis, and you know, he got him off? He put up with a lot to do it in that courtroom, but he's talented. Got the right balance of bluster and the humility you say he lacks.

"The others—including your brother-in-law—weren't convinced. They still question whether someone from national can abide by our work and our way of life. You see Percy still ain't changed his mind. But Simeon just needs to get settled. With Matthew back in DC, and Abel minding his single man's extracurriculars, he needs to see how a young, married man lives here. I pushed for him, so that makes him my responsibility. It would mean a lot to me if you gave him a chance. It'd be nice not to fight for him in the meetings *and* at home," he said, which made Simeon our responsibility, another cross to bear. To be added to the list of names for whom I listened, and for whom I spoke, tethering his fate in the city to my family. My promise, my approval, pushing up the corners of Raymond's smile.

So I can't say for certain whether it was agreement or necessity that kept an invitation open for Simeon at my supper table—this man for whom I would have to deploy my half-truths every time I saw the Tuesday ladies while I was still getting to know him myself. Yes, he was a lawyer. Yes, he was single. He wasn't partial to perch, but loved cathead biscuits and fried chicken, and unfortunately, he'd be in Atlanta during the Christmas dance. Every word uttered on his behalf felt like another length of rope tying us together. But I didn't say, and couldn't say, that he had ready-made answers for everything. I didn't say, and couldn't say, that I wanted him gone. And I didn't say, and couldn't say, that if he was found out, me and Raymond would never escape suspicion for twice being associated with an instigator in New Jessup.

TWENTY-TWO

Behind my eyelids, there was nothing at first—not the wrecker rumbling to the curb; not my missing pocketbook or the nowhere-to-be-found bag from the men's store; not my shoes, kicked off and laying on the pavement; not the chill of an amethyst dusk at the peak of rush hour; not the man at the other end of the bench with his newspaper; not the panic in Raymond's voice—until he shook me awake. I wasn't hit over the head or otherwise harmed except by my own ego telling me I could push my body harder than the flesh wanted to go. The only thing that had beat me was pure fatigue, and I fell into a deep sleep at that bus stop. In fact, behind my eyelids, the nothingness was so pure and vast with possibility that the entire world lay ahead; like just the *idea* of time was waiting to be born. There was no north or south or east or west. No up or down, left or right. Just an entire, blank landscape again until my body awoke with one sharp breath.

I opened eyes to Raymond squinting at me, mere inches from my face.

"What are you doing asleep on this bench? Are you alright? Where is your pocketbook?" He gasped rapid-fire questions as his agitated hands felt about my head, neck, and shoulders for the reason

I would be out cold in the middle of town. The older man who must have arrived while I was asleep watched with mild interest from the other end of the bench. "I told you she's my wife," Raymond snapped at an elder, who responded with a shrug and turned back to his newspaper like somebody who had seen it all. With eyes back on me, Raymond continued patting me over, checking for injury, not believing, at first, when I told him I was fine. When he asked about my pocketbook again, I noticed the empty spots on the bench to my right and left.

"I must've . . . left it in the car," I said to him as I opened my eyes to the fact that I had actually been robbed.

"And I told you to stay by the car. Where is that? Why are you sleeping out here on Booker Ave.?"

"It's up the street." I yawned and pointed towards the men's store and Blue Lightning at the opposite end of the block. When I turned back to face him, his eyes had not followed my finger, but stayed squarely, intently, on the side of my head. Under his examining gaze, I tightened my jaw, causing my face to tremble, fighting back another yawn. But unwilling to be suppressed, it snuck up and escaped through my half-open mouth some seconds later. The release caused his frown to sink even lower.

That was one of the weeks when exhaustion smothered me. Nearing year's end, with Chase's opportunities to call my phone dwindling, he was summoning my men more than he wasn't. I was Thursday tired after being up three nights in a row. Monday, with Bea, yes, because she was colicky, even after Raymond and Percy arrived home from their meeting. Then, there were calls from across the woods for Raymond Tuesday, and Pop on Wednesday. Now Thursday was Raymond's birthday.

The day had started with the best-laid plans, which, by four o'clock, felt like they were laying over me. By the time the December evening turned stone gray, the cake was cooling, and the chicken was slaughtered, cleaned, and butchered, leaving only an hour for me to get downtown and pick up Raymond's birthday surprise before the store closed. While Dot stayed behind with the babies, she took charge of frosting the cake and getting the chicken in the oven, allowing me to race out the door to contend with rush-hour traffic. Inside my pocketbook were bills carefully counted and separated from those in my wallet, which was full of walking-around money from Raymond.

This was my coffee-can money—the last of my earnings from working for Mr. Marvin and Miss Vivian, meant to be spent on my own treasures. This little portion in the envelope was for a gold wristwatch Raymond would wear on special occasions and to church. One the salesman had assured me only his most discriminating clients chose for their husbands. The extra for the engraving was well worth his imagined smile when he opened the gleaming present from me and Bea "with all our love." The salesman wrapped it up and put it into a bag, sending me on my way before he locked the door and closed the store behind me.

But when I slid behind the wheel of Blue Lightning—nothing. Finding my car dead drained the excitement propping me up and made the whole world heavy again. The last thing I wanted was to be the reason any of them fired up the wrecker the night of Raymond's birthday surprise. It was bad enough when the Fitzhughs called . . . now me? But lacking any better idea, I trudged towards the pay phone and called Campbell Auto for a tow. Twenty minutes, Raymond told me. He'd be there in twenty minutes, and to stay near the car.

Standing at the payphone, flattened by the fatigue, the car seemed farther away than I remembered. I sat on the bench, meaning to rest my limbs for just a moment before I headed back. But settled at the bus stop, the world passed by slow and even: the cars crawling through traffic with their engines thrumming a steady rhythm, the constant *click* of heels passing by on the sidewalk. I blinked, blinked again, and found myself in a world without north or south.

Now, my pocketbook, and the beautiful wristwatch bought with my own money, were gone.

This was my first time inside either of the wreckers—two beefed-up pickups, each around ten years old with a long arm on the back and a crank on the side with a handle. Inside the cab, a broken seat spring squealed underneath me, and the seam at my shoulder blade was ripped like a puckered, open mouth. Raymond climbed into the other side and the door screamed shut, resting the rugged heel of his work boot in a hole worn through the floor mat by years of braking and accelerating.

With the sun setting on Raymond's twenty-eighth birthday, he pulled an illegal U-turn into traffic, angling the truck to clog up one full lane and a little of the other. He backed up as close as he could get to Blue Lightning, which was parallel parked and resting peacefully. As he surveyed how to turn the car into the street, horns and voices abused him for further jamming up rush hour traffic.

After some moments, reluctantly, he looked up at me sitting in the cab of the wrecker and asked me to get back behind the wheel of my car. I steered as he told me, braked as he told me, while he ran from front to back, back to front, pushing, yelling through clenched teeth. We inched it together, forward, then back. Finally, exhausted, perspiring, he sent me back to the cab of the wrecker while he finished hoisting Blue Lightning. With those working man's hands, he grabbed the lever attached to the crank on the side of the truck—pulling down to nearly squatting before bursting up to stand on tiptoe. Over and over, with great effort, the crank tightened the line hooked under the front bumper, lifting the car's front tires from the ground inch by inch. After some minutes' fight, he climbed into the cab covered in perspiration, stuck his hand out the window to signal that we were pulling out, and eased the truck and the car—lurching and groaning together—into evening traffic. By the time he finished, my mouth was agape seeing how much of their effort was going across the woods.

"*This* is what towing is like?"

"Yeah. Sometimes. So what are you doing asleep over here?"

"How would you have done this if I wasn't here?"

He sighed, exasperated. I wasn't answering his question.

"What do you mean?"

"I was parallel parked. How would you have gotten me out?"

"I would've waited for the car either in front of you, or behind you, to leave."

"Oh."

"Now my turn. Why are you out here asleep at a bus stop?"

"It was just supposed to be a quick trip to the men's store," I said, still trying to hold on to the surprise of supper. Not that it mattered, with his brow furrowed the way it was and the blank way he stared into traffic, whispering a question more to himself than to me.

"When was the last time I serviced your car?"

We drove in silence for a while as the winter sun fully set— the only sounds, the CB radio and the rough metallic jolt of Blue Lightning at the stoplights. I closed my eyes and woke to his hand shaking my knee. He asked, with that same worried brow, if I was feeling alright—a brow unconvinced no matter how many times I told him I was just a little run-down. Every pool of streetlight we drove underneath revealed shadows of worry on his face. It didn't matter that the car dying was none of my fault. Whoever owned the failure, his fear, his hurt, was mine. Nobody stirred Raymond from the depths of himself like me. I knew how to slow his every breath or quicken his every heartbeat with a single word or touch. So each shadow of worry on his face was another bruise I meant to heal. Every time. Every time.

"Hey," I said, pushing my sweetest smile past the fatigue. While we sat locked in traffic, he looked at me with soft grays inviting me into the depths. I got exactly the gentle laugh I was looking for, watched the shadows lift from his face as he smiled when I said, "Happy Birthday, Mr. Mayor."

TWENTY-THREE

By April following, the phone's ringing, and its silence, could actually be trusted. In the early months of the year, Chase tried to act like the world had not turned its calendar to 1961. The first time, we were sitting down to leftovers of collards and black-eyed peas when Pop left the table and went to hook the car. But the next time, Raymond answered the phone in the middle of the night. After some minutes, he returned and slid into bed, pulling me back atop his chest. It took a long, silent while for his heartbeat to slow and his breath to soften back into sleep, but he stayed in our bed until morning. At grits o'clock, I found the telephone receiver laying on the kitchen table, and when Dot arrived, she said hers was the same way.

That happened a couple more times before the calls stopped. The expectation of that blackdamp coming through my phone at all hours was slow to evaporate, though, making overnight quiet hard to trust for a while. Not that the phone silenced completely; but when it did ring, it was normally Simeon, asking what he should bring for supper. By April, he was at my kitchen table two, three nights a week, and after five months of coming around, he had started growing on me. He was easygoing, with an agile mind, if always talking that big Georgia talk with that big Georgia laugh. Whenever he started

pulling those ready-made lines from the shelf, I barbed him a little, and the crinkles at the corners of his eyes let me know the message was received. Behind all that bluster was a sincere awe tinging
his voice about New Jessup that was unique to those of us not
grown up in town. He marveled, talking about an all-Negro police
department and how he had stopped expecting the sight of whitefolks on the bus or the sidewalk or . . . anywhere on our side of
the woods.

Over smothered pork chops one night in early April, he was in
the middle of such expressions of appreciation when he opened his
mouth to say, "Y'all have been so generous with me since I came to
town. If you'd allow it, I'd love to treat you to a pig roast."

As an apartment-dweller in the city proper, it was unclear to me
how he planned to "treat" us to anything. In Rensler, as in New
Jessup, roasting a pig was the domain of men. Women made the sausage, cleaned and cooked the chitlins, and preserved the fat and leav-
ings for cooking lard and lye soap. So the closest I ever got to the
actual cooking was my daddy coming home perfumed of pork and
hickory smoke and the molasses sopping sauce turned acrid from
dripping on the coals. It was no different with the Campbell men,
who helped hunt and gut the animal, dig the pit, and tend the hog
for the family reunion hosted by Pop's older brother, A.C., every
July. So maybe Simeon had ideas that I had never been privy to.
I doubted it.

"Treat us?" I asked. "You come upon some acreage all the sudden?" His eyes stayed full of good humor, and he readied those
Georgia dimples to take a little teasing as the table shook with laughter. Behind his smile waited those giant "yes, ma'am"s and "no,
ma'am"s he always rattled off in play, though I had asked him a hundred times to call me Alice. But I didn't mind it so much anymore,
because his affection for my family, and our way of life, was blos-
soming into genuine.

"No, ma'am," he said. "And it may be presumptuous of me, but I thought we could possibly do it here. I'll get the pig and everything."

"And where would you get this pig, Simeon?" I asked.

"The butcher near me in town." The laughs continued. Including Percy, who exaggerated his chuckles to make sure everybody knew just how tickled he was.

"That's where y'all get y'all's hogs in Georgia? The butcher?" I said. "It's just . . . you *are* from Atlanta."

"Yes, ma'am, born and raised. But I've got family all over the state. Some of my fondest memories are of pig roasts as a child. Fetching firewood, running back and forth all night for coffee and shine, getting my own sips and listening to grown men tell lies."

"Alright, but you ever actually killed it?" I asked.

"No, ma'am."

"Gutted it?"

"No."

"Built the pit?"

"Usually, by the time we pulled up, they'd already dug it."

"Cleaned the chitlins, then, or helped make the sausage?"

The air trembled with his low, raspy chuckle.

"No, ma'am," he said. "By the time chitlins and sausage got to me, they were ready for hot sauce."

Though the rest of us were enjoying a good laugh, Pop's gaze had quietly turned to a corner of my yard through the window. After wordlessly picking a spot for the pit, he turned back to the table and lifted an eyebrow at his boys. They smiled. Then, he said, "We shoot hogs around here, Simeon. Right out yonder, on our land. Still, for all y'all's fooling, it ain't a half bad idea."

So Simeon popped some cans and bottles at the edge of the corn with one of the little CZs a couple times, and then he took that rabbit rifle into the woods with Raymond, Pop, and Percy thinking they'd get something right-sized for our two families. The CZ was hardly gun enough to bring down a wild hog, but he carried it with him while me and Dot stayed behind and left them to it. Maybe he even shot it once or twice. Who could tell with Percy coming back after their second hunt, bragging to the heavens about the monster he bagged with his Winchester? One big enough not only for us behind the pines, but for Raymond and Percy to call the fellas, their families. So Pop called his brothers, their families. Then Dot called her people, who included a brother-in-law who she despised. And if he was coming, then no need keeping it to blood relations since it was too much meat even for that list of folks. By the time our phones stopped dialing out about that hog, it had turned into a Sunday pig roast for nearly half of New Jessup.

On Friday night, while Pop and Percy were out gathering wood, me and Dot set up on the porch with our heads together making lists: to-do lists, "who's bringing what" lists, shopping lists. Raymond and Simeon were digging the pit in a corner of my yard where a whisper was a shout. Where men with deep voices wrongly believed they could be seen, but not heard, and engaged in a conversation meant to be between them alone. It was a corner where the gravel met trees so thick with magnolia and white oak and longleaf pine that the forest refused to let the words slip through. Instead, voices drifted over moon-glow gravel, past the cars, up the steps, through the pickets, and directly to me and Dot's ears on my front porch. We could see every sideways glance and hear every sigh. The words were sharper than anything coming through my telephone, and more telling. Particularly words whispered by one voice matching the piano's lowest register speaking to another from the bottom of a deep well.

In the middle of saying something, Dot shushed me with eyes in that way sisters understand means *hush*. *Listen*, she wrote on the back of the grocery list. Stormy voices rumbled from the whispering corner right to us on the porch. With our heads huddled together as if still talking about groceries, just about every time one of them spoke, me and her fast-scribbled.

"All I'm saying," Simeon said in a sharper tone than I'd ever heard from him, "is that we should be recruiting. Keeping the membership so small and secretive is no way to show strength and demonstrate how much the vote means to the community."

What is this Negro talking about? I wrote on my paper. She shook her head slow.

"We have no results with municipality," Raymond said. "Nothing to show New Jessup that the NNAS has done any good here. We need to get established as a city first so our folks can see that the NNAS is invested in our community, and ain't just about agitating." Even the sound of the shovel ripping into the earth echoed from the whispering corner.

Set him straight, Raymond, she wrote, and I nodded.

"Y'all get me the rest of the signatures we need, and I'll rush the petition to the courthouse. Even still, judges take the time they take, and it could be pending a long while. In the meantime, we just sit and do nothing? Nothing while folks all around us are pushing for the vote in Alabama? I understand you wanna bar the door, but c'mon, Raymond." Raymond grabbed a sip of his coffee from a nearby stump, so Simeon kept on. "We should be on the front lines, out there getting people to the polls."

Me and Dot exchanged looks then, but neither of us wrote as we waited.

"We are on the front lines. In New Jessup. Establish our own city. Vote on our own city council. Solidify independence so everybody sees that the NNAS ain't pushing desegregation here. After that, I'm with you, man. This way, we get New Jessup to the polls to vote for folks who represent *us*. But if you violate the Rule of Three? Hold some membership drive? You'll be a man without a friend around here."

Without a friend in the world, I wrote.

Not a single one, she wrote back.

"But it isn't just city council," said Simeon. "It's county, state-wide, federal offices. You've said it yourself that we're entitled to vote for everything from dog catcher to president."

"And we are, but we gotta start somewhere. Otherwise, you're asking New Jessup folks to go against sixty years of peace here. To fight hurdle after hurdle trying to register, only to be met with violence at the door. And for what? To cast ballots for candidates who care nothing about us? There ain't any appetite for that here right now, or to hear anything about anybody's NNAS."

"Hear me out then."

"Simeon, we've been over this time and again—"

"Hear me out, Raymond!"

I shot up straight then. This man, at our house, raising his voice at my husband? I almost leaped out my chair as a pause settled between them.

Pull back, Dot wrote, pushing her palm towards the ground over and again to add: *This is NNAS business.* Simeon broke their silence before my chest stopped heaving.

"Fine, no recruitment drive. But say, for instance, your pop knew. He serves with a bunch of these men on that business council across the woods. Including judges. He already knows about municipality, and he could help grease the wheels to get our paperwork pushed through. Maybe we don't tell everyone in town yet, but we at least tell him so he's not operating in the dark."

Raymond did not hide that mention of Pop got his back up.

"Me and Percy have told you more than once to leave our old man *outta* this. Don't you ever ask my father to grease wheels for you or speak on your behalf on the other side of the woods. Get that in your head and remember it. Hear me? We never wanted him going to those meetings to begin with. Even if they never tell all, you'd best believe Cap, Mr. Marvin, and my father find ways to deal with agitators. Don't believe me? Ask Patience about getting run outta here. Everybody knows you're talking to her since she moved to DC and started working at HQ."

Simeon's shovel sliced the ground, but before he pulled the dirt, he craned his neck up for a long look at Raymond.

He's doing what? I wrote. *Did you know that?*

She shook her head and responded, *Trifling. Both of them, just trifling.*

"She wasn't run out because of the NNAS," Simeon said.

"But she *was* run out for agitating. So go on and ask her what it was like. Not only are y'all plotting insubordination against HQ," Raymond kept on, "but she's my best friend's girl, man. He stood up for you, for all that you're doing behind his back. I'm telling you to leave it alone."

Dot hummed a quiet response and I told her, just as quiet, to hush.

"It's not like that with me and her. We just agree that the NNAS can do a lot of good here right now. And you said yourself how much it bothered you that none of us cast a ballot in 1960. Not for president or city council or anything."

"Nobody's denying that."

"I'm trying to meet you halfway, Raymond, but you've got to give me something."

"This was all settled long before you came to town. You said you understood that, which was why me, Matthew, and Abel vouched for you."

"I came here from HQ, Raymond. That vouching and voting business is y'all's local creation. I agreed to abide by y'all's decision, but I didn't have to. I could've just brought the NNAS to New Jessup and stayed regardless of what you said."

Anger and sadness stilled my pen. I don't know why Dot stopped writing, but Simeon's presence all the sudden felt heavy and inevitable to me. Not exactly menacing, but not free of threat either.

"And you would've gotten run out like anybody else. There are still a couple of fellas waiting for the go-ahead—my brother included. But I opened my mouth and put my name behind you to men I respect: New Jessup–strong and coming from generations of those who stayed and built this town. I did that because you gave your word.

"There is no halfway when it comes to my family and this town, you hear me? We've invited you into our homes, Simeon. So you come in and jeopardize this project, put us all at risk? You won't have to worry about Cap running you outta town. It'll be me leading the way. Believe that."

"I appreciate that y'all have welcomed me into y'all's homes, and I do love it here," Simeon had the nerve to say before he told my husband, "but hearing you now makes me wonder if maybe the NNAS isn't right for New Jessup, because our goal is equal rights."

Now, it was Raymond who stopped digging mid-shovel. Leaving it in the ground like a leaning fence post, he rose tall with the utter disbelief on his face that was similarly roiling my insides. Feeling heat rising in my chest, I had to breathe deep and tell my heart to stop thumping so hard so I could hear better.

"You *dare* stand here on Campbell ground talking this shit? Trying to tell *me* what is, and ain't, for New Jessup? You think just because we wanna protect and build on what our grandparents started that we don't want equality? This is our birthright, man, and if you can't get behind us, it's probably better for *you* to push on."

"C'mon, Raymond. We agree on so much, and you've been like a brother to me. I'm talking the future, same as you. I wanna cast a ballot in Gilliam County, same as you."

"Not same as me, though, because I'm talking about New Jessup, Alabama—past, present, and future. Risen from the swamp—you hear me?—on my family's back and others like us. So let me tell you like this, Simeon: you're gonna stop talking this mess about putting our business in the street right now. Municipality first. Then, the vote. That's the way. It's been decided."

Disappointment and anger steamed from my head. I had invited

this man into my home, trusted him enough to speak for him, teth-
ered my family's fate to him, because he had promised to abide
by our way of life and the fellas' path for preserving our town for
future generations. This tangle of some-truths, half-truths, and
nontruths—all in service of the NNAS—and now, Simeon was
pushing to out us before we had anything to show for our sacrifices. Just one slip of his tongue could cost us business, or get us
sent away, and that was if they didn't find out across the woods
first. With those wide-open, appreciative eyes, and big Georgia
dimples, Simeon had proposed this pig roast. And now, in less than
two days' time, half of New Jessup would be in my yard because
of him.

WE ALREADY KNEW it would be big. It was bigger still. The buzzing began Saturday morning when generations of Campbell women
descended on my house with mason jars full of peaches, potatoes,
corn, carrots, and whatever they had left over from the prior year's
canning. At the home house, some cleaned the innards and made
chitlins and sausage while others picked our garden clean of every
blackberry, string bean, collard green, turnip, pecan, and strawberry.
Two of Raymond's uncles set out on the Tombigbee for catfish that
they would take charge of frying on Sunday, but the star of the show
was a 175-pound carcass that became a twenty-four-hour hog.

Men came and went to sit alongside Raymond, Pop, Percy, and
Simeon, who were out there poking coals, telling lies, and drinking
shine. There was no sign of tension between Raymond and Simeon,
no additional hostility between Percy and Simeon, and no change
at all between Pop and Simeon, either. As I snapped beans or sliced
potatoes or washed dishes, through the window, they seemed normal. In fact, the biggest commotion occurred when Mr. Marvin
pulled up Saturday evening with his father, Mr. Sir Johnson, who
was confident his was the only way to finish that hog. He baptized

the roast with his own special sauce while declaring it a sin and a shame that these men had almost ruined this beautiful animal and thank the good Lord he arrived when he did.

Mr. Sir hovered over that hog all day Sunday, serving stories as folks piled meat on their plates. Meal-crusted catfish swam in barrels of roiling, popping grease until golden fried and laid atop plates heaped with green beans, potato salad, and crackling cornbread. Little hands and faces were streaked pink with frosting from the strawberry cake, and Raymond's aunts Johnnie Mae and Melanie each watched closely for any indication that folks preferred one of their pecan pies over the other.

And I could hardly stomach a bite. Uneasiness left no room for food or drink as folks parked cars lining the service road and streamed through the pines on foot. The yard was thick with friends, family, and people I didn't even know. A head above the rest, Simeon was easy to spot as he moved around. I watched him dare children to stick hands, then arms, then bodies into the woods at the edge of the yard, bellowing that Georgia laugh as they squealed with delight pulling unscathed limbs back from the edge of fright. Saw him wander into some almost-blue joke between Major and Cap; made sure him and Pop and Pastor and Abel had enough food to fuel a heated spades game; and saw him clap Raymond's back after my husband took up for him during one of Mr. Sir's dressings down.

After awhile, I took Bea to the porch for her bottle, and Simeon searched me out carrying a plate. Lifting my daughter from my arms, he handed me the food with that smile like there was more to it than a friendly offering. He fed Bea, insisting I put something on my stomach, saying his mama always told him the hostess never eats.

"What's he talking about over there now?" I asked, nodding my head at Mr. Sir, who was in the middle of another big show.

"Still talking about how he had to poke us time and again with that crutch for catnapping over the pig last night."

"Well, he is one tough old bird. Had to be," I said in a tone that shallowed the dimples on his face and turned down the wattage on his smile. Neither Dot nor I mentioned anything to anybody about what we heard from the whispering corner. Nor did we intend to. But his cautious eyes suggested he recognized something amiss, which, if I'm honest, was enough. I wanted him to be troubled about smiling in my face after he talked the way he did about upending our lives. When I told him it was a blessing to have the old heads around reminding us where we come from, his eyes crinkled at the corners. We sat quietly for a while after that. As I picked at my plate and Bea finished her bottle, me and him sat there watching the kids brave the edge of the woods, watching the old heads in conversation with the young. My daughter fell asleep in his arms, and my anger even simmered at him for lulling her into a trusting sleep.

He broke the quiet by asking whether mine was also an old New Jessup family, and he was genuinely surprised when I told him I grew up in Rensler.

"Rensler, huh? Indeed. Let me find out you and I have something else in common. That we're transplants to New Jessup," he said.

"Thought you knew that already."

He shook his head with the furrowed brow of a man still trying to read me.

"You talk about New Jessup like you've been here all your life."

"I should've been so lucky." He had Bea's head too far back, so I laid my plate down and started to take her. He apologized and righted her quickly, keeping his hold on the most precious piece of me in this world.

"What's the other thing you say we have in common?" I asked, sitting back down.

"You have a sharp mind. Know how to turn a phrase. I bet you'd be a formidable adversary in the courtroom."

"Maybe, but you have nothing to worry about from me. I have no ambitions to become a liar."

He drew breath and parted his lips to say something, but my face blanked for a smile or a frown. He took the jab with nervous good humor and said, "*Heh, heh.* New Jessup: where the warmest folks tell the coldest jokes."

"You are enjoying yourself here, I hope," I hinted. Bea was sucking her lips slightly in a milk slumber, and we both turned eyes to watch her. "This is the best place in the world for us."

He looked at my daughter with the kindest, sincerest eyes I had ever seen on the man.

"You know, Alice? I do love it here. In this great land, there's nowhere better for a Negro to rest his head."

THE MOON WAS SO BRIGHT that Sunday that revelers treated the night like the day, staying long after the stars blanketed the sky. Even cleaning could not dampen Pop's recollections of the party. While him and Raymond folded up the tables to carry back to the shed, he recalled with fondness how Mr. Sir guarded that pig, serving up stories about roasting the Negro Jessup way; about how Mother Dear Blakely told of coming home from Tuskegee in 1895 with a nursing degree and a determination to get Negro doctors practicing in their own hospital. With pride, Pop smiled that others had recalled to him how Big Poppa often bragged that he got that Tin Lizzie up to "forty-two—*forty-two!*—miles an hour" the day he spent riding Booker T. Washington himself around! Every time I returned from carrying dishes inside, an endless stream of stories poured from Pop's mouth. Although plenty of shine and beer had been drunk, he was high on remembrance, which flowed easily into excitement about the future.

"All this today has me thinking," I heard him say just as I was on my way inside with another armload of dishes. He was folding one table, and Raymond another, for a stack while Percy tended the trash fire nearby.

"About what?" Raymond asked as he stacked another table on the pile so they could move a bunch, together, at the same time.

"I know I gave you a hard time about municipality at first, but we had families here today—some of four generations, from great grands to great-grandbabies. Look at what we've built! How far we've come, but also, we're keeping our traditions. Old and new."

"Old and new, that's right. It was a good time," Raymond said.

"We should do our own roast every year; maybe even take over the family reunion from A.C.," Pop said with a gleam in his eye.

"Alright, Pop. Calm down. You're getting yourself excited," Raymond said, chuckling softly.

"I'm just proud that it's my sons—my sons—gonna be the ones to give us our own. Y'all always had a good group of guys around you."

"Thanks, Pop. That means a lot."

I headed inside to the kitchen and dumped my armload. Nothing sounded out of the ordinary; they were just talking. In fact, me and Dot saw and heard them jawing through the window for the few minutes I stood there drying, chatting, helping put stuff away. Making my way back to the porch, the first thing I noticed was Percy's neck snap towards Raymond when Pop said, "And I'm thinking—maybe don't put us old heads out to pasture just yet."

"What do you mean?" Raymond asked.

"Let us help you. With municipality. Whatever we can do."

"You're already talking it up to Pastor, Cap, other folks. That's a big help."

"But, I mean, let us put something into the work. Come to your meetings on Monday nights. There's gonna be a lot of planning to do moving forward, and most of y'all are hardly outta short pants."

"We're talking through it," said Percy with wary eyes fixed on his brother, the embers from the trash fire floating around like lightning bugs. "The way we figured it, we're the third generation to keep New Jessup going."

"Yeah, Pop," said Raymond as he and Pop picked up the stack of tables. "We've got a handle on things. It's our turn now."

"We could show y'all a thing or two, I bet. None of the guys you have right now is over thirty. You could use some guys like me, Cap, Marvin—men a little longer in the tooth."

"No, Pop," Percy said now, trying to keep his voice steady. "You can't. You just can't. None of you. This ain't for you."

Pop stopped moving towards the shed, stopping Raymond as well. The flames dancing in the trash barrel threw deep shadows across Percy's face. Pop's cooling mood chilled the air, but there was no other indication of a brewing storm—only the scents of fire, the remains of the feast, and the cowcumbers. No rain, or even a cloud worrying the midnight sky or its stars. Still, I slowed pace gathering dishes as Pop stood to his tallest self and looked Percy in the eye.

"Excuse me, Percy? What—"

"Did y'all see these children running into the trees today?" I cut in. "Jumping their little sticky bodies through right here, probably attracting every—" Pop cut me off with a glare and turned back to Percy. Raymond's *be easy* eyes in my direction asked for cooperation, patience for him to handle the situation, so I obliged.

"Tell me how this ain't for us, too, Percy?" Pop said.

"He doesn't mean anything," said Raymond, drawing Pop's heat. "It's just—"

"But he said it. Y'all got something against these men? They practically raised you."

"No, of course not! Calm down, Pop! He didn't mean it like that. You've already been a big help," Raymond told him. "Now c'mon, let's move these tables."

"Then why not? I ain't heard a good reason yet." Raymond and Percy traded looks, and then my husband took a deep breath.

"Because, Pop. We're working on something."

"I know, that's what I'm saying. Let us help."

"No, you don't know. And Percy's right, you can't."

"You ain't making sense. What don't we know? Why can't we help, Raymond?"

After another look at Percy, then me, and a final deep breath, Raymond said, "Because what we're doing, it's . . . with the NNAS. I mean . . . we're all NNAS."

Pop's eyes glazed at his end of the stack of tables in his hands. We all stood, stalk-still, waiting on his reaction to Raymond's own violation of the Rule of Three. Overhead, even the black silhouettes of trees leaned closer to listen inside a night still fragrant with pork and magnolias. The ancestors peeped through their windows; all of nature watching, bearing witness to Pop, now a man alone among his kin and his woods, as he realized that we were all involved in this secret in some way.

"What 'we all'? You?" His words cracked at Raymond like a rifle shot, and he nodded. Then, at Percy, then me alone, with Dot still inside at the sink. "Y'all knew?" I nodded. "What 'we all' are you talking about, Raymond?" The tables crackled and groaned under the pressure of his trembling grip as Raymond came clean about the fellas, the plan, and about how they brought the NNAS to New Jessup; about Patience and the articles; about Simeon's real reason for coming to town.

The sky vacuumed up the air like it did before a storm when Raymond mentioned the bus boycotts. My men stood there with eyes locked on each other, at opposite ends of the tables and the world. Pop's was the first thunder of the tempest. He heaved his end of the tables to the ground, causing Raymond to lose his grip. The wood shattered, and Pop was hollering before the splintered pieces settled in the gravel.

"Y'all need to stop this mess. Immediately," he hollered.

"It ain't that simple, Pop."

"I don't give a good goddamn whether it's simple or impossible! End it. Now. Get these instigators outta New Jessup, and quietly so you don't have Cap or anybody else coming down on your heads."

Staring steadily at Raymond, Pop pulled his keys from his pocket. He turned on his heel to leave in the Cadillac for his house. Raymond talked at Pop's back, first trying the same reasoning he always used about not wanting mixing and keeping our community to ourselves. But Pop's feet skidded to a stop on the gravel when Raymond's thunder boomed.

"Well, what were *you* planning to do, old man? Keep shucking and jiving for these rednecks across the woods? They'd sooner hold a gun to my baby's head than allow her to *think* about attending Jessup schools, nevermind the fact that we don't want her over there in the first place! I'll fight for our family, New Jessup, and our way of life with my last, dying breath, and if that means having the NNAS behind us, then so be it."

Percy smiled, nodding encouragement at Raymond because words he would say without a thought now streamed out my husband's mouth. But I was too stunned to share his enthusiasm. Me and Raymond had promised that we would never send our child to a desegregated school. But his words made me think not about the gun in our face, but the one the courts put to our backs. To send our daughter across the way, or desegregate New Jessup schools, whether we wanted to or not.

"Shucking and jiving, you said to me? *Hoo!* Lord Jesus, if my boy didn't find his voice and lose his entire cotton-picking mind! 'Shucking and jiving' because I'm telling them we ain't agitating over here? I know you ain't talking to me like that, son. I raised four kids, including your ass, in New Jessup, and we've lived this way for almost sixty years."

"Courts integrated the schools *after* the last of your children graduated. There's something entirely different brewing here, and we need to be thinking, acting, with haste if we wanna keep our community together. Preserve our way of life. We telegraph across the woods that we ain't interested in mixing, now, or ever. Yes. But with our own schools and everything, we maintain our independence. How can you argue with that?"

"Nobody's arguing with it, which is why it astounds me that y'all brought the NNAS here."

"This idea needed support, resources, organization, to move forward. They have all that. But they needed local boys, too, and they knew it. We know the lay of the land. How separation can work for Negro communities. Got them thinking about equal rights a whole different way. A way that doesn't mean upending lives, risking ourselves for integration that folks don't even want! NNAS HQ is already talking about repeating this in Montgomery, Chicago, New Orleans, Oakland, Atlanta, all over." Pop breathed deep and glared, the words boiling inside him until they spilled over.

"Me, Marvin, and Cap ain't shucking and jiving for anybody, hear? How dare you talk to your own father like that when we only wanted to keep agitating off the radar."

"Nobody's agitating," Percy jumped in. "Stop with that. And you need to quit those meetings. We're maintaining separate, saying give us our money, and keep your doggone lunch counters. That's more than enough." Pop cut eyes at Percy, but bounced his keys in his hand, looking back at Raymond.

"I can't quit the council, and y'all know it. Especially not with what y'all are telling me now. Who's in charge? Who came up with this scheme in the first place?" Raymond's closed mouth and tight jaw told on him. "Of course it would be my own son."

"Pop, we're really just trying to protect what the town fathers built—that's it. No mixing, no agitating."

Slowly, Pop took a deep, deep breath, and shook his head as he put his keys back in his pocket. Then he leaned down, picked up a piece of broken table, and nodded towards Raymond to do the same.

"You better know what you're doing. Keep these men in line, hear? Don't tell Simeon I know anything, and don't any of you say a word to another living soul."

TWENTY-FOUR

The envelope contained one of my most unwelcome surprises in four years. Not that he knew that, or maybe he did, but either way, the setup was elaborate. In July of 1961, somehow Raymond had even convinced the sun to melt celebration gold across the horizon, its shimmering heat forcing us underneath the black walnut tree at Waverly's that stretched from the end, to the end, of town. He told me to rest my legs (my "beautiful legs") while he stood in line for our supper. Another of the evening's suspicious events I happily ignored as I sat entirely free for these few moments—nothing to do, nowhere to go, and nobody to take care of but myself, as he had even arranged for Pop to spoil Bea back at the house, giving me and him an evening alone by the river.

He returned with mustards, hushpuppies, fried perch, and a Cheshire Cat grin that said he'd done something. The secret behind his smile lasted all throughout the meal, while he tortured me with words as flirtatious as they were spare.

"What's gotten into you?" I asked.

"Nothing." He chewed and kicked up the corner of his smile.

"Then what's that look?"

"Nothing." He flicked his grays, ticked his smile another notch.

Because nothing? There's nothing so big as nothing. "Just hoping your meal tastes as good as you look eating it."

My cheeks flashed as the mama on the next blanket sucked teeth. These were private words, dance-floor words, words inviting me from sleep's caress into his own. Words spoken straight from his lips to my ear and never to be heard by anybody else. But his smile kicked up another notch at seeing my surprise, so I allowed my butterflies to flutter in anticipation of some sweet sneakiness.

We finished eating and lingered long after the moon rose. Some people stayed, but most packed into cars and drove off. Mr. Waverly closed the awning and left us stragglers to enjoy the night, so, with outstretched legs, I leaned back on my elbows to moonbathe. Raymond propped on an elbow next to me, longwise, with his finger tracing Little Turtle. With eyes closed and facing the heavens, during a pause after saying nothing memorable, he asked what I would think about finally taking that trip to DC.

I blinked eyes at Raymond's moonlit grays and his bit-lip smile.

Conflicts had mercifully arisen to keep us from visiting DC over the years—it was always "dress season" until Raymond got me fired from the shop, and he didn't dare ask me for months after that—not when I was plagued with dizzy spells, a sick stomach, and disappointment about Taylor Made. Then after Bea came, she was too small to travel. Matthew did his internship at Freedmen's Hospital up there, and was scheduled to come home permanently in the summer of 1961 to start his residency at Blakely Memorial. That would have closed our window of opportunity had Matthew not promised Patience he would stay in DC permanently if she joined him from Detroit.

My intuition was blunted, intoxicated by the honeysuckle-scented river mist and Raymond's sweet flirtations.

"We couldn't possibly," I said, brushing it off with a laugh. "Who would watch Bea?" The moon was full, yellow, but I ignored its efforts to illuminate the plotting behind his smile. When I closed my eyes and relaxed back into moonbathing, a small, cream envelope kissed the stomach of my dress. His lips parted with sly excitement when I finished reading the paper, bolted up straight, and looked him in the face.

"This says you and me are going to Washington, DC, in three weeks."

"Does it?"

"You know it does."

He was all relaxation, still on his elbow—his grin confident that I wanted to visit Washington, DC. So convinced of the rightness of this grand gesture that he pretended not to notice how quickly I returned the envelope to him. He just slid it into his back pocket and kept talking to Little Turtle.

"Well, we have an anniversary coming up, in case you forgot. You were working, then last year, you were expecting, then, we waited for Bea to get a little bigger. I thought we might finally take a proper honeymoon. I can show you around DC. Show my wife off *to* DC. And we can catch up with Matthew and Patience. What do you say?" he asked.

"'Thought we might,' indeed, Raymond. This cake's already baked. But we can't go to DC. Like I said . . . it ain't proper to travel without the baby." I clutched the blanket so hard the soil's dampness seeped through the wool.

"Pop and Dot are over the moon to fatten her up all week. She'll be in great hands." He glanced at my ankle and asked, "So what else is on your mind?"

"Nothing."

"Nothing?" His cocked eyebrow told me to find a better lie or tell the truth.

"Nothing. Why? What's that look for?"

"Because your foot is fidgeting to make poor Little Turtle seasick, darling."

Front doors were on my mind—walking through without a thought since the shoeshine man assured me that's how New Jessup Negroes did. No soda fountain, or water fountain, was marked as COLORED ONLY because all the folks were Colored since I arrived in '57. Bronze to brown; dusky to deep night—the closest I knew to white were Matthew and his mama. So thinking about whether doors would welcome me or not had turned my Little Turtle into my Judas.

"If you wanted a vacation, we could just stay at the Collier House for the week," I suggested. "We can eat wherever we want, go wherever we want right here."

He saw right through the door I was trying to close and opened it gently.

"DC is no New Jessup. That's true," he said. "It's no Jessup, either. We're gonna eat well, see the sights, watch Sam Cooke play, and spend a week entirely alone in our hotel room—no Pop, no baby, no Dot causing a ruckus in my kitchen at four-thirty in the morning. Just me and you and those beautiful legs."

"Now you trying too hard, Raymond. I get it . . . you wanna visit DC. But keep in mind—I ain't thought about a back door, or a WHITES ONLY sign, in almost four years."

"And I wouldn't take you anywhere like that. I visited Matthew back in '57. No signs, darling."

"That make it better or worse?" He chuckled softly then—really, a small sound that could be mistaken for contentment, or the shift of getting more comfortable. A small, closed-mouth *umph* that he tried to hide behind a smile to convince me that a hurt no longer hurt. Sometimes from gashes or bone-deep bruises from searching the boneyard for parts—still aching as they healed from deep purple to yellow to just the twinge.

"You'd rather have folks shouting hate to your face?" he said.

"My face is just fine in New Jessup, Alabama, Raymond Campbell."

"I know it is," he said, the flirtation in his voice cut short by that false contentment again. He sat up.

"What's aching you?" I asked him.

"Nothing to worry about. Hit my shin at the shop."

"You didn't tell me that when you came home."

"Hardly hurts. I was just lying on it funny. Besides, I was trying to get you out the house before you got ahold of me with one of your ointments or potions."

"I don't hear you calling them 'potions' when I'm out gathering marigolds for your aches and pains, or when that ointment takes the swelling down."

"No. You're right."

"Where we stay in DC? I bet they won't even have marigolds. Probably just aspirin and ice." The moonlight played with the flecks of green and yellow in his grays and one side of his mouth kicked up—his willingness to take some light sparring after the fates had already called the round for him. And I genuinely wanted him to be happy, though I also wanted to remind him that this trip would force me to dress myself in armor I had shed years before.

"Probably no marigolds, no," he said. "But we'll see Matthew, and Freedmen's Hospital is there if we really get into a scrape."

"We have Blakely Memorial right here. And marigolds. Acres of hydrangeas, azaleas, real pretty ficus—"

"There are lots of pretty flowers in the world. Different, too."

"Because of the soil. The climate."

"You know more than most in this town about the world outside New Jessup."

"Sure do. Know how to grow things. Know what makes them wither, and what makes them thrive."

In the heartbeat between injury and pain, his eyes flashed. Whether because of his shin, or because of my words, I don't know. But my heart caught to see it either way.

"Look, Raymond, it's just that, coming up, even if there were no signs, there were signs, you know?" He absorbed my words with a slow nod. "Here, there are no signs welcoming or refusing me. No signs telling me my place because everyplace is my place."

"I know you love it here, and it makes my heart soar that *you* don't have to deal with hatefulness. And you won't."

The tender case he made brought a smile of concession to my lips. Still, *you* lifted his tone, meaning to stand out whether he intended it or not. Hovering as a reminder that he *did* have to deal with signs. Like weeks before, when the Fitzhughs had called looking for the rear fender and door from a Cadillac 62 and he had scoured the boneyard looking for the car. It came apart easy enough, and Raymond carried the parts across the woods. Chase burst through the front door before Raymond could make his way around to the back (no need trying front doors over there)—meeting him in full view of the audience waiting through the plate glass inside the waiting room. He loud-talked my husband, saying that he had asked for a whole car, and true to Campbell form, Raymond had only turned up with the pieces.

Victorious by the Tombigbee, Raymond went back down to his elbow, adjusting his leg to avoid the bruise again. He urged me to uncross my ankles to let him play with Little Turtle. Happily obliged, he traced my birthmark and talked about our itinerary until deep into the purple night. After he stood and pulled me to my feet, we yawned and stretched the kinks. He looked at his old, beat-up watch.

"You're keeping me up late tonight, darling. Me and Lisle wanna drop a transmission over to Fitzhugh's tomorrow before church."

"On a Sunday?" I shook the blanket.

"This way, Chase won't be there to act a fool in front of their customers again."

"I still can't believe he would say something stupid as that. 'Ask for a car and get the pieces,' like you didn't bring exactly what he asked for," I said.

With my arms spread wide to fold the blanket, he told me, "Yeah. Trying to claim we used to tow the cars in more wrecked than they should be, and it drove their customers' repair costs through the roof. Said that's why they ended the towing." Everything stilled except the catfish thrashing its desperate, dying breaths inside my chest.

"Raymond, stop lying."

"God heard me speak it, darling."

"You never told me that part. About the costs. Not to mention that he said *they* ended the towing?"

"Well, that's what the man said."

"Ain't that rich? Weren't those cars already cracked up to begin with, which is why they *needed* the wrecker?"

"You got it."

"So they were upcharging their customers? Ripping off their own folks?" He nodded. I needed something to take my frustration, so I snapped the blanket a couple good times to shake every crumb of dirt loose. But the stink of this news lingered. Dirtmouthing my men and their work to rip off other whitefolks? I was too through. "Trifling! Chase Fitzhugh couldn't fix a training wheel to a bicycle, to be blaming us for all that. He should be ashamed of himself."

"Should be. But trust me—he ain't."

"And what about his father? Where was Mr. Doing-Business-Since-Toy-Trucks this whole time?"

"Inside. Through the window. Doing something behind the register to avoid my eye."

"That's because he knew their high bills were none of our fault. He was right to be shame-faced about it. He shoulda yanked his son's chain long ago."

"Some folks figure it's better to go along to get along. Fitzhugh keeps saying he's retiring soon. Got one foot out the door. And besides, he treated that phone call with Pop like they were doing us a favor to end the towing."

"Let me call him up, then. Remind him that Campbells never worked for anybody but Campbells. I'll tell him exactly what they can do with the money and the aggravation that comes with it."

"I don't think so, darling." He laughed softly. "Thank you, but I think it's just as well you never meet the Fitzhughs. No. Let's both lay it down. I brought you here to talk about a trip and an anniversary," he said, laying a hand on my shoulder. Time for my heart to stop racing again.

This time, throbbing because the Fitzhughs were once again out here proving that they were nobody's Negroes. Not self-reliant. Or talented. Or resilient. And only creative enough for this sleight of hand with their customers. They were nothing like my husband who—according to some quick math in my head—had planned this trip less than a week after this happened across the woods. A man of the fullest measure, proving indignity away by grand gesture, if a gesture that had me reaching for excuses and alternatives.

"I thought you'd like to get away for a while," he said. "That's it. DC's not New Jessup, no, but I've been before, and Matthew and Patience are there now. We'll find our folks and have a good time." He pulled my hand to his lips, kissed my palm, then pressed it against his cheek and closed his eyes. Pressing his flesh into my hand the way one who radiates nightglow pleads for trust, support, and forgiveness from the ones he both protects and needs most. The real cross of a Negro man and the reason a Negro woman like me clenched teeth and swallowed bitter pills like candy.

"All this today, buttering me up to tell me about this trip? You coulda just told me," I said.

"I did just tell you."

"Without Waverly's and the river, I mean."

"I love perch and love watching you eat perch," he said, his voice molasses with flirtation. "The way you pick at it with those long fingers, and your pretty lips shine with grease."

"There you go."

"I just wanna see that smile."

"Here it is, baby."

"And look—I booked you some time with Miss Vivian on Monday. You know how hard it is to get an appointment with that woman?" When I raised an eyebrow to remind him of just how well I knew it, he blushed and flashed that guilty grin. "But she squeezed since it was you." I started to object to the extravagance. I clipped coupons to stretch dollars he never asked me to stretch. But I liked being the reason for the light in his eye.

So on Monday, Dot watched from the corner while me and Earnestine had differing opinions over pins. Resting a hand atop a stomach already rounded by Clifford's little brother (*brother*, she was sure), Dot talked and distracted our babies with toys and baubles from the dressing room while I slipped in and out of outfits for alteration. The appointment was a crowded one, made more so by Earnestine, who was fitting me, pinning me, doing all Miss Vivian had done for me in the past. But Miss Vivian was busy with Mrs. Wicks on the neighboring pedestal, leaving me with her daughter to place pins I could place myself.

"Well, isn't it nice to be Mrs. Raymond Campbell? Washington, DC," Miss Vivian sniffed in that quiet, musical way of an impressed mama. I smiled and warmed inside.

But before I could open my mouth, Dot said, "*Hmph*, I'll say," with her lip poked out. "I married the wrong Campbell man, Miss Vivian."

"You think you may have wanted to figure that out a little sooner, Dorothy?" said Miss Vivian, flicking her eyes towards Dot's belly. My sister-in-law's cheeks turned cherry red.

"Miss Vivian! Isn't that just the wickedest thing to say to me?"

"Call it what you like, but with so many young ladies around here expecting, it might make sense to start making maternity clothes. Right, Earnestine?"

One day, Mama kissed and hugged me and Rosie and promised to be there when we arrived home from school. But while we were away, and without warning, she collapsed in the cotton, the thread of her days snapping so violently that the moon should have never continued to rise and set. My everyday had already ended with Miss Vivian, but another piece of my eternity died when she uttered Earnestine's name where mine belonged.

"Alice?" Mrs. Wicks said.

"Yes, ma'am?"

"I asked you about Matthew Washington."

"Yes, ma'am, what about him?"

"How he's doing," she said with the irritation of repetition. "They introduced the new residents at the Blakely Memorial benefit, and I was surprised not to see him among them." She had no cause to be surprised when everybody in town knew that Matthew and the Washingtons were still pegged as sympathetic to Patience and her troubles. The sweet shop lines had recovered some but were still far from the crowds of old whenever I passed by on the street, and he had only been home once or twice since the river. Patience moving to DC was none of anybody's business. Besides, I was already nervous about seeing her for the first time since she was sent away, and had no desire to bring her up in my appointment and remind Miss Vivian about my role in Patience's undoing.

Mrs. Wicks coursed bankers' money through her veins, and she had a hand in every social club and activity on our side of the woods. She was forever bragging about her family lineage—her father and her husband and her sons. All Morehouse men. All bankers or bankers-in-training. Women clamored to touch the hem of her garment or scrambled to stay out of her way. But not Miss Vivian, who had been working on dresses for Mrs. Wicks since her grandmere taught her to sew inside the first Taylor Made.

"We need our young people to come back here, be leaders here," Mrs. Wicks said. "Take my boys, for example—"

"Stay still, Brandy," Miss Vivian repeated calmly as she slid pins into the fabric around Mrs. Wicks' waist.

"I'm being still, Vivian. Anyway, Raymond remembers my Joseph, I'm sure. He tutored my son in math all through high school, and now, Joseph is home, recently promoted again. At the bank, you know. Anyway, I thought Raymond and Matthew would come back as professional men, too—become real Negroes of high esteem in New Jessup. They are both from old families, and that helps, I suppose, but . . . well, maybe not everyone is meant for professional life. Matthew though," she said, and *tsk*ed.

Miss Vivian's quick eyes flicked up from sticking pins. She had worked her way to Mrs. Wicks' generous left thigh and was making progress around the curves when Mrs. Wicks launched into another brag about her sons—the banker and the business student, both destined to lead a community full of Campbells, Taylors, Royals, Greenes, and others who had cast their buckets, and used those buckets to drain the swamp. So it didn't surprise me one bit when Mrs. Wicks shouted, "*Ow*! Vivian, you stuck me!" Miss Vivian, still with eyes on the dress, scolded her quietly to keep still again. Mrs. Wicks rubbed the pinprick and frowned, but Miss Vivian would never stick her hard enough to draw blood and ruin the fabric. "I didn't mean any harm." Her voice trembled with indignation.

"Who says you did, Brandy? I warned you a number of times to keep still."

"Vivian, honestly. I've known you too long to be playing silly games with these pins."

"Yes, we have known each other a long time. And I dare say that folks like me, and others without a college degree, have also become *your* Negroes of high esteem."

"Of course. No one is saying otherwise."

"But what you are saying isn't far off from all that talk that almost tore our community apart in the swamp—that the educated few should lead the uneducated masses. We lost a host of our professionals back when my parents, and yours, refused that thinking and the purse strings that came with it. In a community rich with talent and creativity of all sorts," she scoffed, "who are the few, and who are the masses?

"Now again, just the other day, some young people were outside my shop distributing flyers about desegregating the schools because *they* think we should. But I never wanted my girls in an integrated school, nor did you want your boys in one, Brandy."

Without changing a note in her voice, Miss Vivian's words set me to high alert, and I readied myself to tell whatever truth the moment required. So when she asked whether Clifford and Bea would be attending school across the woods, I said, "No, ma'am. Not in my lifetime. And what group would push for such a thing here, of all places?"

She shrugged.

"The name escapes me now. Some alphabet soup organization with which I'm unfamiliar," she said. She had mentioned the NAACP, the SCLC, and the NNAS in plenty of prior conversations, so I figured she would call their names. "Earnest already knew about it when I gave him the flyer, but it does make you wonder why the few outside my window get to make decisions for the rest of us. Who ordained them?" she asked.

With icy, casual disdain, her accusation flowed into a dressing room where pins pricked and words drew blood. Ordained. It was easy to understand why folks felt the way they did about the NNAS— there was hardly a headline about integration around the country with its name unattached. But New Jessup was baptized in the wellspring of self-reliance. It wasn't the NNAS who brought me through the water, raised Raymond from a baby, or ministered to us, taught us to appreciate, and maintain, our way of life. Our wishes and sacrifices for the community were as inseparable from New Jessup's own desires as a splash was inseparable from the river.

"Well, thank goodness Cap already knew about it," I said.

"Oh yes, he's never far behind an instigator. You remember those articles," she said coolly, without looking up from her work.

"And did you ever see what she wrote about us?" Mrs. Wicks asked. "Such an ungrateful child this world has never known."

"Yes, well, all the more reason it was better that Earnest ran her out. We don't want the sheriff coming through here indiscriminately, thinking we all share her views. But you are right, Brandy . . . no one wins when we lose all of our young people," she said, tugging the hem to straighten the seam on Mrs. Wicks' dress. With a satisfied nod, Mrs. Wicks bunched the skirt in her hands and descended the pedestal to change into her next outfit. Miss Vivian came over to my mirror and shifted some pins around on my dress while she waited for Mrs. Wicks to return.

"I know Patience was your friend, and it was hard to see her go," she said. "But I hope you understand that if there are people who need to be dealt with—" She shrugged the last of her thought as she moved another pin, and I readied another half-truth for the community.

"Yes, ma'am, I suppose you're right. But whoever it was outside here, they'll move on just like the rest of them. Ain't nothing for them in New Jessup."

"*There is* nothing for them here," she corrected, another lesson atop the lessons already playing in my head: *Hold your head high. Stand up straight. We hold ourselves with distinction here at Taylor Made.* "And I know I'm right," she said.

We moved on in conversation the way you do when you have minutes, instead of days, to wander through topics at your leisure: my airplane outfit and our DC itinerary; Bea's diet; Miss Vivian's war with the abomination polyester; whether I had tickets for Mrs. Wicks' school benefit dance. After more than two hours in the mirror, with Mrs. Wicks finally gone, Miss Vivian wrote the mile-long order onto my account—dresses, suits, new jewelry, and a new handbag for my first time ever leaving Alabama.

"You come back in two weeks, and we'll have all of this finished for you, Mrs. Campbell," she said. A formality she considered—judging by her smile—to be a playful pinprick, it nonetheless stuck me to bleed.

"Miss Vivian . . . what's this 'Mrs. Campbell' business?"

"That *is* your name?" she said, like she was reminding me.

"Yes, ma'am, but whatever happened to just plain old Alice?" I asked.

"I'd consider it a great personal failing of mine if you believed yourself to be 'just plain old' anything," she told me. "Still, if it's 'Alice' you prefer, then you'll get 'Alice' from me."

MISS VIVIAN WAS STILL ON MY MIND when Raymond's question about the window or the aisle seat jolted me back into the plane. The sun was shining through the window onto seats 22A and B. The light was bright, bright white enough to make the back of my right eye throb. Across the aisle, a white man growled at a boy sandwiched between him and his wife to keep still. I twirled my pearls, realizing that there would soon be thirty thousand feet of blue sky between solid ground and my shoe leather. But standing there, watching that man, as we moved to take the seats across the aisle, the whole sky had already opened up between me and New Jessup. Because sifting through and deciphering between the good, middling, and dangerous was something I had not had to do for four years—not since my time in New Jessup had given me freedom from perpetually wondering about whitefolks' intentions.

"These are our seats? You sure?"

"Positive, darling. 22A and B." Raymond showed me the tickets again, but over top, all I noticed was that white man grimacing apologetically about his misbehaving son. In his shy smile, I saw Fitzhugh, who had refused Raymond's eye weeks before. And I wondered how often Mr. Shy Smile had looked away when the time came. How often had Mr. Shy Smile been "the time coming" himself? How often had he ginned up a pile of lies and spread them like infection, or snatched a Negro college boy off the street? How often had he showered Negro girls with red clay dust and Big Red soda, or been the silhouette over somebody's grieving daughter in a cotton field? How often had he thought a Negro's time had come? And how often had he done more than thought it? The unspeakable, the unthinkable, the monstrous and unimaginable except to those with imagination for spilling Negro blood. His hands seemed scrubbed and manicured that day across the aisle, but our blood never washes from hands always thirsty for it.

I nodded and smiled at the man, trying to squint my headache away as all that wondering raced through my mind. When I asked Raymond, for a third time, "You sure these are our seats?" He reached around me, pulled the shade, and ushered me to the window.

LATER, THE HOTEL DOOR SHUT BEHIND US, closing out all the *click-clack* footsteps on tile, the babies fussing, cars honking, jets blowing, folks shouting, second-guessing, breath-holding. With no more need to smile politely for Mr. Shy Smiles, Mr. Deep Dimples, Mr. Square Teeth, and any other time-comers, I took my first good exhale in hours. As I unpacked and hung our things, Raymond pored over the itinerary, looking for the place where we had reservations for supper.

But more than food, I wanted to be with the Alabama I'd felt in his first, sleep-hazed words of the morning. His long arm laid heavy over me after I hit my alarm, squeezing me just before I slipped from our bed. Like he would do sometimes when he was dreaming or shifting to get more comfortable. It was hours before his alarm, and he seemed deeply overcome by the sandman's dust—relaxed, inhaling and exhaling early dawn. But my body was rigid to his ease.

As though dreaming about our conversation from Waverly's about the trip, words continued across his lips in a soft, sleepy voice. "Yeah, but nowhere is truly New Jessup but New Jessup."

"Raymond, baby," I said, trying to rouse him with light taps. "You talking in your sleep again."

"I'm awake, darling. Thought the squeeze let you know." His chuckle in my ear was almost drowsy enough to pull me back asleep.

"Oh. What are you saying then?"

"Nowhere else in the land is New Jessup, that's true. No matter how many Negro cities, towns, there are, or ever will be."

"No. I guess that's right."

"But you ain't who you are because of New Jessup, Alice. You got off that bus with your blood already spiced." I laughed. "Soft voice and skilled shooter? Your deadly smile and catamount heart? The way words flow from your tongue, and the way you draw them from mine? There's never been another like you."

"You talking like you half-sleep, baby," I said with a smile in my voice, rubbing his forearm gently in appreciation.

"Maybe. But the way I see it, that's why we can visit DC. Go anywhere in the world. You brought all that here, and you'll carry it wherever we go. You're Alabama, girl," he said with a smiling, twilight voice. "Wherever we go."

TWENTY-FIVE

The curtains slid open the next day, with the day, like I had not signed up for a vacation from the dawn. By the time the soft sunlight surprised the sleep fog from my eyes, the shower faucet squeaked, revealing Raymond's whereabouts. I rolled over and enjoyed the sheets, pulling the covers to my chin and the blankets back over to trap the heat of his still-warm spot. I turned my face into his pillow and his scent, and away from the sunlight, listening to the shower running and the barely-there sound of traffic six stories below. The same sort of traffic sounds that used to lull me to sleep in my old apartment. With each deep breath, I told myself I would get up on the next exhale. But the next one came and went, came and went. Came. And. Went. Until I opened my eyes and his gloating smile was looking down at me.

"Vacation looks good on you, darling. I can't ever remember seeing you sleep in."

We dressed and walked arm in arm up the sidewalk without a single sign in the window—even if there was plenty of unwelcoming: a pocketbook clutched closer at the sight of us; an up-and-down glance chastising our insolence for sharing concrete. Involuntary tics reminding us that not all unwelcoming is posted in the window at eye level.

We arrived at a high-rise, rode the elevator to the top, and ended up outside Dr. Matthew Washington's door. Raymond straightened his lapels and took a deep breath before he knocked, but Matthew—tipped off by his doorman—yanked the door open before the first tap.

"Hey, young boy!" Matthew smiled, half-smothering a yawn and scratching at some new hair on his face. He wore rumpled pajama bottoms and a white T-shirt looking due for a good cleaning. "Y'all finally made it! But . . . it's seven-thirty in the morning."

He opened the door to a modest apartment—not much bigger than my kitchenette over Taylor Made. Except it had a massive L-shaped leather sectional that ate up most of the floor space in the living room, and there was a square, crystal-topped coffee table taking almost all the room inside the L. Tall windows faced a full, southern view, and Matthew's longing eyes glanced briefly towards morning in Alabama. The comforter was only disheveled on half the bed, there was a clean bathroom with his and hers toiletries, and a kitchen with a table and two chairs. The seat cushions were moss-green plastic—one, split open with a valley of egg-yolk yellow foam running front to back, and the other, with thousands of veins cracked into the plastic. A macramé shoulder bag hung from that chair, and on the tabletop in front of it, an advertisement was circled in red pen:

> Why buy a house for your landlord?
> Whether you rent, or whether you buy,
> you pay for the house you occupy!

The ad had a picture of a little house with some trees around it on some postage-stamp-sized-looking land.

Off the back of the torn seat hung Matthew's blazer. A chill shot through me at the sight of *Washington Afro-American* headlines familiar enough to be a fingerprint.

LEADERS PREDICT WASHINGTON RACE RIOT UNLESS
COP BRUTALITY, NO JOBS STOP

HOW GHETTOES GROW: PEOPLE FORCED TO PAY HIGH
RENT FOR RUNDOWN HOUSING

"THEY ALL LOOK ALIKE TO ME" SAYS COP IN ARRESTS

"We're working on replacing my bachelor furniture," Matthew said. "Got the sofa and coffee table new, though." He winked his preview to a smart comment ahead. "And, of course, the bed."

Next, he squinted into the Frigidaire. Seeing only some cold cuts and slices of processed cheese, half a gallon of milk, a paper bag of some sort, and no eggs or vegetables of any kind, he scratched at that hair on his face for breakfast ideas and apologized for being ill prepared to receive us.

"Between Patience's schedule and mine, seems we never quite make it to the market, or even know whose turn it is to get there," he said. "She's gonna try and catch up with us this week, but she spends every waking hour either working a headline or downtown at NNAS HQ."

He dressed and we piled into his little Datsun for a drive over to Freedmen's Hospital, where he worked and took most of his meals. Pushing trays through the cafeteria line, Matthew piled food high on his plate, and when we reached the table, he poured maple syrup between every pancake in his stack. Curds of scrambled eggs floated atop the lake of overflowing sweetness.

"Thin as you've become, Matthew, I can hardly believe you'll finish all that," I teased as he bit a sausage link in half. He snorted a laugh and scratched his chin again. "And all that hair on your face must be itchy."

"Damn, I miss Alabama." He smiled as he chewed. "Nobody talks to me like that except my mama."

People in every shade of the fall forest filled the cafeteria wearing white coats from short to long. But there were also younger students like Mama was supposed to be, and Rosie was supposed to be, and I was supposed to be had I ever filled out my Stillman application. Serious, studious men and women digging into mounds of food and hovering over steaming coffees as they talked through the open pages of medical texts. And Matthew basked among them, introducing me and Raymond to nearly every passerby with his trademark smile and eyes sparkling with that same freedom as the little girl from the playground slides all those years ago. All that New Jessup confidence on display like a boy grown into his daddy's shoes; who knew the world yet glowed with self-assurance despite the world. While watching Matthew in his element, I quietly promised the universe that Bea would always know a New Jessup way of life so that my daughter— my mama's granddaughter—would finally take a place at Stillman.

Raymond hung a new Polaroid around my neck, and over some days, we bounced around DC seeing the sights. Often with Matthew, though sometimes he had to work. But we three took photographs in front of the Capitol building, and next to the Hope Diamond at the Smithsonian. We ate hot dogs from a street vendor on Pennsylvania Ave. before queasiness overtook me as the elevator raced to the top of the Washington Monument. And I burned through almost an entire roll of film photographing the two of them jostling and elbowing and boisterously recounting their last time together on the Washington Mall.

"Give us the ballot," they repeated, imitating Dr. King and his demand for the Negro vote from the steps of the Lincoln Memorial in 1957. His echo was in their words—the sincerity and conviction, full-throated and soaking into the trees and the green blades of grass. Negroes with their own Polaroids walked by smiling, some shouting *"Yassuh!"* and *"Give us that ballot!"* at my New Jessup men. I snapped photos that had no hope of capturing the happiness that blazed in their eyes and inflated their chests. Matthew and Raymond, intertwined at the taproot, if grown their separate ways.

We finished that evening at the White House.

"The house where Kennedy lives," Matthew announced. With the fountain going and the house lit up, I could see Camelot. The water danced, its reflection splashing in Raymond's softening grays, Matthew's hopeful browns. It was beautiful—majestic, even—like an American castle. But none of us had voted in 1960 or had anything to do with placing Kennedy on his throne. Still, I clicked picture after picture, making them laugh when I supposed that maybe Harold Jenkins would build something just as grand for one of them as the mayor of New Jessup.

In the frame, in that light, Raymond's smile caught me in my throat. That smile! I fed that smile, loved that smile, gave that smile a baby. Trusted that smile, laid with that smile, cherished and obeyed that smile. But there was an ease to him with his arm around Matthew, happiness so bright as to be careless and too big to fit inside the frame. They laughed and talked so much that the tickle returned to Raymond's throat. I fished through my pocketbook for a lozenge.

Because although Raymond's voice commanded attention, required you to take notice, more and more in the summer, he arrived home from his meetings needing hot salt water for his throat. For a voice like his to go hoarse meant that somebody wasn't hearing him. Or not paying attention.

AFTER A LAZY FRIDAY MORNING IN BED, then an afternoon wandering the zoo, me and Raymond changed clothes and headed into the evening. We found Matthew Pinckney-Ave.-leaning next to a no-name door on U Street where Negroes streamed inside. He smiled politely at all the perfume floating by and nodded friendly at the cologne until we caught eyes and he waved us over. But with every click of my heels, his head wilted further to the side.

"Got-damn!" he said, his voice constricted, holding cigarette smoke. "Ain't you somebody's mama to be out here, looking fine as all that?"

I sucked my teeth at his stupid tease—a meaningless flirtation meant to raise Raymond's eyebrow more than mine.

"I ain't dead, Matthew, for all this you doing. And you see me on my husband's arm," I said. Yes, my sheath was cut a little tight, but it wasn't bothering Raymond or anybody else. With one last night before our flight home in the morning, Matthew was again meeting us by himself. Though it was fine with me, I asked after Patience to be polite. He blew the last of the smoke and shrugged.

"She sends apologies. She's working on a story. Next time," he promised with a dampened smile as he ushered us inside.

The wait for Sam Cooke was an eternity. We suffered through a corny comedian in a U-shaped booth near the edge of the stage, mere feet away from the band. The club was dark and smoky and packed with bodies calling drink orders, leaning on support poles, whispering to each other. All the sudden, Patience—velvet midnight as ever—appeared through the haze behind Matthew. My body tensed for an unforgiving encounter in our first time seeing each other since the river. For any hint on her face of knowing, blame. But she smiled slyly with a finger to her lips, pulling us together into the playful secret of her surprise. When my eyes gave her away, she slid into the booth next to him with a forgiving chuckle. After a kiss hello, she wrapped fingers around Matthew's glass and took a sip.

She drowned out the ventriloquist who had taken the stage with talk of her doings in the couple years since the river: about working as a reporter; living in Detroit; the letter from Matthew that finally convinced her to move to DC. Her and Matthew shared their drink, their cigarette, their sentences and gazes that spoke nothing of full Frigidaires and furnishing a home, yet everything of two people for whom a lover's touch was nourishment and shelter.

Raymond pried Matthew away to the bar when the drinks were low, and the show, imminent. While they were gone, she asked how I handled being a wife and mama while working at Taylor Made. But her question surprised me, I think, more than my answer surprised her at first. Each word, its own question about my loves, my longings, my duties. Wife. Mama. Career woman. Each separate, competing role adding up to my worth. When I told her I no longer worked with Miss Vivian, her saccharine, "Is that right?" suggested she knew already. But when I told her that I chose to resign, she cocked her head to the side and asked, "Is that right?" again. This time, her voice deeper, her interest piqued.

"Raising Bea, keeping a home, and working the land keeps me more than busy," I told her. "My workday starts when I open my eyes and ends when I close them."

"What'd you say to her when you quit?"

"Not much. We agreed that, as an expecting mama, it was time."

"So did you quit, or did she fire you?"

"I resigned. We just agreed, is all. She took it well and said I could come back whenever I wanted."

"Would you go back? Maybe when Bea starts school?"

"We'll see," I said, not wanting to tell her that Dot's rounded belly was making me nostalgic for Bea's smaller days. My daughter had taught me what it meant to be enchanted by love, and I prayed thanks every day that she had chosen to teach me as her mama. The place in my heart touched only by Bea panged as I sat in a nightclub a thousand miles away from her, wondering if another baby would be just as sweet. Another baby that would likely delay any return to Taylor Made, if there was ever to be a return at all. My baby, my babies, were too precious to be pitted against the piece of my heart still aching over the dress shop. Especially by Patience, who was still waiting for more of an answer than "we'll see" when our men returned with the drinks.

They slid glasses in front of us just as she asked where Bea would attend school. When I told her New Jessup Primary, she turned a needling, mischievous eye towards Raymond and said, "Oh, of course New Jessup Primary." He leaned in closer, smiling slightly, trying to hear over the din of the nightclub. "What, with HQ's excitement about the way your segregation project is coming along. I mean, where else would she go?"

The smile faded from his lips. He glanced at Matthew, then finished sitting.

"You know she's just trying to get under your skin, man," Matthew said. "Don't let her."

"No, really!" she continued. "Alice and I were just talking about Bea going to school."

"Yeah?" was Raymond's only response.

"And she mentioned New Jessup Primary."

"Yeah."

"And when you walked up, I kicked myself for even wondering because, if anyone is going to keep their kids in New Jessup Primary, it's the man leading the segregation project."

Raymond said nothing about the *municipality* project or anything else—just sipped his drink. Matthew cut in. "DC seems to agree with you, Alice! I hope you've enjoyed your visit to the capital city. We'd love to have you back again sometime."

"It's been nice, though if I'm honest, it's just a bigger New Jessup."

She sucked teeth, but with a smile unique to Alabama's Negro women: sweet as a blackberry, barbed as the thorn, with pursed, curled lips and eyes sparkling in mild challenge.

"DC is *nothing* like New Jessup," she said coolly. "I could've showed you if y'all had come to see me at the newspaper, or even a meeting! I know folks are eager to meet the man behind the segregation project, and"—she chuckled softly—"the woman *behind* the man." I didn't care for the dismissive tone easing past her lips and, judging by Raymond's sigh, I was in good company. But determined not to be the one spoiling Raymond and Matthew's last few hours together, I sipped my drink and stilled my tapping toe.

"We're on vacation, Patience. And I don't intend to bring Alice to meetings in New Jessup or DC or anywhere else," Raymond told her.

"Alright, you two," Matthew said. "We're here to have a good time. Check all your differences at the door."

"Oh, Matthew, he knows I don't mean to ruffle feathers," she said, waving her hand in the air at us to make any offense a problem of our imagination instead of the intention in her words. "I remember a time, though, when Raymond Campbell used to have a sense of humor, used to enjoy playing the straight man.

"Now, you're just . . . straight" was her final barb before the saxophone growled.

The drums rattled next, and somebody strummed a guitar. On the stage, feet away from us, the emcee was calling for a response to draw Sam Cooke to the stage. Mr. Soul! The spotlight pointed to the side, and he emerged from the darkness in a maroon velvet jacket to caress that microphone not twenty feet from me. Though I was not the only woman by a long shot, I screamed. Before Patience could utter another word, Raymond slid out the booth and offered me that working man's hand. Together, we eased to the dance floor, leaving Patience and Matthew to their lovers' looks and sweetness and thorns and whatever else they thought to do with their night. Because this was supposed to be me and Raymond and Mr. Soul taking us to church. I pressed my ear to the chest of my Alabama man, dancing and swaying and doing the cha-cha-cha until my legs could take no more.

Just when I thought I couldn't move another step, it is no lie of mine that Sam Cooke looked down from the stage at me and Raymond and said, "Looks like Cupid's been here already, but we'll do this one anyway."

With the smoke licking around the room, the music warming my good humor, the promise of a song just for us, and the feel of Raymond against me, just before my eyes floated to a close to enjoy the song against his heartbeat, with the last look to my left, through the shadows, Patience cut eyes at me from inside Matthew's embrace.

We should have just said goodnight after the show, but we rode back to their place for a nightcap. Matthew poured four short glasses and we sank into the leather couch. Raymond and Patience were next to each other on the inside corner of the L, our knees all inches from the edge of the crystal coffee table. After we toasted to friendship, Patience quietly inspected the liquid swirling around her glass. Matthew and Raymond filled most of the space with their voices, but when talk turned to Dot expecting again, Patience set her glass down with a soft click.

"I always thought Dot would do something more than just lay down and have Percy's babies," she said. "She won all those math prizes, you know?" My blood simmered. I was tired of her hints that her way was the only way and tired of holding my tongue about it.

But still determined not to be the one ruining the last of our hours together, I turned my own Alabama smile back on her and said softly, "Well, wait till you get those black wedding pants and let's see if we ain't talking about you and Matthew's babies one day."

Matthew furrowed his brow but shrugged, seeming to dismiss it. She insisted, and quickly, "Not me. Never me. I have bigger aspirations."

"Yeah," he said with a little laugh, "Mrs. Patience Washington? With a baby on her hip? Could y'all ever imagine it?" He squeezed around her shoulders, smiling at her. Confusion poured over my head since she was the one who told me once he would never get her milk free. When I opened my mouth, she cut me off.

"I have too much work to do. I've documented the Freedom Movement from almost every angle, you know. Even been back to Alabama. Not New Jessup, but Anniston, as a Freedom Rider. This

May, I rode and wrote when every stop was another terror. I sat-in at the Greensboro Woolworth's last year, and I've interviewed folks from SNCC, whose students feel like the movement is stagnating. I've interviewed just about everyone with something to say about Negro progress in this country—"

Matthew squeezed again, this time, with warning in his tone.

"Patience, we agreed, sunshine, not to do this—"

"You *told* me, Matthew. We didn't agree on anything."

"Still, let's not."

She ignored him, turning to me. "Like I said—"

"Patience—"

"Matthew," she barbed him.

He stood at the other end of the L and offered her his hand.

"Let's you and me talk in the other room for a minute, huh?"

She turned her back on him and looked squarely at me.

"The one article I haven't written is about how Negroes can fight *against* equal rights—"

"Patience, let's go—"

"How folks in New Jessup can be content to embrace the tyranny of the Old South. I'm wondering whether you have any comment on that, Alice." After she unsheathed these switchblade words, my voice trembled slightly, holding back fire as best it could.

"Comment? On tyranny?" I said.

"Embrace . . . ? What's this about, Matthew?" Raymond asked.

"Patience," Matthew said again, much harsher than his normal sweet tone. "Enough."

"You don't run me, Matthew. If she has a word, let her say a word. It won't kill y'all to let the women speak for once."

A fist reached behind my right eye and squeezed. My head had not throbbed like that since the light bothered me from the plane. I took a couple deep breaths as she raised an eyebrow at me—waiting on an answer to her accusation that I was laying down for Old Jim Crow.

"I have no comment."

"Well surprise, surprise. Alice Campbell has no comment about oppression," she mocked.

"You've been trying me all night. Why?"

"By asking you to raise your voice for something?"

"Patience, why *are* you antagonizing her? Matthew—" Raymond said. Matthew sat back down and leaned in to say something in her ear, but she moved away and narrowed eyes at him.

"It's *just* like y'all to take her side. Again."

"This ain't about sides, Patience. We're all friends in this room," he said. Only, long gone was the woman with whom I shared a laugh about black wedding pants. She glared at me, so I stood with my pocketbook to go. The coffee table made it so Raymond had to scooch sideways down the couch before he could stand, leaving no room for two people to pass between the sofa and the glass edge at the same time.

"I don't have anything to say about your article because I believe in equal rights," I said.

"*Ha!*" Her laughter snapped my head around, rousing anger so hot I could've burned footsteps into the rug. "C'mon, Alice, you're smarter than this. You do understand that segregation is bad for us, right? And integration is good?"

"It's that black and white to you?"

"*Ha ha.* It is that black and white, yes. To anybody with sense."

"Now you saying I have no sense?" She answered with the defiant jut of her chin. "So the way you came up was bad?" I asked her.

"You saw the textbooks."

"Yeah, I saw the textbooks. So your solution is to put my daughter in the same classroom as the children who wrote that hatefulness in the first place? With the teachers who allowed it?"

"Can I quote you on that?"

"Not on your life."

Raymond had made it to the end of the sofa and was waiting on me to move so that he could stand up. But when she said she could hardly tell the ventriloquist from the dummy between us, he pushed up anyway, toppling into me when he knocked into the table.

"Let's go," he said, righting himself. She was all smugness on her face.

"You have nerve talking to me like this," I said. "Grown up in New Jessup to sit here and badmouth the way of life that gave you every opportunity under the sun."

"Not every opportunity. I am a Negro woman, remember. Same as you."

"Not nearly same as me! Not nearly same as me!" I shouted.

"C'mon," Raymond said, urging me, gently, by the wrist. "Come on, darling. We're leaving."

I pointed my finger at her with my free hand. "I wanna say something to her first, Raymond. And not as ventriloquist or dummy."

She stood there on the opposite side of the table, waiting with her lip curled in disgust.

"You dare try to tell me about being a Negro woman? While you were growing up with whitefolks across the woods, buying store-bought, going to a high school full of classrooms, with each classroom full of books? Getting served at a diner where your worst trouble landed you in the suds and your police *protected* you! You have some nerve.

"You had doctors to care for you, Patience. Went to college. I got two parents in the ground who wished college for me since before I was born! You wanna talk to me about being a Negro woman?" I swallowed hard, barely able to grit a whole truth behind my teeth. "Did the only landlord you ever knew evict you, shouting 'nigger bitch' at your back like it was your Christian name? Don't you sit here telling me nothing about you and me being the same. I know plenty of life outside New Jessup that would crumble you to dust, so you'll never hear me apologize for loving our city the way I do and wanting it for my family."

"You love it enough to have me sent away?"

"You have something on your heart, Patience? Ask me a question, I'll tell you the truth."

"Did you tell Cap about the articles?"

"I ain't told Cap nothing."

"You're lying! It had to be you. I didn't tell anybody else."

"Let you tell it, you told everybody else! How many people around New Jessup did you complain to, make your little slick comments to? You have yourself, and only yourself, to blame for your mess."

"Ask you a question, you'll tell me the truth?"

"Come on with it."

"The swamp."

"What about it?"

"That day you took me out there. You thought about shooting me, didn't you?" That thought had never crossed my mind. Before I could get a shocked word in edgewise, Matthew cut in.

"Patience, that's enough, now! For Chrissake!" he said.

"The air must be real thin up here for you to accuse me of something like that."

"Your hands, your feet, your rifle, that's what you said."

"Patience, what reason would I have to shoot you in a swamp? Listen to yourself!"

"You didn't think it, not even for a second?"

"This is you trying to turn Raymond against me again. But do you know how crazy you sound?"

"That's not a 'no.'"

"'No,' then. The thought never crossed my mind to shoot you. *Shoot*, if I had really wanted to harm you in that swamp, I would've just left you in that swamp."

"Alice!" said Raymond. "We're leaving! Now!" He grabbed my wrist with a firmer grasp this time and started leading me out. But Patience came around the table hot on my heels, yelling in my ear as Matthew banged his leg trying to get to her.

"There she is! There she is, fellas!" she said. "There's your Little Miss Pretty Perfect, fitting the mold of the good wife since the day she dropped from heaven."

I twisted my wrist free of Raymond's grasp. His momentum carried him forward, but he stayed on his feet while I spun on my heel, squaring up to her nose to nose.

"You'd be balled up calling your mama in the kinda heaven where I came up."

"Let's go," said Raymond, taking my elbow this time.

"Y'all never saw see this side of her, did you?" she yelled after us. I made every footstep a heavy one, and Raymond was struggling to get me out the door. But his hand was firmly inside my elbow, and Matthew's in hers, as they pulled us apart—whatever friendship, whatever world we had foolishly tried to build, split in pieces.

"All of them, smiling, slapping Raymond on the back in the corner at our meetings, talking about you, what a great woman you would be for your man," Patience continued. "Those guys couldn't say enough about you every time they checked you out—"

"—Patience, that's enough!" Matthew said.

"—Matthew, get a handle on your woman!" Raymond shouted as he struggled with me.

"—Matthew, with stars in his eyes about you and I becoming friends," she kept on. "Friends? I had friends. Them! Eight men I've known all my life, and all they wanted to talk about was *you*." We got through the door, and into the hallway, and she was still yelling. "People *want* to believe you, Alice, and would never believe that Miss Pretty Perfect would leave someone to die in a swamp! But I knew you had that side to you, as sure as I know my own name."

"Then you know nothing! And have nerve calling me a liar after how you used me and my sister!"

"Your sister!" she shrieked as the clarity broke her voice like a shattered dish. "Of course you were the one who told! It *was* you! I told you I didn't know! Did y'all tell her about the death records, the arrest records? You—"

"Patience, shut your goddamn mouth! This is over, right now! You hear me? Over!" Raymond bellowed. I had never before, and have never since, heard him cuss a woman.

Up and down the hallway, Negro faces appeared in door cracks, listening. Patience's promises had revived my hope once and dashed it like a boat hitting a rock. For years, I had collected the remaining splinters, trying to convince myself that my sister was lost only to me and not the world. The elevator wouldn't come, and Matthew couldn't, or wouldn't, tussle her inside the apartment, so we four stood breathless with the struggling, the shouting, and now, the pause. She used her free hand to wipe tears from her face. I let mine fall. Raymond pulled me towards the staircase at the far end of the corridor.

"You haven't told her, have you, Raymond?" she called after us in a casually mocking tone.

"Haven't you done enough, Patience?" Matthew said.

"Y'all are still doing it. Still protecting her!"

Raymond hustled us to the staircase but couldn't open the door fast enough.

"Hey Raymond! You need to tell her what NNAS men and women are doing *for* her since we all found out about that eviction!"

I snapped. Planting my feet as hard as I could, I pushed my beloved husband with quadrupled strength and sprinted at her when she mentioned my sister being evicted, possibly homeless, in Chicago. Thinking that Patience knew something about Rosie that I didn't set me off because I couldn't stand for her to revive my sister, then shatter my hope, then put danger on her name in that corridor. With every step I ran towards her, I made my plan to slap Rosie's name from her mouth and beat her to the ground. I was on her in a second, before Matthew could even step between us, raising my palm to strike her down, only remembering at the last second that I had taught her to fight back myself. She forgot, too, and brought hands to her face right away—cowering, neck bent, she waited on the blow.

The last blow of an entire world, the final rejection of New Jessup, Alabama, lacing the palm of my hand. My mere presence in town and my embrace of the lifestyle and its freedoms had been reason enough to exile her from the place we both called home. I was exactly the woman the town fathers, the town stewards, and now the town grandsons envisioned carrying New Jessup forward for the next generations; everything she started fighting against since long before I stepped off that bus. I needed say nothing to Cap to serve as her betrayal because my arrival was the disloyalty. No slap would send her lower than she had already fallen in the eyes of the men she grew up with and the town that raised her. When the strike didn't come, she turned her head up towards my face, her eyes burning with hate for me. Even then, I couldn't break her all the way down.

She thought I was going to keep inhaling that blackdamp because of where I came from, because of my sister. Breathing and breathing it to fuel my rage until I killed myself, my spirit, thinking, always thinking, about whitefolks. But they had to reshackle my daddy to get him back in that mine, and he died regretting the lifetime he spent thinking about dying. New Jessup was supposed to be freedom from all that—from talk of sunset silhouettes dragging me from the field and Mr. Shy Smiles invading my every waking thought. Not every Negro needed to adopt our way of life—that was their choice. But I wanted the freedom of that choice; wanted Raymond to be successful so others had it, too. Including Rosie—who I prayed, every night, would return safely to Alabama.

So just before I lowered my hand, I told Patience, "I didn't betray you. I didn't leave you in the swamp. Next time you fix your mouth to say my sister's name, you remember that. And you remember this."

ME AND RAYMOND walked together in silence—my single, solitary thought, the mint-green dress. I swam through half-closed, tear-filled eyes to that field of goldenrod where I'd seen her in my dream. But all that was there, as if swaying in the breezes of a clothesline, was her mint-green dress. Not her face, her voice, her long braid, or her beautiful skin.

"Is she dead?" I asked the field. Raymond answered.

"No one has found a record of her death."

"Arrested?"

A breeze caught the dress when he said, "I don't know."

"Do you know where she is and you ain't telling me?"

"No. You said you wanted to know when there was something to know. Nothing has changed. I told you we'd keep looking and we're still looking. That's just where we are now. Arrest records and death records, and that's *if* she's still in Chicago. We haven't stopped looking. That's just . . . where we are. The records."

Inside hazy vision, my tears stretched the starlight, as if my people were trying to wrap arms around me and Rosie from the heavens.

"We never gonna find her, are we? I'm never gonna see my sister again, am I? Never. Never. Never? Not *never*, Raymond!" I repeated, too weak to push myself from his embrace. I didn't care about the signs passing by on DC faces just then; I cared about hurting the regular hurt of being unable to see my sister's beautiful face in that mint-green dress. I cared about the crush of knowing that the best I could hope for was Rosie jailed or dead or vanished into thin air. I cared about the wide-open nothingness of sky between me and her and just another touch.

THE SUN WAS STILL RISING the next morning, still working to burn away our overnight words, as me and Raymond sat at the airport. We were quiet, waiting, every so often giving each other a weak little smile, as the pallor hung over us. After awhile with no words, a hand slid onto my shoulder from behind me.

"Don't swing, slugger," Matthew said. Ever the peacemaker, he showed up at the gate after me and Raymond left the hotel in a cab instead of waiting on the ride he promised. "It's just me. Wanted to make sure y'all got here safe. Mind if I sit?" I tilted my head towards the seat next to me. He tapped my leg in a brotherly, affectionate way, too tired to pretend flirtation. "I couldn't let y'all leave without saying goodbye."

"It doesn't have to be goodbye, man," Raymond said. "It's been two years. Let me talk to Cap. Maybe—"

Matthew bent over with his head in his palm. Without looking up, he waved the other hand at Raymond, telling him to go no further.

"Even though I can go back, she can't. And even if she could, she wouldn't. The only way I got her here was by turning down the residency back home. We're still figuring things out. Last night didn't help, but neither does this foolishness with Simeon . . ."

"I warned him about that once," Raymond said, about the night they dug the pig pit. Matthew shook his head.

"It's bigger than just me, young boy. They're looking for cracks in the dam. Any weakness in our plan. They wanna pull leadership back from municipality and push, full steam ahead, with voting."

"Matthew, come back, man. Can't you change your residency or something, and just come home?"

Matthew sat up, looked at me, then looked across me.

"And forget Patience? I know I don't have to tell you how much I love that girl. We're still just . . . figuring it out."

Then, resignation hunched Matthew back over, and he folded our whole conversation into silence until it was time to board. My arms wrapped around Matthew in wordless invitation to join us on the plane back to Alabama. Though he squeezed me too, he eventually tapped my shoulder asking for release. When I spoke, it was to remind him to put some meat on his plate and his bones, and to call often—reverse the charges if need be.

"I haven't lost an ounce since I've lived here," he said. "Not one."

"You hardly throwing a shadow, Matthew. You better start eating right, taking better care of yourself."

"Yes, ma'am," he promised, ushering us towards the door.

From my seat, I raised the shade and watched him watching us pull away from the gate and take off home for Alabama.

TWENTY-SIX

In 1961, the rains arrived on the tenth day of October, and lasted every day for the next three weeks. It was the patient, rotting kind of rain that waits until every inch of soil is tilled, waits until the weeds are chopped; waits until the crop is whispering about the harvest—until it falls, this too-much rain. Some days steady, some days torrential, and some days, hardly a mist. But it soaks everything it touches, causing crops to wither, and things to die, this sort of rain.

The first clouds crept in during my appointment with Doc Patterson. While Dot watched Bea and Clifford in the waiting room, I smiled as I sat in the guest chair at his desk. These were the last few moments before he would confirm that my dizziness, my sick stomach of late, meant I was expecting again. For weeks the physical discomfort had been accompanied by pangs of guilt whenever I regarded Bea, wondering if it was selfish of me to want two of her. Until I realized my unborn child would have a different heart and soul; need a love not yet invented. My love for Bea would be unique, and no less full than it would be for another, for each child has their own special heart.

Doc Patterson had had an air of competent confidence when he'd told me I was expecting my daughter—"Congratulations, Mrs. Campbell! I am happy to tell you that you are with child. How's your diet? Good,

good. More greens, though, and let's get that blood pressure down so these dizzy spells go away." This time, instead of sitting in his chair, he hovered at my shoulder, flipping through the pages of my chart until he settled on one.

"Why don't we retake your blood pressure?"

I offered my arm and started to ask, but he shushed me as he listened. When he finished, he closed the chart without correction.

"So, am I, or am I?" I joked, still smiling, but nervous. The knot in my stomach was unmistakable for food since I had not touched my breakfast that morning.

He shook his head. "I'm sorry, Mrs. Campbell. Not at this time."

"But that can't be right. I've been sick for weeks. It's all the same as it was with Bea."

"Did you ever find out whether anyone in your family had high blood pressure?"

"Not that I know of, no."

"When your mama passed—was she complaining about head-aches, dizziness, stomach problems, anything, when she collapsed?"

"I don't know. I was in school," I said. My mouth was formed around the word *Why?*, but the answer broke like the dawn and I didn't ask.

He nodded slightly with the little smile and soft eyes of one know-ing the view on the other side of a bricked window. Instead, he wrote a prescription for clonidine and a referral to a cardiologist named Doc Underwood. Any other words he said next floated around in the place without north, south, east, or west, refusing to stick in my memory, since my dizziness, my sick stomach, had assured me for weeks that I was having a baby. I was ready, it was time, and I had finally allowed the excitement of Bea having a little brother or sister to push back my guilt over these last days with her as my only child.

Doc Patterson finished writing and stood, urging me to do the same. As he walked me towards the door to his office, he said, "Well, I am sorry to tell you this news, but it is a relief to know you aren't expecting with your pressure this high. You have plenty of time for children, Mrs. Campbell. But until we get your blood pressure under control, I cannot advise that you try for another baby." He opened the door to the waiting room, where I saw Dot's belly before the light in her hopeful eyes. She was bouncing my sleeping Bea gently while Clifford slumped, napping at her side.

"Not this time," I managed quickly, and we left.

Doc Patterson's words had already left the hair at my nape soaked with perspiration, so the day's sudden chill hit me as soon as we stepped onto the street. Above, patches of white and dove gray crept along silently as though attempting to draw the hurt steeping into my muscles and blanching my bones. Some clouds were so thin they still allowed the quiet hope of blue through from the other side. And then, without any other warning on that first day of the rains, a light shower fell on us. These no-rain rainclouds hurried Dot and the babies into the car while I stepped quickly into the drug store—for iron pills and vitamins, is what I told her.

Later in the day, the rain paused in time for a gentle sunset. For a few stunning moments, the night was a muted mist of amethyst and amber, marigold and ripe watermelon, some gray, a touch of lavender, a hint of cottontail white—yet still a little cloudy like the second Goody's powder I was stirring that afternoon. Sometimes, New Jessup sunsets blazed coneflower pink, but this evening it settled into a soft mauve the same as the color on the walls of Bea's nursery.

My daughter clutched my heart inside infant fists, summoned laughs when she giggled baring rabbit teeth, and entranced me with the patches of soft wool growing on her head. She absorbed stories about her namesake until her eyelids grew heavy and she drifted into milk slumber; her innocence, a song only I could truly understand. And whenever she was away from my arms that day, her spot in, and on, my heart craved the warmth of her weight. I sang sweet lullabies to her as both apology and a prayer.

Trying to seem hopeful, I told Dot to look out the kitchen window at a sky worthy of my baby girl. But my sister-in-law sucked teeth and glanced at the sunset before settling her eyes on my glass.

"I asked how you're feeling. You've been mixing Goody's powder with sodium bicarbonate all afternoon." After the appointment, as the day wore on, she had been pretending not to notice my distracted mood, and her words were stern but cautious. She slid the bowl of chicken in buttermilk to me. "You're always changing the subject when somebody's trying to talk to you, but you're going to ruin your stomach trying to settle your stomach."

"My head is just aching, is all. I ain't changing the subject—just noticing outside." She looked me up and down, then started to slide the bowl away from me.

"Well, all that pink in the sky just means when it's time, it'll be another girl." She wrinkled her nose with pity. "Why don't you go lay down, honey? The babies are asleep and I can fry chicken, easy."

The sunset disappeared behind fresh rain clouds and drops popped against the windowpane. I started to hold my post to make sure the chicken was seasoned my way, though it hardly mattered who was standing over the stove those days. By then, our recipes had become a little of her, and a little of me. Over the years, everything we'd cooked took on the flavor of hers, and mine, becoming ours—my extra dash of vinegar in her collards; some friendly fire about the way she seasoned the chicken; and no one really knew who started the cayenne pepper in the macaroni and cheese. The chicken only needed dredging and frying, but as soon as I stuck my hand in the bowl, the touch, sight, and smell of the clammy skin brought my stomach racing to my throat. I pitched the Goody's but swallowed a whole glass of bicarbonate and took Bea out to sit under the awning on the porch.

A short while later, Raymond's Studebaker pulled up with our men. Percy nodded his head and went to his house to shower, and

Pop and Raymond lined boots up next to the door, draping coveralls over the rail. Before he went inside, Pop pecked my head and took Bea. Raymond sat next to me, silent, his face fighting disappointment.

"Chicken's done," Dot announced, coming through the door. "I'm going next door and get Percy settled." She passed as quietly as she had somehow told the men there was no baby.

Raymond sat down and rocked us in the swing, asking all the right questions and saying all the right things. But the faraway sound of his voice confessed his sorrow. I tried to gin up something inside me to salve his hurt; to convince myself that I'd had all afternoon to sit with the news, and that it was his turn for sadness. But my grief seeded itself and blossomed from the place where a baby should be nestled, growing. It sprouted, filled my chest, choked my throat— fertilized by the powerful fears of being sick and failing my family. I wept and could not empty—the tears just called more tears. I had nurtured life all my life, and was now, again, at the mercy of fate— when the sun shined and kept shining, or the rain came and kept coming. The season of wait-and-pray had arrived, and with it, the memory that crying never changed a thing.

I calmed to the steady rain pattering a forest of leaves, telling me to *hussssh*. Gentle, polite thunder rumbled overhead like heaven's heartbeat, and Raymond's breath cloud mingled with mine. It was cold, and he was only in his T-shirt and slacks, with nothing on his head or feet. Nothing protecting him from the world.

"You gonna catch your death out here," I said. The cold air sliced into my nose with each sniffle.

"Didn't wanna get grease on you." He squeezed me, still smelling like rust and motor oil from the day. "Feel better?" I nodded. "Did Doc Patterson say anything about your stomach, these dizzy spells? Is it your pressure again?"

Fretting never stopped the rain or brought it, and asking the sun's mercy often drew its wrath instead of easing it. So as me and

Raymond entered this wait-and-pray season, not wanting to heap more atop what he was already feeling, I told him, "He said it was nothing to worry about, baby. The usual: more rest, more greens, take some vitamins, iron pills."

"He can't give you anything, though?"

"You know he was always cautious with medication. Said it caused a lot of side effects. He didn't offer it, and I don't wanna take it."

"What about—"

"Raymond, I know you like to fix things." He smiled a little. I had his number. "But maybe, you trust me to handle this? I'll follow the doctor's orders and be right as rain in no time."

DURING A HEAVY DOWNPOUR on the third night of the rains, Pop, Cap, and Mr. Marvin ran to a Business Council meeting. The rest of us crammed into the Campbell booth at Mr. Marvin's, where Percy launched into the story of Raymond's high school track days ending on a disqualification. At all the funny parts, Dot rested a hand on her stomach—rounded by the baby kicking along with her laughter. I held my daughter close, laughing when I still felt like doing anything but.

Percy stopped mid-gesture, mid-sentence, with his attention over my shoulder. His mouth shut and tightened in a frown watching Pop and Mr. Marvin drag in the door. Through the plate glass, Cap's tailpipe steamed, and his brake lights glowed, as his patrol car eased from the parking lot.

Fitzhugh had announced his retirement date at the meeting, and Chase had acted out in celebration. When they said November first, just a few weeks coming, lightning zapped behind my eye and thunder exploded. Soon, Chase would have untethered freedom to act like nobody's Negro. I dug my thumb into the side of my head trying to massage away the ringing phones; overnights; broken wreckers; misdirected blame; sunset silhouettes; sweetgum blood; Big Red

bottles; creeping blackdamp; unanswered letters; half-truths; clonidine; deep-well voices searching for cracks; fused trees; newspaper
articles; starry skies; and now, an empty womb.

"We hadn't reported on our side of the woods yet," Mr. Marvin
said, "so they asked us to wait outside so they could get the boy sorted.
Not in the hallway, mind you—*out*side. In the rain," he said, standing at the table edge next to me, his lips pursed, his fingers drumming
all those curse words I knew he wanted to say through the repeated
tap-tap-tap-tap-tap of fingertips on the tabletop. I pulled a Goody's
from my pocketbook, snaking my hand inside gingerly, encouraging
the sound of conversation to continue so nobody would see, or hear,
the pill bottle next to the packet and the lozenges. Placing the powder
on my tongue, I chased it with some water and waited, hoping that
the Goody's could keep my headache down to a dull throb.

"The boy was inside long enough for me to have a couple of cigarettes under the awning. He burst through the door and ran past
then, making sure to call us out our names before he sped off. But—"

"Alice, what's the matter, darling? You alright?" Raymond's
watchful grays were filled with questions about the headaches and
the stomach pains still not going away. I finished swallowing the
paste and smiled.

"You worry too much, Raymond. I'm fine, baby. Just a little headache is all. Go ahead, finish your story, Mr. Marvin."

Pop's slow blink could have been mistaken for a headshake. In
any case, Mr. Marvin changed the subject.

TWENTY-SEVEN

Sometime between midnight and twilight during the gentle tapping of the sixth early morning of the rains, Raymond tried to slip from underneath me undetected. But I was awake with insomnia from my pills. Still, I sighed in fake slumber when he pulled the last of himself from the bed and laid my wrist atop the pillow, allowing him to think he made good his escape. But I watched. Although the window was completely dark with the gentle rain and the starless, moonless sky, he stood silent for a moment with the loving respect for our land glowing on his face. I lay still watching the silent prayer overcome him.

Then, he took large, tiptoeing strides around the bed to avoid the known creaks in the floor; pulled his long johns, wax canvas hunting pants and jacket over his body; and eyed, then tied, the cap on his head, all the while smiling to the moonless woods through the window where, soon enough, he would stalk pheasant with Pop, Percy, and New Jessup's chosen, chosen few.

He came to pull covers to my chin, and I giggled with closed eyes. After he kissed my forehead, he said, "So every shut eye *ain't* sleep. Did I wake you?"

"No. Just turning over."

"You feeling alright? You were pretty restless again."

"I hope I didn't keep you up."

"No. I just . . . well, you still ain't sleeping well, eating much."

"That little indigestion? You know that's just from Miss Stephanie's cooking the other night."

"I've been eating the stone biscuits at Marvin's Diner for twenty-eight years of life, Alice, and I ain't never had more than a rock in my stomach."

"Well, what can I say? You a better man than me, Raymond Campbell."

He chuckled softly, but by trying to hold it in so much, he rocked the bed, quieting every so often, raising fresh laughter every time he repeated "better man than me."

"You better know it, darling," he told me after he finished chuckling. "But I can skip this pheasant hunt. It's just an excuse to walk around the woods with the fellas."

"What'll you do instead? Fix breakfast? Get Bea ready for church? No. You go on ahead. But y'all better bring something back or you'll be eating rabbit straight out the deep freeze for supper." With that little playful tease, little challenge, little threat, he stopped with all his questions and left.

With nobody to feed but ourselves at grits o'clock, me and Dot settled, shoulder to shoulder underneath a blanket in the porch swing, hardly speaking as the fog tinted lavender-gray with the rising day. Instead, we watched squirrels and birds appear, then disappear, into the thick mist. The babies were fed and sleeping in the playpen next to us. Other than Major's baying hounds or a shotgun blast every so often in the distance, the fog swallowed every other sound. My headaches were smoothing over so long as I took my medication first thing, although my appetite was still gone.

Without warning, Dot pushed up and walked inside. Her words floated through the screen door with the occasional clink of plates.

I pulled the thick quilt closer around me to keep all the warmth of our bodies inside. She returned with two plates of scrambled eggs, toast, and the same ham that I had pushed around my plate the night before, holding it in my face until I reluctantly unwrapped myself and took the food.

"Good." She nodded her head and sat down. Everything I normally loved rested in my lap cooling. When she was halfway through her breakfast, she looked at me.

"A table holds the food. A woman eats it. You a table or a woman?" she asked.

"You asking if I'm a woman and you the one sitting here with feet dangling from this porch swing?"

She sucked teeth, but then her eyes, her sigh, pleaded for answers.

"Are you sick, or do you have no appetite?"

"What's the difference?"

"Put something in your mouth. If it comes up, there's your answer."

"I have no appetite, then."

"Then try and make one, honey. Just a couple bites and I'll leave you alone."

She slid a fork into her food and motioned for me to do the same. Mine slid through the eggs and grabbed ahold of a good chunk of ham. I picked it up, considered it, and whether my stomach really wanted it. My mouth watered, assuring me that I was starving, and after I made quick work of my plate, she brought some banana pudding in two bowls. Once finished, we pulled the quilt back up to our necks, and I rocked us back and forth with my toe. It was warm under there, and we sat quiet for a while, our shoulders touching again.

"Thank goodness whatever Doc Patterson gave you must be working. What is it again?"

"Iron pills. Some vitamins."

"Well, they must be doing something. Your head seems better and you were just being stubborn about your appetite."

"Maybe, although you put your foot in those eggs, and your banana pudding is *too* good."

"Well, tonight, I'm going to make you my Auntie Carolyn's yams." She jabbed me with her elbow. "So we can see if those vitamins are really doing the trick."

"Yams? That's just an old wives' tale, Dorothy." She giggled.

"Maybe. But told by some old wives with lots and lots of children."

HALF-TRUTHS, SOME-TRUTHS, AND NONTRUTHS was tricky business those days. As my body adjusted to the clonidine, sleep slipped beyond my grasp night after night. When I did sleep, I had such violent nightmares that nights laying awake staring at the wall or listening to Raymond's heartbeat were a blessing. I was so tired the tenth day of the rains that when Raymond filled the family room archway—his face etched into a frown and his jaw tight—it took me a moment to realize that his coveralls were still clean. He had been gone at least an hour, driving my car over for its tune-up, and he was supposed to bring it back at lunchtime. But here he was, beckoning me with a crooked finger on one hand, and my pocketbook clenched inside the other.

We left Dot to finish some ironing while we went to the bedroom, and he closed the door behind us. Although his palm was open, inviting me to sit on the chaise at the foot of the bed, his stone silence felt like no kind of welcome. Over the years, Raymond's thrifty use of words had rarely been an issue between us—in fact, only that time after Patience and the river. Until the day when he silently demanded that I sit without opening his mouth. Instead of words, my pills swished as he gently shook my pocketbook.

After a chest-filling breath, he asked what he was about to pull from inside. It was supposed to have been my car keys—keys always in the place I could lay hands on them. The place where small things not to be lost or forgotten were automatically put. For Raymond, Pop, and Percy, the edge of their dressers; for Dot, a little bowl by her front door; and for me, the little zipper pocket inside my purse where I also hid my clonidine.

My body shuddered—a quick head-to-foot chill—as he sank down next to me. He rested elbows on his knees and leaned forward, staring at my purse clasped between his two tense hands. I knew I had to find him where he was, draw him out—especially since I was the one who caused him to go inside. After he asked three times what was in my pocketbook, I knew only the truth would do.

Except it was also true that I was tangled in a world of stories. For him. This was only one of the sticky threads that I had willingly cocooned myself inside since the day I agreed to keep the NNAS a secret. I was duty-bound to tell some-truths, half-truths, and non-truths to everyone I knew and loved. Including Raymond. Especially Raymond! To protect him at all costs from disappointment and worry that could easily become distraction. And here he *was* . . . distracted. Because instead of going to the shop, to work, taking my car and bringing it back, he had settled into the office and called Matthew straight away, not only confirming why a doctor would prescribe this medication, but also learning that someone with pressure high enough to need it had no business trying for a baby.

But when he called me a liar to my face—not a storyteller or a tale-teller or even "a lie" in play—I was actually stunned that he could speak such ugliness to me. That word constricted everything I'd done for him until my love, my wanting to protect him, was engorged, misshapen. I didn't lie; I didn't *tell. Lie* was a brutal word to put on my intentions.

"I take these *too*," I finally said. "In addition to the iron and some vitamins."

He released another chest-filling inhale from his mouth in a hollow wind.

"Alice, I'm trying my best to keep my cool here because Mama took pressure medication, heart medication, remember. Doc Underwood's name is on this pill bottle. You've been seeing him? He prescribed them?"

"I have, and yes, he did."

"He tell you that he treated Mama for years? That he was the one that prescribed this same medication for her?" Doc Underwood had mentioned Miss Catherine when I first met him, if not her medications. Still, when I nodded, Raymond's jaw clenched and bubbled.

"So I only called Matthew for him to tell me what I already suspected, and he says more than I ever bargained for. Did Doc Underwood tell you that carrying a baby with pressure this high could kill you *and* the child?"

"Yeah, but—"

"You and Dot, teasing me about yams and fish dreams? You, talking about another baby, you and me . . . And you're taking pressure medication?" His voice was strangled with anger. "At twenty-six years old?"

"She didn't know neither. And it's no reason for us not to be intimate together."

"It's *every* reason for us not to be trying for a baby, and it gives me no comfort to know that you lied to her, too."

"I didn't lie, I told you. I take clonidine *too*."

"You ain't helping yourself right now."

"Why? Because I don't tell you everything that goes on in my day?"

His face twisted up in astonishment. "What else are you keeping from me?"

"Nothing you want to hear about!"

"How do you know?"

"You wanna know how many times I changed Bea's diaper today? Or that I need black thread? Who I ran into at the market?" He looked at me and drew breath to speak. But during a pause, his eyes flashed like he was changing his mind about what he wanted to say to me.

"Let me ask you something."

"Shoot."

"How is this any different than me keeping secrets from *you* in those early days?"

"You ain't really asking me that question, are you?" He said nothing, rubbing his long fingers back and forth over his lips waiting on my answer. I had been so hurt, so angry at Raymond for keeping the NNAS from me that I had set him out in the cold for weeks. I could have said he made a fool of me, talking about me behind my back to his friends, I suppose, but gossiping behind my back was no reason to quit him. No. His secret had lain, a quiet ember lingering among dry brush those first few months of our going together. A single spark waiting on the gentle swish of a leaf, a slight breeze, to feed its need to become a flame. To erupt. The blaze caused by my secret fed itself on the silence growing between us in the bedroom until he bowed his head and squeezed the bridge of his nose between his thumb and forefinger. Unable to tell any meaningful difference between his lie and mine, I said nothing. Breathing deep, he breathed the first words to break the silence.

"Alice, Mama was in her forties when she started with these medications, and fifty-six when we lost her. You're twenty-six years old."

"I knew you would worry like this over something I'm handling. That's all I'm saying. My pressure is improving, and both doctors agree that we can have another baby. Lots of them."

"What about you, though? I don't wanna raise lots of babies by myself. *Or* with somebody who lies to me." His *or* struck a nerve, turned his worry into chords of ingratitude. It was an assumption that I was incapable of making a singular decision about the well-being of my family when taking care of home was my whole life.

And having this problem, being sick and tired, especially with Dot walking around expecting, was already hard enough on me. I was handling my feelings, and his feelings, as best I could, and his tone burned me up.

"I didn't lie to you," I snapped. His eyebrows flicked at the volume in my voice. "But there ain't been a day gone by since you hauled me into this NNAS business that I ain't told a story for you, neither. Not one! You checked me out, trusted my judgment, remember? What use is it telling you all this? To worry you, get in your head? You couldn't do nothing but watch and wait while I had pressure problems with Bea, and they went away. I've been seeing, and will continue seeing, the doctors. I have it under control! Now that you know, ain't nothing for you to do *but* wring your hands. That doesn't help me or you. I've told half-truths and kept things to myself around here for years. Years, Raymond! For you. So call me a liar all you want, I guess, but you'd better thank me while you calling it."

Silence shattered the room, though I hardly felt better seeing purple creeping into his face, or his eyes shimmering. We panted storm-cleaned air on the same rhythm—me, from the shouting, and him, from the hearing. Water pooled at the bottom of his grays as they reflected my words back to me. I thumbed his cheek, intent on catching any tear that I caused to fall. After some moments, he spoke slowly.

"I asked for your hand because I believed I could give you the life, love you like you deserve. Not because I wanted to be the one worrying you, hurting you."

"I know that, baby. In all my life, my wildest dreams couldn't have dreamed you up." A small, appreciative huff escaped him. "All I'm saying is that you came to the park asking me to trust you, and I did. Sometimes, the way I do that, the way I protect you, take care of home, maybe I keep to myself. I do that because I love you, not because I don't."

TWENTY-EIGHT

The phone rang on a Saturday when small became big. Wind had howled through the midnight hours, ushering in cold rain that pelted down with such demoralizing force that the first cake I baked fell in protest. The phone started jangling with regrets and polite questions intended to elicit news of a postponement, so by one o'clock, it was the Campbell family and a couple of Bea's "uncles" from the shop waiting on me to light Bea's first birthday candle. Hurrying to find the matches, I let the phone ring on the wall until it stopped. But as I was walking back out the kitchen, it rang again right away.

Sparks rained down my spine as "my old buddy" Chase Fitzhugh announced himself on the line asking "who's on deck" for a tow. It was only days until all Fitzhugh Auto decisions would be his; when he would be free at last to prove forever and again that he was nobody's Negro. His small banter assured me he'd tried them at the shop, "but maybe no one works Saturdays like Fitzhughs," he said. The expectation in his tone boiled my blood and made my heart race. The plastic handset crackled in my grip.

"We're celebrating my daughter's first birthday today," I said.

"That's wonderful! Just wonderful! Beatrice, right?"

"That's right," I managed, wanting to snatch my daughter's name out his mouth. Maybe he was waiting for me to brag on her a little more, or offer some friendly, motherly details of the day. But I was not inclined to reveal anything further to this man. If Campbells brought the pieces, like he claimed, I meant to offer him only a piece of conversation.

"Okay, well, ain't that just a blessing. And look, this won't take long. It's closer to y'all's side of the woods than some of the other jobs. They'll be back in a jiffy. So be a good girl and get one of the men on the phone, *hmm*? Whoever's on deck."

"We're celebrating—" Raymond appeared in the doorway, the excited, expectant look on his face melting to wonder as he outstretched his hand for the phone.

" . . . Can we talk about this another time? . . . Chase, we're celebrating my daughter's birthday today. . . . Yeah, but that was always meant to be only sometimes, you know, like a favor . . . "

As told by the surprised way Raymond pulled the phone from his ear and regarded it, Chase hung up. He cradled the receiver, but stood with his hand on the phone, thinking for a beat until Bea's squeal of delight pierced the air. Dot shouted for us to "come on, Pop already let her have some frosting!" Whatever had just happened on the phone, one look was all we needed between the two of us to package it away.

Pop had already cut the cake and was feeding it to Bea by the time we got back. Those two—peas and carrots. Every day, Bea became something new. Discovered something, cut a tooth, took a step, said a word, gained an ounce, grew an inch. Every day. And by her first birthday, Pop had hardly missed a single heartbeat of her life. When she stubbed a toe, his ached. If she cried, his eyes watered. Her heart pushed the blood through his veins. He fed Bea her first sweets, and I was overjoyed to leave them to it—to give everybody the gift of keeping that phone call quiet enough to disappear.

Supper was cold fried chicken and leftover potato salad that we could barely manage after two cake-covered babies whipped five adults into near exhaustion. In the middle of eating, the phone rang again. Raymond reached around his back and slid the receiver from the wall. His tone flowed flat and even when he offered to swing by later in the week to look over the Fitzhugh Auto wreckers for them.

"Maybe some of your guys wouldn't mind the overtime," he said. "I'd be happy to take a look and get y'all's trucks back on the road."

Perhaps the offer was the insult—the courtesy of showing a white man how to handle his own business, particularly when that business was misdirection. An opportunity to profit in money, and also, in the currency of reputation. *Campbells towed your car in. I'm sure sorry about your bill, but you know how they do.* An accusation turned to pocket lining for Fitzhugh Auto, and placing us squarely between a white man and some coin. Maybe that was the reason he reacted the way he did, or maybe it was some other thing. "Why?" is hardly a question worth asking because it can never be answered to the satisfaction of those of us just wanting the thumb off the scale and the boot off our back.

The light mist outside had been enough to allow the sun to go down in secret—day slipped into night sometime between Bea having her first sweets and when the phone rang again. This time, with New Jessup's eyes and ears whispering from the other side of the woods. The babies were finally asleep, and we were all settled in front of the television in the family room. Meantime, the cook from Julie's called his friend who called his friend who called her friend who called the Morris boys, who called us up and told Raymond and Pop and Percy that Chase Fitzhugh was riling up some men at the bar to come over with gas cans and matches to show *us* how to handle wreckers. Floorboards rumbled underneath men's heavy feet traveling from the gun case to the front door—three separate freight trains strapping rifles on backs, knives on ankles, tucking shotguns

under arms, pouring extra ammunition into pockets, giving directions to each other, and ordering me and Dot to stay home. Then, the
Studebaker came to life and disappeared through the pines.

After that? Nothing. Driving off, they took all the sound away.
Nothing filled my ears, filled the room, filled my house, big and wide
and without north, south, east, or west. Only now, a direction beck-
oned me. I walked past the babies, asleep in their playpen; past Pop's
armchair with his blanket lain askew; past the sewing machine and
the basket full of mending, and straight to the still-open gun case.
My hand skipped over the little CZ I used for rabbit, and wrapped
around the smooth, mahogany wood grip of my Winchester. Used
only to hunt deer until then, it would put a hole right in Chase
Fitzhugh's eye.

Eight months along, Dot placed herself between me and the front
door, refusing to budge when I told her to stay and watch the babies.

"Alice, listen to me. There's a whole mess of New Jessup men
on the way who can handle this. You and me need to stay put and
take care of home. Don't leave me here by myself." Her plea was
dusky, demanding, and a little bit scared, and it split me in half as
I was filling my mind for how to get Chase in my crosshairs. It was
already dark, but even in the daylight, a straight-shot bullet from our
front porch would have to travel through pine forest, across a field of
hydrangeas, past a mess of azaleas, on off through the cornfield, over
top of an acre of thick and thin grass, through Pop's yard, and down
the driveway to find its targets at the wreckers. At that distance, I
needed a missile, not a bullet. Miss Catherine's garden was full of
shadows and my best way to get close. The light from the home house
and shop would blind them to my presence in the corn. I had the
cover of night and, above the mist, my folks in the stars.

But Dot's dusky plea was right—we needed to stay together.

"Listen to me," I told her. She was shaking her head already.
"Listen. We gonna put some brandy on the babies' gums to keep

them asleep, strap them to us, and go into the garden." Her mouth and eyes turned to disbelieving Os.

"It's dark as sin outside. You're the one always telling us to get in before *can't see*, and now, you want me to go lurk around in the garden?"

"Please do as I say. Right now. Because if something happens while I'm here fussing with you, I'll never forgive you, Dot. Never." Rosie's stricken face after my words to her flashed in my mind as that same shock overcame Dot. And I took a deep breath, needing to harden to them both.

"You're serious?"

"No time to be otherwise."

"What would you do if I didn't move? Bea and Clifford are asleep right in here. You planning to knock me down with a baby in my stomach? Or just run out the kitchen door to leave me by myself?"

"Please, Dot. Get the brandy and let's go."

She took two deep breaths and cut her eyes at me before moving towards the liquor cabinet. "I can't keep up with you running through the garden. You know that, and you aren't leaving me, either, so the car'll have to make it into the camellias through the tractor rut. And when we get back, Alice? You listen to what I'm telling you: when everybody is home, safe and sound, you'd better believe I'm going to tell all."

Without lights, I drove Blue Lightning through the woods hiding us away, turned left on the service road, and right into the garden. But it led straight towards the back of the home house, not the yard or the road. I had to run the last few steps, leaving her in the car with the CZ and the babies and instructions to shoot or shout, if necessary, but not to walk up on me in the dark.

I sprinted those last few feet to the edge of the corn, dropping like a stone to the ground when Pop, Percy, Raymond; the Morris boys and their father, Clint; Cap and a couple of his deputies; Hugo and his pop, O'Connor; Major, with his daddy and uncle, Lieutenant and Duke; Abel Gaston and his brothers, Sage and Bobby; and even Simeon Jones all looked in my direction from the yard. Generations of New Jessup-strong—fathers, sons, uncles, nephews, grandfathers and grandsons; secret-holders shoulder-to-shoulder with the ones from whom they held the secrets—all with rifles and the business of keeping this threat off Campbell land. The group was too thick for them all to even fit inside my scope, but I watched them watching my direction until a night-black Ford raced into the yard and fishtailed to a stop.

Then, I raised up to kneeling, with my right leg tucked underneath my seat, and left bent to support my elbow. The safety disengaged soundlessly. Not that anybody would have heard, particularly the way Chase popped out the car spouting off, followed by three more men. The scope allowed me to watch it all and see what they had in their hands. Nothing at first. Not even the gas cans, which I assume stayed in the car when these men, thinking they could get away with this mischief under the cover of darkness, arrived to find eighteen armed New Jessup men waiting on them.

But with a carload of men there to watch him not be a Negro, my only confidence was that Chase Fitzhugh was capable of the unthinkable. With my rifle steady, I inhaled the scent of fertile Black Belt soil—earthy and pungent with the mist. Exhaled long to calm my heartbeat. Inhaled to extinguish the painful lightning cracking behind my scope eye. Exhaled to clear my mind of Dot and Rosie's disappointments. Some sort of beetle or millipede tapped its way across my leg to continue on its way, and an owl sailed past my sights as New Jessup-strong formed a line between the home house, the shop driveway, and the Jessup men. Pop, Percy, and Raymond met him face to face in the yard.

In the blink of my scope eye, Pop had moved into my shot, pointing his finger back at Chase's car. Chase only reached to his shoulder, and with my father-in-law's arm outstretched, his bicep blocked the sandy-haired curls on Chase's head. Suddenly, Pop jumped back, and New Jessup–strong closed ranks around the four. Eight white hands peeked into the air. Slowly, the group broke apart one by one, with Cap in the middle of it all showing palms towards New Jessup men, telling them to *be easy*. Then, him and his deputies walked the white men to Chase's car. Still, I watched through the scope until those white men slid back inside that black Ford, and my scope eye stayed on them until his red taillights disappeared from view.

I hustled back to Blue Lightning, concerning myself now with getting back before the men and keeping Dot quiet about our doings. But when I reached my car, Hugo Greene was in the driver's seat with Major Royal as his passenger. Dot had the babies in the back seat, and after a brief, disappointed glance in my eyes, she turned her face away from me.

"Two shots in the air means all clear out here," said Major, his Army tattoo stretched tight over his flexed forearm resting on the windowsill. The back of his jaw bubbled with tension. I pointed my muzzle to the sky, pulled the trigger twice, and climbed into the backseat.

TWENTY-NINE

Raymond talked with Major and Hugo in the corner opposite the one that carried whispers in my yard. I heard nothing, but with nowhere else to go, I took a seat in my porch swing. Inside my house, Percy was pacing in and out of the family-room picture window, stopping every so often to scowl at me through the sheers. Hugo had had difficulty backing the car through the tractor rut, and we arrived to the hot, confused glares of our men in the yard. Though Pop stayed with some men at the home house, waiting for more trouble, Raymond and Percy had come behind the pines to check on us, and were getting back in the Studebaker after finding the houses empty and Blue Lightning gone when we pulled up. So some went inside, some went to the corner, and I sat and waited on the porch.

Raymond finished with them and stood before me in the porch swing. I had never felt smaller than with him looking down. He stood silently for a long time, well after Major and Hugo took Percy's Studebaker through the trees.

"You almost got your head blown off, you know. Had Dot, Clifford, and Bea out there in the sights of twenty trigger-ready men. What the hell were you thinking?" I was looking towards the ground, playing with the end of my hair. "Look at me," he demanded, making no effort to hide the disappointment in his eyes. "You called yourself out there stalking? Ready to kill a man tonight?" I nodded, feeling tears bubbling. The steel I had felt in the cornfield had given away to a froth of nerves. "What stopped you?"

"I couldn't see nothing in his hands, and then, y'all surrounded him, and I couldn't see nothing at all. What happened? Why'd y'all crowd him?"

"Ain't important."

"Something happened to Pop. What happened to Pop? Is he alright?"

"He's fine," Raymond said with teeth clenched.

"But—"

"Alice, he's fine, I said. But you? You had Dot, our babies, out there. Do you have *any* idea what coulda happened?"

"They were gonna burn up the wreckers, the shop, the house, who knows what."

"I told you to stay home. We had other men coming."

"I didn't know who all was coming, who would be here in time. I didn't wanna leave Dot and the babies, and I didn't know what else to do." His chest inflated and deflated, pushing out a deep breath.

"Stay home like we told you! And then, to not even hear Major and Hugo coming?"

"My eye was on my shot. My mind was on my shot."

"You know how lucky we are that it was them that saw you, found you? Did you think of that? What if we saw that corn moving and just decided to shoot? Did you think of that, Alice?" His rumble filled out and echoed against the pines. His words, the cold, snaked into my bones. The muscles in his neck tensed. "Did you?" he asked sternly, his voice shaky and deep.

"No."

Finally hunched by disappointment, he crumpled into the porch swing with hands over the back of his neck, his face shielded from me.

"I thought about you, our family, our home, and how little time I had to make a decision. I wasn't gonna let him take you away from me. He doesn't just get to come here and take my men away from me."

"*Christ*," he muttered. "Jesus Christ." He looked at me.

"Raymond, you know I was taught to fight back—"

"—Listen . . . listen—"

"—It's men like Chase and Fitzhugh who'll live to their dying breath taking from Negroes to prove they ain't nobody's Negro—"

"—Alice, baby, look, I know it's a lot here right now—"

"—That redneck came over here to destroy our wreckers, burn everything to the ground, ruin our lives any way they could imagine—"

"—I didn't marry you to worry you to death—"

"—All that chaos and destruction just to prove he ain't nobody's Negro! I wasn't gonna let that happen—"

"—to make you sick, have you stalking around in the garden—"

"—I may not have built cars for the boycott, may not write articles, may not ride off to the swamp every Monday, but I ain't sitting at home doing nothing to protect us, neither. I—"

"—I can't . . . do this!" he thundered to himself, as he rubbed the heels of his hands to his eyes. I jumped, startled, and then started pouring words, trying to find the right ones.

"Raymond, baby, look, baby. Listen. You asked me to stay home, take care of home. This is the best I know how."

"How on earth am I supposed to make New Jessup a city, build New Jessups all over this country, if I can barely keep my own family safe?" he asked himself and the listening trees.

"You already doing it! You doing it! We safer here than any place."

He looked me squarely in the eye and broke my heart with a calm and steady voice.

"Alice. Darling. You, me, and Bea are going to DC for a while. Simeon once mentioned that the NNAS keeps an apartment there. Should any of us ever need it." His grays were so close—each one, its own soft moon—his nose, the curve of his perfect lips, the sad, hazy glow of his face in the low light, was right there in my face. But we had also drifted to opposite ends of the horizon because of my illness, my decisions, my failures.

"Raymond. Think about what you saying, baby. Nobody—"

"—Please don't fight me on this. It's too much, and with your health—"

"—gets to drive us from Alabama—"

"—and you're taking heart medication, not telling me. Got these headaches that don't go away, hardly eating anything, and now, you almost got yourself killed trying to snipe a man from our—"

"—This land is ours! Our generations have walked this soil. It provided for them, nourishes us—"

"—garden. We'll get settled in DC and—"

"—Our folks have been watching over us from these stars since time began. Every night, right through their windows up there. That's here, Raymond, in Alabama—"

"—make a fresh start. This is serious to me. My family's safety is paramount. You know I—"

"—You ain't listening to me. This is our peace, our quiet, our sky—"

"—lost my mama to a heart attack. I can't lose you, too—"

"—I've lived under this night, this moon, since I was a little girl. And the moon! It's special here, baby. Please, Raymond, listen—"

"—and you had my daughter, Dot, Clifford, in a field with rifles trained in this direction. Even Simeon—"

"—Even the sunset. It's the color of coneflowers sometimes, and sometimes, mauve. But the mauve is really a lot of different colors mixed together. Listen, baby—"

"—and he still hardly knows what to do with a gun! He raced over here, had my back. Even though I'm constantly arguing with him these days—"

"—like cottontail white . . . and lavender . . . even some coral . . . sometimes . . . across the horizon. You ain't listening to me! Listen to me, Raymond. Please, baby—"

"—I just can't figure it out. I can't fix it—"

"—Raymond! You ain't listening to me!"

"—I hear you talking fast. But are you *listening* to *me*, Alice?"

"Our life is on this land, baby! The sunset, the moon, the night. They're ours. Out here, it's all ours. In New Jessup, Alabama."

His shoulders sank. "You're talking around things, making excuses, but I'm not blind or dumb. You're taking heart medication. Not eating. Not sleeping. Now this? What do you expect me to say?"

I turned away from him to watch new rain pattering the leaves and assaulting the gravel in our yard. It bounced from the porch rail, dampening and chilling the air just like the first night that Raymond had protected me from the world with that umbrella over my head. I watched the drops crash to the earth, unable to look at him.

"Hey." He tapped my leg softly to get my attention, but I refused his eye, even if I would never refuse his words. Instead, I watched the heavens cry my angry tears about leaving. "I'm going inside to call Matthew," he said. "Tomorrow, I want you to start getting us ready to go."

I STARED AT THE CEILING overnight and didn't even need my alarm, silencing it seconds before it was set to go off. Raymond had come in shortly before, and left Percy to take watch on our porch, so he only stirred a little when I pulled myself from the bed, leaning appreciatively into the warmth I tucked under the covers as I was leaving. Everything was quiet. From our bedroom, there were two corridors: one straight ahead, where Pop and Bea's rooms were, and one to the right leading to the rest of the rooms in our house. I usually went straight first to check on Bea and Pop, but this morning, coffee floated to my nose, though none of the men had ever brewed a pot in my house.

Up the hallway to my right, a pool of light rounded from the kitchen into the dark, where Dot was sitting at the table with her chin resting on praying hands, her eyes on the pill bottle that had been her first big disappointment in me. She never showed before four thirty, when she completed the rounds in her own house. But this morning, she was waiting with the same sad, tired eyes she'd had a couple days before when she found out that I'd kept my condition from her. Her nose was red as I sat down next to her in my chair.

For some moments, it was just the owls' trembling voices outside and the night bugs' softening song. Then, Dot reached out and rubbed her palm in slow circles between my shoulder blades—my sister, this time, there at the daybreak after we fought. This time, it would be me leaving. But this morning, with me and Raymond's things needing boxes and suitcases, a moving truck to call, a million things to arrange at the time of day when me and her planned and chattered, the quiet was the loudest. Instead of laughter, we sat. In the earliest hours, the morning birds were singing a happy trill.

"What do you think it's like to be an animal?" she asked out the blue. Her voice was deep with congestion and she sniffled.

"What do you mean?"

"Like, an animal in these woods," she said. "You think it feels different being different kinds of animals? I mean, like, a deer versus a bird versus a frog versus a snake? Or what about field mice and city mice? You think they're different?"

I had never thought about the feelings of an animal until then. The ones in the DC zoo came to mind. World-sized elephants imprisoned in their enclosures; lions and tigers sleeping on concrete instead of roaming free. Then a mockingbird trilled like a police whistle—like the one belonging to the officer directing traffic my first moments stepping off the bus. And when I heard it, thought about the concrete enclosures being no place for life, and the police whistle welcoming me to my new life, I said the only word that came to mind.

"Free. I think the animals outside my window feel free."

She nodded and let her hand come to rest on my back, allowing the nothing in our words to fill the space again until we went to fetch every egg that had been laid from the chicken coop.

BY THE TWENTIETH DAY OF THE RAINS, Blue Lightning had finished its windings around town in preparation for our leaving. By then, news had spread around New Jessup about Chase Fitzhugh at our place, so whispers and pitying glances greeted me and Dot at the market when we went to fill her Frigidaire but not my own; greeted us when we stopped to pay the house accounts, return library books, pick up my prescription from the drugstore. When we stopped at Mr. Marvin's for lunch, he sighed and lingered after placing our order on the table himself. Handing Cap the payment with my last parking citation, he tore up the ticket and handed my money back.

We drove around and around until finally ending up in front of Taylor Made, where I had no business except saying goodbye. Dot waited in the car with the babies while I stood, dripping wet, in the entryway trying to figure out what to say. Voices were coming from the back but I stood frozen. What was I supposed to say to the woman who picked me with a million girls clamoring for that job? Who gave me a place to wear my shoe leather into the carpet? Who set me up in an apartment and charged me next to nothing for rent when landlords were supposed to expect *everything*? Who worried me about my posture, my diction, my etiquette, and the scuffs on my shoes? Who dressed me for my first date, my wedding, every-thing in between, and almost all things after? Who so believed in me that her intuition, and not my words, became the reason Cap put

Patience out—threading that needle so those articles would never attach themselves to me? Who helped me pick every paint color and stick of furnishing for my house? Standing there, in a puddle of my own making, I wracked my brain and came up with nothing to say. But *nothing* was a powerful lot to say to Miss Vivian.

Just when I decided I couldn't say goodbye and turned to leave, Earnestine came out to see who made the door chime.

"Oh, good afternoon, Alice. Did you have an appointment? I don't remember seeing you in the book." I shook my head and stood there dripping. "Well, Mama's in the thick of it fixing the train on an original," she said, pulling imaginary glasses over her eyes. "Something I can help you with? Are you okay? I heard about your troubles. I hope everything is getting back to normal."

"We're fine. Thanks. And . . . no need to bother Miss Vivian right now. Sounds like she's tied up. But . . . can you just tell her that I'm sorry I'm missing her?"

"Of course," she said, and I left.

EVEN THE STAINED GLASS was angry on Sunday. Usually streaming color as varied and brilliant as the shades of Negroes worshipping in rainbow-colored Sunday best, the dark clouds promising rain turned the figures into gloomy, ominous-looking forms. With plans to leave on Monday, this was to be our final goodbye to New Jessup. But Pastor conjured the brewing storm with the one atop his heart. He lumbered to the podium and scanned his flock from side to side before his eyes settled on Simeon briefly—a head above the rest and smack dab in the middle. Then, his gaze moved between men I knew to be in the NNAS—including Raymond and Percy—to hold each in his own momentary stare.

"Brothers and sisters, can I get an *amen* for the choir?" And the church said "amen" as he tuned up the music in his voice. "I hope y'all don't mind, but your old pastor has something on his heart this morning. A little different than what I prepared. (*All right*) But a word is speaking to me that needs to be spoken, so, I pray y'all's indulgence. (*Take your time, Pastor*)

"I thought I'd never return to New Jessup after seminary. Truth be told, I never thought I'd make it to seminary at all, but I did. (*God is good*) My daddy started this church. Was nothing more than a clearing in the swamp and a vision in his head. (*Say a word*) And from my daddy's vision, in the muck, this community came together to build Morning Star Baptist. (*Yes it did*)

"I was called to this very pulpit. (*C'mon, Pastor*) Those of you who knew me as a young man know I wasn't always on the right path to get here. (*Testify*) Spent a lotta time engaged in worldly pursuits, thinking there must be something better than this (*That's the world*), maybe music, or maybe the Negro leagues. Only your old pastor can't carry a tune or swing a bat, no. (*Heh heh. That's alright*) Instead, my path led me up the stairs outside (*Tell it*), past the brick laid by Milton Jenkins (*Yassuh*), through the doors, past the pews (*Mmm-hmm*), to the podium in this pulpit (*Preach*), all of it, hand hewn by Milton's father Desmond and his brothers Early and John. (*Yassuh*)

"And did any of y'all ever starve? (*No, sir*) Ever go hungry or without books or clothes on your back? (*No, Pastor*) Know why? Because my own mama, Hagar Brown, kept the "fellowship" in the fellowship hall as long as there was an hour in the day. (*Yes, she did*) Women like Clara Campbell, then Catherine after her, my mother-in-law Nanette Rose, worked and offered and canned and kept food to make sure no man, woman, or child would ever starve! (*Bless their names*) Mother Dear Ann Blakely led the effort to rebuild our hospital, taking every pain to comfort the sick and attract doctors while they built (*Yes, she did*), and Nadeen James made it her life's work to make sure New Jessup had schools where young and old could learn to read and write. (*Tell it*) Men and women in this congregation lifted me, supported me, this town is in me. (*Yassuh*) I am here to tell you that there's nothing better on this earth than being the pastor of Morning Star Baptist Church (*Say it plain*) right here in New Jessup, Alabama."

Hallelujah!

Tell the truth!

"I was a young man once, though, with a restless spirit, and the devil was in my ear. But y'all know that the devil is a liar—amen? (*Amen!*) Lying is his business, and it's a nasty one at that. Those who engage in treachery and deceit do not follow in godly ways. Amen, amen? (*Amen!*)

"Now, I'm not asking you to believe me. I am merely His vessel. (*C'mon*) But my daddy used to shout out Proverbs 12:22 whenever he caught me sneaking into the house late (*That's alright*), fast-talking about where I'd been. And with whom. I hear some of y'all laughing because y'all know what that's about. (*Tell the truth*) 'Lying lips'"— he sang as a shout—"'are an abomination to the Lord, but they that deal truly are his delight.' (*That's right*) Now, I could've gotten up here and preached to y'all about John, 8:44, which says, 'Ye are of your father the devil, and the lusts of your father ye will do.' (*Mmm-hmm*) 'He was a murderer from the beginning, and abode not in the truth, because there is no truth in him. When he speaketh a *lie*, he speaketh of his own: for he is a liar, and the father of it.' So, the devil is a lie, you see. (*Mmm-hmm, the devil is a lie*) But you know what we're gonna talk about today? We're gonna talk about truth. Telling it straight."

Talk about it!

Come on, now, Pastor!

Tell it straight!

Without calling a name or mentioning the NNAS, Pastor looked hard at Simeon. Around the sanctuary, ears and faces glowed red and purple listening to him preach about lying lips and speaking truth.

Percy glared over top of my head at Raymond, who was clapping and *amen*ing to my left as whatever Simeon had apparently said to Pastor came back to bite us all during the service. While around the church, some fanned themselves and hummed affirmation of Pastor's condemnation of "others," certain "others" frowned and worked knots in the backs of jaws while still "others" turned necks coolly in search of a sympathetic eye.

After service, me, Dot, and Eddie Mae Green were waiting inside the vestibule for Pop and Hugo to pull cars to the curb so we could make a rainy dash to the street. The rain popped so loud on the roof that we missed Mrs. Brown's soft footsteps approaching, and her gentle throat-clearing. She tapped our shoulders to get our attention, then opened the outside doors, where Raymond, Percy, Pop, Hugo, and Abel were all marching across the street to the parsonage behind Pastor. She snapped her umbrella open and we followed suit.

We stood in the family room where I had spent my very first days in New Jessup. Pastor regarded us all with such judgment as to seem Godlike. Simeon was nowhere to be found. Pastor looked to Raymond.

"That big old Georgia boy told me a story this morning that I can't hardly believe. With you, Raymond Campbell, in the starring role."

"Sir? What'd he say?"

"Don't 'sir' me like you respect me and then lie to my face. You're smart enough to know what he said."

"Yes, Pastor, I am a smart man. Smart enough not to let another man speak for me. And smart enough not to take the weight of accusations without knowing what they are."

"Fine," Pastor said through clenched teeth. "He told Mrs. Brown, an hour before Sunday school, that he had an emergency and needed to speak to me right away. I was going over my sermon when he came and sat down, all shrunk into his shoulders. 'Pastor, I've got a confession,' he said to me. I told him out with it. We ain't the Catholics.

"He told me about the NNAS here—in New Jessup, Alabama—and called all *y'all's* names. He said he's been worried that New Jessup stands to catch hell because of this Fitzhugh mess, and wants to bring more folks here. Lawyers. Organizers. Agitators. Like we haven't been dealing with the other side of the woods since way before any of y'all were even a gleam in your daddies' eyes. Said he plans to approach the men of the cloth in this town to ask that we spread a message of welcome to the NNAS. So that's what you saw today. Now service is over, and he's vanished, leaving y'all holding the bag. So now that you know the weight, you care to explain? As the star of this show?"

"Pastor, I don't mean to contradict you, but whatever he said ain't entirely right. We've been trying to calm him down for about a week now. But our work is to bring municipality to New Jessup. Independence and a safe vote in the future. That's all." He looked around at the other guys, their wives, Pop, then me, as if needing all our permission. "I'd appreciate a chance to talk to you about it more, though."

"I baptized every last one of y'all," Pastor said. He closed his eyes and shook his head, and when he opened them, they landed on me. "Except you. No, *you*, Mrs. Brown and I welcomed into this very parsonage, made sure you were safe, took you in when you had not a single friend in the world. We told you how dear we hold New Jessup, invited you to stay here so you wouldn't get cast out in the cold—for you to turn your back now and get involved in all of this?"

Raymond opened his mouth to answer, but I cut in because this was my question from a time before I knew anything about Raymond Campbell. When Pastor and Mrs. Brown certainly could have turned me away with sausage-thick bruises on my arm and a half-used bus ticket. It would have been easy to tell him I had disagreed, or been tricked, or that I got involved against my will. I had never gone to a single meeting, never plotted with this group of men. But my complicity was love—for Raymond, of course, but for this town and its folks where I had thrived. So was I involved? Alone?

"You too, Pastor," I said. He cocked his head and lifted an eyebrow, daring for me to explain.

"Excuse me? What are you—"

"What I mean is that we all involved. You said so yourself today. This town raised you, is in you. Well, I am his wife, and yessir, I support him, love him. Pop and Miss Catherine raised him. But you are his pastor, sir; you ministered to him to live right and in the service of others. Our New Jessup teachers taught him his lessons, and our doctors keep him healthy and strong. Mr. Marvin fed him and Cap protected him so he could grow from a boy to become this man who loves, wants to protect and maintain our way of life. They are these men because we've all made them these men. So if you look at it like that, yessir, this whole town is involved." The room drew a breath, everybody ready to say something. He raised his palm, meaning *stop*. Scanning face by face, his glare settled on Pop.

"Y'all get outta my face. Every last one of you. Right now."

IT HAD BEEN A WARM FALL, but the cool rain brought winter to my mind. Rosie's letters had assured me that it was brutally cold up north, and I had nothing appropriate for my baby, my husband, myself. No heavy boots or thick gloves or coats warm enough to keep illness away. After we got home from church, I sat on the bed, surrounded by the clothes I had yet to decide whether to pack or leave behind: Bea's little dresses and baby sailor suit and leather booties too small for her nearly walking feet; things needing to be mended, making me wonder if there would be a sewing machine. The hunting clothes, the gardening clothes, his Campbell Auto coveralls all in the "leave behind" pile. The memories of our house, our clothes and what we were doing when we wore them, swirled around and around while the men were gone for a couple hours closing Raymond out at the shop. He appeared in the doorway with the light lowering outside, pulled my dungarees and heavy jacket from the "leave behind" pile, and laid them on the bed next to me.

"This can wait. I wanna take you somewhere," he said. "Just you and me, but you'll need to put these on."

We climbed into the Studebaker and drove towards the home house, towards the fork in the road, and then, after about a mile, maybe mile and a half, he turned left into the woods. He slowed and we entered the dark trees where I had driven past a thousand times and never even imagined a driveway. The Studebaker groaned along a soft path as black as the back of my eyelids; the dark eating the light of our headlamps. He seemed to be driving by feel more than anything as we rocked and rolled from side to side, progressing slowly, with him calmly behind the wheel.

"What you said the other day? About the sunset?" he said to me. "You're right, you know. I never opened my eyes to it, and lately, I've been looking for it. Hoping to see what you see. You're always opening my eyes to something, Alice." A branch scratched down the side of the car as we rolled along, listing to the left.

"It's been raining. But it's up there, I promise."

"And what you said to Pastor this afternoon? Everybody in the parsonage got a tiny glimpse of my Alice and they ain't quit talking about it since."

"I thought y'all were at the shop. They were there, too?"

He shook his head.

"You ever regret staying here with some fixit man in New Jessup?"

"Don't diminish yourself, baby," I said. "That's the world's work, not yours. I couldn't be prouder of you, or love you more, if there were a thousand of me being proud of you, loving you."

"You and your words. I think of you and your words when things get hard for me out here."

"Yeah?"

"Yeah. Like when you say things like that. A thousand of you, loving one of me?" He paused and let the silence speak his appreciation, kicking up the corner of his mouth. "When you call me 'Mr. Mayor,' or talk about this as the town Campbells built. Or when you said what you said to Pastor today? Your tallest tales. Your story about getting off the bus, with the shoeshine man? Sends shivers down my spine at how quick you coulda gotten away. As silly as it sounds, I even think about those first, simple words you said to me."

"I don't even remember what I said. You know I'm always talking."

"Don't do the world's work of diminishing yourself either, darling," he mimicked sweetly. "Your face lit up, and you said, 'Oh, *you're* the Raymond Miss Catherine was always talking about. It's a pleasure to make your acquaintance.' Trying to be all proper with that sweet country in your voice. But those words, spoken by someone as beautiful as you? That *you* remembered me, and lit up talking about my mama? I was gone."

My tears flowed. Some from the lighter memories, some, from the heaviness in my heart, but who could tell the difference drop by drop?

"And Alice? I thank God every day you got off that bus to stretch those *beautiful* legs. Are you sorry? It breaks me to see you cry."

"I ain't sorry for getting off the bus. My only regret is that Rosie never got to see it." He tapped my leg.

"We'll find her, darling. One day. On that, you have my word."

We drove on with him squinting into absolute darkness. At that pace, over that terrain, it could have been fifty feet or a mile that we traveled.

"Where are we?"

"Greene's property."

"We never came this way before."

"Nope."

"What are we doing out here? I gotta finish packing if we ever gonna get on the road."

"So today, we weren't at the shop. We scrambled the guys together, talking about what to do. Simeon was there, and with HQ's blessing, we voted to send him back to DC. I warned him once that I'd lead his undoing if he stepped outta bounds. He's such a great lawyer, Alice, and truly a good man. It broke my heart today to keep my word.

"Afterwards, the fellas needed to go home, cool off, and think. Even though municipality is close, it ain't finalized. But the way this is playing out, we'll need to announce ourselves as NNAS sooner rather than later. Make sure New Jessup understands our goal is family, community first. So if we stay—"

"What do you mean 'if *we* stay?' You and me?" He nodded. "But what's changed?"

"Nothing, exactly."

"Ain't nothing so big as nothing, Raymond. What are you saying?"

"You know Doc Underwood treated Mama. Matthew was supposed to start his residency, study with him, remember. Still wants to . . . still might. Anyway, he assures me you're getting the best care with your doctors here. So, I'm leaving it up to you. We make our home where you wanna make our home."

"What about Pastor and folks around here, though? And Chase?"

"You saw Pastor's face after what you said. Thought his head was gonna explode. It did a little. But after I met with the fellas, and he had some time to think on it today, I took a chance and ran by the parsonage. He gave me a few minutes just before I came home to get you. He's more curious than angry now, and agreed to meet with all of us, hear us out, later this week. My hope is that him, and others like him, will be a big help in paving the way for folks to understand just what you said today. That this is for all of us. That we're all *of* this town.

"But at the end of the day, we can't control Chase or the Chases and Fitzhughs of the world. What we can do is live for, love, and protect our community." He snorted softly. "This was just an idea one day among a bunch of friends—to protect our way of life while finding the best, safest way to bring the vote to New Jessup. For us to find a way, and a reason, to cast a ballot in Alabama."

"I hear you, baby. But why bring me out here?"

"I really don't know. I just saw you sitting in the bedroom, surrounded by clothes, looking how I feel about leaving. And I just wanted to . . . I don't know . . . maybe I wanted you to find a little of your magic for me."

The car lurched and groaned to a stop. Old man pines, tall, straight, gnarled, and hunched were overcome by silvery moss and thick vines, and the ground was soft, wet mud, never dried in history. He cut the headlamps and all the night eyes disappeared. But he flashed a flashlight past me, to the right, and, sure enough, there was the old father's cottage—of the earth, and looking like the earth was coming back for it. In the dark, you would never know it was there, except for the few hardy moonflowers glowing and open with perfume. Above, our saints jeweled the onyx sky and the moon was bright. We stood from the car, and I reached high—high enough to hold it, to hold on to Alabama, in the palm of my hand.

ACKNOWLEDGMENTS

First and foremost, my deepest gratitude to Gloria Young Minnicks—my mama—for every moment she spent protecting me, honoring me, and believing in me. I carry the pride of Black womanhood because she was the embodiment of determination with dignity and grace. Though our time together was too short, and she rests among the stars, she remains my beacon in this world. I am forever blessed that she spent a piece of eternity here on earth as my mama.

I extend my infinite thanks to my family for keeping our history alive and blessing my life with stories. For understanding when I need space to create, when I need to get lost in your embrace, and for always holding me up with love. Thank you for countless phone calls that last long after, "Well, let me let you go"; for hours on the road ferrying me to and fro; for documenting and passing our stories through the generations. Your love and sacrifices take me places, and *take me places*, and have gifted me so much of the rich context for my life and the lives inside these pages: John Young, Jr., Margaret Young, Clara Martin, Ann Black, Harrison "Bill" Black, DeBorah Giles, (the inimitable) John Young III, Carolyn Young, Bobby Young, Althea Young, Leona Walker, Harriet Black, Sakinda Skinner, Milton Young, Nadeen Ivory, Hagar Young, Betty Young, Vernon Martin, Stephen Martin, Matthew Minnicks, Thomas

Minnicks, Eugertha Minnicks, Sterling Minnicks, Vicki Minnicks, Arlene Minnicks, Liz Hooper, Clinton Minnicks, Barbara Minnicks, Carolyn Wyatt, Marion Goode, Omari Minnicks, Samia Minnicks, Danielle Minnicks, Omar Minnicks, Johnnie Mae Sankey, and Melanie Richburg.

My sincerest thank you to Barbara Kingsolver, whose intrepid pen is a testament to the fact that stories can be powerful, transformative. I am eternally grateful for the phone call that changed my life, and your encouragement that *Moonrise Over New Jessup* invites people into my family's Alabama for a spell. I wish to also thank Heidi Durrow and Sunil Yapa for believing in the power of my story, and for your deeply moving words about Alice and her journey. Heidi, I am eternally thankful and amazed that you took my phone calls, and kept taking them! Not only am I a Bellwether winner because your jury saw the beauty in my story, but I continued to take risks and grow as a writer because of all of your personal advice and support. I thank you for being one of the strongest believers in my work and my voice.

Many, many thanks to my sister and dearest friends for reading these, and other, pages time and again. The phone calls, text messages, emails, and long walks you've gifted me are moments that I will treasure always. Your limitless enthusiasm to devour these pages resulted in a sharper, fuller book from first to final draft, and I am forever indebted to you for your generosity of time and spirit: Shani Whisonant, Terri Johnson, Mariama Liverpool, Chiedozie Dike, Nicole VanderLinden, Melissa Moore, Lekesha Campbell, Sarah Navarro, and Kevin Gregory.

I am immensely grateful to my literary agent, Michelle Brower, for not only believing that the sky is no limit for me or my stories, but also for being so remarkably adept at pushing the sky when it needs pushing. Thank you for championing my book and my voice, and for your endless encouragement to dream bigger than what may be polite or possible.

ACKNOWLEDGMENTS

Endless gratitude to my brothers Jason Mott and Robert Jones, Jr., who have so completely embraced me as "lil sis," and to Deesha Philyaw for her kind and supportive words from the earliest days. Thank you for your commitment to my art, and for your commitment to teaching me the business of this art. Jason, through your willingness to mentor me from the first "hello," unwavering support, positive pragmatism, and readiness to troubleshoot big and small (usually, through the occasional dad joke or 1970s meme), has developed a friendship I will cherish always. Robert . . . thank you for recognizing The Ancestors in my spirit and my work. The way you shared your real-time love of Alice, and New Jessup, text by text; our countless hours on the telephone; and your beautifully encouraging words about my book, my career, and my people, have been the rarest form of blessing to my life. And Deesha . . . thank you for taking my call, the time you spent encouraging and supporting my art, and all your advice that continues to light my path.

Many thanks to my editor, Kathy Pories, for her sharp and incisive pen, curious mind, and encouragement to bring Alice's truest voice into the world. I am indelibly grateful to have you in my corner helping to make my art. I also owe an enormous debt of gratitude to Betsy Gleick, Brunson Hoole, Steve Godwin, and Cathy Schott for your careful attention to the edit and design of this beautiful book, and Michael McKenzie, Debra Linn, Stephanie Mendoza, and Annie Mazes for your extraordinary effort to get *New Jessup* into the hands of readers. With your help, the world will meet New Jessup on its own terms, and I am extraordinarily grateful to have such an amazing team with the singular goal of representing Alice's story for true.

And finally, thank you to my husband for holding the umbrella over my head that first night, and continuing to do so as we navigate through this adventure called life.